The News in Small Towns

(Small Town Series, Book 1)

Iza Moreau

I0638293

Books for people who like to think about what they read.

The News in Small Towns

Black Bay Books
7500A Wigfield Road
Mobile, AL 36619

ISBN-13: 978-0-9624878-8-0
Library of Congress Control Number: 2012947278

First Printing in 2012

7a

There is no note on any instrument that has not been
played before. That said, *The News in Small Towns* is a
work of fiction. Any resemblance of names, places,
characters, and incidents to actual persons, places, and
events results from the relationship which the world
must always bear to works of this kind.

Books by Iza Moreau

Small Town Series
The News in Small Towns
Madness in Small Towns
Secrets in Small Towns
Mysteries in Small Towns

Elodie Fontaine Mysteries
Tank Baby
Ghost in the Piano
Horses Wild
Desert Girl
Billy's Legacy (with R. E. Conary)
Stormy Weather (with R. E. Conary)

Stand-Alone Works
The XYZ Mysteries
The Five
Swamp Girl
London, Falling
Persephone's Mare

When your horse shies at an object and is unwilling to go up to it, he should be shown that there is nothing fearful in it, least of all to a courageous horse like him.

—Xenophon

I see it. It's not dangerous. Walk on.

—Cindy McKeown

Prologue

On my last day in Baghdad, I woke up in a bed with a sagging mattress, rumpled sheets, and a naked Crow Indian from Montana by the name of Lieutenant Ossie Enemy Hunter. He was sleeping off a booze and sex binge—one of the first he'd been able to have since being deployed to Iraq several months earlier. I was hung over from the same binge, but it was not nearly my first. Lt. Enemy Hunter was in his late twenties, bronze and very tall. Although I was a half dozen years older, I had never met a Native American before, much less slept with one, and I had fallen in love with his stature more than anything else. Of course the term "fallen in love" is a euphemism, but the night had been more pleasant than most.

I had been in Baghdad for almost six months, living in a compound of journalists in the eighteen-story Palestine Hotel, once one of the most popular and expensive places to stay in Iraq. When I arrived it was still expensive, but mortar shells and rifle fire had damaged the façade and blown out many of the windows. The lobby had lost any elegance it may once have had—the carpets were stained, the ceiling had been torn apart for wiring repairs and never replaced, the furniture was ramshackle, and the service was nonexistent. Plumbing was iffy, and electrical blackouts were common. The room was hot and humid even in the early morning, and the open window admitted only the shadow of a breeze.

Outside, I heard the thumping fan blades of a rescue helicopter, carrying wounded to the Baghdad Hospital. I sat up in bed and looked at the clock on the nightstand. Six a.m.: just before sunup. Everywhere in the city, Muslims would be on their knees facing Mecca before going about their daily duties. My own duties would begin later, meeting with others in my bureau and getting brought up to speed on car bombings or firefights or *fatwas* from the *imams*. I would read copy and study photos from the day before, then make assignments. Maybe I could work up a story to send home, maybe not. Maybe I'd just visit the few shops in the compound, drop in on other bureaus, add something to my diary, sleep. The truth is, I had arrived on the ass end of the Baghdad story. At one time journalists could freely wander around the entire city without escort; now it was too dangerous. An American—especially an American woman—walking along Baghdad streets alone would have a less-than-even chance of arriving back safely. And to go out with an escort was putting the escort in danger as well as yourself. Better to stay inside and go crazy. Better to let wannabe Iraqi reporters get whatever news there was that was fit to print. Many of the news organizations had packed up and gone home. I knew I would be leaving soon, too. Not soon enough, though. The months of fighting in the streets, the distrust, the religious decrees that marginalized women, the infighting between members of the coalition government, the waste of billions of taxpayer dollars to opportunist private companies with their hands crammed all the way to the elbow up the asses of the Bush administration—all of it—had put me into a deep depression that made booze, sex, loud music, greasy food, and frantic bouts of typing on my computer necessities of life.

The Enemy Hunter stirred in bed and opened his eyes.

2

He blinked a couple of times, then smiled. "Hello, beautiful," he said. Oh, yeah, his voice. I loved that voice, too—deep and hollow like it was coming up from a brick well.

"All American women in Iraq are beautiful," I told him. I gathered my shoulder-length hair in both hands and twisted it behind my head.

"Sue," he said. "Susan."

"Sue-Ann," I told him. "Sue-Ann McKeown. Listen, I meant to ask you; do you shoot archery?"

"Bows and arrows?"

"Yeah."

"Not since I was a papoose. Why ask something like that?"

"I'm not trying to stereotype you," I said. "It's just that I do. I thought we might have something in common. Something we could talk about."

"You do what? Shoot bows and arrows?" He ran a hand through his jet black crew cut.

"Yeah. I was, um, on the Olympic team once. I've studied Native American archery tackle; I tried to make one once but I couldn't get the rawhide the right consistency. Did you know that some Indian bows were so powerful that they could send an arrow completely through a running buffalo?"

The Enemy Hunter shifted toward me on the bed and sat up so that we were face to face. "You're interested in my culture?" he asked.

"Well, sorta, at least the archery aspect of it. Ironic I guess, being as we're surrounded by Ghurkas with AK-47s."

He stroked my bare leg. "I wish I did know," he said. "Because I would like to talk to you about those things. But not many Crow use the bow and arrow any more.

3

What about horses?"

"Horses?" I asked. "My mother has horses. I ride them sometimes when I'm home."

"I can talk to you about horses," he said, showing his long, perfectly white teeth. "I can take you to see horses."

"What, you're going to take me to Montana?" I smiled.

"No, there are horses here in Baghdad. I can take you there."

"Are you talking about old work horses?" I asked. The only horses I had seen in Iraq were even more to be pitied than their owners; pulling crickety carts filled to overflowing with loot or debris. Those that died were pulled to the side of the road.

The Enemy Hunter had seen them, too, and answered quickly. "No no. Pureblood Arabian horses. At the Zoo. Very beautiful."

"Horses at the zoo?"

"That's where they are now. For their safety."

"When do you want to go?" I asked.

He reached out and pulled me gently down on the bed. The sparse stubble of his beard was raspy against my cheek, but I didn't mind. There was a lot that I had learned not to mind. "Maybe in an hour?" he smiled, and turned his attention to my nipples.

"Wait," I began, squirming, "I saw something in a brochure somewhere. It said that the prophet Muhammad was a master of archery and horsemanship. How's that for a coincidence?"

"Shhh," he said, and moved on top of me. I shhh'd.

After a cold shower and breakfast downstairs in the restaurant, Ossie (short for Oscar, I found out) and I walked out of our safe compound and across the Joumhouriyah Bridge toward the Green Zone. We ran into a couple of men from his unit on the way, and they escorted us up to the gates. The Enemy Hunter wore a holstered pistol on his belt. In his boots and fatigues, he was almost a foot taller than me. I felt pretty safe, really.

The Green Zone, which some people referred to as The Bubble, was a four-square-mile bulwark of safety against anyone who might want to harm the people inside with rifles, mortar shells, or suicide bombs. It was here, inside seventeen-foot-high concrete barricades, that were housed most foreign nationals—not only diplomats and "advisors," but employees of companies like Halliburton, who were in charge of staffing and maintaining the hotels, or Blackwater USA, who provided private security guards to whoever had enough moolah to afford them.

I had known that the Baghdad Zoo was located in the Green Zone, but it had never occurred to me to go there. On the many previous occasions when I had gone into The Bubble, I was always strapped for time scheduling interviews, getting press briefings, and trying to get back to my hotel before dark. Too, I was put off by stories I had heard about the zoo: cages being opened during the invasion and animals stolen by looters. Birds and goats— even one of the giraffes— had been eaten by the looters or sold on the international black market. Other animals had starved for days in their cages because zoo workers were afraid to come to work. Maybe I'm not a zoo person. I hadn't known I needed a horse fix, but the opportunity to see the Arabians Ossie had mentioned was perking me up as nothing had in months.

After we had shown our credentials at several checkpoints, we walked through streets relatively empty at this time of morning. Rows of date palms and other lushness actually thrived in the Green Zone, but pedestrians often missed the greenery because they had to keep their eyes on the ground in order to avoid falling over rubble or stepping into a deep rut made by an army tank. Nevertheless, we hadn't gone three blocks before two western women jogged past us wearing shorts and t-shirts. One was wearing earphones. It was a different world inside the Green Zone. Anywhere else in Iraq, women not wearing veils and voluminous, ankle-length skirts could be harassed by clerics and kidnapped by criminals. In fact, the repressive gender dynamics in Iraq had gotten worse since the invasion: some Iraqi women I had interviewed told me that, fearful of being attacked on the street, they stayed in their houses with the curtains closed.

"Did you know that Baghdad has a track?" the Enemy Hunter said in his rich, bricky voice.

"What, you mean like to jog around?" I asked.

"A horse racing track. The Equestrian Club of Baghdad at the edge of the city. I went there with some of my unit. It's very popular—more now than before the Operation."

"Why is that?" I asked.

"Because Saddam's two sons owned a lot of thoroughbreds and liked to race them. They always won."

"The other owners were afraid to beat them?" I asked.

"Uday and Qusay didn't like to lose, no, but they could afford to buy all the best horses—except for the Iraqi National Herd."

"What happened to Uday and Qusay's horses?"

"Stolen by looters, same as everything else in Baghdad. But fine horses are sacred in Iraq. A lot of them were recovered."

"And taken to the zoo?" I asked.

"No, no. To the Equestrian Club stables."

"But you said—"

"It's the National Herd that's at the zoo," he said.

"So, what's the National Herd?"

"It's easier to show you. We'll be there in a few minutes."

We were passing the British compound, where we saw a sign posted on a lightpole that said, "You're not paranoid: Everyone IS out to get you." Music wafted out of one of the Halliburton trailers from Freedom Radio—a station that specialized in classic rock and patriotic patter. I waved to a British journalist I knew, then turned back to Ossie.

"Why your interest in horses?" I asked. "Is it a cultural thing?"

"Partly," he said. "Mostly. That's why I joined the 1st Cavalry Division." He pointed to the insignia on his lapel—a yellow shield with the black profile of a horse's head. "Back at Ft. Hood, I was a part of the Horse Cavalry Detachment—we take care of the Army's horses and mules—mostly ceremonial stuff. When we found out about the National Herd, some of us volunteered to come over and rebuild their barn."

"You *volunteered* to come to Iraq?" I asked incredulously.

Ossie shrugged. "You did, too," he replied. He stopped in front of the thick iron gates of the 2,500-acre al-Zawra entertainment park and looked through the bars. "This is it," he said.

Inside, we strolled for a few minutes through rows of cages in various states of repair. If I remember correctly there was a porcupine, some German Shepherds, a lion cub, and a few camels. We stood there for a few seconds, admiring the camels, wondering if they would be fun to ride. Eventually, though, we passed out of the purviews of the zoo proper and came to an area with twenty newly constructed stalls of timber and iron. The area was cleaner than the rest of the zoo and I could see horses resting in stalls. Ossie greeted a soldier pushing a wheelbarrow filled with manure. The front of his sweaty t-shirt read "1st Cavalry" in brown letters.

"So, um, you work here?" I asked.

"When I'm not drilling or going on supply runs." He walked up to the first stall and stroked the mane of the small, fine-boned white mare within. We made a tour of the stalls, and Ossie gave each horse a squarish alfalfa cube from a storage room. He called each one by its name and explained to me what the names meant. They were truly magnificent, proud creatures. He showed me the acres of pasture that they had for turnout and the large supplies of hay and feed, all of it donated by Western equine charity organizations. We sat down on a stack of lumber and Ossie told me a little about himself—that he has a wife in Billings, for instance. She is from another tribe, the Gros Ventre. He has two young boys and had been a high school history teacher before he enlisted. Maybe he would try to get his master's when he got back, try to get a job at the college in Crow Agency. He could teach Native American History, maybe throw in some information on the bow and arrow. He smiled as he said this.

"So tell me the history of the Iraqi National Herd," I said.

Ossie tilted his head back slightly, then began. "Their line goes back to the ancient Sumerians—the oldest civilization on earth. It was located right here at the Tigris and Euphrates conjunction."

"Sometimes," I said, "I walk out on my balcony and look into the Tigris and wonder how many millions of stories have passed down its currents. I mean, Iraq is exotic enough now, but imagine how it must have been when it was part of the Ottoman Empire!"

"And it was Babylon, too," he told me.

"Tell me about the Sumerians," I said.

"For one thing, they kept records on clay tablets."

"Cuneiform," I remembered. "The first newspapers, kind of."

"Yes. And many of them, thousands of them, survived the centuries. Some of the records were about breeding and domesticating horses."

"I didn't know that," I said. "God, my mother would give anything to see those."

"Me, too," he said. "But the information in those tablets was passed down through generations, and when the descendents of the Sumerians and the Babylonians became wanderers of the desert, they took their horses with them."

"Do you find a lot of similarity between Middle Eastern Bedouin tribes and American Indian tribes."

"A little. The tribal systems still exist in both cultures."

"Both have respect for the horse," I added.

"Yes. I mean, we don't use the horse to get around any more, or to carry our homes from place to place, but the idea of the horse is still ingrained in us. The Iraqis kept and nurtured a special herd of over a hundred purebred Arabians."

"My mother told me once that the Dutch government owns some of their country's best warmbloods. It might be the same in Germany, too. They have hundreds of years of selective breeding."

"The Iraqi National Herd has five *thousand* years of selective breeding. And like you say of the Dutch, they didn't belong to Saddam or his sons, they're not Sunni or Shiite, and they don't belong to one city rather than another. They belong to the Iraqi people as a whole. In a way, if you help the horses, you help the people."

I closed my eyes and visualized a herd of magnificent

Arabian horses running free over miles of pasture land, free to fight and race and breed. Then I opened them and looked toward the dozen and a half stalls.

"Where are the rest?" I asked.

"The rest?"

"You told me that there are over a hundred horses in the herd but there are only, what, twenty stalls."

The Enemy Hunter looked toward the stalls and a sadness came into his eyes. "When the first Army units deployed into the city," he began, "there was a firefight. A cruise missile destroyed their old barn. Only nineteen horses survived."

"They were killed?" I asked stupidly.

Ossie nodded.

And there, then, the barrier I had been building up inside myself to keep from feeling any real anger or sadness or futility started giving way, not with a mortar shell or a bomb, but more like its atoms just fell apart and crumbled to dust, and I was suddenly engulfed in grief.

"Wait. Let me get this straight," I began, tears starting to come. "To protect the oil flow to American gas guzzlers, the military slaughtered more than eighty 5000-year-old pureblood Arabian horses?" The tears were streaming down my face. It was the first time I had cried since I arrived in Iraq, and I have cried many times since.

"Collateral damage," he said. He paused, looking away, then added an afterthought. "It was a Tomahawk".

"What?" I felt dumb in so many ways and had no idea what he was talking about.

"The cruise missile that took out the horses. It's called a Tomahawk."

When I couldn't find anything to reply, he said simply, "I want to go back home."

"Me too."

As we walked back to the hotel, the life seemed to go out of both of us. I suppose we talked about our future plans, what we would do when we got back home, although I'm sure I didn't have a clue. I do remember one thing more before we parted in the lobby. I asked him if it were possible for me to see the old cuneiform tablets with the inscribed breeding information that had been preserved so carefully for millennia.

"Gone," he said simply.

"Gone? What do you mean gone?"

"The museum was hit by another missile. Whatever wasn't pulverized into dust was stolen by looters."

The next day I got my wish to go home. My mother had been bucked off her three-year-old filly and killed.

Chapter 1

By the looks of my bedroom, the last few weeks had been bad ones. Dirty sheets lay heaped up in a corner surrounded by almost a month's worth of clothes. Against the wall, my blue iMac computer splattered with yellow stick-it notes sat on a small desk littered with flint arrowheads. A dozen tightly crumpled sheets of paper lay on the floor by the printer where I had dropped them in disgust. On a nightstand, an unopened bottle of tequila kept company with a digital alarm clock and a conch shell ashtray. An overhead fan created a slight draft that wafted marijuana smoke toward an open-curtained window. And below the fan blades, I was lying naked and damp on a rumpled queen-size bed.

Almost eleven months had passed since my mother's funeral, which I missed when the transport plane I was supposed to catch out of Amman had been grounded for two days because of a bomb scare. I still loved journalism, but was sick of reporting on war and death. After leaving Baghdad I quit my high-profile job with *The Richmond Times-Dispatch*, staged a fight with my boyfriend, and moved back to my home town of Pine Oak, a small city in the Florida panhandle, where there was not much else but forest, breeze, and a twice-weekly gossip sheet called *The Pine Oak Courier*. I got a job with *The Courier*, which paid almost nothing, and moved to my parents' farm, empty now except for me.

A couple of months before, I had started dating

someone new, but being with him had been too much like war.

I reached out and placed my roach clip carefully in the conch shell. Marijuana is generally not my thing, but a supply of the stuff had recently dropped into my lap and I was languidly high. Not high enough to forget that I would be spending Friday night at home again, but high enough, if I concentrated, to slow down the fan blades to the point where I could read the letters that were scrawled in lipstick on each one: D-O-N-N-Y.

Never trust guys with 5-letter names. They'll write their names on your fan blades. Later, they'll begin on your shoulder blades and work their way down and around until their names are inscribed throughout your whole body.

But Donny was gone now. Was with Linda C now. Looking back on it, I realized that it was partly my illness that had driven him away. Breathlessness, fatigue, and general depression had crept over me so slowly that I at first assumed they were the effects of my mother's death combined with the hopeless knowledge that I had uprooted myself from a situation I had worked all my life to attain, only to return to a place I had once vowed to escape from. But it had gone beyond that now and I often found myself staring at those dark fan blades, my heart drumming like galloping hooves. I was starting to think I had some kind of combat fatigue that was lingering far longer than it should. It was getting worse as the months went by.

Getting high is for shit. I was reaching toward the whirring fan to smear out the letters when the harsh notes of a jangling phone cut through me like shards of glass. I grabbed blindly for the receiver, knocking the conch shell onto the bare wooden floor with a clunk, spewing ashes everywhere. The hooves were trying to kick through my chest. I let the phone ring once, twice, until I was calm enough to answer.

"'Lo?"

"Sue-Ann? Hey, it's me, Mark."

"Hey, Memark," I answered.

"Listen, Sue-Ann. Are you busy right now?"

"Busy?" I asked.

"Mr. Dent just called me on my cell. There's something going on down at Meekins' Market. Can you get down there?"

The shock of the ringing phone was wearing off and I tried to will myself alert. I failed. I was stoned and tired deep through to my bones. I looked at the digital clock. Nine twenty-five p.m. I stalled. "What is it?"

"Not sure; something about a dead goat. But there are supposed to be cars from at least three law enforcement agencies."

"Cal Dent called to tell you about a dead goat?"

"He heard it from Billy Dollar."

"Dilly called in another story?"

"I guess."

"Why tell me, then? You're the fair-haired boy."

"Come on, Sue-Ann," he wheedled. "I can't help it if the boss has been using a lot of my stuff lately. But I can't do this one. I'm drunk."

"You don't sound drunk to me. Besides, who isn't?" In the silence that ensued, I heard voices in the background, the sound of cars on a highway. "Where are you?" I asked.

"Some little speakeasy in Forester. And listen, Sue-Ann, I'm not alone, do you know what I mean?"

I propped my back against the cool headboard and tried to think it over. Billy Dollar—who drove the only night patrol car in Pine Oak—got ten bucks every time he tipped off Cal Dent that there was a story to be had. It was supposed to be a secret from the other officers but even the sheriff up in the county seat knew about it and used it as an unspoken excuse not to give Billy a raise. A few of his tips had been good ones, though, like the time an eighteen wheeler had jackknifed and scattered bricks of high-grade marijuana along both shoulders of the interstate. I was currently reaping the benefits of that story.

"Okay, Mr. Hormone. Tell me about the goat."

"Thanks, Sue-Ann. Only thing I know is that the guy down at Meekins' found a dead goat in his dumpster."

"Somebody murdered a goat?"

"Right, that's what I heard."

"And Cal wants you to go down there and find out why?"

"Maybe there's something to it." His voice told me that he thought nothing of the kind.

"Yeah," I told him. "Sure. I'll get over there as soon as I can."

"I owe you."

I hung up.

Right. I was going to rush out into the night and try to get an interview with the last person to see the goat alive. I thought about rolling another jay, but fell asleep instead.

It was a fitful sleep, a few hours of unconsciousness followed by an hour of drowsy discomfort, trying to shape my pillow into a mass that fit my head, searching for a cool spot on the bed or a comfortable position. When the fluorescent numbers on the clock read 5 a.m, I gave it up for the night. The air was cool, made more so by the slowly spinning fan, but I was covered with sweat. Still, I felt surprisingly rested and alert. The marijuana seemed to have done some good after all. I flung on a terry-cloth robe and padded into the kitchen to turn on the coffeemaker. Kitty Amin, my black shorthair, was asleep on a blanket on one edge of the sofa. The cat half-raised his head as I passed, then settled back down into his nap.

Waiting for coffee to brew is worse for me than waiting in line at a party for a bathroom to be free, but five interminable minutes later, I returned to the living room, coffee cup in hand. I switched on the radio, dial set all the way to the left, then sat down on the sofa next to Amin with the intention of going through a pile of mail that had been collecting for a few days. The voice on the radio was that of a young woman, giggly, maybe a little drunk or high. Probably the deejay who called herself Gamma. She was giving a recipe for okra stew but her voice kept fading out, as if she were moving around in the booth and only occasionally talking directly into the microphone. I had discovered the pirate station while channel surfing a couple of months before and was fascinated. It had no set call letters, sometimes claiming to be W-O-R-M or W-F-U-K. Sometimes the number of letters didn't seem to be important and I had heard W-E-I-R-D and W-I-C-K-E-D.

Gamma was on the air again. "And if you don't like it, you can always toss it in your mulch pile. Hey, I found an old Yma Sumac record in the Goodwill store yesterday for a dime. I mean, it was marked a dime, but I ripped it off." She giggled again. "I'll play a few cuts from it, then read you a poem I just wrote."

Abruptly, a series of needle pops came over the air followed by the highest pitched voice I have ever heard, scatting to a kind of Brazilian big-band beat. It was the kind of thing I had come to expect from the station— something totally unusual or outrageous. I was glad someone was on tonight—sometimes days went by without a peep and I worried that the FCC had closed in on the mysterious station. I listened with a kind of sensual tranquility as I leafed through a Dover Saddlery catalog,

16

through junk circulars and credit card offers. My sweats had stopped and the coffee was working its spirited magic.

I took up a letter from my insurance company and ripped open the side as the high voice in the song descended several octaves into a kind of bear growl. My rates were going up. I remembered the TV advertisement the company had used to entice me into buying it: "And if you buy your policy now, your rates will *never* go up." Maybe it depended on your definition of "up" or maybe "never." Either way, I was screwed. My savings were next to nothing and it was obvious that Cal Dent was easing me out of my job. Telling me to rest, take it easy, giving all my stories to Mark.

Oho, a letter from my father, postmarked where? Italia. Me o my o. I slid it onto the coffee table to read later and trudged back into the kitchen for another cup of coffee. I glanced through the window; the full moon was just visible through the ridge of pines beyond the pasture. The faint popping of rifles passed through the window from hunters far out in the forest. It was a sound that always gave me a jolt, a phantom bullet passing through my heart.

On the radio Gamma was reading her poem. It was way out there, as her stuff usually was; a flurry of adjectives descending on an idea that I couldn't latch onto, although I had a vague suspicion that one existed.

> *It was whistly, grisly, blood on the moon*
> *a ripening tripening, diapered cartoon.*

Gamma went on for a few more lines in that same vein, then, without stopping for effect, said, "And now, apropos of absolutely nothing here on eighty point oh the recipe station, is a whole side of Mick, Keith, and the boys doing their version of the album they call *Goat's Head Soup.*

Get your five-thirty a.m. asses out of bed and dig it."

I jerked my head up involuntarily. Goat?

There was a dead goat at Meekins' market. Coincidence? Maybe. Probably. Certainly. But Gamma—and most of the other nattering deejays at the pirate station—sometimes gave me the heebie jeebies. Maybe that's why I tuned in. Five-thirty? Check out a goat in a dumpster at the edge of town?

I didn't have anything better to do.

~ ~ ~

A dozen Styrofoam coffee containers were hip-hopping along my floorboards as I sped along the rutted dirt road. A dry few weeks had turned the road into a long washboard. When I first moved back to Pine Oak I had gotten mad at the young bucks for speeding down the rough road at double the posted limit; later I learned that the faster you went, the less you bounced. Tonight, my old Toyota pickup sailed over the ruts with just a little shimmy. The few houses out this way were still dark and my headlights showed the way clearly. No dust meant that no one was up and about yet. When I turned onto the highway I switched on the radio. The Stones were still playing. I like them okay, but I'd never heard of *Goat's Head Soup*. It was all right, I guess, something to get through the couple of miles I had to drive. But I made a mental note to check on whether the Stones had ever actually made a record with that name.

I had been shopping at Meekins' Market pretty much all my life. Situated on the very edge of town, it was the last place to get groceries for most of the folks living in the rural areas—like me—and the first for people driving in from Forester. And its unusual two-part structure made it one of the strangest places in this part of the country. The front building was just a rectangular stall paralleling the highway, thrown together with two-by-fours and chicken wire. But as you entered, the walls gradually conformed themselves to fit into a Quonset hut that old man Meekins had bought off the Army for twenty-three cans of shoe polish right after World War II. I had gone to high school with the current Meekins—Clarence—who had been a talented athlete but turned down a football scholarship at Wabash College to run the family business. Hadn't made many improvements in those sixteen years—the chicken wire was probably from the same roll that his granddad fished out of an abandoned construction site back in the forties; nevertheless, it had become the best place in Jasper County for pretty much whatever it carried on a given day. No one knew how Clarence was able to get the jump on the Piggly Wiggly, but the produce boxes crammed onto the old wooden shelves held the freshest fruit and vegetables in the area. Customers could also find various kinds of nuts, herbs, seeds, locally produced honey, even sugar cane in season. You could also buy azalea and boxwood plants for your front yard and a straw hat with a green sun visor to wear while you tucked them into the soil. Then there were the more unusual items: boxes of used harmonicas, containers of glass spools that formerly sat atop telephone poles, rows of vintage postcards, and issues of *Look Magazine* and *TV Guide* from the 1950s. People liked to browse the crowded aisles back in the darkened Quonset hut—it would be rare to find something you were actually looking for, but almost impossible to come out empty-handed.

But if Clarence's purchasing wizardry was a mystery, so was his strange habit of closing up shop for weeks at a time without a word. Anyone looking through the chicken wire would see every shelf completely empty. Yet when he opened back up—a week or a month later—everything would be as fresh and exotic as before, although maybe switched around some location wise. And somewhere in the burgeoning aisles would be a box or rack of items that was not there before.

Thing is, though, Meekins' didn't sell goats, didn't sell meat of any kind. I pulled off the road and stopped in front of the market. I switched off the ignition and the headlights. It was still dark, although the light haze of a rising sun could be discerned through the trees. The place would be opening up soon and I could ask some questions. In the meantime, I wanted to see the dumpster. I grabbed a flashlight from the glove box, got out of the truck, and began walking around the side of the stall toward the back of the Quonset hut. Halfway there I heard a harsh clatter like the heavy door of a dumpster being opened or closed. Had Clarence gotten there ahead of me? I hadn't seen his car, but he lived just across the street and could have walked over. Or maybe his mom, who tended the register nearly every day from sunup to sundown. I walked faster.

"That you, Clarence?" I shouted. "It's Sue-Ann." Another clatter and a hush of voices, then hurried footsteps. I rounded the aluminum building and cast the light from my flash at the square green dumpster sitting just inside the tree line. But no Clarence. I shone my light at the trees and caught what looked to be the shadow of running legs and I heard the crunch of heavy boots on dry leaves.

"Wait!" I called loudly, and sprinted the last twenty yards to the treeline. I moved the light back and forth, lasering the trees and shrubs but caught no sign of the person I thought I had seen running away. I wanted to follow whoever it was—the flashlight revealed a faint trail through the high grass—but even that short run tuckered me out and set my heart groaning. I had to go down on my haunches to rest. I went through a litany of curses—some in different languages—but none did any good.

Clomping footsteps approached from the direction of the market and I heard a familiar voice shout, "Who's back here?"

I managed to stand up and compose myself. "It's me, Clarence. Sue-Ann."

I clicked off my flashlight as Clarence came into view. Clarence was a big man, and he looked bigger in the semi-darkness. He was wearing his inevitable brogans and blue overalls and his hair was slicked back like he had just gotten out of the shower. The only odd thing about him was the shotgun he was toting. The stock was held in his right hand; the barrel lay loosely in the crook of his left elbow. "God's balls, Sue-Ann. What are you doin back here?"

"Working on a—" I had to stop and take a couple of breaths. "Working on a story about that goat," I managed. "For *The Courier.* You figure on using that shotgun on me?"

"Not if you ain't killed no livestock and put em in my garbage."

I started to retort, but Clarence waved away my words. "Just kiddin, Sue-Ann. Saw your truck pull up just as I was ready to come over. Thought you were an early customer." Clarence walked over to the dumpster and peered inside. Then he looked back at me. "You open the door?" he asked.

"No, I . . . I was going to, but somebody was already here. I chased them for a while. . . ."

"Wondered why you were huffin and puffin so. Did you see who it was?"

"Too dark. And whoever it was heard me coming. Ran off into the woods right in there."

Clarence walked to the edge of the woods and peered into the darkness. When he turned back around he looked pensive. Holding the shotgun in his left hand he walked back to where I waited. "Still workin for *The Courier*, eh?" he asked.

"Yeah. But if you want me to talk you've got to give me coffee."

His face brightened as more of the sun crept through the trees. "Got some fresh beans yesterday morning," he told me. "Had to drive down to Panama City to get em. Got some ground and ready for the pot."

"Let me get my purse out of the truck."

Ten minutes later we were sitting across from each other at the counter made of nailed-together 2 by 12s, drinking hot, rich coffee from hastily washed-out cups. Banks of rudely mounted fluorescent lighting cast a ghastly glow over everything.

"Okay, Sue Ann," Clarence began. "Doesn't *The Courier* have better things to write about than some kid's prank?"

"If you think it's a prank, why are you carrying around that twelve-gauge?" I parried.

Clarence shrugged his big shoulders and sipped from his cup. "Guess you got me there. Truth is, the whole thing makes me a little uneasy."

"What was a dead goat doing in your dumpster, Clarence?" I asked.

"I can't imagine," he said. "Unless some kids thought it would be a good idea to leave a carcass at a vegetarian grocery."

"They would have left it where people could see it," I told him. "Probably right in front there."

"Yeah. I guess."

"Who found the goat, anyway?"

"Me. When I went to throw away the day's garbage I saw it. Called the sheriff, but he just sent Dollar out."

So much for the law enforcement agencies of three counties, or whatever Mark had told me. "Did you see what kind of goat it was?"

"No mystery, there, Sue Ann. It was a young Alpine— just a regular dairy goat—mostly black. Belonged to Ray Colley."

"How'd you find that out?" I asked.

"He's about the only one in Jasper County who keeps dairy goats—I've probably sold you hunks of cheese that came from his place. After Dilly left last night, I loaded the goat in a produce box and drove over there. It was one of his all right."

"Colley's a County Commissioner," I said, but I was really thinking out loud. "Do you think somebody might have gotten mad at him and killed one of his goats as kind of a revenge thing?"

"Colley lives half a dozen miles from here," Clarence answered. "And just like you said earlier, if it was to snipe at him, why not just leave it where he could see it when he got up in the morning?"

"I guess you're right about that."

Clarence sat silently over the dregs of his coffee.

"But if somebody was back there just now," I asked, "where could they have run off to?"

Clarence was silent. "Clarence?"

"Sorry, Sue Ann. What were you askin?"

"If somebody *was* back there, where would they go? Who owns those woods back there?"

"God's testicles, Sue Ann, there are thousands and thousands of acres between here and Hanson's Quarry. "I own a few; paper company owns a lot more. Some of it's swamp, some forest."

"Are there any roads?" I asked.

"None that anyone knows about. Used to be a few farms way on back there. Remember Rabbit Foote? I heard that his grandpa used to own a couple of hundred acres back there, but that was a long time ago. Rabbit never came back from Kuwait and the rest of his family are dead now. May Barnes had a place out there, too, somewhere. I remember going out there with Pop to pick some radishes and carrots once. She let me sit on her tractor, but she died when I was about five. Guess the forest has taken all that back for itself. Even the dirt road we took to get there is probably gone by now." Clarence hesitated for a moment, then went on. "There was another crazy old family out there, too. Must have been way out because nobody I've ever talked to ever seen the place. Family's name was Tilly or Tolliver or something like that. But they must have cleared out, or died off like the rest."

"Listen, I see your mom coming over, so let me ask you one more thing. How was the goat killed? Was it like one of those cattle mutilations you read about?"

Clarence thought for a while. "It's possible, but I doubt it. The throat was slit—and that's how you're supposed to slaughter a goat—but it was a messy job. And then there was a big cut in the belly. Some entrails had been half pulled out—or maybe pulled out and half pushed back in."

"Maybe a ritual of some kind? A sacrifice?"

"Sacrifice?" Clarence thought it over. "You may be on to something there, but I still think it was a kid's prank. Probably on some kind of drugs and the thing got out of hand."

I had to admit that Clarence was probably right. I got up and began to browse the shelves. I already had enough honey. Apples, too, and I doubted that I'd need any of the dozens of what appeared to be Vietnam service medals and ribbons. I generally shake my head in disbelief at least once per visit, and I did so now. Then I came to a rough box piled high with small, rectangular sandbags. When I picked one up it felt like it was filled with rice. It also had a pleasant but medicine-y smell.

"What are these?" I asked.

Clarence came over. "These are pillows you put on your eyes. Eye-pillows. Home made."

I lifted one to my nose. "What's in em?" I asked.

"Some flax seed, eucalyptus oil, bunch of other stuff."

"Did you make them?"

"Naw, but I know some people," he said. "And don't worry, they don't sting your eyes none. I use em myself. Good for headaches, stuffy sinuses, and it relaxes you like nothing this side of rotgut whisky."

Just then Gladys Meekins, dressed in a flowery print dress and white orthopedic shoes, walked in the door carrying a black handbag and a dish covered in tinfoil. I fished around in my purse for a couple of bills.

"Up early today, aren't ya?" Gladys asked. We didn't know each other well, really, but we usually spoke a few words whenever I came in.

"Couldn't sleep. Need some coffee. Give me a pound of that stuff we just had, Clarence. And this eye-pillow."

As Clarence went to fill a small paper bag with some whole beans, his mother set her dish down near the register and placed her handbag under the counter. The plate reminded me I hadn't eaten since lunch the day before. "That smells really great," I told the old lady. "What have you got there?"

Gladys looked over at her son and cackled. "Goat cutlets," she said. "Hee hee."

I shook my head. All the Meekins were kind of weird.

In fact, Clarence's dad, who had worked the market for almost forty years, simply disappeared from Pine Oak just after Clarence got out of the army. I was in graduate school then, but on visits back home I heard various rumors: that he had run off with a customer to a retirement community in Lake Worth, that he had become an itinerant beggar-for-god, that he had died. I asked Clarence about his dad once, but he had quickly changed the subject.

I stuffed the eye-pillow in my purse, picked up my sack of coffee beans, and went out. Instead of driving out to the highway, though, I pulled back around to the dumpster. I had an idea and wanted to check it out now that it was full light. I walked out to the part of the woods where I thought I had seen someone running and looked closely at the leafy ground. Lots of scuffing, but nothing that I could actually identify as a footprint. Just to the side of one of the scuff marks I spotted a reddish blotch in the sand. I bent down and moistened my finger with my tongue, then passed it along the stain. It came up red and sandy. Blood, almost for sure.

Whoever had left that goat in Clarence Meekins' dumpster had not just stolen it and carried it six miles, they had presumably taken the goat into the woods and killed it. But why? One thing I was sure of: it was too elaborate to have been a prank.

Well, I had my story, at least part of it. But how to get the rest? The healthy part of me wanted to traipse into the woods and see if I could track the goat killers back to where they had come from. Trouble was, the healthy part wasn't in control right then. I knew I couldn't get more answers without more rest.

But a story was a story, especially in a quiet town like Pine Oak. Back in the pickup I began to develop it in my head, feeling phrases take shape and nudging them into polished sentences, a task made easy by long practice. By the time I got home all I had to do was type it up and drop it by the office. Maybe a shower first, though. Maybe a nap . . .

But when I arrived home and went inside, I saw that my living room had been ransacked. Desk drawers strewn against the wall. Papers were everywhere. The bedroom had been treated similarly. Bureau drawers yanked out, pillows on the floor, the closet door wide open and clothes thrown down in heaps. Even the mattress was askew. The realization hit me like a gust of freezing wind that whoever had done this might still be in the house. I was frightened, but I carefully searched the rest of the house until I was sure I was alone. Then I called the sheriff's office. The only things I touched were my roach clip, which I hid, and the remnants of my joint, which I carefully swept up and threw outside in some bushes.

What next? It would take hours to go through the house and see if anything was missing, even longer to go through all the police bullshit with the sheriff or whoever he sent out. I heard a muffled scuffling in the kitchen that almost made me run back out the front door before I realized it was only Amin coming in his cat door. I picked up the cat and stroked it. "Did you see who did this, boy?" I asked hopelessly. The cat just looked back at me silently, trusting that I would fix whatever needed fixing or solve whatever needed solving.

"Guess it's lucky you're not a goat," I told him.

Chapter 2

The offices of *The Pine Oak Courier* were tucked away in the corner of an L-shaped shopping center just off the main highway. The shorter wing was taken up by the Piggly Wiggly grocery store. The longer wing consisted of a row of smaller shops and offices: *The Courier*, an attorney's office, an empty space, a used bookstore, and a laundrymat. I pulled my pickup into a space alongside Cal Dent's new Ford Explorer and shut off the motor. I was way late for the morning briefing. I threw my purse over my shoulder, grabbed the yellow legal pad I always carry in the truck, and hurried through the glass door.

The Courier made do with just a few rooms. The first three—Cal Dent's office, my office, and a slightly larger conference room—took up most of the front. The rest was divided by portable walls into half a dozen cubicles, each with a computer hookup. A couple of drawing boards were set up against the back wall for paste-up. I had worked more than a decade for a far more sizable paper and, by comparison, *The Courier* was a cramped, stuffy little place. But I still liked it and often drove the five miles in to the office just to type up my stories in its muffled-clackety environment.

As I approached the conference room I saw five heads glance up from their notes. The man at the head of the rectangular table, Calvin Dent, was a man in his mid-forties with graying hair. He was the editor of *The Courier* and as usual he was nattily dressed, this time in a dark, pin-stripe suit and baby-blue tie. The others were Mark Patterson, handsome, twenty-three, and just out of journalism school; typesetting and paste-up specialist Betty Dickson, plump and dowdy; Paul Hughes, pot-bellied ex-Marine major in charge of writing about local politics; and too-pretty Ginette Cartwright, who was not only the sales representative and office manager, but was also sleeping with Cal Dent. Ginette and I had a strange rivalry that went back over twenty years; I'll explain when I have a moment.

"Sorry I'm late," I said. "I—"

"Weren't expecting you at all today, Sue-Ann," Cal Dent said. Concern showed in his face, which embarrassed me. "In fact, we . . ."

"I'm fine, Cal. Rest is for people who are dead."

"We heard your house got broken into," continued my boss.

"Oh, that. How did you . . ." But I didn't finish the sentence.

"Dilly Dollar called," said Ginette. "But all he knew was a bunch of nothin. Any ahdea who it was?"

"No idea at all. All my stuff got thrown around."

"Anythin stolen?"

"Don't know yet. Dilly told me not to mess around with things before he dusted for fingerprints. By the time he finished, all I had time to do was jump in the shower and get over here before the meeting was over."

"Dilly wouldn't be able to fahnd a fingerprint even if there was a dozen burglars and they had all just dipped their fingers in a bottle a ink," said Ginette. Oddly, of the six people in the room, only Ginette had lived all her life in Pine Oak and was the only employee of *The Courier* who spoke with the small town's unique accent. I used to speak exactly the same way, but the accent had been drilled out of me in the dozen years I was away.

"I thought his name was Bill," said Betty.

"Prahvit joke," said Ginette, who had not warmed up to the baggy, middle-aged typesetter in the months since Betty had been hired—even though it was Ginette's old job that Betty had taken over.

"We started calling him Dilly in junior high," I told Betty. "I forget why just now, but it stuck."

"You went to school with him?" Betty asked me.

"Me, Ginette, half this town," I told her. I turned to Ginette. "I just saw Clarence Meekins. He's another. And, hey, I may have something for Friday."

"Something about the break-in at your house?" asked Cal, interested.

"Not that," I replied. The last thing I wanted was to be the subject of a news story rather than the reporter of one. "It's that goat thing."

"Right, the dumpster goat," Cal said. "Someone got mad at Ray Colley and killed one of his goats."

"Well, that's what Dilly thinks, but—"

"Mark agrees with Officer Dollar this time," Cal said. "How'd you find out about it anyway?" he asked.

A glance was all I needed to see that Mark had gone rigid. The little twerp. He must have told Cal that he had checked out the story himself instead of getting me out of bed. Well, I'd keep his secret this time, but it was going to cost him.

"I—I went out to Meekins' Market to get some coffee," I said. "Clarence told me about it."

"Clarence is a square shooter," Ginette said. "What's *he* think?"

"He doesn't really know. Probably agrees with Mark"—I gave him a look. "But I think there's more to it than that. Something kind of ritualistic."

"You mean Satanic or somethin lahk that?" asked

Ginette. She took a pack of cigarettes from a small purse and put it in front of her on the table.

"I don't know about Satanic," I replied. "But haven't you ever read about cattle mutilations, or heard stories about people going around poisoning cats and dogs?"

Paul Hughes spoke for the first time. It's hard to describe his voice other than saying that it was deep and kind, but also subtly condescending—a voice that would be more appropriately used in speaking to children or mice. "Right now it's just one goat, Sue-Ann," he said. "I'm not sure that's enough for a story, know what I mean?"

I did know. He meant that it would embarrass Commissioner Ray Colley, who was a decent guy and who was always good for a story, no matter how boring, about local politics. But he was also someone who kept his private life private.

"I agree with Paul," Cal said. "But if there are any more killings or mutilations we'll pounce on it. Mark, keep your ears open."

"Yes sir." Mark Patterson looked down at his notebook and scribbled what looked like two wavy lines.

"Let me do some more work on it," I said. "There are a couple of weird things I noticed at—"

Cal Dent cut me off. "You have too much on your mind already," he told me. "Take some time to get your place back in shape. Get some sleep."

"What else do you have for Friday?" I asked.

"We settled that before you got here," Cal told me. He looked down at his own notes. "A revival, a city commission meeting, the schedule for hunting season. I'm going to work up a report on how the real estate market is doing since the election." He looked up. "And the usual stuff from the community columnists. A few letters to the editor. If you want to write something, do a story about this year's Plank Festival. Maybe some kind of history from the beginning until now."

"That's more than a month away."

"You'll have plenty of time, then. If you want, there's some kind of rodeo going on next weekend in Forester—you can cover that. Not a big deal though." Cal looked around the table. "Anything else? Okay—that's it."

I stayed seated after the others had left. Maybe Cal was right. Maybe I needed to get my house in order and forget about chasing stories for a while. I sighed and got up, tucking my pad under my arm, and made my way out of the room. Betty was sitting at one of the back drafting tables lining up ads in columns for the next issue's shopper. Ginette sat in one of the cubicles, phone in one hand and a Rolodex in the other. The former local beauty queen had been the paper's typesetter for years until she began taking on other duties. In high school she and I had run in different crowds and were only classroom acquaintances. She had been popular, I had not; I had been a pretty good student, she had been average. I always had the idea that she was kind of flighty and aloof and I'd been surprised when her tenacity and gift of persuasion raised both the paper's circulation and its advertising revenue. Ginette looked up at me as I passed and gave a little nod. We had never been friends, but as long as she was good for the paper, I could work with her.

Cal was in his office talking to Paul Hughes and Joe Rooney, the attorney who occupied the office down the row. The three men often played golf together.

Mark Patterson was nowhere to be seen.

On the way to my pickup, I caught sight of a hunkered-down little man struggling to unlock the front door of The Best Little Bookstore in Pine Oak. It was the *only* bookstore in Pine Oak and I was a regular visitor. I liked to read; in fact, I had a pretty good background in English literature. Lately, though—ever since I got back from Baghdad—I found myself in more and more of a trash-reading mood, mainly the fat fantasy novels favored by my ex-boyfriend Donny. The fact that Donny was totally screwed up should have made me take a step back, but hey, reading about the lives of dragons and warriors kept me from thinking too much about my own life. And The Best Little Bookstore was eclectic if nothing else. I threw my notebook and purse on the front seat and walked over.

"Hey, Benny," I said.

The man was so intent on the lock that my voice startled him and he dropped his key and stammered a "Hey hey, little lady, long time no see." He retrieved the key and poked at the lock again.

"I think you've got your key upside down," I told him

"Umm. Right. Aha. Had an idea for a new kind of lock," he said. "Clumsy people's lock, ha ha."

"How's it work?" I asked.

"Touch. Fingerprint recognition. Sensor units. Just push on the door in the right place and it unlocks automatically. Presto! No keys."

"Got you this time, Benny," I told him. "They already have some of those on the market. They're called biometrics. I did a story about one that they installed in a prison outside Baltimore."

"It was a good idea, then, huh?" he asked.

"It was until some prisoners revolted, cut off one of the guard's fingers, and used it to escape."

"Ewww." He finally conquered the twentieth-century lock, walked inside, and flipped the sign from Open to Closed—something he did about every other day. His name was Dominic Benedict, but most people just called him Benny. Benny was a man of many interests and I enjoyed talking to him as much as I enjoyed browsing his shelves. Not only did he know a smattering about just about every subject he carried, but he was—on a small scale—an inventor, a playwright, and breeder of Manx cats. And strangely enough, he had a college degree in Journalism. After he flicked on the lights, I followed him in, correcting the Closed sign to Open. A tiny bell jingled over my head.

The first time I had been in Benny's bookstore—on a holiday visit a couple of years before—Benny had confided in me that he invented things. In that same conversation he had told me about an idea he had to use Chinese gongs for yardage markers at golf driving ranges. "Bong! Bong!" he chuckled. I had just shaken my head.

Inside, Benny sat down in a wicker chair behind the card table he uses for a front desk. A dozen or so boxes bulging with paperbacks Benny had purchased sat clumped in uneven rows nearby. The same boxes had been there for weeks.

Benny was a short, pudgy man somewhere in his fifties. He was wearing khaki shorts and a black Metallica tee shirt. Flip flops revealed crooked feet and toenails that hadn't been cut recently. Sometime in the last few days he had dyed his hair white and given it a spiky look. As always, there was a band-aid on the side of his face right under mid-ear. The strip didn't quite hide the red, angry-looking skin condition that crept up into his sideburns.

"I came by a couple of times last week but you were closed," I told him. As it happens, Benny was not only the owner of the store but the only employee, and he came in pretty much when he felt like it. It wasn't unusual to see his lights on in the wee hours, with him arranging books on a shelf or pecking out words on the portable typewriter he carried around in his Jeep. Although he had yet to publish his first piece, if the definition of writer is what he gave it out to be: "someone who writes," then Benny was a writer. From my many visits, I knew that he had begun his writing jag as a desk jockey in the Air Force, where he had contributed to the base newsletter. Then he had studied journalism at the University of Florida on the G. I. Bill before drifting down to Jasper County, where he married a woman whose previous husband had left her a small house, a few dollars, and a cattery. The bookstore had already assumed several guises. When he first opened up, he had been writing fiction and had called it Hemingway Heaven. In his poetry phase, which lasted only a few weeks, he had renamed it Ozymandias Books. His playwriting turn had given it its present name. Just before that he had gone through an Alasdair Crowley phase and toyed with the idea of changing the name to Equinox Boox. I talked him out of it. These phases, though, had good results, because he had an eclectic, if limited, selection of fiction, poetry, drama, and occult books.

The little man pursed his lips. "Umm," he said, shaking his head. "I wish . . . ah . . . well, you know. Umm, heh heh, lost my cat. Little bugger disappeared."

It wasn't unusual for me to have to interpret what he was saying into a context that made sense. "That's why you couldn't come in?" I hazarded.

"Yeh, umm hmm."

"Find him?"

"In the cupboard. Wife shut him in by accident. Thought he might be dehydrated, harumpff, so I took him to the vet."

Benny was the master both of the non-sequitur and of human noises. But he used noises like other people use body language. I had done a small interview with him for the business section of *The Courier* several months back and had the hardest time squeezing out anything I could put quotes around. Yet the piece had gotten Benny some extra business and he was grateful.

His card table desk was covered with large sheets of paper containing numbers, musical notations, and odd-looking grids, like tic-tac-toe boxes with hundreds of squares. The pages were professionally printed, like blueprints, but with Benny's chicken scratch added here and there.

I knew I shouldn't ask but couldn't help myself. "What are you working on?"

"These? Ah! Know how when you drive over a bridge?" He stopped, waiting for an answer.

"Uh, yeah. I've driven over a bridge," I said, already regretting my question.

"Know how when you drive over a bridge that has an iron grating you hear a hum?"

"Yeah. Most big bridges have those grates. None around here, though."

"Well, hah, think about that hum. That hum is a note, like C or F sharp, depending."

"Depending on what?" I was becoming more interested.

"On, uh, lots of things: the thickness of the metal, the spacing of the grids, how fast you're going. You know."

"And what does that have to do with anything?" I asked.

"Well, ah, about a year ago—before you moved back—I had a thought. Hmm. I had a thought that if you put together metal grids of different thicknesses, it would make different types of hums. Notes. At a particular speed, say the speed limit hah hah, you could . . . you could play a song with your car." He stopped and looked into my eyes.

"Heh heh," he added.

"Like, what, 'Twinkle twinkle little star?'"

"Yah. Something simple. Sure."

"Benny," I told him. "That's either one of the most brilliant ideas you've ever had or you're just completely crazy. It's one or the other, no in between."

"Well, hoo. Maybe it's nothing, we'll see in a month or two. I've invented a new type of manure fork, though. I've got it in the car. Want to see it?"

"Maybe next time," I told him. "I just came in to pick up—" Actually, I wasn't sure why I had come in, but now it struck me. "Listen, do you know anything about cattle mutilations?"

"Aliens," he said, cackling. "Crop circles."

"No, not like that. Like somebody killing a goat and slitting its belly."

"Ha. Santeria. Yiii! Heh heh."

"What, voodoo?"

"Might be. Know-nothings think that Santeria is some spooky, scary, hip religion. Black cat bones and chicken feet. Boo! Ha ha."

"So what is it really?" I asked.

"Kind of like being Catholic."

"Have you had anyone in here looking for books on Santeria?"

"Yow. Might have. Some punkoids over in that section a couple of days back. Goths, maybe. Giggled some, but left without showing me any dough-re-me. Might have stolen something, though. Eww, didn't think of that."

"Goths?"

"Dark and dreary. Siouxsie and the Banshees, the Cure. Arghh."

"Who were they, do you remember?"

"Nah, I was typing on the play. Had this page I

wanted to get right."

"Back to your play?" I asked.

"Yeh. I finally figured out what was wrong with it."

"You did?"

"Ummmm. I just needed to justify both the right and left margins."

I thought for a moment. I knew that despite Benny's interest in technology, he had never owned a computer. "What, on your typewriter?"

"What else?"

"That would mean that every line would have to have exactly the same number of spaces."

"Hmmm."

"I guess if you added an extra space here and there between the words . . ."

"But that would be cheating," he smiled. "Had to find different words, different ways of saying the same thing so that every line came out exactly even. Took me three days."

"You finished it in three days?" I asked.

"Finished two pages. Whew!"

"That's great." What else could I say?

Benny snorted and blew his nose on a handkerchief he produced from his shorts. "Ah, I found out something about your boyfriend," he told me.

"Donny?" That puzzled me. "I thought I told you we broke up last month."

"Naw. Nope. The surfer boy. One you work with."

"Oh. Mark Patterson. Right. You said you knew somebody in Gainesville who . . ."

"Yow. He's an instructor there now. Turns out that Patterson was in a class of his about a year ago."

"Good student?" I asked.

"Didn't ask. Found out something else, though."

"What, that he's a prick?"

"Naw. Nope. He left sans degree."

"He didn't graduate?" I asked, very surprised at this information.

"That's your story for the next edition. Ha."

"Do you know why he left?" I asked.

"Making the beast with two backs. The old in-out in-out. Whee!"

"Come on, you can't be expelled for having sex," I said.

"Umm. Didn't say he got expelled. Got caught boofing his major professor's new young wife. Decided that retreat was the better part of valor." Benny blew his nose again.

I wondered if Cal knew. Had Mark lied about graduating in order to get his job at *The Courier*? It was worth checking into, but in the meantime it gave me some leverage over him, if I needed it. *More* leverage. I had no quarrel with Mark's work; he was a little green but worked hard and took Cal's red pencil like a trooper. Still . . .

I turned toward the fantasy books, but before I got there I spotted a book in the mystery section with a horse on the cover. A horse mystery? Well, that would be a change. I took it to the table where Benny was actually going through books from one of the boxes. I had to pull out the eye-pillow from my purse to get at my wallet.

"Whazzat?" Benny asked, looking at it with interest.

"It's called an eye-pillow. Never seen one before?"

"Uh, uh." I passed it over to him and he hefted it in his hand. He smelled it. Held it up to his ear and shook it. "Hmm, wheat husks, eucalyptus, some, um, peppermint. Aromatherapy, yah."

I plunked the paperback and two dollars on the card table. Benny picked up the book and looked at the cover. "Horse mystery, eh?"

"I've been thinking about getting back into riding," I told him. Actually, I had only been thinking about it since I saw the book on the shelf, but it seemed like a good idea. "I need something to balance me. Maybe I'll get you to order me some riding books."

Benny stuck the two dollars in his pocket. "Will do," he said. "Just lemme know."

I put the book and eye-pillow in my purse. "Thanks for the information about Mark, Benny. And good luck on your play."

"Oh. Um. I'm working on something else now."

"Something with Santeria in it?" I guessed.

"Umm. Well, heh heh."

Chapter 3

My dark mood returned when I opened my front door and saw the cyclonic mess in the living room. I shouldn't have been surprised since it had been the same when I left. Maybe I had been hoping that someone had come in and cleaned up the mess or better still, that the break-in had never happened. Cushions from the couch were upended, drawers were pulled out from the secretary and their contents strewn everywhere, my father's matched set of Zane Grey books toppled off their shelves and onto the wooden floor. All the rooms of the house had been similarly treated. Both my parents' rooms were trashed as bad as the living room, maybe worse. The furniture in the guest room had been taken apart or rearranged. Food from the cupboards littered the floor of the kitchen. It was like being hit on the head in a raw, bruised place. So much work to do. It wasn't fair. I had been crying a lot lately, and I started again. I couldn't help it. I just cried and cried, sagging down in the open doorway and burying my face between my knees. And not for the first time in the last several months, I gave myself up to total self-pity. I was being eased out of my job, my boyfriend had left me, I was sick as hell half the time, and now some asshole had violated my space. My thoughts ricocheted from if-only-this to if-only-that until I sank so deeply into misery that I almost couldn't breathe. If only my mother was still alive with her gentle confidence and ability to see things through. Or if only my father hadn't run halfway around the world to try to find a reason to live without her. If only I had stayed in Richmond, where things had once been good. If only I had the nerve to walk out in the woods somewhere and die.

But you can only cry for so long before you run out of tears; and it's only a matter of time before self-pity turns to self-loathing. I was vaguely aware that I was staggering along a border I was not ready to cross and slowly raised my head. I don't know how long I had been insensate, but the front of my shirt was wet.

I lowered my knees until my legs were straight out along the floor and used the edge of my sleeve to wipe my eyes. I was feeling a little better. My life was still totally fucked, but now at least I felt ready to evaluate the situation rationally. And rationality told me I was in danger. Not the immediate danger I felt when I thought that criminals might still be in the house, but a subtle and pervasive sense of cold unease.

The destruction of the house added to my fear. What did the burglar want? My computer was intact; hadn't even been touched. My father's TV was on the floor of his bedroom, but it didn't look broken. The stereo system was just moved cockeyed on the shelf. If someone wanted some quick cash for crack, all that stuff would be gone. It was something more sinister, more creepy. I briefly wondered if I should call Donny. No. Bad idea; I was way too pathetic. And I didn't need a protector; I needed some kind of weapon—a pistol or shotgun in case—

A weapon. I jumped up so quickly it made me dizzy and staggered across the living room, through the kitchen, and out the back door to the barn.

The back of the house gave out to a small, weedy yard. Beyond that, on the right, there was a row of four stables where my mother had once kept horses. On the left was a red barn with a tin roof and huge double doors. I ran to the doors and struggled to pull one of them open, then flipped on the lights. The barn was home to a green John Deere tractor with a mower deck attached, although it had been many months since it had been used. Spread out in the barn were other tractor attachments, a riding lawn mower, and various paraphernalia that were once used to keep my mother's training arena looking smooth. A couple of large cardboard boxes filled with tack and a couple of saddles sat next to my mother's traveling show box, which held more tack, braiding equipment, lead ropes, and medicines. Kitty Amin was asleep in a wheelbarrow. A complement of hand tools hung on the walls, but I wasn't concerned about any of these things. I headed straight for my archery room, a large rectangular office built into the left-hand wall. Like everything else, I never locked up the place and now regretted it. I opened the door, fumbled for the light switch, and breathed out my relief. The thief had not been here.

The room had once been my mother's office and tack room. It was a splendid room while she was alive, brightly painted and well lit, with slatted wooden ceilings and trim so tightly sealed that an ant couldn't get through. And although the saddles and bridles, blankets and bits had been packed away, her books taken from their shelves and sold, the room retained its special purpose as a kind of museum and trophy room. Instead of tack, though, the walls were carefully pegged for my collection of archery equipment. With a peg under each limb, the bows were arranged in rows down the long wall. Most were recurves—my bamboo-backed Saluki Ibex, a Wapiti takedown laminated in exotic woods of green and brown; my beautiful Black Widow Osage. All were made to my own specifications and had my name written next to the serial number. There were a dozen other bows on the wall, including two longbows and—the most unusual stick of all—a seven-and-a-half-foot-long Japanese yumi bow that had cost me over three thousand dollars, not including shipping from Osaka. And they were all there; not a peg was empty. My mother's mahogany trophy case still stood in the right corner, a bit dusty, but now filled with trophies and other memorabilia that I won in formal competitions or informal outdoor target shoots and 3-D events. There was even a National Championship medal in there.

At the far end of the room sat a work table I had installed to use in building or repairing my own tackle. I made a quick inventory of the table and was satisfied that all my fletching jigs, bare shafts, and stock of feathers, target points, broadheads, and nocks were untouched. Whoever had ransacked the house did not know that the only things I really valued were here in this room. It had been weeks since I had touched a bow—longer probably—and I had sorely missed it. Archery always had a calming effect. On the range I could lose myself in the target and put off worrying about things until later. And although I hadn't planned it, I realized that that was exactly what I needed at that moment; the thought of having to face the wrecked house again was too much to bear.

I took my Black Widow down from the wall and ran my fingers over the finish. There were thin layers of cocobola and bocote alongside the osage orange. But it felt much heavier than usual and I dreaded the idea of having to string it to its 45-pound draw weight. I put it back and turned to the half dozen or so rectangular bow-carrying cases arranged on shelves. I selected a cherry-colored wooden case and opened it on the desk. It contained a Groves Spitfire takedown—one of a kind and fashioned for me before the company went out of business a few years before. The riser was a golden maple and lay in a padded foam indentation. Above and below were two sets of limbs, both with the brown and golden basketweave design I preferred. Without thinking, I reached for the 40-pound limbs, then with a sigh, picked out the 30-pound limbs instead and bolted them to the riser. I fished a bowstringer from a drawer and, after struggling for a half minute, succeeded in stringing the bow. I clipped a hip quiver to my belt, picked out a dozen arrows of the approximate stiffness for the bow, and left the room. For the first time in a long time, I felt my shoulders draw back in anticipation of what was to come. I stretched my rib cage and took a deep breath.

Outside, just beyond the barn and stables, was a rectangular open space about half the size of a football field. It used to be my mother's regulation dressage ring, but I took out all the lettering and fencing a few weeks after I moved back to Pine Oak. I converted the judge's box into a target shed—a three-sided enclosure six feet high, four feet wide, and about four feet deep. It sheltered a single square bale of cotton that took up almost the entire volume of the shed. And the bale was large enough to accommodate a regulation 80-centimeter bullseye target. Today, though, it was bare save for a three-inch black circle painted about three quarters of the way up the bale—about the height of my chest.

Four fence posts stood between the barn area and the shed; one at 70 meters from the target, one at 50 meters, one at 40 meters, and the closest at 30 meters—all of the regulation shooting distances. Each was equipped with a clip on one side and a hook on the other. The clips, which I had lined with thick pieces of felt, were strong but soft, designed to grip a bow without scratching the surface. The hooks were for quivers.

I went directly to the 30-meter line, clipped my bow to the pole and began my stretches. At the top of my game I usually spent ten or fifteen minutes warming up, beginning with 50 jumping jacks and continuing with several exercises designed to stretch most of the muscles in my arms and abdomen. This afternoon, though, I was content just to raise my arms over my head a few times and even then I felt my heart begin to complain. I put on a three-fingered shooting glove and strapped on an arm guard.

Facing the target, I took the first arrow from the quiver and fitted it onto the string. Pulling the string back with three fingers was surprisingly difficult, even with my lightest bow, and my bow hand began to tremble. That didn't bother me too much because the first few shots were always the hardest, even when I warmed up properly. Sighting down the arrow, I let the string roll off my fingertips like a wheel rolling off the edge of a cliff, and saw the arrow miss not only the black circle, but the entire cotton bale, burying itself in the tall grass a few feet short of the target. Was I that weak? I aimed much higher with the next arrow, but it flew all the way over the shed. I quickly nocked a third, which buried itself with a thunk in the wooden edge of the shed. Shit. That was going to be a bitch to pull out. And forget about ever finding the one in the grass behind the shed.

I clipped the bow back onto the post and swung my arms around in circles a few times. I arched my back, took a deep breath. Try it again. I took up the bow and, steadying my arm as best I could, sent the arrow into the bale, missing the black circle by only a few inches. I took up two more arrows in quick succession and managed to hit the outer edge of the black circle with both.

"Good shootin!" The voice behind me almost made me jump out of my shoes, and I spun around. I was greeted by the sight of a smiling Ginette Cartwright in white sweater, lime skirt, and matching lime-green shoes.

"Fuck a duck, Ginette!" I sputtered. "Give me a heart attack!"

"Sorry, Sue-Ann." Ginette was walking across the grass toward me. "Ah never saw anybody shoot one of those before. Ah mean, in person." With her blonde, expensively done-up hair and immaculate clothes, Ginette looked like a runway model lost in the woods.

"What are you doing here, Ginette?"

"Well, ah do guess ah'm about the last person you'd expect to see."

I could think of one or two, but not many. When I had gone to work at *The Courier*, I had not been pleased to find that Ginette worked there too. There was some consolation in the fact that she was only a low-paid typist. Later, when Ginette had gotten a promotion to sales and had become the girlfriend of the boss at almost the same time, I connected the two events as I would have a bow and arrow.

"That's about right," I said.

"Ah'm, you know, jist worried about you." I tried to express some degree of disbelief but Ginette hurried on. "Cal told me about your bein sick."

I burst out: "God damn it! Cal promised not to—"

"Don't blame Cal," said Ginette. "A person'd have to be a bat not to see that somethin's wrong. You've got bags under your eyes and you've lost enough weight to make a stew. And look at how your hands are shakin."

I stared at my bow hand and shook my head. "I need to sit down," I said. "Come into the office so I can put this stuff away."

"Office?"

"In the barn."

"Ah'll follow you."

"Will you bring my quiver?" I asked. "It's hanging on the pole there."

Without a word, Ginette gathered up the quiverful of arrows and walked beside me into the barn. In the office, I set the bow on the table without unstringing it and sat down heavily in my armchair in front of the desk. I motioned Ginette into a matching chair nearby.

"The only thing I told Cal," I began angrily, "is that I haven't been feeling very well for the last couple of months. Sometimes I get weak and shaky, like you saw outside. Maybe Cal thinks I have cancer or something. But that's not it. I'm probably just anemic. It's nothing. I can take care of it."

"You've been to see a doctor?"

"I'm thinking about going. Haven't had the energy."

"Not pregnant, are ya?"

"Not much chance of that." The bitter words came out before I had time to think. "Anyway, I had my tubes tied when I was twenty. Why I told you that I have no idea."

Ginette raised her eyebrows, but passed over it. "Donny Brasswell hasn't come back?" Ginette began. "Don't look at me lahk that. Ah hear stories. Ah even know who he's been seein. Why'd y'all break up, anyway?"

"Who said it was your business, Ginette?" I replied loudly, standing up.

Ginette stood up, too. "Forget it, Sue-Ann," she said. "Guess ah'll jist go." The look on her face was so hurt, so—almost—innocent, that I was suddenly ashamed. More so because I had a sudden memory of seeing that same look once before, when we were teenagers.

"Sit down, Ginette. Fuck." I sat back down myself and combed my fingers through what felt like a mess of unruly hair.

"Nobody wants to be around a sick person," I complained. "I don't really blame Donny; I was hell to be around. No reason for you to go, though. Sorry I shouted. How'd you know where I live?"

"Ah do the payroll," Ginette said. "And if ah didn't there'd still be the phone book. Or ah could've rustled up Donny and ast him. Maybe even——"

"Okay, okay."

"When ah drove up, the front door was open wide as the big blue sky. Ah saw how your place got all trashed up. Called out, but nobody answered. When ah saw that the back door was open too, ah came on out and saw you shootin." Ginette looked around the room in amazement. "Is this stuff all yours? All these bows and arrows and ah don't even know whatall?"

"All mine," I answered.

"And those trophies and things?"

"Yeah. I used to be good."

"You looked great to me," said Ginette sincerely.

"You must have missed my first three shots," I said.

"Maybe ah was lookin at the stables," Ginette answered. "You have horses, too?"

"All the horses are gone," I told her. "Look, you want me to talk you have to give me coffee. Got your cigarettes with you?"

"In the car."

"If you want me to talk you have to give me cigarettes. I'll make the coffee. Meet me back in the house."

In the living room, I hastily swept the debris away from the couch. I picked up an ashtray from the floor and put it on the coffee table, then went into the kitchen and changed filters on the coffeemaker. As I ground some of the beans I got from Clarence, I tried to make sense of what was going on.

The first thing I had to get straight in my head was the fact that Ginette Cartwright was concerned enough about my health to look up my address, drive who knows how many miles, and get up the gumption to walk through my front door.

I mentioned earlier that Ginette and I were never close friends, but that doesn't even begin to describe the incredibly complicated, subtle, and wrenching emotional roller coaster that we had once ridden together as we grew through our teens. She was the bright shining star of Pine Oak High School, so popular that all the other popular girls looked up to her like little yapping dogs look up to a collie. Gorgeous, yes, but also both hard and original. She took the term "southern belle" and refashioned it to fit her the way an apple fits inside its skin.

I was more like a dark star, strong but untouchable, unfathomable. I had my own popularity, but it was with the teachers and with those students blessed with brains but not big breasts or, in the case of guys, big balls. I need to make another point here, though, because my star metaphors leave a lot of white still on the page—in my teens I was pretty hot-looking, but not as hot as Ginette. She radiated, I smoldered. Sometimes I would smile at her across the cafeteria or as we passed in the hall, but I hated her. I hated her but wanted to be her so bad it almost killed me.

When we graduated, she got more fanfare for being invited to go straight to work in the cosmetics counter at the brand-new WalMart than I got for winning a free ride to the University of North Carolina. We never fought, never argued; only smiled and watched and, at least in my case, learned.

And here's something you didn't know. When I came

back to Pine Oak, I decided that the only guy worth dating was Cal Dent, who was going through a messy divorce at the time. Three kids were involved, that kind of thing. But my few hints to let me take his mind from his problems didn't seem to make an impression. Actually, they were more than hints. It took months for me to wise up to the fact that he was secretly seeing Ginette Cartwright. In fact, I assumed that Ginette was responsible for the divorce. What's worse, I secretly suspected that she was also responsible for Cal giving me the bum's rush and giving Mark Patterson most of the assignments that had earlier been given to me.

So I was feeling more than a little confused when Ginette came back in and placed a pack of cigarettes and a lighter near the ashtray. She sat on an arm of the couch where I could see her from the kitchen. "Funny how we've never really talked before," she said. "Specially since we've known each other since forever. Haven't you ever wanted to?"

"Wanted to what?" I shouted from the kitchen.

"Jist have a little talk. Ah mean, we see each other at least a couple tahms a week."

"Sure," I said. "I guess. Look, don't you find this kind of awkward?"

"Some, ah guess, but ah don't care. It's tahm we had it out."

I put the coffee in the new filter and turned on the machine while Ginette folded a blanket she picked up from the floor and draped it neatly over the back of the couch.

I didn't answer. As the coffee dripped, I tried not to notice Ginette as she got up and started picking up my dad's books from the floor and placing them back evenly on their shelves. "Ginette, quit that," I told her.

When I walked in the room with two full cups and

some packets of Splenda, Ginette was sitting on the couch straightening the pile of mail she had gathered up from around her feet.

"Had what out, Ginette?" I asked testily.

She stacked the mail carefully in the far corner of the coffee table before she answered. "Damn it, Sue-Ann," she said. "You're spose to be the smart one here. For us not to trah to be friends is jist plain stupid. It's *always* been stupid!"

"I don't know what to say to that."

"You can laugh if you wanna, but ah've admired you since we were in the tenth grade, maybe even the sixth. Didn't ya know?"

"You *admire* me?" I asked, astonished.

"Raht," said Ginette.

"I thought you despised me."

"Ah don't, though."

"But you were the queen of Pine Oak High. You hung out with the best crowd and went to all the parties while I was stuck in the mud like some old dinosaur bone. Even now, look at us. You're still the best looking woman in the county and you're seeing one of the only decent guys I know. I look like a scarecrow and the closest thing I have to a boyfriend is a cat."

"Maybe we both see things backwards," Ginette ventured. "Ah lahked those parties and all the attention, sure ah did. But what ah really wanted was to be *involved* in things. You were always busy workin on the yearbook or the newspaper. You were on the bowling team. And you were *learnin* things while ah was only goin to class." She took up one of the cups and blew into it. "Then you went off to college—outta state no less—and later we all knew you were workin on a big newspaper. And then we heard you were in the Middle East. Heck, we ran some stories about you in *The Courier*. Ah typed em up mahself."

"I think that's where I got sick," I said. Yet I still had a lingering suspicion that Ginette's visit wasn't all she said it was. "Listen, are you sure Cal didn't send you over here?" I asked. "Or that bastard Donny?"

"Darn it, Sue-Ann. Nobody told me to do nothin. Ah'm worried about you and it's that simple. Why're you so aggravatin?"

"Sorry. You were Miss Sawdust, weren't you?"

"That was half a lahf ago and don't go tellin me that you'd lahk to trade places cause ah'd do it in a heartbeat."

"I can't believe you knew I was on the bowling team," I said.

"Ah'm sure there's lots of things ah know that you wouldn't believe."

"Did you ever think of going to college?"

"Been there and done that," answered Ginette.

"Sorry, Ginette, I didn't know."

"Two years at JCCC and another at FSU before ah quit. Ah was twenty five and ah'd just got divorced from Jimmy Jepperson. When we split the property ah came out with a little bundle a cash and thought ah'd use it to make somethin outta mahself. Didn't have the grades to go raht into a four-year college."

"Why'd you quit?"

"Same ole same ole," she replied. "Started seein one a mah professors and got pregnant. Ended up miscarryin, and after that ah just kinda stopped goin to class. Me and the guy broke up after a few months. Ah traveled around some, then came back here. Kinda soured me on school. Learned some office management, though, and enough accountin to get by most places."

"So you never had any kids?" I asked.

"Nope. Not yet. Ah'm still thinkin about it, though."

"With Cal?"

"Mebbe yes, mebbe no. But lahk you said, he's not the worst guy in this wild world. Listen, Sue-Ann, ah know you were puttin moves on Cal when you got back to town. It didn't bother me none—you didn't have any way of knowin we were together."

"But when I found out, it made me try harder," I said.

Ginette gave me a cold stare, kind of the way she used to look at me in high school. She took up the pack of cigarettes and lit one. "Bring it on," she said. "But Cal is as high as ah can go. You're better than this little hole of a place. You've even got rid of your accent. Ah mean, listen to me talk; ah sound lahk Melanie Wilkes."

"That's what four semesters of broadcast journalism will do." I took the pack from Ginette and lit one for myself. I hadn't had a cigarette in months and the first inhalation sent my head spinning.

"Ah don't mean to pry, Sue-Ann, but what made you come back here?"

"Lots of things," I replied. "Lots and lots of things." I drew deeply on my cigarette. "First, it was the war. Being in the Middle East for six months is like being in the lower reaches of hell. Bullets popping, smoke everywhere. People dead in the street. Nobody safe. And the way women are treated over there is a crime worse than the war. I couldn't stay neutral, and not being neutral is the kiss of death for a journalist. We—the press, I mean—had our own little haven with razor wire and private security men, but we still went out. I didn't see a tenth of the things I might have seen but it was plenty. Don't tell Major Paul, but I just didn't know why we were over there at all, I mean, except to keep the black gold pumping. I ended up sleeping with a coworker over there I didn't even like. Then a couple of soldiers. Maybe more than a couple. Damn, Ginette, I don't even remember most of their *names!*" I stubbed out my cigarette in the ashtray, surprised at my own emotion. It was something I had never revealed to anyone before.

"Listen, Ginette," I said. "You want to get high?"

"Wouldn't be the first tahm," Ginette replied. "Wouldn't be the second neither. And you can call me Gina if you want."

I rummaged in my purse for my stash. "I didn't know people called you Gina."

"They don't," Ginette said.

I folded a pinch of weed into a paper and rolled it with unsteady hands. "You're kind of weird, you know that? Gina?"

Ginette broke into a smile that revealed white, even teeth, and reached over for the box. "Here, let me do that; you'll spill it all over creation." With a perfectly manicured hand she picked a speck of marijuana from my knee and put it in her mouth. Then she finished rolling the joint with a dexterity that surprised me, licked the edge softly, and held it up as if it were a wineglass. "To your health," she said, then lit it with her lighter and took a hit.

We passed the joint back and forth for a few minutes without speaking. I still didn't completely trust Ginette, but by the fourth hit or so, it didn't matter. I was glad that she had come, whatever her reason. I watched her languidly as she fished for a pair of tweezers in her purse and used them as a roach clip. She handed it to me and laid her head back so that her long blonde hair cascaded over the back of the couch.

"Wowie zowie," she said.

"Gina," I said.

"Hmmm?"

"Nothing. Just Gina. I'm trying it out."

"Ah kinda lahk it," Ginette said. "So are you goin to

finish tellin me about the musical beds you were playin in Iraq?"

"I was finished with that part," I answered. "I was about to say that I'd been there almost six months when I got a phone call that my mother had gotten thrown off a horse and died."

"Ah heard about your mama and ah'm so sorry."

"I left Baghdad on the next plane but the next plane in Iraq doesn't necessarily leave when you need it to, and I missed the funeral by a day."

"Where did it happen?" Ginette asked.

"You mean where did she get thrown? Right out in back there. Pretty much where I was shooting. She was practicing her dressage, like she did almost every day. Something must have happened to spook her filly—a rattlesnake, gunshot, whatever. She got bucked off and she hit her head against one of the railroad ties around the ring. Broke her neck."

Ginette was silent, looking at me intently, listening with more sympathy than anyone had in a very long time. Finally, she said, "Who found her?"

"My dad. Must have been a couple of hours after it happened. He went outside looking for her, saw Alikki grazing near the stalls in full saddle and with her bridle trailing on the ground. It busted him up. When I finally got here he seemed pretty crazy so I stayed a day or two before I went back to Richmond. Guess I should have stayed longer. After I left he either sold or gave away Alikki and the other two horses along with everything else he could get rid of in a hurry. If I hadn't boxed up some of her tack when I came home after the funeral, he would have sold that, too."

"Hold that thought," Ginette said. "Where's your bathroom?"

"Back through the bedroom," I told her, pointing the way. "Don't trip over anything."

I put my head back against the couch and closed my eyes. I didn't feel as bad as I had earlier. My heart rate seemed closer to normal and I was calm. I gave myself up to daydreaming. A kaleidoscope of images rushed by— some disquieting, some peaceful— ranging from Army Jeeps to my mother riding in a dressage show in Kentucky only a few months before she died.

"Do you still rahd?" I opened my eyes, but Ginette's voice came from the bedroom. I squinted and saw that Ginette was making my bed, smoothing down the blanket and fluffing the pillows. I jumped up and crossed to the bedroom.

"What are you doing?"

"Cleanin up some."

"I don't want you to."

"Sure you do. Everybody wants somebody to clean up for em. Almost nobody ever gets that particular wish granted, but today, you do. So lay down there and tell me about your rahdin."

"Forget it," I answered. "Anyway, I haven't ridden in I don't know how long." Instead of lying down, I went to the open closet and began picking up the clothes from the floor, brushing them off with my hand, and slipping them back on their hangers. "When I was growing up we lived on Decatur Street, near the library. My parents both worked full-time jobs. You probably knew my dad; he was the art teacher at Pine Oak High."

"Ah never took art," said Ginette, "but ah knew who he was. And ah knew your mama. She sold us the house we lived in when Jim and I were married."

"She was a really good saleswoman. It was her father's—my grandfather's—business, but she pretty much

57

ran it from the time I turned ten. It was about that time that one of her customers got her interested in horses. *Back* interested, I mean—she had ridden when she was a girl. She started taking dressage lessons on weekends. I went with her every once in a while, but I think she preferred to ride alone. That's when I went through my little hunter-jumper phase that you already know about. I liked it, but there are a lot of other things a girl can do when she's growing up."

Ginette was rolling my pile of dirty clothes in one of the sheets she had found on the floor. "Tell me about it," she said.

"It wasn't more than a year after I went off to college that Granpapa died and Mom inherited some money and some property. She sold the business, renovated this old farmhouse, and she and Dad moved out here. She had the barn and stables built at the same time. She bought horses, went to riding clinics, and competed in shows. But I had gotten into archery by then so I only rode when I came home for holidays or whatever. Still, I think it was kind of extreme for my father to sell everything without even telling me."

"But you were supposed to be telling me whah you moved back to Pine Oak," Ginette said, toting the bundle of clothes out of the room. I ran after her and showed her the laundry room. When the water was hissing into the machine, she walked back to the couch and carefully rolled another joint, licking the ash-thin paper, then toking hard on one end while holding her lighter to the other.

"I forget what you asked," I said. I was feeling muddled and strange, and a hit on the new joint didn't help.

"Whah you came back."

"I was getting to that," I said, "and it's simple: When I

58

got back from Iraq I didn't like my job anymore. That and the fact that I broke up with my boyfriend."

"Your boyfriend?" Ginette asked.

"Oh, didn't I mention him earlier? While I was screwing my brains out in Baghdad, I had a boyfriend in Richmond."

"No you didn't," Ginette said, looking shocked.

"I did," I told her. "And the first thing I did when I got back to Richmond was tell him everything. Took him a while, but he split to a motel until I finally moved out, and I didn't really care; Jack's a nice guy, but he stifled the shit out of me. Damn, Ginette—I mean Gina. I've never seen better looking fingers wrapped around a joint before. Tell me who your manicurist is."

"*Ah* used to be a manicurist, didn't ya know? Ah learned to take care of mah hands pretty good. Feet, too," she said. I looked down and saw that Ginette had slipped off her shoes and was wiggling her toes. They were perfectly proportioned, neatly filed, and painted the same pretty shade of red as her fingernails. I took the lit joint from Ginette and inhaled, still staring. I was high as an astronaut.

"You must have good genes," I told her.

"Beauty's only skin deep."

We passed the joint back and forth and I could tell that Gina was getting as ripped as I was. "Anyway, that's my story. I came back here, got the only job I could. Now I'm trying to make ends meet and stay alive at the same time. Ever date Donny?" I asked.

"Too young for me."

"Two years, yeah," I answered. "If we were still in high school I wouldn't have given him a second of my time. It might be different with you," I smiled, "but when I reached my thirties, younger guys got more appealing and I got a lot easier to flatter. I should have known that sometimes boys will remain boys. Donny's nice enough, and has a good body, but he doesn't have much courage. I mean, he'd rather run from problems than face them."

"And you were his problem? Gina said.

"It was more like he was my problem," I told her. "But he had some doozies of his own. Usually I can handle other people's problems, but I haven't been up to it for a while—ever since I came back from Iraq."

"What about your guy in Richmond?" Gina asked.

"Same thing. I'm a magnet for helpless men. I can never say no and it's only in the last year that I've learned to say git."

"And in all the datin ah've done," Gina said, "ah've never had anybody that needed me at all."

"Cal needs you," I pointed out.

"He needs me for *The Courier*; ah'm not sure he needs me emotionally. That's sad, ain't it?"

"It's sad and odd, too." I didn't know how it had happened, but I knew that Gina Cartwright and I had, over the last hour or so, formed some kind of tenuous bond. And what was even more surprising was that I felt glad about it.

We sat silently for a while, but finally Gina said, "Ah had an affair with a woman once."

I sat up rigid. "Gina! *You*? With a *woman*? I'm totally shocked. And why would you tell me something like that?"

"You told me stuff. Seems only fair."

"Well I'll be a . . . " I shut my mouth in mid-sentence and looked sideways at Gina with wide eyes. "Did you like it?"

"Boy howdy!" Gina said, and we both burst out laughing. "It's . . . it's not really funny, ah guess. Ah mean ah'm not a lezzie or anythin. It was just a one- or two-naht thing years ago. College girl ah met in a bar in Tallahassee. Her name was Carrie. We spent the weekend together. Never saw her again after that. Kind of ashamed, ah guess."

"Does Cal know?"

"Hell, no!" We laughed again.

"How did you meet Cal?" I asked. "There at the paper?"

"Raht. Ah'd had a few different jobs after ah came back from travelin, but none of em lasted more'n a few years. This one ah lahked, an ah think ah may actually be good at it."

"You *are* good at it."

Gina glanced at her watch. "Hells angels! Ah told the guy down at the Exxon station that ah'd bring him his ad by the end of the day. Ah forgot all about it." She slipped back into her shoes and stood up unsteadily.

"Can you make it?" I asked her.

"Ah'm a drivin fool," she said. "Do you want me to come back and finish cleanin up?"

"I think I can manage," I said. "But thanks."

"Don't forget to put your clothes in the dryer. If you don't they'll get sour."

"I'll remember. And Gina, thanks, really."

I opened the door for her and stood there while Ginette walked a few steps, then turned around. "This was nahce," she said. Then she was gone.

Chapter 4

Let's step backwards into 1990 for a few minutes and let me catch my breath. I was sixteen and I was riding in my first jumping competition in quiet Connitchee Horse Park, just outside Panama City. The course was small with a rich grassy infield dotted here and there with small puddles, as it had been raining the night before. The jumps were all fairly easy, made up of different arrangements of logs. I remember that one of the jumps was a single tree trunk about two feet in diameter; others were built of smaller logs set atop one another. Red and white course flags tacked onto the jump standards added a touch of gaiety to the surroundings.

I was proudly wearing a new riding outfit, and my heart was thumping for all the right reasons. I was sitting on a roan mare belonging to the barn where my mother was just starting to learn dressage. Roanette was a safe, well-trained schooling horse and I was both scared and excited about actually riding before judges for the first time. Dozens of other girls, along with a few boys, rode up and down the practice area, awaiting their turns on the course. An occasional voice came through a loudspeaker, but it was impossible for me to listen—I was too busy watching other riders on the course, trying to make sure I would ride the correct pattern when my turn came. My mother was nearby; she had the order of go and knew who I would be following, so I left it to her to give me my cue.

The girl riding the course—she was three or four

riders ahead of me—was astride a black gelding that must have been 17 hands high. Both horse and rider were magnificent—simply one creature with two heads—and they made most of the logs seem like twigs as they flew over them. In reality, it was not a clean run; the gelding's back hoof tipped over at least two of the logs, but that was unimportant to me. I knew I was way outclassed. There was applause and the rider exited the course and rode past where me and Roanette were waiting. The girl's eyes were shining and triumphant knowing that she had done well, that she would finish high despite the penalty points. But when she happened to glance at me, her gaze hardened and she gave her horse a nudge with her leg. It was only then that I recognized the rider as Ginette Cartwright, the Barbie princess that went to my school and who I hated. I hadn't even known she rode, much less that she was so accomplished.

I didn't even see the next riders, although my eyes might have been pointing in that direction. I was thinking about the monstrous coincidence that Ginette and I were probably the only two competitors from Pine Oak—over a hundred miles away. The coincidence was more blatant in that the two of us had been competitors in school ever since we had become aware of each other. First it had been on the playground when we were little kids; I found that I could outrun every girl in school except her. In turn, she found out that I had better hand eye coordination in games like softball or volleyball. As we grew older, she became the better gymnast, and was on the cheerleading squad, which I then talked trash about; I led the bowling team to an even record—the best it had ever done—while Ginette stayed away from any organized team events. In the classroom it was the same; if I excelled in a course, such as English, Ginette would let it slide with a toss of her long blonde braids, but when she outtested me in home ec and typing classes, I pretended that I would never have any use for those particular skills.

The most recent conflict had to do with boys, who we had both only just discovered. Ginette had a boyfriend first, of course, because she was prettier and much more social than I was. But when her boyfriend, whose name was Marty, was assigned to be my lab partner in honors biology, I suddenly became worldly and flirty. When, a few weeks later, I received my first kiss from Marty as he walked me part way home after school, Ginette heard about it and was livid. I stopped flirting with Marty almost immediately—not because of Ginette, but because I had started being friendly with a boy who played the lead in our school play that year. I felt warm around him, enjoyed talking to him about the theater, and people knew we were a couple. Ginette knew too, and although it took her a few months, she managed to make him break up with me; made it a point to walk past me in the hall holding his hand before she lost interest.

There were many other examples of conflicts between me and Ginette, yet none ever led to words between us; we had never had an argument or even deigned to notice that we had appropriated each other's boyfriends. It was a mental thing and so far, on that Saturday at Connitchee Horse Park, it was a stalemate.

This is what was going through my head as my mother's voice woke me from my reverie and told me that my name and number had just been called. Ginette was nowhere in sight, probably grooming her horse. That was good. I took a deep breath, looked over the course—its jumps now looking impossibly high—and gave Roanette a gentle nudge with the heel of my boot. That was all the incentive the mare needed, and she shot forward onto the course in a canter.

The first two jumps went smoothly, although my time was nowhere close to what Ginette's had been. As I rode toward the third, which was made up of four logs fastened to two long poles set in the ground, the wind suddenly whipped up, causing the colorful banners on each side to flap furiously. To Roanette, the plastic pennants must have sounded like fierce animals stalking through brush, because she shied just before the jump, then stopped abruptly. My momentum almost carried me over the mare's head and into the logs, but my left foot caught in the stirrup and I went over sideways instead.

My foot still entangled in the stirrup, I hung almost upside down with the sound of flapping banners in my ears. Roanette was trained well enough and long enough for her to be aware that I was in trouble, and had it not been for the wind, there would have been no danger of her spooking further. As it was, she took a step in one direction, wheeled, and took another in the opposite direction. She knew her job—which was to stand perfectly still—but she was also frightened, and didn't know what to do with the contradiction. With each step she took, she dragged me with her, wrenching my ankle. I was crying out when I saw a man run out onto the course and reach for Roanette's reins. It was one of the officials, but his movements were so clumsy and his voice so loud as he shouted "Whoa! Ho! Stop!" that Roanette shied away from him as she had from the banners.

I was gritting my teeth and trying to reach up for the stirrup, thinking there was a chance I might pull myself up before the pony bolted, when I heard another voice, female this time. It said, in a carefully modulated but firm voice. "Git away." It puzzled me until I realized that she was talking to the official. "Git over there and rip off those banners," she told him. My heart sank like an anchor into the muddy turf when I realized that it was Ginette's voice. She had taken the reins in one hand and gripped Roanette's nostril in the other and I could feel the mare's wildness lessening. As soon as the banners had been silenced, Ginette let go of Roanette's nose and, reins still in one hand, she unbuckled the girth so that both me and the saddle slipped to the ground with a solid plop.

Ginette handed Roanette, calm now, to the official or someone else that had come onto the course. The whole episode had taken no more than ten or fifteen seconds. And in that few seconds, Ginette had been superb. I, on the other hand, had become scum, but I was too worried about my ankle to have more than a fleeting idea of how this was going to affect my life. I felt Ginette's hands, firm but gentle at the same time, lift my leg and carefully extricate my foot from the stirrup.

She looked at me without triumph, with the concern she would have felt for anyone in her sport that had gotten injured. "You okay?" she asked.

"I—I guess. My ankle hurts." I was trying my best not to cry but I knew that tears were streaking my face and that I had mud in my hair and on my new clothes. Vaguely, I noticed that others were hurrying onto the course. I heard my mother's voice and running footsteps.

Ginette picked up my saddle and I struggled to a sitting position.

"Um, thanks," I said miserably and forced myself to look her in the face. "You want me to do your homework or somethin?"

Ginette dropped the saddle at my feet. Then she lifted her head, turned and walked away without a word. After a few steps I saw her waver, stop, and turn again. The expression on her face was almost impossible to describe, but it was a mixture of sadness and hauteur, pride and hurt. But what she said was clear enough.

"Mebbe you should rahd more and do homework less," she said, and walked toward the stables, her head as high as it had ever been.

I remembered that look as clearly as a reflection in a still pool; it was the same one I had seen in the last chapter when Ginette had stood up in my archery room with the intention of leaving me alone with my misery.

Back in the present I worked on making my house livable again. It was less difficult than I thought because Gina—it was now impossible for me to think of her as Ginette—had not only picked up all my dirty laundry, but had carefully put away the things that had been pulled out of my dresser. The computer desk had been straightened and dusted and the wads of crumpled paper—false starts for several articles—were in the trash can under the desk. But the strangest thing, and the thing that moved me more than all the others, was that she had carefully wiped the lipstick letters off the blades of the fan above my bed.

She had told me she admired me; had typed up stories about me for the paper. She had said . . . but my mind stopped there; I was stoned; all my sensations were altered, heightened and I couldn't trust them.

My high wore off slowly, and by the time I finished making my bedroom and living room presentable, I was conscious of a growing fatigue. I was also very hungry, so I picked my way through the debris of the kitchen and made myself a tuna sandwich. It made me nauseous but I ate it anyway, then gave the rest of the tuna to the cat. I drank half a glass of water and decided to retrieve the arrows I shot earlier before they got exposed to the elements.

Passing the stalls always brought up vivid images of

the horses that had been such fixtures on my trips home over the years. Although they generally lived in the fenced-off pasture beyond the dressage ring, they always trotted in for their scoop of feed morning and evening. And Cindy McKeown had always brought them in during thundershowers.

It feels odd to refer to my mother as Cindy. It seems like the name of a younger person, and it is certainly one I never called her by. It was always Mom or Mother. Yet it's likely that I'll have to mention her many times in these pages and I want to portray her as more than just somebody's mother. Cindy. I kinda lahk it.

The stables were constructed of sturdy two-by-six pressure-treated boards nailed to tall six-by-six poles and protected with a corrugated red tin roof. The floors were dirt, but had been bedded occasionally with shavings or straw so that they seemed clean and inviting. There were four stalls, although Cindy only had three horses. The fourth was for friends who sometimes trailered out to the farm to ride for a day or a weekend.

Each horse had its own stall. The stall nearest the house belonged to Facilitator, a black Hanoverian gelding just past his prime. The next was where Trifecta stayed. She had been Cindy's top riding horse—a mare that had been trained and competed at the highest level by one of the top riders in the U.S. But I knew that her pedigree and training came with a high price tag. Cindy had bred Trifecta to a top Hessen stallion and the result had been Alikki. That third stall had been hers. Cindy had doted on Alikki and had insisted on training the filly herself. Alikki, at three years old, had only been under saddle a couple of months when the accident happened.

Alikki's stall door was halfway open; the ground inside held scattered shavings and the dusty patch of what was once a small pile of manure. Her blue water bucket was dry and dusty.

Now all three horses were gone, scattered around the south—or around the world for all I knew. I had never asked my father where they had gone, and I should have. Cindy's death affected me deeply; my time in Baghdad and my ensuing illness made it impossible to concentrate on anything that was not right before my eyes. Although I had only ridden Trifecta once and Facilitator a dozen or so times, I always loved to be around them, to press my face into their necks and smell the fresh clean horse scent that is far more exciting than any perfume, any flower or breeze. I badly wished I could have seen them all again, to say goodbye. I wished I could have said goodbye to Cindy, too.

I pushed myself away from the stalls and walked toward the target shed. The first arrow I shot had almost managed to bury itself completely in the tall grass in front of the shed. But not quite—the white nock was still peeking out. I bent down and carefully pulled the end toward me, succeeding in getting it out without bending the aluminum and with a minimum of damage to the feathers. I smoothed them out. Good as new. I extracted the three that were in the target without much difficulty, then looked at the one that had stuck in the woody edge of the shed. I grasped it firmly near the point and was surprised when it came loose at once. The shot had been weaker than I thought. *I* had been weaker. In back of the shed the grass was so high I knew that finding the last arrow was futile, but I dutifully searched anyway. When I bent down to see the ground better, my nausea returned and I sagged to my knees, vomiting tuna, water, and bile. The stench was repulsive and I spat several times to rid my mouth of the taste. I felt better, but there would be no finding the last arrow. It wasn't the first arrow I've lost and won't be the last.

But I was glad that I had hit the mark when Gina was watching.

Back in the house I faced the problem of what to do about the other rooms. The living room and my bedroom were almost back to normal and I found that Gina had done a quick pick up of the bathroom. The kitchen was very messy, but the guest rooms wouldn't be too bad—the furniture had been moved around some but there were fewer small items for anyone to scatter about. Cindy's room would be the hardest; I decided to put that off until I was stronger. I also thought I would leave my father's room as it was so that when he came home he would be able to tell if anything was missing.

It was only then that I remembered his letter from Italy that I had put aside without reading. It must have been scattered along with all the rest of the stuff in the living room. I sat down on the couch and picked up the pile of letters and circulars Gina had stacked on the coffee table.

The letter was near the bottom. I opened it.

> *Susie:*
>
> *I've been staying in the Villa della Trattoria here in Florence for a few weeks now. I've been doing a lot of sketching—here in my room, down in the square with pigeons flocking around the fountain, in the museums, wherever I can. I suppose I'm just reliving my college days but those were happy times for me. I had good friends here, all lost to me now. I wonder how I could have let those friendships lapse.*
>
> *I have made a few new friends, though. One is helping me to improve my Italian. She works as a*

guard in the Uffizi Gallery and has aspirations of becoming a painter. I have seen a few of her attempts and I think I may be able to give her some advice. I was a teacher for 25 years after all!

I'm thinking of setting up an easel down in the square and doing pencil portraits of tourists for a few euros. I have purchased a porkpie hat and have grown a goatee.

I hope your job is working out and that you are happy back in Pine Oak. As for myself, I can't imagine it any more. Luckily, I have enough money to stay here; maybe buy a small house in the city and renovate it. It will be a place where I can be alive again and a place that you can visit if you ever get the time.

I hope you were able to sort out all that paperwork I left you. Cindy's will made my work easier, but she had a lot of interests and I did the best I could with whatever she had not already put in your name—bank accounts, taxes, the files in her room. You might sort through those files for the breeding papers on the horses. I seem to remember that I promised to send them to the new owners.

Write me when you can.

M.M.

I put the letter back in the envelope, got up from the couch, and stretched. It was the kind of note I expected from my father, heavy on his own doings and making it tacitly understood that he was uninterested in mine. It didn't sound as if he planned to ever come back. I remembered now that while he had been a student at Florida State University, he had spent a year in Italy—or was it two?—on their Florence program. He had, when I was much younger, often reminisced about the places he had seen and the four or five close friends he had made there. It seemed strange to me now that I had never met any of them.

A goatee? Sketching tourists? I wish you well, Daddy.

The files he mentioned were now probably strewn around Cindy's room like big confetti. And his letter had not mentioned who the new owners of the horses were so what was the point of looking for the papers?

Instead, I went into the kitchen to survey the damage. Most of the dishes in the cupboards had been left untouched, as it was pretty obvious that nothing could have been hidden behind or in them. But most of the food in the pantry had been pulled from the shelves, cans had tumbled out, loose cereal and flour were mixed on the floor. Boxes of rice-a-roni and packets of sweetener had been trampled under someone's feet. I sighed, wishing Gina hadn't had to leave, and began salvaging what I could. I dumped the rest in two plastic garbage bags and swept most of the cereal and flour outside. I was busy washing the dishes in the sink when I realized I was about to collapse. I walked unsteadily to the bedroom and saw that the red light was blinking on the telephone. It must have rung when I was outside picking up arrows. Without checking the number on the Caller ID, I pressed the replay button.

"Sue-Ann? This is Jack. Listen, Sue-Ann, I'm sorry about what happened. I don't know whose fault it was but I'd like to talk about it. I thought that I was okay with it but I'm not. I'm . . . look, I'm driving to Miami for a meeting in a few days and I'd like to stop by and see you. You've got my phone number. Please call me back." The message ended.

I collapsed on to the bed, then stood up again. The

call was exactly what I didn't need. Jack Stafford—my boyfriend in Richmond—was a photographer for the *Richmond Times-Dispatch*. Thirty-six, black wavy hair, blue eyes, rugged good looks, and gentle manner. His only flaw—and a flaw that I think I am the only one ever to see—was that his camera understood more than he did. In some impossible-to-explain way, his use of light, angle, focus, you name it—all of which came as naturally to him as bowhunting came to Fred Bear—gave his photographs unique personalities, allowed them to tell tales like the best storytellers, and conveyed marvelous aspects of life that only a very few people ever get to witness. His worst photos were good enough for most magazines; his best were like diamond rings given with love to young maidens. The problem was, he almost never understood why he took a particular photo until he developed it. Although he had unbelievable people skills, he had trouble imagining why they acted the way they did. Had trouble imagining why *I* acted the way I did. He was high on the list of people I never wanted to see again. I had no idea what to do about him and thinking made me tired.

I turned on the radio and began to undress.

The pirate station was playing a recording of William S. Burroughs reading something dreadful. I leaned over to turn it off when one of the deejays, male this time, interrupted, "Thanks, Bill. That was great. Really. Yeah. No, we'll call you, okay?

"This is Smokestack here on W-A-K-O, your wacko radio station broadcasting from the wilds of tree country. I'm gonna play a few songs by The Carpenters now. Betcha thought now that Karen was dead, people would have thrown all their Carpenters stuff away, and you might be right but they would be wrong. She was way cool; I even wrote a story about her once, but I won't go into that.

Instead, I'll play a song about her by Sonic Youth that kind of captures in three minutes what I tried to get over in 20 pages. It's called "Tunic."'

The song that he played was both raucous and touching—a paean to the anorexic singer with the soft and beautiful voice. I had heard the song once before—a soldier in Baghdad had played it for me. It was about creation and death.

I lay down on the bed Gina had made, and put my eye-pillow carefully over my closed eyes. It was cool and put a soothing pressure on my eyelids. The aroma of eucalyptus and peppermint was indeed therapy and I loved how everything was suddenly so dark that I felt like I was floating in an isolation tank. Not only was the light blacked out, but most of my sensations were, too. I felt like I was drifting on a cloud and could no longer feel my arms or legs. I was aware only of the sound of Karen Carpenter's voice fading in and out as song after song began and ended. I must have nodded off because the next thing I was aware of was Smokestack's voice on the radio. He was speaking in the pseudo-professional disk jockey voice he sometimes assumed when he was being facetious, which was usually.

"Let me remind you that this program is brought to you by—. Oh, wait, this is a pirate station. In that case, let me tell you about one of my new favorite things. It's called an eye-pillow. Why is it called that? Because it's a pillow that you put over your eyes. For a cool refreshing sleep, try an eye-pillow."

I sat up with a start. The coincidence was way too much! There were a few seconds of dead air, then another voice came over the waves, no longer the voice of Smokestack, but the whiny, raspy, singsong voice of the man called The Creeper. I listened intently; The Creeper was a mysterious commentator who was sometimes mentioned by the deejays, but who rarely came on the air. I had heard him only once before, but I hadn't forgotten his disquieting, almost annoying up and down timber with just the hint of a not-of-this-earth accent and a style of speaking that used correct pronunciation but odd grammar. That first time I had heard only the very end of the tale he told, but it was enough for me to gather that he spoke in parables as portentous as they were baffling.

"Here's a story for you little kiddies out there," he began in his *sarcastic whine. "Once upon a time, at this very moment in fact, there was a very old man they call Papa Gede. Maybe he's white and maybe he's black. Some say he was born in Africa, others say Haiti or other islands in the Caribbean. Some even say New Orleans. Papa Gede can do magic, yas; can heal the sick, can make little children rich. All the people who see Papa Gede try to get him to give them favors or eternal life, try to get him on their side in softball games. But Papa Gede is tired. Papa wants to rest. So Papa comes here to the timberland and to the swamp to get out of doing miracles all the time. He wants to be alone, hear?*

"But somehow, little boys and girls hear that Papa Gede comes and want him to give them candy and teach them to rustle cattle. They want to find Papa Gede, but how do they do this? They can't find him in phone books, no, so they look in other books, books written by people who have seen Papa Gede in Africa or in Haiti or New Orleans.

"So little children learn how to dance, they learn secret signs that only the dead supposed to know, and they find out how to call Papa Gede to them. They make an altar, yas, they make a sacrifice; they draw on the ground secret symbols. They draw a circle to sit in and they wait for Papa Gede to come. And Oho, Papa Gede do come and he be a frightening old guy and little children shake and little children toss their cookies and little children cry and weep. But Papa Gede

point at them in their white circle and say 'Boo!' and the white circle becomes a black hole that kiddies fall down through. They fall down and fall down and fall down and maybe they never come back up. And Papa Gede say, 'Let me be!'

"Moral of story: Leave shit alone."

Almost before the last tones of The Creeper's voice had faded came the first notes of what sounded like primitive African drumming.

I was sweating. It was impossible not to be frightened. First the commercial about the eye-pillow when I had the only one—outside of Meekins' Market—that I had ever seen. Then The Creeper's story, which was so unsettling that I fired up my computer to do a Google search for Papa Gede. I quickly scanned the first article I clicked on. A voodoo god of some kind, very powerful. Life and death, creation and conclusion. Healing. With mounting concern I looked over a list of characteristics and symbols, appropriate offerings. I pushed the off button on the computer without even shutting down and sat still and quiet for several moments.

One of the offerings to Gede was a black goat.

In the background, Smokestack was back on the radio. "We're back, Jack, and here with some Siouxsie, some Bauhaus, some Robert Smith and The Cure, and then, maybe, some really dark stuff like Crüxshadows. Oh, boy! This is W-D-E-D, all goth all the time."

I turned off the radio, flicked off the light, and got back into bed. Almost at once I fell into a deep but restless sleep rife with animals, knives, and vomit. I slept almost until morning, and when I woke up I knew what I had to do.

Chapter 5

It was 4:30 a.m. when I stepped out of the shower. I put on jeans, a long-sleeved flannel shirt, and walking boots. It took only a few minutes to make coffee and cinnamon toast, and only a few minutes more to choke them down. I walked out to the barn, taking up the bow I'd used the day before and attaching a clip-on quiver with three arrows. A shoulder quiver was nice, but it added too much weight and was too noisy. I filled a fannypack with a shooting glove, a wrist guard, extra string, a bow stringer, some razor-sharp broadhead arrow points, and a small pair of binoculars. At 5:30 I parked behind Meekins' Market and stole into the woods, taking the same direction in which I'd seen the shadows moving two mornings before. It was early enough so that Clarence wouldn't see me and ask what I was doing with a bow and arrows in his woods. Despite his treating it as a prank, I wanted to find out who it was I had seen running away. I knew I wouldn't be lucky enough to encounter them a second time, but that didn't mean I couldn't follow the path and find out where they had gone and what they had been doing.

Although I used my flashlight continuously, it was slow going. The trail was narrow and might simply have been a deer path, but it was large enough to follow. I've never found a way to comfortably carry a strung bow—especially one with a quiver and arrows attached—and several times it knocked into low branches or got caught in high weeds. I didn't even know why I brought the bow, but it comforted me to carry it, knowing my arrows were within easy reach.

Every few minutes I could hear a car whoosh by on the highway, but these sounds grew fainter until, after a while, they faded into the quiet of the trees.

I had to walk slowly, conserving my strength and watching my footing. At the end of an hour, I doubt if I'd gone even half a mile, but the sunlight filtering through the trees allowed me to switch off the flash and transfer it to my pack. Almost immediately I came to a small clearing—an area thirty feet or so in diameter, surrounded by several tall pines and a gigantic live oak. Dead limbs and newly cut brush told me that the area had been cleared deliberately and recently. Near the center was a big white circle with other white splotches outside its perimeter. I looked more closely. Possibly letters or symbols, but partially scuffed out by heavy boots. Near the oak was a log a foot and a half high, and around this I spotted signs of civilization: cigarette butts, empty cans of Miller Lite beer and an empty box of corn starch. That must be what the circle and other lines were made with.

There was a stench and I heard the buzzing of flies. Something was dead. I looked around without seeing anything, but the sound was coming from within the corn starch circle—from a dark, sticky-looking patch of red. Blood, but from what or who? I saw more flies covering a small lump of something a few feet away and kneeled down to examine it. Phew! It wasn't blood, but vomit, no more than a couple of days old.

I didn't see anything else of interest, so I sat down on the oak log to rest. I rummaged in my fannypack and found a plastic bag containing a new bow string. I took the string out and replaced it with several of the cigarette butts that were lying around. There were at least two different brands, maybe three.

A few pieces of a story were starting to form in my mind. It was pretty obvious that this must be the place where the goat was killed—in the center of the circle. A sacrifice to Papa Gede, but the presence of the beer cans made it look like more of a party than a ritual. The vomit told me that one of the gang had a weak stomach.

What happened after that was anyone's guess. Why carry a heavy, bloody goat for half an hour just to put it in a dumpster—especially after you've just killed it? It made no sense. And who had been crazy enough to steal a goat in the first place? I had a few ideas about where to start, but that would be the easy part. The hard part was figuring out how the pirate radio station was mixed up in this macabre business. Playing the entire *Goat's Head Soup* LP was no coincidence. Nor was The Creeper's parable about Papa Gede. It was like a warning to stay away, but a warning to *who,* and to stay away from *what?* He had used the words children and boys and girls, so it was a warning to young people. What had Benny called them? Goths, punkers. And they were being warned away from here—from these woods, probably from this very clearing. But why? Scarier still was the fact that The Creeper had been in this clearing himself, may have sat right where I was sitting, had seen the circle and the vomit. For all I knew he might have been the one who had rubbed out the symbols. The whole thing was starting to weird me out.

I wished I had someone with me that I could talk all this over with, Gina Cartwright maybe, although why Gina would flash into my mind at that time was another mystery. There's no reason that Gina would think any differently than—

I became aware of faint sounds behind me. Voices, but not from the direction I had just traveled, but from further down the trail. The voices were a ways off yet, but coming closer. I quickly took up my bow and moved to a position behind the oak, which was broad enough to hide three of me. I crouched silently, listening. Presently I heard hurried footsteps and was able to make out a few words.

" . . . see us!"

"No way. Sunday morning, remember?"

The first voice was feminine, the other masculine. Young, but not children. They passed along the trail without stopping at the clearing. After a few seconds I ventured a glance around the tree. The girl had wild and fluffy hair the color of the inside of a peach, and was wearing athletic trainers and a long, flowery dress. The guy wore jeans and a red t-shirt. Long hair, but not shaggy. Neither appeared to be much taller than I am and both were wearing backpacks. That was all I saw before they disappeared around the path out of sight. I hadn't seen their faces. I stood up to follow them, then had another idea. I crept back to the path and headed in the direction they had come from.

The trail I followed was distinct, but bordered by thick brush and high grass. It wound through the pines and oaks the town was named for. Occasionally it opened out into a grassy glade, but always the forest eventually closed back around me. I walked as briskly as I could for half an hour without seeing or hearing anything unusual. My heart was beating rapidly, but I was enjoying myself. I was closing in on a story that no one else believed existed, trying to solve a mystery that only I recognized.

The trail sloped slightly upward into a grove of cedars. The air was clean and fresh and the leaves were brilliant green. Great old logs and trunks were evident here and there. On one of these I spotted a pine cone, although the nearest pine tree was fifty yards distant. Someone must have put it there; maybe one of the two hikers I had seen, maybe someone else. I stopped to listen, but heard nothing but the wind and a few crows calling far in the distance. I knew I was being careless, but years of stumpshooting wouldn't let me leave such an obvious target unmolested.

I took an arrow from the quiver, nocked it, aimed at the pine cone, and let the string flow off my fingers. It sailed high by a few inches and swicked into the ground. I pulled another arrow from the quiver and pierced the pinecone through, sending it flying several feet, still impaled by the arrow. I smiled. Not too bad for someone sick and out of shape.

I stepped over brush and limbs and retrieved the arrows, pulling the pine cone loose and tossing it away. I sat down on the log to rest for a moment before I went on. The path I was following went through the cedar grove into an unusually thick growth of ground cover. Beyond that, there was more forest, dark and brooding. What would I find there? A hunting lodge? A logging trail? Maybe a swamp or small lake. It seemed impossible to think that there could be houses, farms, or civilization of any kind way out here, yet there must be something; Clarence had hinted at it when he told me about the farmers who had once peopled these woods. I figured that as long as there was a path to follow, I would keep on.

I had been sitting quietly enough to hear the wind wafting through the tops of the cedars, but now I heard something else—the rustle of leaves. It was coming from behind a huge cedar maybe twenty feet from where I sat; too quiet a sound for a human to make but too loud for the wind. I slowly stood up and peered intently in the direction of the sound, but what I saw made my skin shiver down to my very cells. It was a rattlesnake, larger around than my forearm, slithering slowly forward. When it sensed my presence, it stopped, raised its head, and threw out its tongue like a tiny flame. Its tail rattled like maraca.

An icy fear in my belly froze me solid for a few precious seconds. But I shook it off; my time in Baghdad—where every step outside the safe zones was a step into danger—had prepared me for fear. I knew that if a snake that size struck me, I would never make it back to my truck. The cedar was an old one, with dozens of low-hanging limbs, but I could see the snake clearly through a break in the foliage. I watched it coil itself up slowly while, at the same time, I reached out for an arrow. It had only a target point and there was no time to reach into my fannypack and change it out for a broadhead. It would have to do. It occurred to me as I slowly and quietly nocked the arrow, that I had been preparing for this shot all my adult life, that all my trophies and accomplishments meant nothing if I wasn't equal to this moment. This was for the entire wheel of cheese.

Very slowly, I pulled the string to my anchor point and sighted down the arrow, hoping the snake wouldn't sense the movement and strike. But just before the arrow rolled off my fingers the rattler's head came up a few more inches. I released the arrow and jumped sideways with every ounce of strength I had left, trying to get the log I had been sitting on between me and the snake. Too late I realized that my foot was caught on a root or vine, making me lose both my balance and my direction. The last thing I saw was the end of the log coming toward me like a truck toward a bicycle.

Sometime later I was roused to consciousness by a sound I hadn't heard since that morning in the Baghdad zoo—a soft whinny. The top of my head hurt like someone had buried a hatchet in my skull. I made an effort and opened my eyes, but everything was blurred and red. But there, towering miles above me stood a gray horse. It was looking at me curiously, cautiously with its very large, brown eyes. The horse seemed to be asking me questions I didn't know the answer to. I tried to raise my head, to reach out and touch the horse, but the pain made me pass out again.

The next time I woke up it was in a hospital bed. My head still ached, but not as much as before. I raised a hand and felt my head wrapped in bandages. I was more than a little groggy, and heavy with sedation. I was thirsty, though. And hungry. "Hey!" I called, but the word came out slurred and made me a little dizzy. The response came almost at once from a lanky figure who was slumped in a chair in a corner of the dim room.

"I'm here, Sue-Ann."

"Clarence?"

The worry on Clarence's face was obvious. "Hey, Sue-Ann," he said. "How're you doin?"

"I don't know. Where am I?"

"County hospital."

"How did I get here?"

"I drove you."

"You?"

"I saw your car parked out back of the market. When you didn't show up after an hour or so, I figured you'd gotten a burr in your bra about that goat and gone in the woods lookin for somethin. God's gonads, Sue-Ann. What did you expect to find out there?"

Then memories began flooding in: the path, the couple with the backpacks, the clearing with the circle of blood, the . . . "Clarence! There was a rattlesnake, I shot at it but . . . I don't remember any more. Ohhh," I moaned, "What happened to my head?"

"You conked your coconut on a log and sliced the top

of your scalp open. They had to shave off some of your hair to put in stitches. I found the snake, though. Somebody'd put an arrow smack through its mouth and nailed it to a tree. It was as dead as I've ever seen a snake."

"I hit it?" I asked happily. The dizziness was wearing off.

"I should smile you did," he replied. "Darned arrow was stuck so deep into the trunk that I had to screw the point off and leave it there. I've got your bow and stuff in the car. Got the snake, too—I'll give you ten bucks for the skin. But don't tell me you went out there rattlesnake huntin."

"No. You guessed right about the burr. I was trying to find out who put that goat in your dumpster."

"Now, Sue-Ann, we talked about that . . ."

I tried to sit up, but it made my head ache more and I settled down again into the pillow. "But Clarence," I told him softly, trying to keep my head from pounding with excitement, "I found the place where they killed the goat. And I saw two people; one was a guy with long dark hair and the other was a strawberry blonde girl . Youngish. Wait," I continued, trying to think rationally through the pain and whatever drugs they had given me, "If you followed me out on that trail, you must have seen them."

Clarence looked blank. "Sorry, Sue-Ann. I didn't see nobody."

"But that's not possible." I began, thinking rapidly. "Unless . . . unless maybe they came out before you went in."

"That's probably it. But are you sure you saw somebody?"

"Don't treat me like I'm blind."

"Awright, Sue-Ann. You don't need to get upset. But it was probably just a couple of backpackers out for a

Sunday hike."

"How did you know they were wearing backpacks, Clarence?" I asked.

"What else would backpackers wear?" he asked innocently.

It was almost like the log had knocked some sense into me, because I was thinking more clearly than I had in months. "Clarence," I asked, "are you trying to tell me that you carried me for over an hour through the woods, and managed to bring my bow, my arrows, and a seven-foot rattlesnake at the same time?"

Clarence stiffened and I knew that something was going on. "Now, Sue-Ann," he stammered, "you just had a hard knock on your—"

Before he could finish, a woman dressed in white came into my peripheral vision. Nurse or no nurse, I glared at Clarence, waiting for his "explanation." The woman spoke first.

"Sue-Ann!" The voice made me forget about Clarence altogether. I made the mistake of turning my head too fast and the pain almost made me cry out.

"Gina."

"Mah gosh, Sue-Ann," Gina said, out of breath. She was dressed more simply that I had ever seen her: white jeans, white blouse, sandals. Her hair was straight and tied back with an elastic band. "Ah came as soon as ah heard. Are you all raht? Clarence, is she all raht? Where's the damn doctor?" Gina took my hand and squeezed it gently.

"She'll be fine, um, Ginette," said Clarence, who looked totally surprised to see her. "Just busted her head open a little. The doctor had an emergency; said he'd be here in a few minutes."

"How did you know I was here?" I asked her.

"Dilly Dollar called Cal at home," she said. "Told him

you'd been in a serious accident."

"But how did Dilly—" I began.

"He was at the hospital when I drove up," Clarence said. "He was writing up a report on some kind of abuse. He helped the nurses get you on the gurney."

"What did you tell him?" I asked.

"Just that you'd had an accident. Guess he thought I meant you'd crashed your truck."

"You didn't?" asked Gina.

"No. I just fell and bumped my head on a log. It's not that serious. I'll be—"

"It's serious enough," came an unfamiliar voice in the doorway. I looked over to see a young man in a blue smock with a stethoscope around his neck. He held a clipboard that he looked at as he spoke. "You had a concussion and a laceration to your scalp that took ten stitches to close. Plus various minor abrasions to your hands and face. Aside from that you're undernourished and probably anemic." He put down the clipboard, looked up, ran a hand through his already mussy hair, and smiled. "But I'm glad you're awake. Are these friends of yours?"

"Yes, sure. In fact, Clarence was just about to tell me—"

"We'll have to talk about that another time, Sue-Ann," Clarence said. "I need to be gettin back to the market."

"But you didn't—" But Clarence had walked quickly from the room. I looked at Gina. "I've a bone to pick with that man," I told her.

"He may have saved your life," said the man with the clipboard, who was now feeling my pulse, now listening to my chest, now looking into my pupils. He looked at me quizzically. "You seem to be feeling a lot better than you should be," he said.

"I'm great," I told him. "Just a little headache."

"You need rest," he said.

"I'm resting," I said.

"Without visitors," he replied.

"Gina can stay," I told him.

"Only a few minutes," he said, looking at Gina, who nodded. "Call if you need anything."

"Right. And hey," I called after him. "Bring some more drugs when you come back." I looked back at Gina. "I'm glad you're here."

"Now there's somethin ah never thought ah'd hear you say," she said.

"Me neither," I admitted.

"Tell me what happened."

For the next twenty minutes, I related everything I knew about what I had started to call the goat story. From the phone call on Saturday night, my talk with Clarence, my visit to the bookstore, the pirate radio station, and so on.

"But I shot at the rattlesnake just when I thought it was getting ready to strike, so I jumped out of the way. I remember tripping over something and evidently hit my head hard on a log. Seems like I came to for a few seconds and . . . and, oh Gina," I breathed, "there was a horse! A magnificent gray horse!"

"A horse?" Gina asked. "Where?"

"Standing over me. *Watching* over me. I only saw it for a second and everything was bleary, but it was a horse! I think I tried to get up then, but I must have passed out again." I looked at Gina thoughtfully. "You know, Clarence thinks I'm bonkers, or at least he pretends to think so, but he may be right. I mean, I saw a horse, but there couldn't be a horse out there. There just couldn't."

"If you saw one, Sue-Ann, then there *was* one," Gina said calmly.

"I've never seen you without makeup before," I told

her.

"I was in a hurry, darlin."

"I like it, though. You look, I don't know. You look pure. Were you, um, at Cal's when Dilly called?

"Ah was, yes. Ah'm not now."

"He asked you to come over and see if I was still breathing?"

"Course not; what do you think. He wanted to come himself, but ah told him to let me come instead. He's workin on somethin, so he was glad enough to let me. He *was* concerned, though. Told me to let him know if there was anythin he could do."

"Call him and tell him to let me write my story." I smiled. "Just kidding. I don't have half the information I need yet."

"Tell me what happened after you saw the horse."

"I don't know. I passed out and didn't wake up until about half an hour ago. Clarence saw my truck out back of his place and he came in the woods and found me. But get this: he said he didn't see the two people I saw when I was hiding. He was lying, Gina. He knew that they were wearing backpacks without my telling him."

"But if he saw em, why wouldn't he tell you?" Gina asked.

"I don't know, but I'ma find out," I said. "Here's another thing. He told me that he carried me out of the woods. That's over a mile of heavy walking. Maybe two miles. Now Clarence is strong and he could probably do it, but he also brought out my archery stuff and a dead rattlesnake that must have weighed thirty pounds."

"He told you that?"

"He sure did. You want to know what I think," I asked.

"What?" asked Gina.

"I think that those two people I saw helped him get me out. It's the only thing that makes sense."

"Ah think you're raht as raisin bran and not nearly as flaky. But ah ask again: whah would Clarence lah about it?"

"Because he knows something he doesn't want *me* to know."

"Doesn't want *us* to know," said Gina.

"You want to help?"

"We're friends, ain't we?"

"I guess. Alright, then."

"So what do we do?" she asked.

"I've got a few ideas. First of all, someone needs to go to the county courthouse and find out who owns all that property behind Meekins' Market. I'd say we have to go out at least ten, twenty square miles."

"That'd be fun," said Gina.

"Second, we need to check out certain hangouts. Clubs, bars, things like that."

"There's not much of that in Pine Oak."

"We'll have to spread out over the whole county. Maybe the next few counties as well."

"What are we lookin for?"

"That's where our third task comes in. We need to find out whether there are any punkers in Pine Oak."

"How do we do that?" she asked.

"I'm not sure. Maybe ask around the high school. We can do it together."

"When you're better," said Gina.

"Shit, speaking of better, my head is starting to fall off. Where's that doctor with those drugs?"

"I'll git him on mah way out."

I felt my face falling. "You're leaving?"

"Ah need to git back. The paper'll be goin to press to-naht."

"Oh, right."

She was silent for a few seconds, then looked me in the eye. "Maybe sometahm," she began, "when you're better, you and me can git together and have a girl's naht out." She reached out and gently pushed a lock of hair out of my eyes and tucked it behind my ear.

I blinked. "Are you hitting on me, Gina?"

"Mebbe yes, mebbe no."

Without really thinking about what I was doing, I gave her hand a brief squeeze. "Talk to me when I'm better," I told her.

Chapter 6

I met Crookneck Smith for the first time just before the end of my second semester at University of North Carolina. Crookneck ran a seedy hunting supply store outside Huckleberry Spring, but he was the only Martin Archery dealer I could find anywhere near my area. I was driving a Jeep Cherokee that my parents had purchased used and given me as a high school graduation present, but the directions he had given me were squirrely and it was almost dusk when I finally pulled up to the address.

The "store" was really one of those rectangular metal buildings that can be put up by a small crew in a day or two. Although it had about the same square footage as Benny's bookstore, it was both higher and wider and looked more like a long garage. In fact it had electronic garage doors on each side. Over the front was a sign older than I was with faded lettering that read "Crookneck's Archery and Hunting Supplies." I looked closer and saw that the left side of the building had its own door, over which hung a new-looking sign that said "Tom's Taxidermy," so I assumed that there were two separate businesses in the same building.

A series of uneven paving stones connected the front of the building with a mobile home in the next lot. There were no other businesses within miles; in fact, although I had passed several houses in the area, none were visible through the trees. It seemed a lonely spot for a business. There were no lights on in the building when I got out of my car and I hesitated whether or not to go in until I saw a gaunt figure limping down the sidewalk toward me.

"You Sue-Ann?" he asked.

"Mr. Smith?"

"Call me Crookneck," he chuckled. "We've talked on the phone so often I feel like we're old friends. Ye'll have to 'scuse my slowness but I had some surgery on my back a week or so ago."

"I could have waited until next week . . ." I began. Crookneck didn't have a crooked neck, exactly, more of a buzzard's neck, long and with a prominent Adam's apple. He looked to be in his mid sixties and his chin and cheeks were grizzled with stubble. He was wearing a clean pair of jeans, ironed white shirt, and serviceable work shoes.

"Oh, I'm fit as a frying pan," he said, reaching out to flip a switch that turned on a bank of overhead fluorescent tubes. It took a few seconds of flickering, but soon the room was flooded in light. If the place looked like a garage outside, it looked more like one inside. The floor was concrete, unswept for months or years. The walls were pegged with hunting paraphernalia—both for guns and archery—sights, grips, cases, straps, and the like. A long and rough wooden bench held containers of arrowheads, nocks, inserts, vanes and feathers, and a heavy metal bowstringing stand was positioned within easy reach of the bench. "I know ye've been anxious to get yer bow," he continued. "So I called as soon as it came in this morning. Sorry ye couldn't find a dealer a little closer to where ye live."

"I talked to two or three others on the phone," I told him. "But you were the only one that wasn't rude to me when I mentioned wanting a recurve."

"Yeah, waal, traditional archery isn't what it was when Fred Bear was alive," he lamented, taking a long white box from a corner and placing it on the bench. He took the top off and reached in for the bow. "Ye know, I remember when ye could find a selection of these in any good archery store. Now all ye find is compounds. Here ye go," he said. "She's a beauty."

What he handed me was a new Martin Mamba recurve, sleek and dark with exotic African woods and a thirty-five-pound pull weight. I almost gasped, although I'm not sure that people do that. It was the most beautiful bow I had ever seen, although, to tell the truth, it was probably the first recurve I had ever seen up close. I ran my hands up and down the smooth finish, looked at the gleaming tips, fitted the grip in my hand.

"How long ye been hunting?" Crookneck asked.

"Oh, I don't hunt," I told him. "I'm just a target shooter. I took an archery class last semester. That was the first time I ever held a bow, but we had to use these old compound bows. I loved the shooting part, but when I decided to buy my own bow, I wanted a nice wooden one."

"Oh, ye'll come back around to compounds eventually," he said. "And ye'll get into hunting, too."

"You think?" I asked.

"Here, let me show ye something." He took the bow from me and replaced it carefully in the box. Then he led me to the back wall, where there were half a dozen new compound bows hanging on pegs. "I'll bet these don't look like the ones ye were shooting in yer class," he said, and he was right. These were more colorful, more technologically advanced, like something out of the movie *Alien*. I couldn't help but admire their impossible twists and turns, their almost bizarre beauty. Crookneck took one off the wall that was so black it could have been a stand-in for night, so black I expected to see his fingers disappear into its finish. It had all kinds of things growing from it—a quiver, a sight that looked like eyestalks on an insect, a cigar-shaped stabilizer. "Try this one," he said. "Don't worry, ye can pull it okay. I fixed this one up for my granddaughter and it has my special sight."

"Special . . . ?"

"I've been tinkering with sights for years. This one is exactly the same as I use on my own bow." He pointed out the back door toward a small shed about twenty or twenty-five yards away. "That's my target," he told me, "that bale of cotton in the shed. Ye see the black circle in the middle?" I did; it was just smaller than a saucer. He handed me an arrow. "Go ahead and try to hit it."

I nocked the arrow, but ran into some trouble because the bow was fitted with a wrist release aid and I had never used one—you didn't touch the string with your fingers, just pulled back on a mechanical device attached to the string and pulled a trigger. To make things even more confusing, Crookneck's special sight moved upwards as I pulled back the string, like it was on a small escalator. But once I was able to fit the tiny red light to the pinhole of the sight, I pulled the trigger and it was almost like nothing had happened. The string was back in place and the arrow was gone, although it had traveled so fast I hadn't even seen it leave.

"Did I miss the whole shed?" I asked.

"Sure hope not," he said. "That's swampland back there and those arrows are expensive." We walked to the shed and, to my surprise, the arrow had caught a good inch of the black spot. Crookneck withdrew the arrow and chuckled. "Ye see, ye'll come back to compounds by and by," he said. "And ye'll feel the lure of the hunt." His faraway gaze seemed to take in the mounted deer heads on the wall.

I didn't reply, but that moment was the one in which I

decided that nothing would ever induce me to shoot a compound bow again. What was the point? With that kind of power and technological accuracy, there was literally no way to miss. I wanted to do something hard; I wanted to be able to use my own senses to determine whether or not my arrow was aimed in the right direction. And although, years later—when I was shooting in national competitions—I again began to forsake craft for technology, I never picked up a compound bow again. And you were there when I killed the rattlesnake in the woods—the only animal I ever shot. But Crookneck did influence my archery: you might remember that my own target—which I set up in the judge's box outside my mother's dressage ring—was patterned after Crookneck's, cotton bale and all.

I no longer have that first bow, but I remember it with pleasure for all the practice I got in on it over the next year. As I gained strength, I soon wanted a heavier bow and the more I shot, the more accurate I became. And if I hadn't been accurate that afternoon in the woods, I probably wouldn't have had to be taken to the hospital. It would have been the morgue.

~ ~ ~

They kept me in the hospital overnight and, to tell the truth, I was glad they did. The young man with the blue smock had given me a sedative and I went out pretty fast.

When I woke up it was morning and the man in blue was standing over me with a pencil in his teeth and a clipboard in his hand.

"Huh ah yuh eelin is ornin?" he asked.

"Take the pencil out of your mouth," I told him, struggling to a sitting position, and propping a pillow behind my bandaged head.

"Sorry. How are you feeling this morning?"

"Better. Head still hurts, though. Are you a doctor?"

95

"I am this week," he smiled. "Actually, I'm an intern. You're my first case."

"Why does that make me uncomfortable?" I asked.

"No need to worry," he told me. "A *real* doctor was standing over me while I sewed up your scalp and prescribed your medication."

"Has Gina been here this morning?"

"That your friend from yesterday? The blonde?"

I nodded, which made my head hurt only a little more.

"I haven't seen her. She married?"

"She's old enough to be your mother," I said. It was stretching the truth, but she did have almost ten years on him. I looked at him more closely and realized that he was a good-looking kid. Five-ten maybe, built kind of slight but well proportioned. Sandy, wavy hair, neatly trimmed mustache. "What's your name?" I asked.

"Will Morris."

"Well, Dr. Morris," I said. "If I see Gina I'll give her your regards. When can I get out of here?"

"Whenever you'd like, as long as you take it easy."

"What does that mean?"

"You know, like go home and stay in bed for a few days. Pop a few pills."

"My kind of intern," I smiled.

"One thing, though." I saw the seriousness in his eyes. "I'd like to do a couple of tests before you leave."

"What kind of tests?"

"Your friend—Gina—told me you were having some problems before you banged yourself up."

"Well, maybe a few," I admitted.

"I noticed a couple of things myself when you were brought in—mostly under your eyes and in your clothes."

"My clothes?"

"They're too big," he explained. "I have a few ideas.

Or, at least, I have *an* idea. I just need to get a couple of blood samples."

"What's your idea?" I asked.

"Ah-ah, Holmes never divulges half-baked theories. Wait until I get it out of the oven."

"Is it cancer?" I asked.

He laughed. "No, not cancer. I mean, you may have cancer too, but that's not what's causing your hair to fall out."

"Why does that *still* not make me feel comfortable?" I said with asperity.

"Sorry. I mean well." He thrust a hand through his hair and grinned. "I have a few more patients to see, but I'll send in a nurse practitioner to get blood samples. Then you're out of here. But really, you'll have to miss soccer practice for a few days."

It was hard not to like Dr. Will Morris. Even though I was old enough to be his mother. Almost. And he was as good as his word. Inside of an hour I was tested, dressed, and wheeled out the door.

But when I got out to the parking lot I realized that I didn't have my truck. It was still in back of Meekins' Market. And it wasn't like I could walk home—the hospital is in Forester, twenty miles from Pine Oak.

I retraced my steps and went back inside to ask the receptionist to call me a taxi. I didn't really have anyone else to call; or maybe I just didn't want to impose on them. It was a good half hour before the taxi came and another half to get to Meekins' Market, where I planned to confront Clarence again about the discrepancies in his story. I paid the driver with a credit card I keep in the truck and walked into the market. No sale there, though. Gladys told me that Clarence had gone out, she didn't know where, Tifton, maybe. Watermelons.

When I got in my truck, I noticed that Clarence had put my bow on the back seat and covered it with an old blanket I sometimes used to keep my legs warm on long drives. The snake was nowhere to be seen.

It occurred to me that I still had unfinished business in the woods—the rattlesnake had stopped me before I had finished following the trail. My scalp told me that it would have to be another day, so I started the truck and drove the few miles home.

But the goat story stayed with me and when I walked through my front door I half expected to find the floor covered with voodoo symbols and bloody fingerprints. Instead, I found my phone light blinking and I recognized Jack Stafford's number on the ID. With everything that had been going on, I had forgotten about Jack's first call. But deep down I had been hoping he would give up trying to contact me. He had been one of the reasons I left Richmond, but at that time I had been so muddled in my own mind that I wasn't sure why I had to get away. No wonder Jack was confused. He was a patient man and had waited almost a year before trying to contact me. Still, I wished he hadn't; I still didn't feel rational enough to deal with him. I pushed the play button.

"Sue-Ann. I haven't heard from you so I got a map to your place from Google."

There was a click as he broke the connection. That was it. Jack was coming to Pine Oak. But he hadn't said when. I suppose I could have called him back and told him to stay away, but I didn't have the energy; in fact, I turned off the ringer and went into the kitchen. I opened a can of Pepsi and took one of the pills I had gotten from Doctor Will. I turned the radio on, but the pirate station was off the air. I was restless, needed something to do with my hands and my mind so, gathering up some courage, I went into my mother's room and began the long, slow process of putting her things in order.

I have mentioned that my mother was a realtor. Although she sold the business soon after she moved out to the farm, she had kept a wooden filing cabinet full of the records of her old clients. All those papers and file folders were scattered on the floor. I straightened her mattress, made up her bed, and sat down with a large plastic garbage bag. I looked carefully at each paper and each folder I picked up. It was difficult sometimes to tell whether the papers had to do with property she owned or property she had sold either to or for someone else in her professional capacity. And, of course, there were other papers having to do with her taxes, her horses, and other things in her personal life. It took a couple of hours, four cups of coffee and another Vicodin before I had sorted them out into several piles. The ones dealing strictly with her realty records went into the trash bag. The others I would have to go through more carefully later. Luckily, Cindy (there—I had to refer to her again, and this time it wasn't so difficult) was very meticulous and very neat. There was a folder for every piece of paper in the room, which would make it quicker to refile the ones I didn't toss in the trash.

The pile that interested me most was the one that contained papers about Cindy's horses and competition results, including a loose-leaf notebook filled with aphorisms on dressage that she had scribbled down over the years. There were certificates, membership papers to various equine organizations, letters from humane societies, registration papers and health certificates for each horse, and correspondence, including emails she had printed out. Some of these would be needed by the horses' new owners, but by the time I had finished my initial sorting, my eyes were too blurry and my head ached too much for me to continue. So I stripped naked and lay back on Cindy's bed.

Minutes—or hours, I'm not sure—later, someone knocking on the front door woke me up. Wondering if it might be Gina, I threw on one of Cindy's wraps and went to the door.

It wasn't Gina.

It was Donny.

He came inside before I could tell him not to and looked at me with a worried expression.

"What happened to you, Sue-Ann?" Donny asked. His voice sounded tired and I could tell he had just gotten off work because his shirt and hands carried fresh grease stains—he drives a truck for Harrison Towing Service.

"Nothing; I'm fine," I told him. "What are you doing here, Donny? Came back to get your bottle of tequila?"

"Somebody told me you were in an accident," he said.

"News travels fast in this here small town," I said. "Know anything about a goat?"

"Don't know nothin bout no goat, no," he said, puzzled.

"Been talking to Dilly?" I asked.

"I saw him, yeah. He told me your house got broken into and that you went out and got yourself in a car wreck."

I didn't feel like going through the whole thing again, so I let the accident theory stand. "I didn't get hurt much but thanks for your concern."

"I *was* a little concerned. But that's not why I came over."

"Why, then?" I asked.

"I wanted to make sure that you know I didn't do it."

"Sit down if you want. I'll be back in a minute." Actually, it took more like five minutes for me to go into my bedroom, straighten my bandage, and throw on the long dress I sometimes lounged around the house in. I'll use that five minutes here to describe my relationship with Donny Brasswell.

I met him in a bar in Forester—there are no bars in Pine Oak or Timberlake, so everyone has to drive twenty miles in (Forester is the hub of a radial county) to party. I don't know why I was there that night; I don't know why I did much back in those days. I had just quit my dream job as an international journalist, left what my acquaintances in Richmond thought of as a successful relationship, and moved back to a family home devoid of everything except a few memories. I had been employed by *The Pine Oak Courier* for only a few weeks and I had just finished an interview with a school board member who was creating quite a local controversy by suggesting that Hanson's Quarry High School be closed and the students bussed into Pine Oak. The interview had gone on longer than I had expected so I dropped into a place called Eat Now: The Home of Food, which had a bar off to the side, and ordered a cheeseburger and a Coors.

It was a Friday evening and the place was pretty full, mostly of young blue-collar types—ranchers, heavy-equipment operators, guards who worked at the prison a couple of miles north. Donny was sitting by himself at a corner table, drinking one Miller Lite after another. I noticed him because, except for me, he was the only one there alone. I knew who he was because he grew up in Pine Oak. And, although he's a couple of years younger than me, I knew that he had gone to Pine Oak High and had been a good athlete of some kind. He looked it.

There was a juke box playing CDs, with a trash basket to the side, above which was a hand-written sign saying, "SMASH THE DIXIE CHICKS." Inside the trash basket were a few dozen CDs, in and out of their jewel cases. There was a buzz in the room, the same kind of a buzz that is in all rooms where people of opposite sexes gather. I wasn't there for a good time; just to eat and wind down. I think I had just begun to realize that I might have a real illness, so I was feeling a little more blue, a little more scared and run down than usual. In fact, the gaiety in the room was depressing me and as soon as I finished my burger and beer, I walked up to the counter to pay. I nodded and said a few words to the woman at the cash register as I was paying. The woman's name was Linda Christian, who will come back later to play a more important part in this narrative. She was the one we always called Linda C in high school to differentiate her from Linda DiLorenzo, who we called Linda D. Although Linda D left the county before we graduated, everyone continued to call Linda Christian Linda C—even after she married and changed her name to Zimmer. I remembered that she had once been one of Gina's crowd, but more of a hanger-on than an equal. Working the cash register in a popular hangout was about the best she could hope for herself.

Linda C was babbling something about having a kid that went to Pine Oak when I heard a commotion coming from the corner where Donny was sitting. Two other men had appeared and were standing at his elbow. They were bigger than him, both in height and bulk, and they both had hair the same dark shade of red. I heard the words "back home" and saw Donny shake his handsome mane of brown hair vigorously. One of the men grabbed him by the elbow but Donny suddenly stood up and shoved both men hard in the chest, sending them both sprawling backwards. "Fuck both of y'all!" he shouted and stormed from the room.

I looked at Linda C with a question.

She shrugged. "His older brothers," she said, as if that explained everything. "Half brothers, I guess I should say."

I walked outside to my car to discover that Donny had parked right next to me and was fumbling with his car key. He was obviously too drunk to drive.

So I drove him home that night. And the next afternoon, I drove him back to get his car.

And my five minutes are up.

Dressed in my house gown, I came back into the room to see Donny sitting on the couch and smoking a Kool light. He held the pack toward me but I shook my head. "I can't find that bottle of tequila," I told him. I figured that Gina had put it away in a cupboard somewhere and I would find it later. I sat down on the chair near the couch.

"Forget the damn bottle of tequila," he said. "Do you think I would have broken into this house to get a bottle of tequila?" As always, clean or dirty, Donny was darkly handsome, his tanned face lightly pocked, his shirt just a mite too small. He set his cigarette in the ashtray and I saw the familiar dark fingerprints on the butt. But when your boyfriend works in grease, you and grease get to be friends.

"I hadn't figured you'd broken in for any reason," I told him.

"You hadn't?"

"You never had any reason to. You know I would have given you anything I have except my bows, and I probably would have given you half of *them* if you'd asked."

"Did they get your bows?" he asked.

"No. Thankfully, they didn't think to go in the barn."

"What about the stash from the semi that turned over?"

"I . . . forgot about that," I admitted. "But except for a couple of pinches I never took it out of my truck."

"If you're not goin to smoke it, you should get rid of it."

"Give me time. You don't want it, do you?"

"Naw, you know that stuff makes me sick. But thanks for askin. Listen, I'm sorry I was so mad the last time I left here."

"Were you mad?" I asked. "Is that why you called me a fucking bitch, drove over the plants I had just put in the front yard, and took a couple of shots at my mailbox?"

Donny leaned over tiredly and put his head between his hands—a gesture I was familiar with. "I don't know why I do stuff like that," he said.

I *did* know, but didn't want to go there right then. Instead, I changed the subject. "Linda C still at Eat Now?" I asked.

"Last I heard," he said guardedly.

"Still seein each other?" I asked. He looked up, meeting my glance. "Small towns, Donny," I told him.

"Yeah, I guess. Off and on. She's okay. A lot different from you, but she has a good heart."

"What's it like dating someone with kids?" I asked, genuinely curious.

"Hmm? It's okay, I guess. Adam mostly lives with his dad, but comes over weekends. He can be a pain—doesn't really like anything the way it is and complains about it."

"Isn't that the way all kids are?" I wondered aloud. "That's how I was. I couldn't wait to get out of here and now look at me."

"Look at yourself," he answered. "I told Adam a few things about you. How you left and got a good education and traveled all over. I showed him a couple of things you wrote in *The Courier*. Thought it might inspire him or something."

"Did it?" I asked.

"Mebbe it did. At least he asked more questions than he usually asks."

"It's funny that you should wind up with Linda C after

the way we met," I mused.

"That's right. It was at Eat. Was Linda working there that night?"

"Sure. That was the night that you had that ruckus with your brothers, but I see that you're still working at Harrison's." I was looking at his hands, but he glanced at the nametag on his work shirt.

"I'm not going back to those damn cornfields!" he said. "They can have every kernel, every husk, and every grain of sand."

"Listen, Donny," I began, realizing that I was falling into my old habits with him but unable to stop myself. "Someday your dad won't be around any more."

"Sooner the damn better," he said in a low voice.

"But stop. Listen to me. Take what's yours. You don't have to grow corn, you don't have to grow anything. Start a ranch. Raise bulldogs, do whatever you want. Build a nice house and live in it instead of renting that leaky room you've got."

"Fuck, I don't know," he said. "I better go."

"Yeah."

"How have you been feeling? I don't mean the head, but that other thing?"

"Some days are better than others, but I just met this doctor who thinks he knows what's wrong. We'll see."

"That's good. Well . . ." Donny got up to go but instead of walking toward the door, he leaned over, put his hands on my shoulders, and kissed me. I struggled a little, but then forgot what I was struggling for. I experienced his mentholated breath, his whiskery rasp on my cheek, his pressure on my lips. Then his hands were under my dress, where he found my breasts uncovered and ready for his touch. Then the dress was up around my waist and I had unzipped his pants and there we were—at it again, him, gripping my breasts with both hands, kissing me hard and groaning the same way he might have if he'd had a broken arm. It took him less than three minutes to finish, then lay panting over me and running his fingers through the part of my hair not covered by the bandage.

As he was lying there, I heard a soft tap, then the front door opened and Gina stood in the doorway. When she saw us, her face went from bright to blank and her eyes became hooded. "Mah bad," she said. "Here ah am walkin into people's houses ah don' even know." Then she turned and went out, not bothering to close the door.

I pushed Donny off me and pulled my dress back down.

"What the fuck?" Donny said, bewildered. He turned around, but Gina was gone. I heard the wheels of her car spin in the dirt as she sped out the driveway.

"Who was that?" he asked.

"Wrong number," I told him, but my stomach had grown so icy I thought I was going to pass out. "Donny, you've got to get out," I said. "And we can't do this again."

"But Sue-Ann," he said. "You—"

"Never mind about that. It was my fault, I should have said no, but it's not going to be my fault again. Go back to Linda C. But take a shower first. No, not here. And remember what I said about the land."

As soon as I had shooed Donny out the door, I took a thorough shower and put on clothes fresh from the dryer. I knew that something definitive had just happened but I couldn't put a name to it. Whatever it was, it made me queasy-sick and very nervous. Without totally realizing what I was doing, I looked up Gina's address in the phonebook. The street name was only vaguely familiar but I wrote it down thinking I might need it some day. I discovered I was almost out of cigarettes and cat food so I left the house and started up the truck. As I drove I took a local map from the door pocket and glanced at the index, which was difficult because the red dirt road was even more of a washboard than it had been a couple of days earlier. I happened to locate Gina's street on the map in case, you know, I ever needed to go there.

My farm is situated on the western edge of the town; Gina's address was several miles to the southeast, but I found myself driving in her direction. It wasn't so strange, when I finally started thinking rationally again, because I knew I had to see her. And once I started thinking again, I couldn't stop. As I drove, my mind was racing faster than the car's engine. I didn't know if Gina would be home—she probably drove straight to Cal's—but I had to find out; I had to see her. I had no idea what I would say to her, was terrified at what she would say to me, but the look she had given me as she turned away had worked its way into my pores and I had to at least try for absolution. But absolution from what? I had told her that Donny and I were not seeing each other and I felt bad for making that seem like a lie. I had also told Gina about my weakness around men and I was disappointed in myself for having let her see that weakness. Still, I told myself that who I dated or slept with was none of her business. But I didn't think of turning the truck around.

Hundreds of snippets of conversation were born and died on that ride, yet I didn't understand why I was so upset. Gina was the enemy; had always been the enemy. Yet she was also the one who had always forced me to the limit of my powers and beyond. And in the last couple of days she had been kind to me.

The sun had gone down and it was difficult for me to see street signs, so when I got into Gina's neighborhood I had to drive up and down a couple of times before I finally found the right street—the green metal sign on its crooked pole was half-hidden by a cedar limb growing on a corner lot. It wasn't a ritzy neighborhood; but it wasn't a poor one, either. Most of the houses looked small, maybe one or two bedroom, and most had brick facades. It was already too dark to see the numbers on mailboxes, but when I had driven almost to the end of the street I spotted Gina's light PT Cruiser in a short asphalt driveway in front of a cozy-looking house—more of a cottage than a family residence. I turned off my lights and parked in back of the Cruiser. In that order. Didn't I want her to know I was there? Did I want to be able to back out? Who knows. I got out of the car quickly and walked just as quickly up to a short porch leading to the front door. There I stopped, not because I had changed my mind, but because I heard the faint strumming of a guitar coming from just inside the door. I quieted my steps and climbed the porch until I could look in the window. Gina was sitting in an armchair, playing a guitar and singing softly. Her voice and the music were country, the words something about heartache. Her eyes were open and she looked straight ahead. She didn't look sad. She didn't look anything.

I knocked loudly on the door, but if I expected Gina to be startled, I was mistaken. She simply leaned the guitar against the far arm of the chair, got up, and came to the door. She was wearing a loose t-shirt, a pair of ragged, cutoff jeans, and nothing else. Her hair was still damp from a shower.

She opened the door and looked at me as if she had expected me, yet she raised her eyebrows almost imperceptibly and asked, "What are you doin here?"

"I don't know."

"Shouldn' you be 'restin?'" Although there was no inflection in her voice I heard the irony. She turned away from me and walked back to the armchair.

"I'll rest after I've killed myself."

Gina sat down in the chair tucking her legs and feet under her like a resting fawn, then looked back at me still standing in the open doorway.

"Comin in?" she asked.

"I don't know."

"Ah thought you were the one who always knew everythin."

"I don't know anything," I said desperately, but I closed the door and walked over and sat down on a couch near Gina's armchair. Just sat there, mute, for what must have been ten or twenty seconds.

"So," Gina began. "You and Donny's a thing again, huh?"

"I don't know," I said. "No."

"No?"

My head had started throbbing again, probably had been throbbing for hours and I had left my pills in the truck. "You think I'm a hose monster, don't you?" I asked, but didn't let her reply. Instead, I continued quickly, "I'm not. I'm . . . I'm a need magnet. There's something that draws me toward guys with problems. Donny just came over to see if I was all right. Dilly told him that story about me being in an accident. I didn't even want him in the house, but when he was, things started, you know, replaying themselves—he started brooding and getting down on himself and generally blaming himself for every problem in the world. One look at Donny hidin his face in his hands and lookin like he was ready to cry and I was just as drowned as if I had jumped in a pond with a tractor in my pocket."

I knew I was starting to babble and I forgot twelve years of self-imposed elocution lessons between one breath and another. "When me and Donny broke up, I missed him some, I did," I told her. "I didn't wanna be lonely, but at the same time I didn't wanna feel sucked on all the time. It's like I'm this big nipple connected to all the answers in the world. I'm about sucked out and I don't have many answers left. I let Donny down just like I let down ten or twenty guys before him."

"Let him down how?"

"I don't know!" I shouted. I looked at Gina and tried to concentrate, to explain what was going through my mind. "When guys are with me, they don't feel like losers. They feel good about themselves, they get motivated. But it takes so much out of me. Why do you think Donny and me split? It's because I was gettin too weak to prop him up. Linda C is perfect for him because she's so good at it."

"It's all she knows how to do," said Gina.

"Wanna hear somethin worse?" I went on. "I got a phone message from Jack Stafford—the guy I lived with in Richmond. He wants to drive down and see me; I think he wants us to get back together. I could've picked up the phone and told him to stay put, but I didn't. An I really, really don't want to see him!"

"Wah not?" she asked curiously.

"Guilt, what do you think? Raw, unadulterated guilt. I'm not sayin that all my old boyfriends are saints, but Donny and Jack are both nice guys. They came to me because they needed me to feel good about themselves. And I left em worse off than they were before."

"That ain't true, Sue-Ann."

"Then I left *myself* worse off, okay? I wasted years taking care of guys instead of gettin on with my own life. And I can't help it, when I'm alone with guys like Jack or Donny I just let em feed. Is it any wonder that I tried to steal Cal from you? Oh, shit, Gina," I cried, leaning forward and putting my throbbing head in my hands. "What's wrong with me? Why don't I think before I do stupid things like lettin Donny mess with me when all I wanted was for him to go home and be happy with Linda C? I hurt everybody I'm around," I babbled, "and someday I'm gonna hurt somebody I love." And with that I lost it completely and started sobbing loudly. Gina let me cry and cry and when I finally quit and raised my head and wiped my wet hands on my pants I realized how I must look.

"God," I breathed. "I'm such a mess."

Gina appeared not to have moved, but I thought I saw a narrow wet streak down one of her cheeks. She slowly uncoiled her body and rested her bare feet on the coffee table. Her cutoffs showed a full twelve inches of thigh and she had removed the polish from her toenails. I stared. They were even more perfect than before.

"That's it, Gina," I said. "Just make me fucking crazy."

"That's what ah do," Gina said simply. "Ah make people crazy. But don't worry, it don't last. People screw me, then screw me over. So you see, you're not the only one who's a mess." She leaned over and began massaging her feet. "It's your fault," she finished.

"My fault?" I said stupidly.

"Didn't ya know?" she smiled.

"I told you," I said desperately, "I don't know anything."

She tucked her feet back under her and looked at me like she might look at a painting in a museum. "Ah always knew ah was better'n you in some things, but ah was always scared that they were the *wrong* things. So ah kept tryin to get smarter, to do things that were more important, to do things that *you* maht do, although ah woulda died if anyone'd guessed. And what ah found out was that ah didn't have any use. After you left and went off to college

111

ah didn't have anyone around me that was worth the inside of a pig's butt, so ah started askin myself questions, lahk, you know, lahk why ah was alahve, so ah started tryin to read stuff, to learn, to trah and find out how ah could do somethin that would have any value. And ah *did* learn stuff, and ah *did* better mahself, but it made things worse. That's how ah lost Jimmy—he didn't lahk it that ah was smarter'n him. If ah'da been stupid, we'd still be together."

"Do you wish you were still married to Jimmy?" I asked softly.

"Of course not, but it's because ah *know* better. Remember ah told you about mah professor in Tallahassee? Well ah lost him because ah never got quite smart *enough*. Even after he knocked me up ah knew he'd leave. All he wanted was somebody that could discuss, ah dunno, Keynes or Heegel or some other dead asshole over the breakfast table."

"And all this happened because of me?" I asked, shyly.

"Gloat if you wanna."

"There's no gloating involved," I told her. "You win, Gina."

"Win what?" She gave me that museum look again.

"This lifelong war we've been having to see who's best. It's no contest. Maybe it was once, but not any more. Look at me—banged up, sick as a drunk, disillusioned about everything in the world you can name. I've been to a place where I saw people die and I've run back to a place where no one knows how to live. I'm a blot on the landscape and you're still the shining diamond you always were. I lied when I said I didn't know anything because I do know one thing, and it makes me feel like a boulder has rolled downhill right into my stomach. I know that you win and I lose."

Gina looked at me. Only her green eyes had any

expression, but it was those eyes—bright and questioning in the lamplight—that calmed me and let me feel like coming to see her had been the one thing on earth that I had needed to do. She got up from her chair and leaned over me. She fiddled with my bandage with gentle fingers. Then she reached out and wiped a smudge from behind my ear with a fingertip and studied it. It was grease. She wiped it on her cutoffs, put both hands on my shoulders, and looked into my eyes. "Sue-Ann," she said softly, only inches from my face, "either we both win or we both lose." She took her hands away and sat back down in her armchair. Still looking at me, she lit a cigarette from a pack on the coffee table, and curled into her resting-fawn attitude.

"What does that *mean*?" I asked, getting frantic. I couldn't believe that I had once considered Ginette Cartwright a bimbo, or that I had ever considered myself intelligent. It seemed like everything that came out of her mouth had about six meanings.

"You jist go home and think about it, Sue-Ann. And figure out how you're going to get better."

And then I remembered. "Gina," I said excitedly. "You know that doctor you saw in my hospital room?"

"Ah remember. He stopped me in the hall when I was leavin and asked me a few questions."

"Like your phone number?" I asked.

"Questions about you," she replied.

"I think he might know what's wrong with me. He did some tests. Said he'd call me with the results."

Gina smiled and straightened up in her chair. "That's great, darlin. But, ya know, that's not what ah meant just then about you gittin better."

Her words sobered me. "You mean, this thing I have with men?" Too late I realized the double meaning in my own words, but I couldn't call them back.

Gina's lips twitched but she pretended she hadn't caught on. "If they're the *wrong* men, yes." she said. "You need to straighten it out, don't ya think?"

"I guess there's a lot of things I need to straighten out."

"And you need to git home and git some rest. Some *real* rest."

"Will you play the guitar for me?"

"Not to-naht," she was still smiling.

"I'll keep asking until you do," I told her, rising from the couch and moving toward the door. "Maybe I'll see you in the office this week."

"Stay home and rest," she told me.

"Thanks for listening to me," I told her. "I owe you."

"An ah'll collect someday," she said.

"What does *that* mean?" I asked.

Gina just kept on smiling.

Chapter 7

I went straight home after I left Gina's but I couldn't sleep. The moon was almost full and shone like a flashlight through the open curtains. I was fatigued and felt my heart running its long-distance race, but I was alert, wide-eyed in the semidarkness. I thought briefly about the sex with Donny earlier, winced, and passed on. My muscles tightened involuntarily as I thought of Gina seeing him draped over my half-naked body; but that, too, I could pass over without much reflection. My mind kept going back to Gina's porch, hearing the chords of her guitar and her soft voice.

I didn't know what to make of her. I had never really had any close female friends—only professional acquaintances or women I occasionally met at archery competitions—no one who could sluice the impurities off my heart as Gina had done. It felt strange, like the first bite of a glorious new dish. Sick as I was, screwed up as I could possibly be, I felt more at peace than I had for years and I finally closed my eyes and drifted off, smiling at the ceiling.

I awoke somewhat later with a headache. I had been dreaming about my mother. I guess coming close to death reminds us of other deaths we have known, and certainly my mother's was the one closest and most frightening to me. I remembered her long legs, her assurance, her perfect balance when she walked and when she rode. Riding had not just been her passion, it was what had molded her as a girl and continued to craft and perfect her until the day she died. And when anyone complimented her on some achievement or some personal quality, she was quick to give credit to her horses. I thought about her horses with sadness. Where were they now? My dad had probably not given a thought as to what kind of homes they had gone to and my overtaxed mind saw them having to stand in deep snow or exercise in a barbwire-enclosed quarter-acre of hock-deep mud. I made another resolve to ask him where they had gone and, sleepily, imagined buying horses of my own, cleaning out the stables, and reconstructing the dressage ring.

Then I thought of Gina again, but this time we were back in high school.

My first rated jumping competition was also my last. Getting dumped by my horse had nothing to do with it but having Ginette Cartwright come to my rescue and possibly save me from serious injury was too much for my sixteen-year-old psyche to handle with any kind of grace. I still rode and I still jumped, but only at schooling shows— venues that would never tempt an experienced rider like Gina. When I saw her at school I would sometimes smile, sometimes nod, and sometimes cut her dead. She would do the same, depending on her mood and, except for a brief contest of wills on this or that school matter, our senior year passed uneventfully. But I remember many episodes in which she influenced me in subtle, almost unaccountable ways.

One incident concerned a Mexican boy named Jorge, who I knew from the boys' bowling team. He was nice enough and fairly good looking—straight teeth, straight black hair. He dressed casually but always looked clean and fresh, kind of like a plate just out of the dishwasher. But his English was poor and sometimes Linda C and some of the others in the popular crowd would make fun of him. I would see Jorge sometimes in the school cafeteria, and we would practice our English and Spanish together over lunch. I really didn't think much about him until one Thursday I saw Ginette at his table as I entered the lunchroom. I was furious at Ginette; I thought we had moved beyond that kind of cheapness. Used to thinking on my feet, I turned and spied an acquaintance on the yearbook staff and persuaded her to walk across the street to Hardees for a Texas sourdough bacon cheeseburger. I was sure Jorge hadn't seen me, but Ginette had; and as her gaze found mine her face was totally expressionless.

The next day, Jorge was waiting for me before school, outside my home room.

"I didn' see you yesterday at lunch," he began, his white teeth gleaming.

"You looked busy yesterday," I told him.

"What, you saw me sitting with blondie?" he said.

"I saw you sitting with Ginette Cartwright," I told him.

"I was waitin for you and she just come and sit down," he said.

"What did she want?" I asked.

"I donno. Just asking me stupid questions bout my family. Prolly just lookin for somethin to tell her friends so they can laugh."

"Maybe she was just curious," I said. "Don't you like her?"

"She's pretty, but stupid like a cow. I tole the bitch she better go back to her own table. Twat mus think I'm a moron."

Jorge never understood why, but that morning I found an excuse not to meet him for lunch, and I found other excuses on other days until finally he lost interest. Ginette was my bitterest enemy, but she was neither stupid nor bovine. On the other hand, if she thought Jorge was a moron, that was good enough for me.

You know, things like that.

I managed to doze off again long enough for the telephone to shake me like a rattle at about 9:30 the next morning. I picked it up before I knew what I was doing.

"Wha?" I answered.

"Good, good," came back a bright, vaguely familiar voice. "I'm glad to see that you're getting a lot of bed rest."

"Who's this?"

"Will Morris, your friendly neighborhood intern."

I sat up in bed, instantly and completely awake. "You found out what's wrong with me," I stated.

"Yes indeedy," he said.

"What?" I urged.

"Hmmm?"

"What do I have?"

"That would be telling."

It took me an hour to shower, dress in the clothes I had worn to Gina's the night before, and drive into Forester. At the hospital it took only a few minutes until I was shown into an examining room, and only a few minutes more before Mr. Blue Smock walked in, pencil in teeth and clipboard in hand.

"Mmmphh," he began, but I gave him a quick vicious look and he took the pencil out of his mouth and said "Morning."

"For another few seconds."

"Time flies when you're cutting people open," he replied. "Let me have a look at your head."

I leaned over and he began taking off the bandages. "What have you—" I began, but he cut me off.

"You need to be quiet while I do this," he said. Very softly, he swabbed my wound with some kind of antiseptic solution. "It's healing nicely," he said. "Is it giving you any trouble?"

"Itches," I said.

"I'll give you some pills," he replied. "Right now I'm going to replace these bandages with this patch. Leave it alone or it'll come off. I'll give you a couple more patches for when you screw up and it *does* come off. But we'll leave the stitches in for another few days. Then you can concentrate on growing out that fabulous shock of dark hair."

"Rat's nest, you mean," I said grumpily.

"Okay, I'm through. Sit up."

Will Morris took a seat next to me and crossed his legs. He grinned and ran his hand through his hair. "You're lucky I played golf in college," he said.

"I'm not sure how to answer that," I told him.

"You have Graves' disease," said Dr. Morris.

"Never heard of it," I responded. "What does it have to do with golf?"

"Ben Crenshaw had it," he answered.

"Never heard of him," I told him. "What's Graves' disease?"

"It means you have an overactive thyroid," he explained. "And Ben Crenshaw was one of the top golfers in the world until he went through a bad slump that couldn't be explained by nerves or a poor swing. I may not be much of a doctor, but I know a lot about golf."

"He had, um, Graves' disease?"

"Right."

"What happened to him?" I asked.

"He was cured by the miracle of modern medicine," he smiled. "And won the Masters a couple of years later."

"What does it mean?" I asked. "I mean, what's happening in my body?"

"Okay. The thyroid gland is located right here." He touched the lower part of his neck, right below his Adam's apple. "It releases hormones that regulate how fast your body uses energy—if you're walking leisurely down the street, looking in store windows, your thyroid tells your body not to burn up a whole lot of energy. If you're playing a hard game of soccer, your thyroid releases a bigger dose of the hormones because you're exerting yourself more. It causes your body to burn up more fuel—more stored fat and anything else your body burns. Clear so far?"

"I guess. Yes."

"That's a normal thyroid. But when your thyroid is overactive it makes more of these hormones than you need. You might still be doing leisurely window shopping, but your body thinks you're running a marathon. You burn fuel, your heart rate increases, you get the sweats, you lose weight, and all without the benefit of exercise."

"How did I get it?" I asked.

"Who knows," he shrugged. "Some say it's genetic, some say environmental; there's a lot of theories. Maybe I'll have my own one day."

"Could it kill me?" I asked.

"It might," he said. "Especially if you insist on running around in the woods playing investigative reporter."

"Can't you give me a pill or something?" I asked.

"It's more complicated than that,"

"I thought it might be," I said.

"Sue-Ann," he began. "There's no cure for Graves' disease."

"But it can be treated," I said. "You told me about Ben Crenshaw."

"Yes. It may take a few months, but you can get pretty close to normal again. Get your weight and strength back, get your heart rate down, get that shock of beautiful dark

120

hair thick and shiny and long again. Right now I'm going to give you some antithyroid drugs that will bring your levels down to normal and some literature on treatment options. Then you'll have to make a choice."

"What kind of a choice?"

"You can keep taking these hormone adjustment drugs. That's the first choice. Sometimes, that will actually fix the thyroid, at least for a while and you can stop taking them. Trouble is, your thyroid might go bananas again at any time, like maybe in the middle of a soccer game. Then you're SOL.

"The second option is to shrink the thyroid with radioactive iodine and take hormone replacements for the rest of your life. The bad news about that one is that you can't have sex for about a week after the treatment. Bummer."

"It will make me sick?" I asked.

"It will make you radioactive," he answered.

"There's a third option?"

"The third option is to have your thyroid surgically removed."

"Like having your appendix out?" I asked.

He looked at me seriously. "Your appendix isn't useful, your thyroid gland is. Without the hormones it spits out, you'll die."

"And I can avoid that how?"

"You'll need synthetic hormones."

"For the rest of my life?"

"Now you're catching on."

"Is the operation dangerous?" I asked.

"Piece of cake."

I walked out of the hospital in a kind of thoughtful daze. I was glad to know that sometime, soon maybe, I would be back to normal. But, although I had occasionally gotten high and had no qualms about taking a few Vicodins for a cracked skull, having to take drugs every day for the rest of my life was an idea that didn't settle in easily. I had been given a lot to digest, and I hardly noticed the miles back to Pine Oak.

My route took me past *The Courier* office, so I stopped, hoping to see Gina so I could tell her the news. I had taken my first dose of the antithyroid drug called PTU and I already thought I could tell a difference. I thought I felt better, that I could see better, that my heart rate was slowing. A similar dose of Placebo X would probably have done exactly the same, but I was feeling pretty good.

I walked into the office, but Gina was not at her desk. I saw Betty toiling over her paste-up board and Cal was bent over some papers in his office with a pen in his hand. I wondered if Gina had gone to his place after I left last night. I took a breath and went in. I was going to keep this short and businesslike.

Cal looked up and, seeing me, smiled widely. "Sue-Ann," he said. "Hey. How are you?" He was genuinely happy to see me. I blinked.

"I'm okay, just banged up a little."

"Listen, I wanted to come to the hospital . . ."

"S'awrght. Gi—Ginette told me you were working on that housing cost piece. Thanks for asking her to come. It helped, having someone there when I woke up."

"I don't know why you were running around in the woods, Sue-Ann," he began, "but I hope it didn't have anything to do with a dead goat."

"Any reason why I can't go stump shooting in my spare time?" I asked.

"What's that? What's stump shooting?"

"It's what some people enjoy doing with bows and arrows in the woods. Shoot at cans and pine cones and stumps. It relaxes me, plus I usually pack out any trash I find."

"You shoot bows and arrows?" he asked. "You hunt?"

"No hunting. I'm a target shooter."

He put his pen down on the desk in front of him. "I haven't seen a bow or an arrow since I was a kid," he said. "You any good?"

"I was on the Olympic Archery team."

"No shit?"

"Well, first alternate, but I got to go to Sydney."

"That's incredible. I'd love to hear about that some time. Have you ever written it up?"

"I kept a diary for the paper I was with at the time, but they never used it. I guess it wasn't such hot news. I've got it on a disk somewhere," I told him, flattered at his interest.

"I'd like to read it," he said. "Really."

"I'll print it out sometime," I told him. "But what I came in to tell you was that I want my job back."

He looked at me with a puzzled expression. "You *have* your job, Sue-Ann."

"I want regular assignments again. I'm not sick any more. I mean, I am, but I know what's wrong. My thyroid is out of whack and I'm getting treatment. I'll be as good as new."

"That's what I like to hear," he smiled. He sat back, pushed his papers aside and asked me questions about my disease, the treatment, and how I was feeling in general. I told him about Ben Crenshaw and asked him how his own game was going. He segued into talking about his twin sons and how he would sometimes take them to the driving range; how he was looking forward to making his baby daughter into another Kelli Kuehne when she got big enough to hold a club. Then we talked journalism for a while. Although he only mentioned his divorce in passing and did not mention Gina at all, it was the longest conversation we'd had since he had interviewed me for the job.

"So can I have an assignment?" I finally asked.

"You have that history of the Plank Festival to get ready."

"You were serious about that?"

"Sure."

"It's still weeks off, isn't it?"

"In the meantime, write about stump shooting," he said. "And what about that rodeo I told you about? This weekend. Ag Center."

"Oh, right. I'll get on that."

"And Sue-Ann. Let's move slow, okay? Let's get your strength back before you start having to drive all over hell at whatever hour a story might come up. Let Mark do that."

"Yeah, Mark," I said, trying not to let any bitterness creep into my words.

"Sue-Ann."

"Yeah?"

"Mark is a grunt. You're a world-class reporter. They're not the same thing. And I'm not just your boss; I'm a fan, and I want to have you at *The Courier* for a long, long time, especially now."

"What do you mean?" I asked.

Cal leaned forward in his chair and intertwined his fingers. "Well, you know, in the last year or so—since you've been here and since Ginette took over the office work and the advertising, our circulation and our revenue have gotten a lot better. I'm thinking about going to three days a week, maybe hiring a sports reporter. When I was researching that piece on housing, I found out that there are more and more people moving in to our area every month, more businesses setting up, people are enjoying a higher standard of living. In a year, two years, we could be a daily with maybe a dozen staff writers. What would you think about that?"

"I'm uh, stunned," I said. "I had no idea that things were—"

"And you would be the bureau chief—in charge of all the other reporters."

"Really? I mean, that would be great, Cal," I managed. "Let me know if I can help."

"You can help by getting yourself back to a hundred percent. Now go home."

I was disarmed. I smiled. "Okay, Cal. Thanks. I'll check in next week."

I left Cal's office liking him more than I had when I went in, and not just because he had told me that my job was secure. He loved his own job, wanted to make *The Courier* the best it could be. The fact that he was Gina's boyfriend, though, set off an alarm with a very unfamiliar timbre.

I looked expectantly at Gina's cubicle, but her chair was still empty—she was probably out selling advertising. Maybe I could call her later.

Outside, I saw Benny's Jeep and thought of the article Cal wanted me to do on the Plank Festival. I remembered that I had once seen a thick history of Jasper County on one of his shelves, so I decided to see if he still had it. Through the window I saw that Benny uncharacteristically shelving books from a rolling metal cart. The bell over the door jingled as I walked in and Benny looked over from his work.

"Hey hey hey," he greeted me, grinning. I noticed that most of the boxes and bags of books that had been piled around the card table on Saturday were now gone.

"How have you been, Benny?" I asked him.

"Better than you," he said. "Mmm. What happened? Somebody hit you with a shovel?"

"You oughta see the shovel," I answered.

Benny shuffled over to his desk, sat down, and rummaged for something in a briefcase by his feet. "Got something to show you," he said.

I walked over and saw that he was holding an eye-pillow—similar to the one I had shown him but stitched into two halves, with a soft bulge in the center of each half. On the bulges were representations of a woman's breasts. He jiggled it in his hands and I heard what sounded like the shake of rice.

"Titties, heh heh."

"I see."

"Found a picture I liked and had it silk-screened on the fabric. My wife sewed it together. She thought it was dirty, ewww, but I told her they were hers."

"This is something I really shouldn't know about," I said. "It's a good idea, though. You can probably sell a lot of them."

"Sell them?" he asked, as if the idea had never occurred to him. And it probably hadn't.

"Here in the store. Get a display for them. It's just what every man wants—an eyeful of breasts."

"Hmmm. Marff."

"On to another subject," I said. "Do you still have that history of Jasper County I saw in here one time?"

"Yah. Right in the corner there." He pointed to a shelf marked Florida History. There it was, lying on its side. I picked it up and gave Benny the money.

"History buff now?" he asked.

"Just research for a story," I told him. "Have you seen any of those punkers you told me about last time I was in?"

126

"Nah, the scratchy little weasels."

"Well, if you do, try and get a license number or the make of car they're driving. If they actually buy something, get a name from a check or credit card. Even the brand of cigarettes they smoke."

"You got a lead on something?"

"I've got something in the works, yes. I'll keep you posted if I find out anything."

"Don't leave yet," he told me. "Heh heh. I got something else to show you. Come on."

He waddle-walked to the back of the store, where he motioned me through the door into a back room. It was as messy as my mother's bedroom after the break in. Magazines were scattered about, hundreds, maybe thousands of surplus books were placed willy-nilly on rickety shelves, and dozens of boxes were piled up against walls. Many of the boxes had books growing from the top of them. Benny picked his way through to the far wall and pointed out a half dozen boxes sitting by themselves. These boxes were sealed tight with clear packing tape. "Ahem," he said. "There you go."

Dubiously, I worked my way through the maze of junk. Benny cut the packing tape with a Case knife he pulled from his jeans. Then he stepped back, dumped some stuff off a folding chair, and positioned it where I could sit down. "Here's you a saddle," he said.

I opened the box he had unsealed and my eyes widened. I saw *Dressage for Beginners*, by R. F. V. ffrench Blake, books by Paul Belasik and Walter Zettl, *The Gymnasium of the Horse*—the box was filled with horse books. "Benny!" I cried. "This is wonderful. What are in the other boxes?"

"Same old same old," he said.

"Where did you get all these?" I asked.

"Your dad," he said. "Yuk yuk."

I straightened up in the chair. "From Daddy? These are my mother's books?"

"Aye, lass. Smart as paint ye be."

"I want to buy them back from you. All of them. I can't pay for them all now, but maybe a couple a week. And I'll give you a deposit . . ."

"Arghh. Yer gold's no good 'ere. The books is yerz, every last page of em."

"But you must have given Daddy a fortune for these!"

"Right ye are, missy, but umm, harrumph, me check bounced. Boing, heh heh."

"And what, he left town before he knew it was no good?"

"Aye, must've."

"You're a lifesaver, Benny, as well as a criminal. Daddy had no right to sell these without asking me. But why haven't you put them out on the shelves?"

"Errr, been pretty busy. Naw, that's not it. Nope. Been keeping them for you."

"What, all this time?"

He became more serious and dropped his pirate accent. "I ordered some of these books for your mom. Sometimes, she, um, talked about you and I knew you used to ride some. The books were kind of a legacy from her, so I got them from your dad and tried to keep the bugs off em. Since you've been back it seems like you've had, ahem, things on your mind, so I saved em. The other day you told me that you were thinking about riding again, so I thought it was probably time."

"I don't know what to say."

"Giddy-up," he smiled. "I'll help you get them outside," he said. "I think I have a hand truck around here somewhere. Hmm, ummph."

As we lifted the boxes into the back of the truck, I asked him, "Here's a longshot for you. You ever listen to that pirate radio station?"

"It's me favorite."

"Really? You're the first person I've talked to who's even heard of it. Is it back on the air? Last time I tried it, all I got was static."

"Last night in the wee hours they played nothing but Irish drinking songs. There's something weird about that station. Like, woooo!"

"Tell me about it." I put the *History of Jasper County* on the front seat of the truck and got in. I spoke through the open window. "Anything else I need to know? Any gossip?"

"Did I show you the horn I invented?"

"Show me next time. Any progress on the Santeria play?"

"Ummm. Got stuck on the setting. Can't decide whether it takes place in Africa or Haiti or New Orleans."

"Maybe in the woods in north Florida," I suggested.

"Who'd believe that?" he asked.

~ ~ ~

It seemed like I made the couple of miles home in only a few minutes, but I had even more to think about than I had before. Pushed aside for the moment at least was the goat story, crowded out by the recovery of my mother's library and the news about my disease. And, oh yes, by Gina Cartwright. Mental snapshots of her came and went as I unloaded the books from my truck. The sky was clouding up and I didn't want to take a chance that they might get rained on. The effort it took let me know that I wasn't yet ready to play in that soccer game that Dr. Morris kept talking about.

The house was as I had left it—no scattered papers or

corn starch designs or dead cattle on my living room rug, and after I had stored the books in my mother's bedroom, I fired up the iMac and began my attempt to read everything ever written about Graves' disease.

DSL or cable had not yet come to most of the rural areas of Pine Oak but my dial-up connection was adequate to do searches, and I read until my eyes threatened to pop out of their sockets. There's no point in going into technical detail here—you can Google it yourself. The important thing is that, in three or four hours, I learned as much about my hyperthyroidism as I could stay awake for, and I think I memorized the booklets Dr. Morris had given me. I became a big Ben Crenshaw fan and found out that Barbara Bush and Christina Rosetti were also diagnosed with Graves'.

Gail Devers, too, the track star. I encountered Gail in 2000; we were both staying in the Olympic Village in Sydney, Australia. She, of course, was the fastest woman in the world and I was just the first alternate on the archery team. She was coming out of a restaurant bathroom and I was going in. We nodded to each other and that was it. Yet eight years before, she had won a gold medal after recovering from a bout of Graves' disease that nearly killed her. As it happened, she came down with an injury in Sydney, so neither of us actually competed there.

Before I shut down the computer I pulled up the file I had been keeping on my goat story investigation and looked over what I knew so far, adding a bit here and there.

And just for good measure, I checked Amazon.com music for *Goat's Head Soup* and as all of you Stones fanatics out there already know, it is a real album. 1973.

After that I zonked out. Not only was my head aching again, but I imagined that all my Graves' symptoms were flaring up at once. I took an Advil and nearly fell into bed, but not five seconds later the phone rang.

It was Gina. Cal had told her about my disease. She was worried, why hadn't I called? Did I have a death wish? What the fuck had gotten into me? She had been trying to phone me for the last four hours but my phone was busy and was I all right?

"Sorry, Gina," I told her. "I was online. I have an overactive thyroid that's making my body think it's a Harley Davidson and I was doing research on it. I'll tell you about it when I see you."

She hesitated and asked if she could come over after work and I said sure. It'd give me a chance to take a nap, and that's what I did. I didn't wake up until Gina knocked.

I answered the door in a robe pulled tightly around me and calfskin slippers on my feet. Outside, the sky looked stormy, but the ground was still dry. Gina was dressed so neatly she could have been just going to work instead of just getting off. Her brown skirt matched her shoes and her light blouse managed to show off her figure without making her look too sexy. She walked in, fumbling with her purse, going past me without looking at me. She sat on the sofa, crossed her legs, and lit a cigarette. Neither of us had spoken a word. Standing there alone at the door I felt like the only one at the dance without a partner.

I don't know what I had been expecting—for Gina to rush in and hug me and make mothering noises, maybe. But her total indifference crushed me. "I . . . I need to get dressed," I managed.

"Raht."

It took me a few minutes to put on some jeans and a t-shirt, and kick my feet into a pair of sandals. When I walked back into the room, Gina had her head tilted back on the couch and was blowing smoke at the ceiling.

I sat on the armchair next to the couch. Gina lit up a second cigarette from the cherry of the first. "So," she began. "Cal told me you have somethin called Graves' disease."

"Right."

"Tell me about it."

Without really knowing what I was saying I told her about my condition and the treatment options, but it was more like I was reading it from a book than explaining it. I told her about the pills, the possible side effects, Ben Crenshaw and Gail Devers. Throughout it all, Gina just sat there staring ahead or at the ceiling, smoking cigarette after cigarette.

"Gina," I finally said. "What's wrong?"

"Whah should anythin be wrong?" she replied. "Ah jist came over to see how you are. Ah was worried."

"Why won't you look at me?" I reached over to touch her arm, but she chose that moment to reach for the ashtray.

She didn't answer, but finally looked into my eyes. The expression there was such a mixed bag of anxiety, sadness, shame, bewilderment, and a dozen other emotions that I had no idea what she was really feeling. Outside, I heard thunder begin to rumble.

"Is there anything else you want to know about my disease?" I asked.

With that, something stirred in her and she came to life. "Shit, Sue-Ann. When Cal told me what you had, do you think ah was goin to wait till now to fahnd out somethin about it? What do you think ah was doin while you were online today? Don't you think ah was doin the same thing you were? Between us we could probly write a book. Have you decided which treatment to get?"

"No," I answered, trying to understand her mood

swing. "Not yet. It'll be a while before the pills bring my hormone levels back to normal. I won't have to decide till then."

Gina stood up and went into the bathroom. She was gone only a minute or two, but when she returned, she was more herself. Outside, the thunder sounded closer and raindrops were pattering steadily on the tin roof. Gina didn't seem to notice. "Here," she said. "Get up a minute."

I stood up and Gina moved my chair so that its front cushion abutted the end of the couch where she was sitting. "Now take off those sandals and sit back down," she said. Puzzled, I did as she asked. She lifted my foot into her lap and started giving it a light massage. "Wh—what are you doing?" I asked.

"Relax, ah'm a professional," she told me.

"But my feet are so—"

Gina interrupted me as casually as if she had just resumed a normal everyday conversation. "Anythin new on the goat story?" she asked.

"Maybe, um, one or two things, nothing to hang my clothes on. Ohhhh!" I moaned.

She gave me an innocent look. "Dilly have anything new on whoever broke in here?" she asked, gently massaging my toes.

"That feels so good I can't stand it," I breathed. "What did you say about Dilly?"

"Ah asked whether—"

"Oh right. No, forget about Dilly. I know who broke in." Outside, the rain began pounding down with force.

She stopped rubbing my instep. "Damn it Sue-Ann. You're the aggravatinist person I ever met. You *know* who broke in and you didn't tell me?"

"I . . . I've had things on my mind."

"How'd you find out?"

"Donny told me. Ouch!"

"Mah bad." She let go of my foot, which she had suddenly squeezed a bit too hard. She took a file from her purse and began filing my nails.

"Listen," told her. "It's just a theory, right? But it's what I have to go with until I hear a better one."

"So it was Donny broke in?"

"No."

"But you just said—"

"Okay. I'll tell you if you promise never to stop what you're doing. Remember that story I wrote about the 18-wheeler carrying weed that skidded off I-10?"

"Coupla months ago, yeah."

At that moment there was a crash of thunder almost simultaneous with a flash of lightning and the house winked into darkness. Both of us twitched with fright and I'm lucky Gina didn't stab me with the nail file. "Yow!" I said. "I guess we're going to need some candles."

"Don't git up. Ah lahk the dark. Go on about the truck. It jackknifed onto the median and turned over, raht?"

"Right, but what no one except Cal knows is that Dilly had gotten a tip about what the truck was carrying and wanted to know whether *The Courier* wanted to be in on a bust. So at about one a.m. Dilly was following the truck down I-10 and I was following Dilly. But when he put his red light on, the driver of the truck tried to get away, lost control, bounced over onto the median, and turned over. And when it did, the back doors flew open and these big brick-sized kilos of high-quality bliss scattered all over. I pulled up maybe five seconds after the semi went over, and when I got out of my truck I almost stepped on one of those bricks. Billy was busy running after the driver, so I quick grabbed it and stuck it under my seat."

"No you didn't!"

"I did. Then I casually walked over to the scene with my legal pad and a camera. I got my story and took some pictures."

"So wait. Are you tellin me that whoever broke into your house stole that dope?"

"They never stole it, no, because I never took it out of the truck—I mean except for that little bit we smoked."

"So how do you know that's what they were after?" Gina asked.

"Remember when Donny was over here yesterday?"

"Is that what they call a rhetorical question?"

"Sorry. But Donny wanted to know if my stash had been stolen. That's really the first time I made the connection between the break-in and the dope. And Donny's the only one who knew I had it."

"What about Dilly?" Gina put my left foot back and felt for my right.

"After he got back from running after the driver, he was too busy stashing his own pickings."

Gina blinked. "You mean Dilly . . . ? But never mahnd about Dilly, what about the driver?"

"He was long gone through the woods."

"So that leaves Donny."

"Who may be half moron, but who doesn't smoke and is pretty honest about most things. No, here's what happened. Linda C evidently has a teenage son."

"Raht, ah think his name is Adam," Gina told me.

"And evidently Adam is a handful, so Donny has been trying to straighten him out and give him some goals. I guess he thinks I'm some kind of role model if you can believe it so he told the kid—Adam—about how I'd gotten a good education and a good job and traveled around and all that baloney. He even showed him some of the stories

135

I'd written for *The Courier*."

"The one about the truck!"

"Right as a razor blade," I told her, "and just as sharp. And Donny is innocent enough to have told Adam about how I'd scarfed up that dope and took it home."

"So a teenage kid came in and tore up your house just for some dope?"

"I'm pretty sure. When he couldn't find any, he took the closest thing I had, which was a bottle of tequila. Unless you put it away somewhere when you were cleaning up the other day."

"No, ah didn't see no tequila."

"Well, that's it then."

"You gonna tell anyone?" she asked. "Dilly? Linda C?"

"I just told *you*," I told her.

"Raht, but you *got* to tell me things. Ah'm your girlfriend."

"You are?"

Gina put her file away and gave my foot a last rub. "Ah dunno. You know whah ah was in such a crappy mood earlier?"

"I wondered."

"Ah was thinkin that mebbe us getting to be friends ain't such a good idea."

It was like she had punched me in the jaw. "You think?" I managed to ask.

"Mebbe, yeah."

"You want to go back to the way we were?"

"Ah do in a way—in a lot of ways ah do. But every time we talk ah get confused; ah start thinkin things I shouldn't." She still had my foot in her lap and was squeezing it gently. I tried to pull it away but she held it tighter and continued. "Sue-Ann, you make me scareder'n ah've ever been in mah lahf. What ah want is—"

But she was interrupted by the lights coming back on. Almost simultaneously the phone jangled in the bedroom.

"Let it ring," I said.

But when the recording came on we both heard Cal's voice at the other end. "Sue-Ann," he said. "It looks like you were right. A woman out on 136 went out to her henhouse this morning and found her dog dead. It was killed just like the goat."

Chapter 8

When we heard the click of Cal hanging up, Gina and I looked at each other without knowing what to say. I slipped my sandals back on and stood up. "I need to call," I said.

Gina nodded so I walked into the bedroom and dialed.

"Cal, it's Sue-Ann. I was in the shower."

"Sorry about that," he said. "But I'm glad you're home."

"What have you got?"

"Between seven and eight this morning, a woman named Estelle Hobbs went out to see to her hens and gather some eggs. She has some kind of a coop in her back yard and when she went inside, she found her dog dead and put up in one of the nests. Throat was cut and belly slit open. Just like that goat."

"Where does this woman live?" I asked. Gina was standing beside me, holding a lit cigarette in her left hand and the ashtray in her right.

"Got a pencil?"

"Of course."

"Okay, she has an acre or so on Peg-leg Road, off Highway 136." I started writing.

Cal went on to give me more precise directions, which included turning down a dirt road and passing a large magnolia tree just before the woman's driveway. As he was talking, though, a thought struck me.

"Cal, if all this happened this morning, why are you

just telling me about it now?"

"I didn't hear about it until Billy Dollar called me not half an hour ago," Cal said simply. "And *he* didn't hear about it until he went on duty. Officer Evers was the one that took Mrs. Hobbs's call, and I doubt he knew anything about the goat. At least, he didn't put one and one together."

"So you want me to follow up?" I asked.

"On everything."

"What about Paul Hughes?"

"I'll talk to Paul."

"I'll drive out there tomorrow morning."

"Be careful, Sue-Ann. Whoever is doing this is sick."

"I will. Thanks."

I hung up the phone and turned to Gina. "I'm back on the story," I said, and in a few words recounted what Cal had told me.

"Will you tell me what you fahnd out?" she asked.

"Of course."

There was an awkward pause. After all, we were standing in my bedroom. "Do, um, do you want to stay?" I asked, then hastily added, "I mean, I've got lots of room."

"Ah wanna, ah do," she said. "But I cain't. Not yet. For one thing, Cal maht be tryin to call me. For another..." She stopped in confusion.

"Yeah," I responded.

"Mebbe we can get together this weekend and do some detectin," she said.

"You still want to?"

"Ah do."

"I'll call you."

Gina gave my hand a light squeeze and walked toward the door. Then she turned and looked at me across the room. "Soon, okay?"

"You're not talking about the phone call, are you?" I asked.

She shook her head shyly and left.

The hour with Gina left every cell in my body radiating energy. I took another dose of my medicine and replayed our conversation over and over in my head. It made me glad that, after so many years, she thought that I was special. I had *always* thought of Gina as special, but I no longer hated her for it.

I tried, without much success, to take my mind off Gina by going through my mother's papers and adding a few more observations to my notes on the goat story. I listened to a couple of hours of the pirate station, which was uneventful until Gamma, in another of her giggly moods, read a new poem. I only remember the first three lines, but they went like this:

> *On midnights dark with fire,*
> *who comes searching for their heads?*
> *The poultrygeists, the poultrygeists.*

Gamma was off and running on a poultry kick. Next she read what she called her own personal recipe for chicken fajitas, which actually sounded yummy, then played an entire side of an album by Country Joe and the Fish, who I immediately brought myself up to speed on by doing a computer search. Another Woodstock-era band whose anti-war stance was reflected both in the titles of their songs and their lyrics. Well, anti-war was good. But when I started reading about the band members I found something I didn't really expect to find, something that made me feel like an insect was crawling up my back: the drummer for the Fish was called Chicken Hirsh.

The dog had been killed in Estelle Hobbs' chicken coop.

What next? Would Gamma play some old Elvis—like maybe "Hound Dog?" Or maybe unearth something like "How Much Is That Doggy in the Window," which my grandmother used to sing for me when I was a little girl? With the radio in the background, I spent an hour reading the horse mystery I had gotten from the bookstore. The mystery was thin, and I heard no songs about dogs. Maybe the chicken thing was just a coincidence. Yeah, right.

That night I rested well and was up early the next morning feeling refreshed. I ate a more substantial breakfast than I had for a long time. I also dressed with more care than usual, deciding to wear a loose hat to hide my patch, then made my winding way to the small farmhouse of Estelle Hobbs. I had no trouble finding the area because I had come this way with Donny a couple of times; the farm run by his father and brothers was just off 136. The last time we had gone there—probably to pick up one of Donny's tools—the west side of the house had been torn out because of termites, and a blue tarp was wrapped around the gap to keep out some of the cold weather. Now the wing had been replaced, but with what looked more like odds and ends than standard lumber. I noticed that five or six pieces of plywood had been fitted together to form the outside wall, and there were gaps between the pieces. I guessed that there was a plan in the works to put on a siding that would hide the poor job they had done, but the Brassfields tended to do things on their own schedule, which was often not at all.

The Brassfield farm was one of many you see in rural areas whose property line is defined by old machinery. As I passed, I saw along one boundary several generations of tractors, a hay bailer, an automobile without doors, stacks of tires, piles of crumpled tin roofing, and tractor attachments I couldn't even begin to name—all rusted and useless. The few pieces of working equipment were kept together with wire and duct tape and were parked in a pole barn in worse repair than the house.

Old man Ed Brassfield, Donny's father, was the worst kind of miser. He might have picked up a few dollars by selling the metal from his useless machines but always held out for a better price than what he was offered by various scrap dealers. In one attempt to save money, he had tried to use old cooking grease instead of diesel in one of the tractors. It had actually worked for a couple of months, but the tractor was now part of the property line. He refused to make improvements to the land and, when successive crops were substandard, he blamed his sons for doing a poor job of planting. When I say sons here, I mean Donny's older brothers, Tad and Chad, the red-haired giants who I had first seen arguing with Donny at Eat Now, although Ed Brassfield blamed Donny as well for not being there to do his share.

Donny hated his father, and I think he had good reason. Not only did he work his sons like slaves, but he had made Donny's mother—Ed Brassfield's second wife—work in the fields as well as cook and clean in a house without air conditioning. She had lost control of her car one rainy evening coming back from the grocery store and plunged into a ditch. By the time an ambulance came, she was dead. This happened when Donny had been thirteen and he had been devastated by his loss. He remembered, though, that Ed had been angry at her for dying, for wrecking the car, and for the money he had to pay for the ambulance and burial. Donny had run away from home a dozen times before he was 18, but he was almost thirty before he broke away for good, with his own apartment and a decent-paying job. There were two things Donny dreamed about. The first was killing his father in a painful way. The second was watching his brothers do it.

Chad and Tad were likeable enough, but were lazy and overweight, despite their long hours in the fields. When they laughed they said "guh-huh" and their red hair was not only uncombed, but uncombable. Their idea of a good time was to drive into Forester on a Saturday night for the all-you-can-eat special at Po' Folks. One thing I had noticed about the Brassfield farm, though, and Donny and I had talked about it more than once, was that with the right management and an infusion of money—not too much—the 200-acre farm could be not only profitable, but had the potential to be a nice place to build a house and raise a family.

I came to the dirt road where Estelle Hobbs lived and found her white frame house without any trouble. It was set near the road, so I parked in front and got out under the large magnolia Cal had mentioned. Before I reached the porch, a stout woman in her sixties opened the screen door and came out to meet me. She wore a pale green dress tied at the waist with a strip of the same material and thick sandals over white socks. The most unusual thing about her was that she wore a metal neck brace that looked like small goal posts rising from her shoulders. She walked with a very decided limp and spoke with the accent of someone who has lived all her life in Pine Oak—which I won't try to duplicate here; I have enough trouble trying to get Gina's right.

"Are you Miz McKeown?" she asked. "Mister Dent called and said you might come by this morning. Are you going to do a story about Lester?"

"Lester?"

"Lester's my dog," she explained. She ushered me into her house, which was crammed with knickknacks, throw rugs, and plump chairs. A sideboard with pictures in frames, lamps with yellowing shades. "It's getting so that it's not safe for people to live these days," she said, continuing through the living room and into the kitchen. "And me with my back surgery comin up next week. Go ahead and sit down there," she said, motioning me to one of two large straight-backed chairs standing at a small table. "I have some coffee made. Would you like some?"

"Yes, thank you."

She continued talking while she served the coffee—the same Maxwell House roast that my grandmother used to brew—mostly about her surgery, not only the one coming up but the many she had in the several years since her husband died. "That's why I named the dog Lester—it was my husband's name. I hadn't had him long—a nephew of mine gave him to me last Christmas to keep me company—but I'd gotten used to him. Wasn't much of a barker, and that's a good thing, because I can't stand those little yapping dogs that everybody seems to like nowadays. And he never went after the chickens; no, I couldn't have stood for that either."

When I could get in a word, I asked, "What breed was Lester?"

"Oh, I don't know. I'm not much on breeds. Kind of a mutt terrier I guess you'd call him. It was a shame what happened to him. I screamed when I saw him all bloodied up and torn apart like that. And right in one of the hen boxes, too. I had to run right out of there and call the police. Then I called my nephew to come and get the dog out of the henhouse. I couldn't go back in there until he'd buried Lester and gone back home. I told him not to get me another dog. A cat maybe. Must've happened sometime after midnight—that's when I usually go to bed and I'm a heavy sleeper."

I finished my coffee and set down my cup. "Can I see

where you found him?" I asked her.

"Come on out this way," she said.

A set of broken flagstones connected her kitchen door with a roughly fenced-in back yard. The yard was mostly mud after last night's rain, and I could see remnants of scratch she had thrown out for the chickens, several of which were hunting and pecking like bad typists. Inside the chicken wire was a shed with unpainted board walls and a tin roof. It was about eight feet square and just large enough to stand up in. The old lady opened a gate, shooed away the chickens, most of which fluttered toward her as she entered, and walked across a well-worn path to the open door of the henhouse. She reached inside and switched on a light that was hanging from the ceiling. She stood aside for me to enter, then followed me in. It was a simple square room with a dirt floor and wide, sturdy shelves along three sides. On these shelves were shallow wooden boxes filled with straw, each box large enough for one hen. In fact several of the biddies were sitting in their boxes and squawked as we entered. Mrs. Hobbs pointed to an empty space along one of the walls. "He was lying right there," she pointed. "His throat cut and his entrails all hanging down. I was scared so bad that it wasn't until Jimmy—that's my nephew—had been gone an hour that I noticed that two of my chickens were missing. No, I don't want me no more dogs. I don't even—"

"Two of your chickens?" I interrupted.

"That's right. Not only was the thief a murderer, but he was a thief, too."

"Thank you, Mrs. Hobbs," I said. "I think I have all I need."

"You haven't written down anything on that pad you brought in," she said suspiciously.

I tapped my head. "I'm a living legal pad."

145

I walked around the house to my car so that I wouldn't track mud into the farmhouse. Then I drove to the nearest gas station and called *The Courier*. Gina answered, as I hoped she would.

"Pine Oak Courier. Ginette Cartwright speaking."

"Hey girlfriend," I said.

"Sue-Ann!"

"Gina, are you up for a little detecting?"

"Raht now?"

"As soon as possible. Can you get away for lunch or say you have to see somebody about an ad or something?"

"Ah guess. Sure. You sound kinda excited."

"I am. Meet me at Meekins' Market in an hour.

"What's it about?" she asked.

"That would be telling."

I had a few errands to do before I went to Meekins' but still managed to arrive a few minutes before Gina. I parked in back near the side of the Quonset hut and walked around to the front just as Gina drove up. I didn't know quite how to greet her, especially as Gladys was sitting at the desk and waiting expectantly for her two customers to come in. I settled on a wide smile; I was glad to see that she had a similar one for me as she got out of her car.

"What's the big mystery?" she asked, but I put my fingers to my lips.

"Tell you in a minute," I said. "Let's go inside first. I want to get some kind of snack and maybe a couple bottles of water."

Gladys nodded at me as we came in. "I told Clarence you was here looking for him," she said.

"He here now?" I asked.

"Naw. Went somewhere. Never sure where. Usually goes out after watermelons but always comes back with something else."

"Chickens, maybe?" I asked.

"Naw. Now Clarence might eat some chicken every blue moon—don't tell anybody—but we don't sell none."

Gina was only half listening as she stared, goggle-eyed, at some of the stuff on the rough wooden shelves. At the moment she was examining a squash that had roughly the shape of a swan.

"Well tell him I'm still looking for him," I said.

Gina walked back into the Quonset hut part of the market and seemed lost in a maze. I grabbed up the water, a couple of peaches, and a package of trail mix and went back to gather her in.

"Boy," she said. "Ah ain't been here in donkey's years. Where do you think Clarence gets all this stuff?" In one hand she held up a pair of castanets while the other hand grasped a used CD that had a black woman on the cover holding a guitar.

"Whatcha got?" I asked.

"Donno. but I lahk hearin different girls playin guitars."

We paid Gladys for our items and I had Gina drive around to where I was parked. I had not cleaned out my truck since I'd gotten out of the hospital and my bow, arrows, and fannypack were still on the back seat. I got them out, along with a change of clothes and a small backpack and piled them on the hood of my truck.

"What's all this stuff for?" Gina asked.

"I went by the house and got you something to hike in. See that little trail just off from the dumpster? We're going in there." I started transferring the snacks and water I had purchased from Gladys into the backpack.

"Is that where you went when you . . . ?"

I nodded. "Now get a move on. Change in my car if

you want, although nobody can see you from the road. Don't worry. I won't look." I took a couple of razor-sharp broadheads from my fannypack and screwed them into shafts. I wanted to be more prepared in case we ran into a snake or anything else that posed a danger to me or Gina.

"Ah won't change if you don't look," she said teasingly. She unbuttoned her blouse and folded it neatly before slipping on a gray, long-sleeved t-shirt. I couldn't help looking as she stepped out of her skirt and laid it down carefully with her blouse. The jeans were too big around the waist and short enough to show her ankles. I handed her a belt. "Can't do anything about the cuffs," I told her. "Think the shoes will fit?"

Gina had taken down the tailgate of my truck and was putting on the socks I had given her. She tried one of the shoes but had trouble getting it over her heel. "Sue-Ann," she said. "Reach into the back seat of my car and get that canvas bag."

I did and handed it to her. She opened it and took out a pair of new-looking white tennis shoes. "Ah always keep an outfit in my car in case ah have tahm to go to the gym," she said, putting on the shoes.

"Why didn't you tell me that before you got dressed?" I asked.

She smiled again. "Ah wanted to wear clothes you've been in. Now where we goin and whah we goin there?" She reached for the backpack, added her cigarettes and lighter, and slipped the straps around her shoulders.

"Just follow me," I told her.

I grabbed up my archery tackle and led the way in to the woods along the same trail I had traveled before. As we walked, trying to avoid puddles below, briars on the sides, and branches above, I filled her in on my visit to Estelle Hobbs that morning.

"That poor dog," she said. "Gotta be the same person who killed the goat, raht?"

"Raht."

"And you think we're gonna find im out here?" she asked. "And if we do, what're you gonna do, shoot im?"

"I doubt if we'll see anybody," I told her. "But have you noticed the tracks?"

"What tracks?"

"Here. You can see it better where there's not much mud. Someone wearing an old running shoe. You can see tracks coming and going." I bent down. "Can you see where this print overlaps that one?"

"Raht."

"It means that whoever left these prints came from the woods, walked in the direction of Meekins' Market, then walked back."

"Back where?"

"That's what I'm going to find out, but not today. Right now we have more pressing business."

We walked Indian file, me leading the way. It was easier this time because it was bright daylight, but also because I felt better. I was about to find one more puzzle-piece, although I knew it wouldn't come close to completing the picture.

It was a hot day and we both began to sweat. Gina rolled up the sleeves on her shirt despite the branches and vines that seemed animate and vindictive. There was no indication of more rain and bright rays of sun slanted through the trees.

Gina and I spoke, of course, but it was general talk about the paper, about our families. Gina told me that her parents were from Tyler, Texas, and had gone back there to live when they retired. She had a sister, ten years older, who now had a family in Canada. They were never close, but they emailed from time to time if anything important was happening. I described my mother, and how she once told me that she was pretty sure she could tell the breed of a horse by its smell. I told her about Cindy's horses and about how my father had rushed to dispose of her things. And not for the first time I had a twinge of anger—but this time the anger was because Mike had lied to me when he said that he had sold the horses because they reminded him too much of Cindy. It seemed now that he had just wanted as much quick cash as he could get so he could try to salvage what he could of what he considered a wasted life. But in doing so had disposed willy-nilly of things that needed to be cared for.

"Ah always heard that them that caint do, teach," said Gina. "But teachin is maybe the most important job there is. Whah should he be ashamed?"

"Daddy was a mild-mannered man with no ambition and no oomph," I explained. "If Cindy didn't tell him what socks to wear he would have gone to work barefoot. Guess he thought that this was his chance to go out on his own and be his own man."

I told Gina about Cindy's books and how I had found them in the used bookstore. How it was going to be very difficult to forgive him for that.

"Yer momma had a lot of books?"

"Dozens, maybe a hundred, all about horses. Most of them about dressage."

"Hey, ah've seen dressage on RFD-TV. Ah kinda lahk it."

"Yeah, me too. She taught me as much as she could whenever I was around. Maybe I'll get back into it someday."

"Gonna get you a horse?"

"Who knows? Maybe if I live I'll think about it. Would

you like to ride with me? There are all kinds of trails out behind the farm."

"Yippie yi ki-yay," she said.

I laughed. "I'll teach you how to shoot a bow and we can do horseback archery."

"Can you do that?"

"I have a book on it."

I slowed down as we approached the clearing where I had found the corn starch circle. I fitted an arrow into my bowstring and put a finger to my lips. We walked into the clearing. It was empty. I looked around for a few seconds, listened intently, but we were alone there with the squirrels and lizards. But the clearing wasn't the same as I had left it. Despite the heavy rain, I could see that a new circle had been drawn over the old one. And some new designs had been added at the top.

But it was what was in the center of the circled area that I had come to find. Gina saw it too.

"Oh mah!" she said.

"Oh my is right," I said.

"So whoever killed that ole lady's dog wasn't after the dog at all."

"No. The dog was in the way."

In the center of the circle—in the charred remains of a fire—lay two chickens, beheaded but unplucked.

"Some kinda sacrifice," she said.

"Yes. It's Santeria or voodoo, or something like it. And here's something else: that pirate radio station has something to do with it."

"You told me about that station before but ah haven't been able to fahnd it. What do you mean about them havin somethin to do with this mess?"

"Last night this deejay, Gamma, played an album by a group that had a drummer named Chicken. And she gave a recipe for chicken fajitas. She read a damn poem she wrote called "Poultrygeist." She *knew*, Gina. Either she was here or she had been told by someone who was here. And they knew about the goat, too. They know about too damn many things."

I looked at Gina. "I'm a little scared," I said. "Not for myself or for you, but for whoever is doing these animal killings. The people on the radio station seem to be playing with them like toys. Sometimes it seems like they're playing with me, too."

"But Sue-Ann," she said. "Dontcha think it's gotta be the people at the radio station that's doin all this wacked-out stuff?"

"I think it's possible, but don't you remember what I told you about that guy they call Creeper? He knew about this voodoo ritual and was warning them away."

"But whah?"

"I don't know."

"What are you goin to do?"

"I think *we* need to find out who's been stealing barn animals and have a talk with them."

"Ah, agree. What then?"

"Then we come back and follow that trail."

I noticed that whoever had brought out the chickens had also left more effluvia round the thick log: a few beer cans, a crumpled cigarette package, a few butts. On a whim, I gathered up three of the beer cans and set them a few inches from each other on the log. "Come over here," I said, walking back beyond the circle, so that the cans were maybe fifteen yards away. I took an arrow from my quiver, nocked it, and nailed one of the cans on the first try. It went flying into the grass behind the log.

"Wowie zowie," she said.

I handed the bow to Gina. "You try," I said.

"Can ah?" she asked, her eyes wide. "Wait a minute, though, Sue-Ann. Ah'm a lefty."

"I knew that," I said quickly. "I just forgot. But you can still get the idea."

I showed her on which side of the bow to put the arrow, what the shelf was for, and how to nock the arrow properly, cock feather out. I explained about using the side of her mouth as an anchor point for the string, and showed her how to sight down the arrow. From my fannypack, I fitted an arm guard to her left forearm and a shooting glove to the first three fingers of her shooting hand.

"What's this thing you put on mah arm?" she asked.

"Protects your arm from the string. Without it you can put a bruise on your arm that looks like a rainbow and feels like somebody ran over it with a truck."

"*You* didn't have one," she said.

"I'm a professional," I smiled. I didn't tell her that I had simply forgotten to don the guard and that the string had brushed my forearm warningly. "Go ahead when you're ready."

Gina had a little trouble pulling the string back to an anchor point and she let go of the string too soon. The arrow smacked into the log below and about a foot to the right of the second can. Both cans topped from the impact, but I quickly replaced them.

"Try again," I told her. "Relax and let the string roll off your fingers like a wheel rolling off a cliff."

She did, and the result was better, although her left arm was shaking with the effort of holding the bow steady. The arrow flew between the cans and swicked down into the grass behind the log. "That was a lot better, Gina," I said with sincerity, as we walked over to pick up the arrows. "You've got good form, but I think you need to start out with a little lighter bow."

"Do they make left-handed ones?," she asked.

"Sure. And it might be a good idea if . . . oh, shit!"

"Sue-Ann! What's wrong?"

I was behind the log and was bending down to get one of the arrows when I saw something else hidden in the high grass. It was that that made me cry out. I picked it up and showed Gina.

An empty tequila bottle.

"You think it's the same one that was stolen from your house?" Gina asked.

I sat down heavily on the log and lay my bow down in the leaves. "It's the same brand," I said.

"Ah think it's the same one," she said. Gina picked out a grassy spot near the log and folded down into her fawn position, torso straight, legs tucked under her. She handed me a bottle of water from the backpack and lit a cigarette for herself. "But what does it mean?"

I badly wanted to ask her for a cigarette, but the state of my health said no. Instead, I sipped my water and bit into one of the peaches. "Let's figure it out," I said. "Okay, if this is the same bottle of tequila that was stolen from my house, then whoever broke into my house also killed a goat, a dog, and two chickens."

"And we already decided that it was Adam Zimmer that broke in to your place."

"Yeah, but see all these cigarette butts? They're different brands, so if Adam came out here, he came out with some other people. At least two others. That makes sense, because I don't think that just one person could have trashed my place so thoroughly."

"So we've gotta find out who his friends are," she said.

"Right as a rainbow and just as pretty," I said.

"So what do we do about Adam?" she asked. She was staring at me fixedly, without seeming to be interested in my answer.

"I don't know," I said. Her eyes were disconcerting me. "I guess we should tell Donny, huh? What would you do?"

"Ah know what ah'm *goin* to do," she said.

"What?"

Gina unwound her legs from under her and moved beside me on the log. I felt her shoulder brush mine, felt her fingers moving softly along the nape of my neck, felt her indescribably lovely hands turning my face toward her. She leaned over and kissed me—a lingering kiss so soft and gentle and so full of words that I just melted into a puddle on the log. For an instant—for maybe a dozen seconds—I was completely enrapt in a bliss I had long ago given up ever feeling. Never, *ever* have I felt so warm and so infused with joy and with life.

It took awhile before I remembered to breathe again. "What," I managed. "What did *that* mean?"

"Ah think you *know* what that meant," she smiled.

"But what do we do now?" I asked.

Gina stood up and repacked the backpack, adding the empty tequila bottle. "Ah gotta get back," she said.

"You don't, um, want to keep following the trail?" I asked.

"Ah do, but ah caint today. Ah've got two clients waitin."

So we retraced our steps and walked out together. Just as in our walk out, we kept to safe topics: *The Courier*, Adam Zimmer, my father's midlife crisis, and the number of horses we had ridden. When we got back to our vehicles, I put my bow in the back seat of my truck. Gina took her cigarettes out of the backpack before she handed it to me.

"Ah really enjoyed that, Sue-Ann. Thanks for lettin me

shoot."

"Do you want to talk about that kiss?" I asked.

"Do you?" she countered.

"I want to sometime."

"Sometahm, then," she said.

"Maybe when you give me back my clothes," I suggested.

"Ah'm keepin the clothes," she said.

Chapter 9

I went home that afternoon trying to think my way out of doing something I considered to be my duty. But how could I tell Donny that his new girlfriend's son was both a thief and a livestock mutilator? And, oh yeah, into voodoo, too. Of course I didn't have a shred of proof—Donny might not even remember mentioning my stash to Adam, and the brand of tequila stolen from my house was a common one. One thing was for sure, though, I *had* to tell him. I felt that Adam was in deep shit; I wasn't sure how deep. He was just a kid: Linda C was my age or maybe a year older, which meant that Adam couldn't be more than sixteen years old.

One thing that kept me back was the three different brands of cigarette butts in what I now thought of as The Clearing. It's possible that Adam was only a follower, that someone else had done the mutilations. But if so, Adam needed to have an intervention. But from whom? I couldn't act until I found out more.

The light was blinking on my machine when I got in. The number was unfamiliar, but had a Jasper County prefix. I played the message and heard a vaguely familiar woman's voice.

"Hi, Sue-Ann. This is Myra Van Hesse. I didn't know you were back in town until someone told me they'd read a couple of your stories in *The Courier*. Anyway, the reason I'm calling is because I never got Facilitator's papers. I guess your dad must have forgot, but I wonder if you could find them for me."

She went on to give her phone number, then the machine clicked and was silent. I had a smile on my face as I wrote down the number and dialed it. Myra had been my mother's friend, mentor, and riding buddy. It had been Myra who had gotten Cindy into riding again and had introduced her to dressage. She had even given me a couple of lessons when I was much younger. We won't actually be meeting her in this story—only hearing her voice—but I want to describe her anyway because of the many reasons Cindy had (and I have) to be grateful to her.

The last time I had seen Myra was a couple of years before on one of my Xmas visits home. She had, I think, just turned fifty-five, two years older than Cindy. She owned a few acres in a fairly high-priced area of nearby Waxahatchee, complete with barn, stables, and dressage arena. She was a good rider, but a difficult back kept her from moving beyond First Level. Cindy had actually outstripped Myra as a rider, but Myra's knowledge of history and breeding was phenomenal. She was an inch or two shorter than I am, which would make her about five foot five, slightly stooped because of her back, and always dressed as if she had only that day received her outfit from L. L. Bean or Eddie Bauer. Her short brown hair was being quickly overtaken by white intruders and the light-toned skin of her face was beginning to sag, as skin will do.

She picked up the phone on the second ring.

"Myra," I exclaimed. "Sue-Ann McKeown. I'm so glad you called. How have you been?"

"Not bad, Sue-Ann. The grandkids are making me crazy, but I still ride a little when I can. I was hoping to see you at the funeral so I could tell you, you know, how sorry I was about Cindy. But I knew you were in Iraq. Cindy always talked about how proud she was of you."

"I was proud of her, too, Myra. And I'm so glad you have Facilitator that I could scream."

"Didn't your father tell you that I'd bought him?"

"We don't talk much. Anyway, he moved to Italy."

"To Italy. Hmm." Mike affected everyone in that way. "Well, Facilitator's fine. He still likes to work in the ring and we go for an occasional trail ride, although the area is building up so much that pretty soon there won't be any trails left to ride on."

"Is it getting bad?"

"Pretty bad, yeah. I thought when we moved out here that it would stay wild and rugged, but there are new developments all the time. Phil and I are thinking of moving further out, maybe to Timberlake or Hanson's Quarry."

"Well, you're always welcome to come out here and ride. I'm so far out that I don't think the developers know there's even an area to develop."

"I'd like that, Sue-Ann."

"Listen, Myra, I know I have Facilitator's papers here somewhere. The house was broken into last week and everything got tossed around, but I've almost gotten everything sorted out."

"My land, Sue-Ann! Do you know who broke in?"

"Potheads, I think. Just kind of trashed the place when they couldn't find anything valuable. I'll find Facilitator's papers and get them to you—this week, I promise."

"I'd be so grateful."

"Do you, um, happen to know who got Trifecta and Alikki?"

"I sure do, honey. In fact, I'm the one who got Trifecta sold. Mike would probably have taken her to an auction. But I got the Poulans to take her to their place down near DeLand. One of the daughters is already winning at Prix St. George on her. I guess he could have gotten a better price if he'd advertised, but I didn't tell him that. Trifecta couldn't find a better home than where she is."

"I'm glad, Myra. Is Alikki there too?"

There was a long silence at the other end before Myra said, "No, honey, she's not."

"Do you know where she is?"

"Oh, my land. I hate to say, but I think Mike sold her to some little backyard breeding place out your way."

I listened in amazement. For Mike to have sold one of Cindy's horses to some cowpoke trainer was so monstrous I couldn't even begin to fathom it. "You're kidding," was all I could get out.

"I'm so sorry, Sue-Ann, but neither of us were thinking straight."

"Thinking straight about what, Myra?"

"Sue-Ann, Alikki killed Cindy. I'd have taken her if it hadn't been for that, but I knew that every time I went out to feed her I'd remember. And I'd never have the gumption to sit on her. I did ask around the local dressage club, but everyone here felt the same."

"I understand, Myra, I do. It's been what, ten or eleven months and I'm only now getting around to thinking about her and Trifecta and Facilitator. Do you remember the name of the place Mike sold Alikki to?"

"No, I'm afraid . . . wait, I do remember. It took me a while before I got out there to pick up Facilitator and Alikki was already gone. I was scared at first that he'd put her down because he told me that she'd gone to Horse Heaven."

"Horse heaven?"

"That's right. Horse Heaven is the name of the ranch."

"I owe you, Myra. Is it all right if I come over some time to see Facilitator?"

"Any time, honey. You can ride him out on the trail if you'd like."

"Only if you ride with me."

"That would be nice."

I looked up Horse Heaven in the phone book and found it in the smallest type. I dialed the number and a woman answered on the third ring. She gave me a soft, kind of tentative "Moon residence." It was the spoken equivalent of getting a dead fish for a handshake.

"Hello? My name is Sue-Ann McKeown. I'm calling to ask about a horse."

"You'll have to call back when my husband's here. I don't know much about all those horses."

"Do you know when he'll be home?"

"Said he'd be back around six or so, but I guess he'll be here when he gets here."

"Well, Miz—" When she didn't fill in the blank, I filled it in for her. "It's Miz Moon, isn't it?

"Yes, that's right."

"Well, Miz Moon, I've been told that y'all have some lovely horses and I'd like to come out and take a look. You sell horses, raht?"

"Yes."

"Can you tell me where you are so I can come and look at what you have for sale? The address in the phonebook isn't much help." The woman hesitated again and I would have gnashed my teeth if people really did that. Instead, I told her, "I won't come until your husband gets back."

"Well, I guess that'll be all right, and we really could use the money. We're out off Highway 77 just outside of Pine Oak." It took the woman another minute or two to give me directions to Horse Heaven Farm; one minute after that I was crying yet again and waiting for Gina to answer the phone at *The Courier*. When she did I interrupted her before she could get out two words.

"Gina," I said, "It's me."

"Sue-Ann. What's wrong? It sounds lahk somethin's wrong."

"Gina. I found Cindy's horses. All three of them, and one of them is on this little farm only a few miles from here. I've got to go see her, but I don't want to go alone. I know I've been bothering you more than I should, but will you come with me? Please?"

"Course ah will, darlin. Is this the one that your mother was rahdin when she . . ."

I nodded, then realized what I was doing and said, "Yeah. Yeah it was."

"Ah'm sposed to do somethin later to-naht, but ah have a couple hours after work. Will that be all raht?"

"I just want to see her for a few minutes. I'll come by *The Courier* around six and get you. It'll be faster that way. That okay?"

"Ah'll be ready when you get here."

Pine Oak, Hanson's Quarry, Forester, Waxahatchee, all the small towns in north Florida are dotted with farms. Some are pretty good-sized cattle ranches, some just an acre or two of dirt, but on most of them you'll find horses. And then there are the backyard horse owners who keep their animals in small fenced-off areas next to their houses or trailers. The lucky horses have a bit of grass, the unlucky ones don't. Ditto with hay, even water. Some horses stand out in the open during thunderstorms and sleep without shelter or blanket on the coldest nights, on rainy, icy nights. Cindy had been frantic about the comfort of her horses, and had taught me to be that way, too.

It was probably a little before six-thirty when Gina and I pulled up to the address I had wrung out of the woman on the phone. Set back twenty yards or so from the road was a stable surrounded by a small, muddy paddock. A too-brown roll of hay sat in the mud along with a rough wooden feeding trough, a pole set into the ground with a rope hanging from a hook, and a couple of upended plastic feed buckets. A few foals were sleeping in the paddock and I saw that most of the stalls were occupied. A faded sign out front said Horse Heaven and a mailbox stood nearby with the word Moon printed unevenly in black paint. A hundred yards further back I saw what looked to be a large mobile home that someone had tried to disguise as a house by adding a deck in front and hiding the crawl space by stacking cinder blocks around the sides. Behind that was what looked to be a small pasture and another set of stables.

I pulled into the rocky driveway and stopped alongside the nearest stable, which I now saw was surrounded by a couple of strands of barbed wire strung between green metal T-poles. Someone was driving down from the house in a golf cart. The driver turned out to be a man in his sixties whose fathers and grandfathers had probably lived all their lives in Jasper County. He was short, stocky, jeaned, and booted, with the ubiquitous white straw cowboy hat set on his head so firmly that it appeared to be glued there.

"Good evenin ladies," he said. "Y'all need directions to somewhere?"

"No. I think this is the right place. Are you Mr. Moon?"

"That's right."

"My name is Sue-Ann McKeown. I'm looking for a particular horse."

"Got plenty of nice horses," he said. "Come on in here and we can talk while I feed up." He opened a gate and walked into the barn, which was made up of a row of stalls set on both sides of a dirt corridor, the entire structure being covered by a sloped tin roof that had probably been put up before I was born.

We followed him through the gate and into the shadows of the corridor, where flies buzzed in uncomfortable swarms and where the manure smell was almost overwhelming. I glanced into the nearest few stalls but didn't see Alikki. What I did see, though, made my gut wrench up. In one, a pony stood with its muzzle against the bars. Piles of manure were built up along the insides of the walls like dunes, and flies were rife. In fact, all the stalls were all like that and I glanced at Gina to see if she had noticed. The glare in her eyes told me that she had.

In the center of the aisle, Mr. Moon was mixing some kind of a pelleted feed with what looked to be chicken scratch. He saw me watching and said, "Cracked corn. Horses love the stuff and I get it for almost nothin. What kind of horse you all looking for? I got some colored horses, geldings, mares, got a lot of foals, too. Bred to my stud horse whose line goes back to Mr. San Peppy and Billie Gay Bar."

"I'm looking for a horse my father might have sold you sometime last year. I'd like to know if you still have her."

"I buy a lot of horses," the man said, not looking up from his mixing. "Sell a lot, too. Not likely I'd still have her. What kind of a horse did you say it was?"

"A warmblood filly. Oldenburg. Golden chestnut. Her name is Alikki. She'd be coming four years old."

"Oh, that one. I never got her papers so didn't know what to call her. I been callin her Biter, because that's all she tries to do. Using her as a brood mare; can't nobody ride her. Doubt if she'll even throw a decent foal, but we'll see."

"You still have her?" I asked hopefully.

"Down in the far stable. Go on down there if you want. I'll be down presently."

We decided to drive down rather than slosh our way through the various mudholes in the driveway. Gina and I were both silent. As we passed the house I noticed a woman's face peering through an opening in the curtains. The curtain drew closed when she saw us looking.

These stables were similar to the first, only rougher. The flies were fiercer and the smell worse. The stalls were made of what appeared to be wood salvaged from an old tobacco barn and reminded me of Eskimo driftwood houses Jack had once taken pictures of when on assignment in Barrow. Only a few of these stalls were occupied, and I saw several geldings searching for browse in the adjacent pasture. We started walking down the row of stalls and I felt Gina's hand on my shoulder. The first horse we saw was old and almost white. She looked up, but the film over both eyes told me that she was hearing us, but not seeing us, as we passed. She gave a low nicker. A louder, stronger whinny, familiar after many months, came from across the aisle. I hurried over—too quickly because the animal inside backed up in fright. The stall was boarded up almost like a casket, with scrap wood nailed everywhere and the door bolted shut and secured with a crossbar. I looked through a small opening and started to cry.

Inside, her eyes almost hidden by gnats and with manure residue covering every inch of her hide, stood Alikki—my mother's pride and joy, who had been a premium filly, had been Oldenburg Horse of the Year as a two-year-old, and who, under saddle was worth many times what all of Moon's horses put together were worth. Looking closer I saw that her water bucket was empty except for a film of algae, she had rubbed her rump almost raw on the sides of her stall, and her hooves flared outward from neglect.

And, although she was grossly pregnant, she was so bony that you could have almost hung your hat on her.

She put her ears up, looked at me closely, and nickered softly.

I didn't know what to say. I just sobbed and sobbed. I even tugged at the bolt, trying to unfasten it, but I couldn't get my fingers to work right.

"Don't be doing that, now," came Moon's voice. He had come up noiselessly in his electric cart. "She's a wild one."

"Why do you have her locked up like this?" I asked, as casually as I could with tears streaming down my cheeks.

"She gets out. Jumps over the door."

"She gets turnout, right?"

"Not after she kicked over my fence for the third time."

"Will you sell her back to me?"

"Maybe. After she foals. But if it's a nice foal, reckon I'll keep her. This is an expensive horse, worth a lot."

"If she's so valuable, why haven't you done her feet? Has she been groomed since you've had her? Does she know what fresh water tastes like?"

"She'll get it when I get to it. I got over thirty horses and I'm a busy man."

"You're a peabrain," I corrected him.

"What did you just say to me?"

"You ought to be strung up by the balls for what you've done to this horse," I told him.

"I don't like to hear profanity in no woman, no I

don't. This horse's not for sale after all," he said. "unless I take her to an auction and sell her to the knackers. Why don't the both of you just git the hell out of here."

I put my fists out and stepped toward him, but Gina somehow got between us, edging me back a little. She faced him instead.

"Raht. Okay, Mister Man," she began.

"Moon," he corrected her coldly.

"Raht. Now ah'd *really* lahk it if you'd sell us this hoss. Sue-Ann's jist upset an don't know what she's sayin. Do ya remember whatcha paid for this hoss?"

"Forget now. Must've been round about fifteen hundred dollars."

"Gina, damn it!" I shouted. "He never paid more than—"

"Be quaht, Sue-Ann. All raht. And how much couldja get for the foal?"

"Five hundred, at least," said Moon confidently, giving me a smirk. "And you ought to pay me board for all the months she's been here."

"Ah guess that maht be fair. And what about the vet bills and the times you had to have her feet trimmed and her teeth floated?"

Moon answered unsteadily. "Well, yeah."

"Hmm, Mister Man, that's quaht a little bundle of money you want. Ah mean, if you'll let us bah her. Maybe if we make an offer you cain't refuse?" Gina was being charming, almost flirtatious, and was wildly exaggerating her accent. I would have been livid at her but I knew her well enough by now to suspect that she was up to something.

"Every horse has its price," Moon said.

"Raht," said Gina. "Now here's the thang. Jist in mah head, it seems lahk you want somewhere round four thousand dollars for a hoss that nobody cain't rahd and that nobody else wants. Here's what ah figger. We'll jist ast Sue-Ann's daddy what you really paid for this hoss, but ah'll guess no more'n two hundred. The price of all the feed for a year would come to bout the same, seein as you get it so cheap and all. The vet and farrier and dentist bills would add just a lot of nothin, so it seems we're pretty far apart on the price raht now."

"What the hell—"

"Ah'm not through talkin, Mister Man," she said calmly, looking him in the face. "Remember what mah friend here said bout you bein strung up bah the balls? Well that's way too gentle for what you've done to this hoss— and all the other hosses you've got here, ah suspect."

"Fuck—"

"Shet! Up!" Gina shouted. "First of all, you can take your four thousand and shove it up your be-hahnd. Ah'm gonna wraht you a check for two thousand dollars for this hoss and her foal and you're gonna deliver it to Sue-Ann's place. To-naht."

"You must be—"

"And in return, Sue-Ann's not gonna wraht about Horse Hell for the next five issues of *The Pine Oak Courier.* What, you mean you don't know that Sue-Ann McKeown is the main reporter for *The Courier?* And here's something else she's not gonna do: she's not gonna call every rescue service in Florida to come in and take away all your beat and starved and neglected hosses. Bah the tahm she gits through doin all that, ah don't think many people in Jasper County are goin to be comin here to do anythin but throw their garbage."

"Get out of here or I'll call the sheriff," was all that Moon could come up with.

"Not raht, Mister Man," Gina corrected. *"Ah'm* the

one that'll be callin im. The officer on duty raht now would be Mr. Bill Dollar, who ah used to date, bah the way. Or, we could call his Sergeant, whose name is Joe Bickley. Now he and I—"

"Give me the money and take the damn horse."

"That's not quaht the agreement. Ah'll get mah checkbook while you hook up your trailer and load up this hoss."

"Damn horse will kick me to death if I try to load her."

"And serve you raht, too. But Sue-Ann and I'll trah to keep that from happenin this tahm. That sound all raht to you, Sue-Ann?"

I nodded dumbly.

"One more thing, Mister Man," Gina said a few minutes later as she handed him a check. "This money is for more than Alikki. It's to pay somebody to come in and clean these stalls and tend to these hosses. Ah'm gonna make sure that some kinda inspector comes out here every week for the next year to see if you're doin it and doin it raht. Raht?"

"How am I supposed to—?"

"Just fahnd a way."

In the car on the way home I sat in almost stunned silence as Gina drove toward home. Moon was pulling a rusty one-horse trailer behind us, a check in his pocket for more than he had ever received for a horse before.

"I can't believe you did that," I finally told her.

"Did what?"

"Took over that way. Cowed that bastard. Got my horse back. Everything. No one has ever done anything like that for me before."

"Sue-Ann, I jist sound the part better'n you do."

"I was fixing to get my bow."

169

"Ah thought you maht. After ah got back to the office, Cal asked me if ah knew that you used to be on the Olympic archery team. Whah didn't you tell me?"

"You never asked."

"You told Cal."

"He asked," I explained.

She sighed. "Jist something else ah can be jealous of," she said.

"Quit," I said.

We drove along in silence for a while, both aware of Moon's headlights behind us but lost in separate thoughts. I broke the silence.

"Did you really used to date Dilly?"

"He wishes. Wasn't a complete lah, though. He ast me lots of tahms."

I smiled. "Me, too," I said. There was another half mile of silence, then I spoke again. "I don't know how I'm going to pay you back," I told her.

"Then it'll be the best present ah've ever given anybody."

I thought about how special Gina had become to me. How indispensable. I thought about the half-starved and pregnant mare following in Moon's creaky trailer. I thought of the recovery of my mother's equestrian library. I thought about my improving health and I began to cry again. I wish I could say that this was the last time I'll cry in this story, but it's not. But at least it wasn't a loud sob, just a gentle tearful interlude. Gina glanced at me sideways.

"What's wrong now, Sue-Ann?" she asked.

"Nothing." I smiled through my tears. "Nothing."

"Whah all the tears, then?"

"All my things are coming home," I cried.

There was another thing, though, that I couldn't get out of my mind: the image of Mrs. Moon's face in the window, the curtain closing over it like a veil.

Chapter 10

It wasn't a long drive, but I was frantic by the end of it. Frantic to see if Alikki had made the three- or four-mile trip alive, frantic to get her out of the trailer and into the paddock, and frantic for Moon to get out of my sight.

But Alikki backed out of the trailer as if she had been doing it all her life. Her nostrils flared as she recognized the smell of the place where she had been born. When I unclipped the rope from her halter she whinnied loudly and took a couple of hesitating trot steps. She stopped and whinnied again, then pawed at a soft, sandy indention, circled it once, then lay down and rolled gloriously, as if she were trying to rub off the layers of filth she still carried on her coat. When she had enough, she struggled to bring up one foreleg, then the other, then hoisted her bloated and emaciated body back to a standing position and shook like a dog just getting out of water.

Moon left without a word. Gina stayed as long as she could, but she had promised to go somewhere with Cal, so I gave her a ride back to *The Courier* office where she had left her car. I was aware of her in the car beside me like I might have been aware of a winning lottery ticket, but I was so preoccupied with my horse that I drove with my eyes on the road, responding as well as I could to her questions about feed, vet, farrier, equine rescue organizations. I hated to leave Alikki even for an instant, but the paddock had plenty of grass and the board fences that surrounded it were high and secure. In the parking lot,

I gave Gina a brief, heartfelt, hug, and watched her drive off. Then I ran across to the Piggly Wiggly and bought five large containers of Quaker Oatmeal, several bottles of molasses, some sugar cubes, a bag of apples, and all the carrots they had. Then I broke the speed limit getting back home.

I stayed with Alikki all that night. I spent an hour talking softly to her in the paddock until she let me get close enough to get a rope back on her halter. Then I led her slowly into her stall, which I had raked clean. I scrubbed out her water bucket and filled it with fresh water, and put a handful of oatmeal into her feed bucket, mixed with a little of the molasses. By the time I had given her half a carrot for dessert, she seemed almost at home again. She was skittish, but eventually she let me curry and comb her in the stall, but my attempt to untangle her tail fell short. I sat with her and told her about what a great dressage champion her mother was turning out to be. I told her all I remembered about the times I had watched Cindy ride Trifecta at Third- and Fourth-Level tests. And when I ran out of those memories I told her about my own flimsy attempt to ride a Training-Level test on Facilitator years before—how I had somehow gotten through the whole test despite the fact that my legs were telling Facilitator to go forward while my seat was telling him to stop. I segued to some of the archery contests I had won and told her that when she had her foal and got her health back we—she and I—were going to build an archery range for mounted shooting and that I was going to ride her every day; that when we got tired of shooting we would pack a couple of saddlebags with apples and sandwiches and ride out in the woods where she could graze while I read a mystery under a shady cedar. And I told her how I was going to name her foal Afterburner and call him Bernie and how, after he was weaned, we could put a rope on him and pony him out with us and maybe we would see deer or wild turkeys.

Early the next morning, I showered off the paddock dust and called every veterinarian in three counties before I was able to get someone to consent to make an emergency call around noon. That left me several hours to run errands.

The first place I went was to Meekins' Market. Not only was it the closest place, but I trusted Clarence to either have what I needed or know where I could get it. Clarence was behind the counter eating breakfast with Gladys when I walked in. When he glanced up and saw me rushing in like an arrow with a purpose, he looked as if he had somewhere else he wanted to be. "God's balloons, Sue-Ann," he blurted out. "Are you still mad about—"

"I need some straw," I told him without preamble.

"Straw?"

"Wheat straw, not pine straw. And I need some hay and feed. I have a pregnant horse and she's poor." I was in a hurry and my words came out in a rush. Gladys had finished eating and was arranging tomatoes in small baskets near the front of the store.

"Where'd you get a horse?" he asked, looking relieved that I seemed to have forgotten our last conversation.

"It was one of my mother's horses. I just bought her back. I mean, Gina did, but I'll tell you about it later. I've got to pick up supplies for her and get back home before the vet gets there."

"Who's Gina?" he asked.

"I mean Ginette. Never mind. What about the bedding and stuff?"

"I got some bales of straw out front under the canopy," he said. "But you'll have to go into Forester for feed. I can probably get some hay delivered here by this afternoon if you want it, but they'll have good hay at Freddy's."

"What's Freddy's?" I asked.

"Freddy's Feed and Seed. Just off the highway on Jefferson. That's the best place for horse supplies unless you go into Dothan or Tallahassee."

"I'll take a bale of your straw, but I have to leave room in the truck for some hay. How much do I owe you?"

"You have ten dollars credit for, um, you know, the snake," he said.

"I guess you know a lot of the hay growers around here," I ventured. "My mother had all this stuff covered, but I wasn't around."

"Plenty of hay farmers in Pine Oak. I buy square bales for the market from a couple of em, but mostly in the winter."

"Can you call someone you trust that has good hay and tell them to deliver about 25 square bales and a round bale to my place?"

"I don't know where your place is, Sue-Ann."

"Here," I told him. "Let me write down the address." I scribbled it out, then added a simple map. "Any time after noon. My phone number's there, too."

"I'll sure do it, and I hope the horse gets better. Is there anything else you need while you're here?"

"Maybe a couple of boxes of corn starch," I told him.

Clarence's eyes widened. "Corn starch. What could you want—"

"Just kidding."

I drove to Forester and found the place Clarence had mentioned: Freddy's: All the Feed and Seed You Need. I spent a busy half hour looking with new eyes at shelves of horse supplies. I bought several bags of Seminole Mare & Foal feed, four bales of hay, fly spray, Fure-a-Zone ointment for cuts, a couple of mineral blocks, and a dozen other things I probably already had in the barn but got just in case.

Back at the house, I coaxed Alikki back into her stall with one of the bales of hay and fed her a couple of handfuls of feed, which she ate ravenously.

The veterinarian arrived a few minutes early and checked her out thoroughly. Moon had given me only a general idea of when Alikki had been bred, but the veterinarian informed me that she could foal at any time and described some of the signs to look for. Alikki was malnourished, weak, rubbed raw in places, but steady on her feet despite not having had her hooves trimmed for who knows how long. Other than that she was healthy. And the foal was healthy, too, as far as he could determine without an ultrasound. He wormed Alikki, put some salve on her raw places, and told me he wanted to hold off on some of the other treatment until after the baby came.

I'll spare you the descriptions of the rest of the day— as well as the next—because it was just more of the same. I had a horse and I was going to keep it alive and if my father ever came back to Pine Oak I was going to take him to Horse Heaven and lock him in one of Moon's stalls. With Moon.

Gina came to visit for a few minutes after work on Thursday and Friday but I was so focused on my horse that I couldn't give her the attention I would have liked. She, too, seemed a little preoccupied, but it wasn't anything I could put my finger on. I know I liked having her there— even more so when she told me that she knew a little about farrier work. She spent half an hour each day working on Alikki's feet, rasping down the worst of the ridges and flares while I watched and learned. Then she would leave, telling me only that she had things to take care of.

I spent much of the rest of those two days searching through my mother's books for tips on delivering a foal, treating cuts, trimming hooves, and whatever else I might have to know. I set up a cozy chair and table in the barnyard where I could read and still watch Alikki as she roamed the pasture, coming in every few hours for long gulps of water from her water bucket.

Once a day I closed her in her stall so she wouldn't wander into my target area, and practiced my archery. First I used a light recurve, then I took out my large yumi bow and practiced my thumb release. I brought out stacks of Cindy's papers and spent hours studying and refiling them. I found Facilitator's registration and breeding papers and mailed them to Myra Van Hesse, along with a note about my recovery of Alikki. I also found deeds to several pieces of property which Cindy had purchased as investments years before. I kept these out—I knew I'd have to sell some of them to pay my new debts, and it was a heavy load off my mind to know that Mike had been in too much of a hurry to clean me out completely. As I stood on the target range, bow in hand, with Alikki munching hay in her stall and watching the arrows fly across her field of vision, with Gina sitting silently close by, I knew I had never been happier in my life. I, too, had come home.

In the midst of my happiness, there was more than a pang of regret that Cindy was not there to share it. You can understand that; she was my mother. What you might not understand is that I wished that Crookneck Smith could have been there too. That's right—he was the old hunter that sold me my first bow. But my first visit to his shop wasn't my last, and as I shot arrow after arrow in the bright sunshine, I let my mind travel backward many years.

When I bought my first Martin Mamba recurve, there was no eBay; you couldn't go on the net and type in different weights and stiffnesses of arrow shafts and locate half a dozen suppliers in a few seconds. So after I practiced at the university shooting range for a month I drove back out to Huckleberry Spring to ask Crookneck Smith for some advice. The old hunter had hinted that he had used wooden bows when he was younger, and he had been kind to me when I had ordered my Mamba from him.

It was a Saturday, I think, windy and rainy and way too cold for the middle of April. A bad day for shooting; a bad day to be outside at all. The wind was strong enough to rustle the leaves off their branches, strong enough to blow the water out of puddles. It was noon when I arrived. I zipped up my red pullover and hurried inside the metal building. Crookneck was with a customer, but when he looked up, he greeted me with a boisterous, "There she is!" and a big smile. I was flattered that he remembered me and, with time to look around, I studied some things along the far walls that I had missed on my first visit, when all I had to rely on for light were the flickering fluorescent bulbs.

Below a small rack of deer antlers, I discovered a row of kernels from the tails of rattlesnakes, some were as long as a dozen rattles; others only two or three. Underneath was a rude, hand-painted sign that read: "WE BUY RATTLESNAKES," and I presumed that Crookneck had obtained the rattles from his customers rather than having shot the snakes himself. Nearby was a freezer, presumably to keep them from spoiling, but I had no idea whether he kept them to harvest the skin, to eat, or both and my stomach got a little queasy. Taped to the door of the freezer with yellowing tape was a dusty, dog-eared poster that announced "Archery Exhibition. Kansas City Auditorium, July 4, 1975" in large type. In smaller letters beneath I read the surprising words "Featuring former

World Champion Jim 'Crookneck' Smith." The man whose photo took up the rest of the poster did not greatly resemble the one who had sold me my Mamba. For one thing, the man in the poster had a dark mustache, trimmed beard, and hair falling halfway to his shoulders. He was wearing an outfit that looked half cowboy, half hippie. But his buzzard's neck was unmistakable, as were his bright eyes and winning smile.

His voice from just behind me nearly made me jump. "That was a long time ago," he said.

"You were world champion?" I asked, trying not to sound too incredulous.

"Waal, there was a time when I wasn't too bad."

"What are you shooting in the picture?"

"That's a Wing Presentation. Wing sponsored me, so I shot their equipment. I tried to get Harold Groves to sponsor me, but Groves already sponsored Jerry Harris. I made him sorry, though; I went out and beat Jerry six times running."

"Why did you stop shooting recurves?" I asked.

"Oh, my eyesight got bad, my nerves got a little messed up from drinking too much. And I started huntin, too, and didn't want to leave a wounded animal sufferin out in the woods. A compound is more like a rifle."

"I noticed that when you let me shoot yours."

Crookneck glanced at the bow that I was clutching. "You ain't still shootin that Mamba are ye?" Outside, I could hear the wind pounding the metal roof and sides of the building.

"I am," I responded vigorously. "I . . . I really like it, but I don't know anything about how to shoot it. I mean, *really* shoot it. I thought you could show me how to tune it and figure out what kind of arrows I should shoot."

"Waal," he drawled, "if you're gonna stick with the

recurve, I guess it's up to me to help you with it, specially since it was me that sold it to ye."

So, in between sporadic customers—I was somehow hurt when he greeted them all by crying out, "There he is!"—who came in to get their compounds restrung, for new sights, or to marvel at the newest broadheads, such as the Guillotine, that could slice the head off a turkey from thirty paces, Crookneck showed me how to tune my bow. It was way too blustery to shoot outside, so he set up a target across the room. He explained what significance an arrow's stiffness had to its performance, taught me how to alter my arrow's flight by experimenting with field points of different weights.

The lesson lasted nearly eight years. In between boyfriends, classes, and jobs, Crookneck taught me the art of archery. He altered my stance, breathing, anchor point, and release, telling me to let the string roll off my fingers "like a wheel rolling off a cliff."

And that's always what I tried to do.

"Bullseye!" Gina shouted.

~ ~ ~

On Friday night, convinced that Alikki was slowly regaining her health, I decided to get up the next morning and go to the rodeo Cal had halfheartedly assigned me to write about. I woke up just after dawn, went out and fed Alikki, then curried and visited with her for a while. It was drizzly out, so I made sure she had water and plenty of hay, then shut her in her stall. After a long shower, I dressed, made breakfast, took my thyroid pill, and reread a chapter of *The Equine Breeding Manual*. When I glanced up at the clock, I saw that it was getting late, so I grabbed my hat and rushed out the door, nearly knocking down Jack Stafford in the process.

"Shit, Jack!" I said, as I nearly fell over sideways to

keep from colliding with him. "What the hell?"

"You didn't call," he said. It was starting to rain a little harder now and Jack looked like a wet puppy that someone had left on my porch.

"I don't have time for this right now, Jack. I have to go somewhere." I brushed past him on my way to the truck

"I'll just wait here."

"No you won't."

He fell into step beside me. "Then I'll come with," he said.

I stopped and faced him angrily, intending to tell him that I was ill, insane, depressed, married, pregnant, or all of the above—anything to get rid of him. But then I saw that he hadn't shaved for several days and his hair and clothes were disheveled. Jack is a neat freak, so something must have really been eating at him.

"What the hell," I said. "Get in."

"I don't want to leave my cameras in the car."

"Fine. Bring them."

I noticed that a road crew had pulled the ditches, bringing up the red dirt from the sides of the road and smoothing it back out in the center, eliminating the ruts. I thought I could feel Jack's eyes on me as I drove, but when I glanced over I saw that he was wrapped up in the scenery. What he was able to see in the scrub oak, pine, and miles of poison ivy vines only he knew: only if he took a photograph of it would anyone else know, but by then he would have forgotten all about it. It made me crazy.

I didn't speak until we got out on the highway. "What are you doing here?"

He pulled his attention away from a billboard advising forest owners to thin out their pines to prevent certain diseases, and looked at me as if he had just noticed I was there. "I came to see you," he said. "Where are we going?"

"We're going to a rodeo," I told him. "And I didn't want you to come here."

"I've missed you."

"We both need to get on with our lives. I thought you *had* been getting on. Is the job all right?"

"Actually, that's what I came to talk about. I'm thinking about going to the Middle East."

I almost swerved the truck off the road. "You what?" I asked.

"Iraq," he said. "But tell me what you've been doing for the last year."

"Iraq is not a place—" I began, but he cut me off.

"We'll talk about that later," he said. "When we have some time and trust each other again. But right now I really want to know how you've been doing. You look thin and there's obviously a bandage of some kind under that hat."

One of the last things I wanted to do was to tell Jack about my life, but the *very* last was to talk about Iraq, so as the windshield wipers did their disappearing act, I brought him up to date on everything I had been doing for the last year, giving him an abbreviated verbal tour of my job with *The Courier*, my father's abdication, and my horse. As far as my head went, I simply told him that I had tripped over some vines in the woods and fallen against a rock. I deliberately left out any mention of Gina or the goat story.

It would be easy to see Jack as too naïve, too boyish, too innocent. He does have these qualities in abundance, but he also has the gift of listening, of giving people the assurance that he not only hears but is interested in what they are saying. It is this that makes him totally charming. It's not fake; it is only his own life that he finds boring. Another thing about Jack is that he is fairly tall and well built—slightly taller than Donny but not as muscled. He has cleanly chiseled features and thick black hair. It is hard for anyone not to like him; hard for any woman not to want to jump his bones at first sight. His old, familiar manner got me to relax so comfortably that I was pulling into the Jasper County Agricultural Center before I realized I had been schmoozing about Clarence Meekins, Benny Benedict, and Linda C as if they were mutual friends.

The Ag Center consists of a covered arena surrounded by parking areas and stables. Horse trailers of all descriptions and makes were parked in the lot or attached to hookups at one end of the stables. And there were lots and lots of horses, more horses than people, it seemed. Some were being ridden, others being walked on the grass and allowed to graze. A few, in full saddle, were tethered to chain-link fences or support poles. Most were Quarterhorses, but I saw a sprinkling of Arabians and Saddlebreds as well.

We got out of the car and headed toward the arena, where I heard a voice over the loudspeaker announcing the next rider. The rain had let up for the moment but it was still wet and drippy. I saw two preteen girls riding together across the wet grass of the grounds and was jealous of their ease and grace. Grizzled cowboys led their mounts toward the arena. Groups of men, women, and horses stood around waiting for their turns in the ring. Almost everyone I saw was wearing cowboy gear, which was not really strange for a rodeo, but many of them also wore pistols on their belts. Two pistols.

Jack, as always, had slung a camera bag over his shoulder and was studying his surroundings with interest. From inside the arena came the sound of galloping hooves, followed a few seconds later by the crack of a pistol. I flinched and scooted behind an iron pillar as a puff of smoke rose up lazily inside the ring. An instant later another pistol shot rang out, then another. Seeing that I was the only one cowering behind something, I peeked out of my hiding place and looked into the ring. A stocky woman dressed like Annie Oakley was galloping toward us, shooting at what looked like balloons attached to the end of sticks. She fired off five more shots in rapid succession and spurred her horse to the end of the arena. People applauded. I stood back up as the announcer blared genially, "That was Teresa Gentilly of Pine Bluff, Arkansas riding Spiffy. Her time was a fast eighteen point six six seconds, but she missed the number four balloon and that'll cost her a five-second penalty. But she takes the lead with a raw score of twenty-three point six six. The next contestant is from right here in Jasper County. . ."

The pleasant voice of the announcer continued its work while Jack and I looked around. In the arena, a cadre of children dressed in frontier clothing fanned out to replace the balloons that had been broken with new ones. It reminded me of a professional tennis match where, after every point or every netted serve, ballboys and ballgirls ran out on the court, scooped up errant tennis balls, and ran pell mell back to their fixed places on the sidelines.

Below the announcer's booth, a half dozen competitors studied sheets that a natty cowboy in a black hat was posting on the wall. I made my way over and saw that it was an order of go, listing the competitors, their mounts, what class they were in, and the approximate times they were to go into the ring.

Jack had disappeared. I waited until the cowboy who had posted the sheets was free, then introduced myself. The man appeared to be in his late forties with an infectious smile and a lot of teeth. Without his hat, he was about as tall as I am; about the same weight, too. He told me that his name was Panhandle Slim, that he was one of the organizers of the event.

"You say you're from *The Courier*?" he asked.

"Yeah. My editor asked me to cover this event, but he thought it was a rodeo."

"Haw haw," he laughed. "This is a twenty-first century rodeo," he said. "We call it cowboy-mounted shooting. And your editor isn't the only one who doesn't know what we do. Gee, I'm glad you're here. Did you bring a camera?"

"Actually, I did better than that," I remembered. "I brought a photographer." I waved my arm in the general direction of the bleachers. "He's out there somewhere, doing his thing."

"Great, maybe we'll be able—"

A new round of gunshots buried his words in their sound, and I looked into the arena and saw another woman, this one dressed in more traditional cowgirl attire—like Dale Evans—riding the course. I turned to Panhandle Slim. "Could you tell me what I'm looking at?" I asked.

Outside the arena, the sky was a bleary gray and rain was beginning to come down again. Horses and riders were having to negotiate patches of brown mud to get into the ring. A light wind had also appeared, wafting mist and a few droplets of rain in our direction.

"Come on over here and we can be comfortable and watch at the same time." Slim led me to a set of dilapidated wooden bleachers about six rows high and running the length of the arena. "Watch your step," he cautioned. "A lot of these boards haven't been replaced in a while." We sat down in the third row. Slim pointed into the arena and, between gunshots, explained the rules of cowboy-mounted shooting.

"Here, lookit," he began. "This next rider's name is Pearl. She's a beginning rider but she wanted to see what this sport was all about." I looked where he indicated and

185

saw a woman in her sixties on a paint horse entering the arena. She had one pistol in her hand and another in her belt. "Okay, she's ready to make her run. When she passes that laser timing mechanism she'll start the timer. There she goes! Go on, Pearl!" Panhandle Slim took off his hat and waved it, revealing a healthy head of hair that I suspected owed its unusual brown-red hue to a popular men's hair-coloring system. Maybe more than one.

Pearl chose to let her horse walk the course, which allowed her to get close to each balloon, level her pistol, and shoot it. "The pistols are filled with blanks," Slim explained. "But each blank has enough black powder in it to break a balloon from anywhere inwards of twenty feet. The first five balloons are spaced out, so you have to ride a kind of zigzag course to get to them all. There at the end, Pearl has to ride around that barrel, holster her first pistol, take out her second pistol, shoot those next five balloons in a straight line, then race to the finish line."

Race was a kind word for Pearl's riding, but she managed to break every balloon and finish the course without getting bucked off. I applauded when she had finished.

I stayed and talked to Panhandle Slim for another fifteen minutes or so and, by the end of that time, I felt I understood and appreciated the rules of this new sport—including the required authentic cowboy getup. In fact, it was similar to horsebow archery, which I had already planned to take up. Slim told me he was a local horse trainer who had just switched to cowboy-mounted shooting from endurance riding. He gave me his cell phone number and told me he'd be glad to answer any questions I might think of later. Then he went off with several other shooters to discuss the lineup for the next round.

As the day progressed, I learned who the best riders

were and where they were from, I learned the pistol of choice, and I learned that many of the winners would get cash prizes. I was writing some of this down on my yellow legal pad, glancing at each rider as they entered the ring and ran the course. It was getting after noon when I saw a young woman on a gray horse enter the ring. She was having trouble holding back the huge gelding but finally got the go-ahead from the ring steward and shot forward so fast that she lost her hat, revealing strawberry-blonde pigtails flying. She missed almost half the balloons but she and her horse were clearly having the time of their lives. Her raw score was somewhere in the middle of her group, but she giggled and joked as she handed her pistols to the ammunition suppliers to reload. There was something familiar about this girl, I realized. Was it her hair? Her voice? She dismounted and was greeted by a handsome young man who—all smiles—gave her an awkward hug. All I noticed about him at first was that he was one of the only men at the event not dressed in cowboy gear. Then I did a doubletake and realized that the girl's boyfriend was our very own Mark Patterson, Cub Reporter.

But that wasn't the strangest part by far. As I looked at the tableau of man, girl, and horse, a frisson went up my back, then increased to a shiver when I realized I had seen that great gray horse once before. I may have been half unconscious and staring up at him from a strange angle and through bloody eyes, but that was the horse I saw in the woods the day I killed the snake.

Jack materialized at my side. He had been popping in and out throughout the morning, only to spot something else in the arena or on the grounds that intrigued him. An occasional flash from his camera let me know where he was. "So this is what you're doing with your time now," he said. "It's kind of fun."

"Jack," I said. "I need you to get some pictures of that girl and her horse."

"I already have," he said. "Got her boyfriend, too. Why? Who are they?"

"Guy's name is Mark. He works with me at *The Courier*." I changed the subject. "It's past lunchtime. You hungry? I suddenly have an almost overpowering hankering for chicken fajitas."

"I guess so, sure."

"There's a good Mexican restaurant in downtown Forester."

"Let's go, then."

As we passed the judge's booth, I hailed Panhandle Slim. The rain, which had been alternating between a downpour and a drizzle throughout the morning, had all but stopped, although the roof of the arena was still dripping in places. Horses and riders had tracked in mud, which we tried to avoid as we walked.

"Not leavin already are ya, Sue-Ann?" Slim asked, showing his line of straight white teeth.

"People to see and places to go," I told him. I tore a blank page from my notebook, wrote down a few things on it, and handed it to him. "Listen, I really enjoyed all this," I said. "If you can write down the winners and maybe a little about them, I'll work up a story for *The Courier*."

"I can do that."

"I wrote my email address on the paper. That's the easiest way to get anything to me."

"I can do that, too."

"I promise to write up the event, but I can't promise that the editor will print it."

"If not, maybe you can send it to me and I'll put it up on our website."

I agreed and led Jack around the ring to where Mark

and his blonde girlfriend were still hanging around the ammunition stand along with four or five other riders and their horses. Mark saw me coming ten yards away and went slightly rigid for a moment, then braced up and relaxed. "Hey, Sue-Ann," he called out. "What are you doing here?"

I walked up as his companion turned around to see who he was talking to. Her natural wide smile and infections laugh disappeared when she saw me. And if people's eyes could actually get larger, hers did. She seemed to check me out from baseball cap to running shoes before her eyes came back to my face.

"My assignment," I told Mark. I glanced at the girl, then back at Mark. "No use asking what *you're* doing here."

The girl was more cute than pretty, with teeth just imperfect enough to give her character. Her cowgirl outfit was light and airy except for a pair of sturdy pointed-toe boots. She couldn't have been much over eighteen years old and for some reason I seemed to scare her to death. This intrigued me.

"This is Krista Torrington," Mark said.

"Hi," I said to the girl, and put out my hand. "I'm Sue-Ann McKeown. I work with Mark at the paper—maybe he's mentioned me?"

"Um, I'm not sure." She took the hand I held out. Hers was small and unadorned, its grip firm, and she withdrew it almost at once.

I introduced Jack to Mark and Krista. Jack was his old hail-fellows-well-met, very charming self, which, for the first time in my memory, made no impression. Krista simply glanced at him, then looked back at me, while Mark studied him with a mixture of curiosity and suspicion. Motioning with his eyes toward Jack's camera case, he asked, "You a photographer?"

"That's the name of my game," Jack smiled.

I let them talk while I moved in on Krista. "I loved your ride," I told her.

Krista tried to smile, but just couldn't do it. "Thank you," she said mechanically. "It was fun."

"You have a beautiful horse," I told her. "What's his name?"

"Trigger."

"You're kidding," I said.

"No," she told me. "That's his name. Trigger."

"He looks so familiar. I think I've seen him before somewhere."

"Naw. He doesn't get out much."

"And it seems like I've seen *you* somewhere before, too," I said.

"Naw. I don't get out much neither."

"Well, then, Jack and I'll get out of your hair and let you enjoy your moment of freedom. Mark, I'll see you at the office. Krista, I have a feeling we'll meet again soon. Maybe we can go riding together sometime?"

Without waiting for an answer, I turned away and, with Jack in tow, headed in the direction of my car, avoiding the worst of the puddles. The sun was beginning to break through the cloud cover.

As soon as Jack had closed the door, he looked at me and asked, "Holy wow, Sue-Ann, what was that all about?"

"What was what about?"

"That girl looked like she thought you were going to shoot her."

"Odd, *she* was the one with the pistols," I remarked. I didn't venture anything else. Krista may not have won her shooting contest, but she had certainly ridden to the top of my Most Interesting list.

Chapter 11

The restaurant I chose was authentic Mexican, decorated inside with original oil paintings—one depicting the painters Frida Kahlo and her husband Diego Rivera, another showing the restaurant's owner astride a black Paso Fino. The walls just below the ceilings were striped in the green, white, and red of the Mexican flag. I ordered some chicken fajitas and a Modelo dark. Jack ordered an identical Modelo dark along with a chimichanga.

I spent some of the time we waited for our meal in writing down more of my observations of the cowboy-mounted shooting event while Jack peered through the viewfinder of his camera to preview the pictures he had taken. I noticed this with some surprise.

"You've gone digital?" I asked.

"Sometimes," he said. "If I'm in a hurry."

"I've never been able to get digital pictures to come out in shaded areas," I told him, thinking of the covered arena we'd just left.

"Sue-Ann," he said, not even bothering to take his eye from the viewfinder, "This is top of the line." I had forgotten that Jack was a technofreak who subscribed to a dozen photographic magazines, but it made me recall that I had heard exactly the same words from Crookneck Smith after he had narrowly beaten me in a friendly match outside Crookneck's Archery and Hunting Supplies. From that moment on, I had never paid for any less than the best archery tackle available. And Crookneck never beat me again.

We were halfway through our meals and on our second Modelos before we actually got around to talking about what was on our minds.

"Jack, I—"

"Sue-Ann—" Jack held up his hand. "No, Sue-Ann, let me talk first." I nodded with resignation, and he went on, "I didn't come here to harass you. I'm sorry it didn't work out between us. I thought we had something special, but then you went to the Middle East . . ." He shrugged. "When you came back, you weren't the same."

"I'd been in a war zone, Jack," I told him simply. "Sometimes that changes people."

"It was that bad?" he asked. "I got your emails—few as they were—and read your pieces. I know you didn't embed with army units or get taken blindfolded to some place in Fallujah to interview Saddam's personal imam."

Jack was right, of course. Like most Western journalists in Iraq, I rarely left my compound. We partied, we slept, and we left everything to our Iraqi counterparts. Some of us played video games on our computers and some of us kept diaries. I kept one, and still do. "You're right, Jack," I answered. "I didn't go hungry or thirsty or get shot or kidnapped. Just about the only inconvenience was when the power went out and the AC didn't work."

"So—"

"It was the everyday things—the tank tracks that I tripped over, the women in veils, the piles of rubble, the hate I felt all around, Bush's cronies lining their pockets with money that was supposed to go to hospitals and schools. It was everything I saw and heard, every day. And Jack, I was lucky. I had friends—good friends—that died doing their jobs. And every day I asked myself why I ever volunteered to come to that awful hellhole."

"Why did you?" he asked.

"Because I needed something different than what I had," I said levelly. "I couldn't believe that what we had in Richmond was all there was. Look, Jack, you're a brilliant photographer—if enough people say that to you maybe you'll start to believe it, but you're not the person I wanted to end up with." I put up my hand to stop him from speaking. "I'm sorry if that's harsh. I agree that someone *like* me is exactly the person you need to end up with." I was tongue tied—not for the first time around Jack—but I pressed on. "A relationship has to be mutual. Shit, why can't I explain this better? It's like, I don't know, it's like I dominate every relationship I've ever been in—the one with you more than most. That's what you wanted—for me to lead, to choose the movies we watched, what kind of beer we drank when we went out—but sometimes it's too much to have to think for two. I needed a break from that pressure. No, not a break. I needed out." I looked down at the remains of my meal. "I'm sorry."

"So you went to Iraq."

"So I spent six months in Iraq, which made me go bonkers. Then my mother died and I went numb, so when I came back to Richmond I just couldn't take care of you like I'd done before. I couldn't do it. So I left and came here and got sick—I have a hyperthyroid condition and probably came close to dying. And that was pretty depressing, too."

"I wondered about the weight loss," he said. "Is it bad?"

"No. I mean, yes, but it's okay. It's treatable. I'll be strong again eventually."

He paused, then said. "I might have something that will cheer you up."

I raised my eyebrows.

"I've been offered a book deal," he said.

I was puzzled. "Book deal?" I asked. "Are you writing now?"

"No, no. A book of photographs."

"That *is* good news, Jack," I said sincerely. "No one deserves it more than you do. Are you talking about a retrospective, or what?"

"It's for work I haven't done yet."

"I don't understand."

"I, um, got a call from somebody I know at Aperture—one of my old students. He told me they were looking for someone to do a before and after book on Iraq. Photos taken before and after the wars—both this one and Desert Storm."

"But you can't—"

"They'll be putting out a call for photographers who were in Iraq anytime during the last twenty years, asking them to submit photographs. I'll make the final selections and take some of the "after" pictures myself. They'd like to have it come out by the end of next year."

"That's incredible, Jack," I told him, "but most of the things you'll want to shoot are in really dangerous places. It's a bad idea. I have enough on my mind without having to worry every day about you getting blown up. Why didn't you just go and not tell me?"

Jack drained the rest of his beer and smiled slightly. "I didn't have any say when you decided to go over, so I don't feel as bad about that as I should. But there's another reason: I've convinced Aperture to let you write the copy for the book."

"Me?"

"Who could be better? You've been to Baghdad. Your stories were read by hundreds of thousands of people. We worked as a team for years before we even started dating,

and no one understands my photographs better than you
do."

"You've thought it all out, haven't you?" I asked. "It
even makes some kind of bizarre sense. I'll think about it.
Probably won't do it, but I owe you that much. I definitely
won't do it, though, if you get killed."

"Agreed," he grinned. "So, you'll miss me when I'm
away?"

"Don't press your luck," I said.

We both ordered flan for dessert and finished eating in
relative silence. I had a lot to think about. The book deal
would take some pondering, that's true. There was also the
problem of what I was going to do with Jack—having him
drop in on me was kind of like finding a new trombone on
the sidewalk, I couldn't play it but I just couldn't leave it
lying there either.

Our talk over dinner had made me realize that
Baghdad had given me a kind of ennui, that I had floated
somewhere outside myself, somewhere safe, for over a year
now. The hyperthyroidism had made things worse but now
I was beginning to focus again, was beginning to be able to
see that just about everything I had done since I left Iraq
was suspect. That whole mess with Donny, for instance;
would any of it have happened if I hadn't been sick? My
goat story might not be real, might be just something I
projected into being through my fantasies, through my
desire to have a focus. For that matter, it was no longer
certain that leaving Jack had been a rational decision. And
what about this confusing and kind of wonderful thing that
was happening with Gina? Was that just my glands talking?

It was likely that the more my hormone supplements
kicked in, the clearer headed I would become. It was truly a
scary moment. I looked at Jack and had the sense that he
was a handsome, creative, intelligent man who I was proud

to know—yet I didn't want to live with him. And as for my fantasies, Cal's "rodeo" had given me another piece of the goat story puzzle, and that piece was very real to me. It excited me, and unless something happened to change my priorities, I had to go with my feelings.

"I want to see those pictures you took at the Ag Center," I said suddenly. "And I really need to get back to my horse."

"You have a horse?" he asked.

"Would that top-of-the-line camera allow you to plug it in to my computer so I can see what pictures you took?"

"Any computer," he answered.

The road from Forester out to Pine Oak alternates between two and four lanes. It's a quick trip with only one caution light between the two cities. Much of the scenery is pine forest, with an occasional new business—a tractor dealership, a truck stop, a junk store. There are also the businesses that failed—a rotting grocery, a small motel without windows or doors, a brick chimney standing alone in a weedy lot. The turnoff to my farm was just before the Pine Oak city limits, then it was a couple of miles of red dirt, farms on both sides, one with cotton stubble, another with huge round peanut-hay rolls wrapped in black plastic. In another long field stood rows of tomato plants with wooden climber stakes driven in the ground every few feet. Mexican migrant laborers had tacked a three-inch strip of tinfoil onto each of the many hundreds of stakes, which, fluttering in the wind, were supposed to scare off birds. From a distance, the fields looked like wind-rippled silver lakes.

When we got to the house, I took Jack to the back and introduced him to Alikki, who wouldn't come within twenty yards of him. Jack snapped a few pictures of her anyway, then went inside while I groomed her and made over her for a while. Half an hour later, I went back inside and made coffee while Jack hooked up his camera to my iMac. With two chairs close together, we sat at my computer desk and went through them. He had been thorough, going as far as taking pictures of each brand of horse trailer on the grounds. He had close-up shots of most of the riders. In some of them you could actually see the almost invisible powder spraying from the pistol and into the bursting balloons. But it was the pictures of Krista Torrington I was anxious to see. When we came to the first one—a picture of her galloping in the arena, I stopped and scrutinized it carefully. There was another of her full-face and one of her with Mark. I zoomed in on her face, trying to recall if I had ever seen it before. I had no luck. Then I zoomed in on her horse and gasped.

"What is it?" Jack asked.

"Here," I told him excitedly, "Just beyond her horse, in the bleachers. Three people—two boys and a girl." The three young people were looking in Krista's direction—into the camera. One of the boys and the girl looked like they were trying to achieve a starved look; the other was a year or two older and had more substance. All had shaggy dyed-black hair, with clothing to match. But none of the three looked familiar.

"No cowboy gear," Jack commented. "I guess I missed that one, huh?"

"No, Jack, you didn't. Listen, I need to print a couple of these out, do you mind?"

"Go ahead, but do you think I could take a shower? Maybe get a shave? I have my stuff out in my car."

"Feel free."

In fifteen minutes I had gone through the pictures again and printed out several, including the blow-up of the three goths in the bleachers. I had pulled up the notes on my goat story and was adding to them when there was a knock on my door. I went to answer it. It was Gina.

"Gina!" I said. "You'll never guess what I've got."

"Somethin for Alikki?" she guessed.

"Not this time," I told her. I hurried into the bedroom for the pictures on the computer desk. Gina followed me in.

At that moment the bathroom door opened and Jack came out wrapped only in steam and a bath towel. Gina looked at him, then at me. Her mouth became a fine line.

"Maybe ah should call before ah barge in," she began. "But as long as ah'm here, whah don't we all go outsahd to your target range and you can shoot at me."

"Stop it, Gina," I told her. "It's not what it looks like."

"Not what what looks like?" Jack asked innocently. He removed some clean clothing from a suitcase on my bed.

"Gina, this is Jack Stafford from Richmond. He dropped in this morning for a visit and now he's leaving, but he took some pictures I have to show you. Jack, Gina works with me at *The Courier*."

"You're a reporter, Gina?" he asked in his innocent, curious Jack manner.

"Office manager," she said thinly.

"Jack, go get dressed," I told him.

"Can I take some pictures of her later?" he asked.

"Absolutely not," I told him.

I grabbed the stack of pictures from my desk and pulled Gina out into the living room, closing the bedroom door behind us.

"What kahnd of pictures was he talkin about?" she asked, casting a glance backwards, as if she wanted to see through the closed door.

"Pictures that will carve you up and let you know what the inside of your heart looks like," I told her. "But really, I know you think I'm a wad of human gum, but we haven't done anything. We've been in Forester all day covering that thing at the Ag Center." I looked her in the eyes and said mischievously, "But were you jealous?"

"Mebbe yes, mebbe——." She stopped in mid sentence and pointed at the pictures I had in my hand. "Those kids," she began. She took the sheet from my hand and studied it.

"Do you know them?" I asked.

"Ah do, yeah," she said. "This skinny kid is Linda C's son, Adam."

"Really?" I asked. Things were starting to make sense now. "Do you know the others?"

"The girl's name is Becky Colley."

"Not the commissioner's daughter?"

"Raht. And, Sue-Ann, you're not gonna believe this, but the older kid, the one with the black fingernail polish, is Pauley Hughes."

"Should I know him?" I asked, not making any connection.

"Short for Paul Hughes, Jr.," she said.

"Paul Hughes from *The Courier*?"

"Raht as a rabbit an jist as fast. Well, almost as fast."

When Jack came out of the bedroom, dressed neatly, cleanly shaven, and with his black hair slicked back, Gina was in the kitchen making coffee. I had filled her in on our morning in Forester and showed her the rest of Jack's photos. Now I was sitting on the couch planning my next move. Jack was a new wrinkle in my friendship with Gina, but one I couldn't think about just then. The goat story was approaching its denouement. All it needed was a little editing, a motive, a couple of i's dotted. Three gothic faces were seared onto my brain like a brand. I toyed with the idea of driving back to the Ag Center to see if they had stuck around, but decided against it. I wanted to see them in their own element. Outside, the light was dimming, it would be night soon. Saturday night.

"We're going nightclubbing," I suddenly decided.

"There are night clubs in Pine Oak?" Jack asked, as Gina came into the room with three cups on a tray. She gave Jack one and placed the tray with the other two on the table in front of me. Then she sat down at the other end of the couch.

"Not in Pine Oak," I told him. "Maybe in Forester. Gina, where do the kids hang out these days?"

"How would ah know?" she said, dragging on a cigarette. "Ah'm jist an old dee-vor-cee."

"Shit . . . Wait! I've got it. Gina, do you have the phone numbers of everyone at *The Courier*?"

"Raht here in mah purse," she said. "On mah cell phone."

"Call Mark Patterson." In filling Gina in on the cowboy-mounted shooting event, I had also mentioned seeing Mark and his young girlfriend. But when I showed Gina Krista's picture, Gina had shaken her head. "No one ah know," she said. But Krista gave me an idea and Mark owed me favors.

"What should ah say?" she asked.

"Just give me the phone and I'll talk," I told her.

Gina fished a pair of glasses from her purse along with the cell phone, played with the buttons for a minute, then held the phone to her ear.

"I never knew you wore glasses," I said.

"Ah'm jist gittin decrepit, ah guess."

Seconds went by and Gina looked at me and rolled her eyes. "He's takin forever—wait . . ." She pulled the phone away from her ear and handed it to me. I put it to my own ear and heard a casual, "Hey, Ginette, what's up?"

"Not Ginette, Mark. Sue-Ann."

"Sue-Ann? But Ginette's number is on the ID."

"She loaned me her phone," I told him. "Listen. Where are you now?"

"I'm home."

"Is, um, Krista with you?"

"No. That shooting thing is an all-day event. She had two or three more rides and I didn't feel like staying. Hey, what's between you two anyway?"

"What did she say?"

"She wouldn't say anything at all. In fact, her mood changed so much after you left that I didn't feel like she wanted me there any more."

"She was probably just concentrating on her ride. Believe me, I was as surprised at her reaction as you were."

"Where do you know each other from?" he asked.

"Mark, as far as I know, I've never seen her before in my life. But I really didn't call to ask you about Krista. What I want to know is whether you saw three kids in the bleachers dressed like zombies at a funeral."

I heard a deep intake of breath and realized that Mark had just lit a cigarette—a habit I hadn't known he had. "I saw them. I almost had to take a punch at one of them."

"You're kidding!"

"The little fucker. He tried to hit on Krista. All three of them kept following her around."

"How did she react?" I asked.

"Kind of like they were flies. Tried to wave them off, but they kept coming back. She finally went up to two or three cowboys she met and whispered something to them. Next thing I know they're escorting the punks out of the grounds and not being too gentle about it."

"Do you know any of them?"

"That's the damndest thing. I saw them once before. They were dressed different, but it was the same three."

"Do you remember where?"

"Never forget. It was the night I picked—the night I met Krista. It was in that place in Forester called something like Eat Me."

"Eat Now," I suggested.

"That's it. Those kids were trying to hit on her that night too, just before I introduced myself. The three of them seemed to flake away after that and I don't remember seeing them the rest of the night."

"Let me guess," I said. "That was the place you called from when you wanted me to check out that goat in the dumpster."

"Hey, that's right. Great memory. I owe you one for that."

"You've just paid it." I said. "See you at the office."

"But what did you call fo—" I hung up on his question and turned to Gina and Jack. "Maybe nightclubbing was too strong a word," I told them. "But we can have dinner while we investigate."

"Investigate what?" Jack asked.

Gina twitched her nose. "Damn, Sam," she exclaimed. "Ah've got some things ah've been meanin to bring over but I left em at the office."

"What things?" I asked.

"Ah went to the Property Appraiser's Office on Friday and found out who owns all that property behind Meekins' Market. Got some maps, too, and I wrote down the address of a website that lets you fahnd out whatever you need online."

"That's great, Gina," I told her. "When can I see them?"

"Ah'll drop them over sometahm tomorrow."

~ ~ ~

Eat Now: Home of Food is located on the main

202

highway just before you enter downtown Forester. It is a square, cinderblock building set apart from other businesses by a parking lot on each side. Over the years, customers in a hurry have left gouges in the corners of the façade with their trucks or rigs so that the whole building gives the appearance of being built of sugar cubes that have been gnawed on by rats. The main dining room consists of a long bar complete with spinning barstools covered with orange naugahyde. A dozen tables and booths take up the rest of the area. A second room, strictly for dining, is reached by going through a door just to the right side of the bar. All in all, its décor can be described as trashy but well-maintained. A back door leads out to a wooden deck that runs the length of the building and is very popular with the smoking crowd. On the whole, Eat Now is an under-35 hangout, although older customers sometimes rent the entire back dining room for parties or business meetings.

We arrived with the place in full swing—customers were eating in booths, drinking at the bar, and milling around outside. The jukebox was playing something by Toby Keith, but not loud enough to inhibit conversation. Although not a pick-up joint per se, it often doubled as one. It was here, of course, that I had first become interested in Donny. For that matter, Donny had probably hooked up with Linda C in this same room. Mark Patterson, it seemed, had met Krista Torrington here.

Jack, Gina, and I entered and sat down at a table next to the one where I had first seen Donny slumped over his beer. It was in a dimly lighted corner near the door leading out to the deck. A glance had been enough to see that the people I was looking for weren't in the room.

Gina took her glasses from her purse and used them to peer at the menu.

"Those glasses make you look, I don't know,

sophisticated," I told her. "I think it would be cool to see you sitting back in an armchair reading Proust or somebody."

"Would ah lahk whoever it was you jist said?"

"I don't think anybody really likes Proust. It's just something you aspire to." I glanced down at the menu for a second, but didn't really see it. I was thinking of Gina reading in an armchair, but in my secret version, her glasses were all that she was wearing. I slapped the menu down and stood up. "Listen, order me a cheeseburger all the way with tater tots and a Corona. I'm going to check out the other room."

"All raht."

I checked out the smaller dining room, but only after I visited the rest room and splashed water on my face from the sink. The dining room was only half full. I recognized a couple of riders from the mounted shooting event, but no one else. I had better luck on the deck. Sitting alone on one of the rude benches in a corner of the deck, smoking, was a very thin young woman dressed in black. It was too dark to tell much else, but I was pretty sure it was Becky Colley, abandoned for a time by her two cohorts. Much of the rest of the deck was taken up by other young people, some in the western garb of the shooting event, others in work clothes or casuals, but all giving Goth Girl her space, as if she radiated a protective aura, or maybe an odor. I checked out both parking lots but saw neither Adam Zimmer nor Pauley Hughes. When I got back to the table, Jack and Gina seemed to have struck up a conversation. They quit as I walked up.

"Talking about me?" I asked.

"Mebbe yes, mebbe no," Gina said with a twinkle. "Fahnd anybody?"

"I did, yes. Becky Colley is out there by herself. Do

The News in Small Towns

you know her well enough to ask her to our table?"

"She wouldn't know me from a tree," Gina said.

"You recognized her picture," I pointed out.

"Cal pointed her out a coupla tahms when we were out."

"So Cal knows her?"

"He's golf buddies with her dad."

"I thought he played golf with the lawyer, you know, Rooney. And Paul Hughes."

"And Ray Colley. That's the foursome. They've been playin golf together for years. Didn't ya know?"

"So that explains the connection between Ray Colley's daughter and Paul Hughes' son."

"Raht," Gina said. "Their families hang out together sometahms."

"Okay, then, I think this is a job for Super Jack."

Our orders came before Jack could reply and I found myself ravenously hungry despite the Mexican we had eaten for lunch. I tore into my cheeseburger and popped some tater tots in my mouth without even letting them cool. Jack and Gina just stared. "What?" I asked.

"Super Jack?" asked Jack.

"Raht. Now listen. I need you to go outside and get into a conversation with that goth girl you took a picture of earlier."

"What, you want me to try to pick up a fifteen year old?"

"Well, yeah. That would be *really* good. But if you don't feel like going that far, I want you to borrow a cigarette from her."

"Borrow a—"

"A cigarette, right. But don't smoke it all. Leave enough of the butt so we can see the brand name."

"Why?" Jack asked.

205

"It's for a story we're working on. An investigative piece. Don't let on."

"Can I eat first?" he asked.

"Eat fast."

Jack took a couple of bites of whatever it was he ordered, then stood up. "I'm not hungry anyway," he said. "Wait for me." He walked slowly toward the door leading to the deck.

"Not a chance," I told Gina, standing up and pushing back my chair. "We'll go around the other way."

"But—"

"No, really. You've got to see this. Jack is something else."

"All raht, all raht."

"And bring your cigarettes." As we hurried toward the front door, we passed our server, gave her a five-dollar bill, and told her not to clear our table, we'd be back. And then we almost knocked down poor Benny Benedict, who was headed for the bar.

I greeted him with a "Hey, Benny," and he turned, startled. "Hey hey," he replied. "The gruesome twosome, heh heh." Now Gina was the one who looked startled, but then said, "You're the guy from the bookstore, raht?"

"Um, well, yeh, uh huh. That's me. I see you going in and out of the newspaper office all the time."

"Ginette is the heart and soul of *The Courier*," I told him, jealously guarding her diminutive. "Meeting someone, Benny?" I asked.

"Naw, nope. Just going to quaff a few before I head on home. You little ladies want to join me?"

"Next time, Benny. We've got to go out for a while. Later."

Outside, we hurried along the right corner of the building, squeezing in and out of cars parked too close to the wall. Our progress brought us to the deck where Goth Girl was still sitting, her back to us. We stopped in the shadow of the wall and lit cigarettes—just two diners who had stepped out for a quick smoke. I know you won't believe me, but I didn't inhale.

Jack was busy being the Jack I knew and had once loved. He was a man who never went right for his object; rather he moved in gradually decreasing circles until he just happened to arrive at the destination he had set for himself at the beginning. It was a ploy that put his quarry at ease and he almost never lost his photo op. As soon as he had gotten outside, he spotted someone from the mounted shooting event, and put on a big smile. I could see the men shaking hands, Jack asking all kinds of questions about the man's life, his horses, and what kind of animals he liked to hunt. The man introduced Jack to others in his group and the same round of questions were gone through again. The men all exchanged business cards and Jack, seemingly reluctantly, looked at his watch and made excuses. Very slowly, he made his way toward where Goth Girl was seated, although I never saw him actually look in her direction. On the way, there was another handshake as he passed another group of people. Another, shorter, round of words spoken.

By the time he had actually gotten within Goth Girl's aura, I was nearly chewing my cigarette butt with anxiety that she might leave or be joined by friends, but Jack's intuitions are almost always precise. Hesitating, he looked at her and cleared his voice. Becky looked up and her back straightened. Jack smiled brightly and said softly, "Do you mind if I sit down for a minute? I'm waiting for someone and I've been on my feet all day taking pictures."

"I might spit on you," she told him tonelessly.

"I guess I can take that chance," Jack smiled, sitting

down across from her, showing his teeth and crossing his legs.

Goth Girl shrugged and reached in her shirt pocket for a cigarette. Jack took a cell phone out of his coat, opened the face, and peered at it. He frowned and placed it on the bench beside him.

"My name is Jack Stafford," he told her. "And I'm visiting from Richmond, Virginia."

Becky looked him up and down, probably trying to figure out what this well-dressed, well-spoken studmuffin was doing in a dingy little burg like Forester. "Visiting who?" she asked. Contact. That was what I had been waiting for and I nudged Gina, grinning.

Jack's eyes opened wide. "Can't tell you that, I'm afraid," he said. "It's kind of a secret assignment." He took a card from his wallet and handed it to her. "For my newspaper," he added. "The only thing I can tell you is that it concerns someone who used to be on the Olympic Team that lives near here. She's been sick and doesn't want anyone to know it."

"You get paid to take pictures?" she asked.

"You better believe it."

"Is that cell phone a camera?" she asked.

"How did you know?" Jack asked.

"My mom's got one. She hides it from my dad, though. I think she has a boyfriend and uses it to talk to him while she's naked. Ugh."

"Well, I don't know your mother," said Jack. "But she can't be that bad if she looks like you. Anyway, I don't— Wait a minute, I think I saw you earlier today, at that cowboy thing."

"You were there?" she asked.

"Holy wow," Jack said, quickly putting his hand over his mouth. "You won't tell anybody that I was there, will you? Listen, can I have one of those cigarettes? I thought I had quit but I guess I haven't."

Becky handed him one from the pack and lit it for him with a plastic lighter. He drew deeply, then blew smoke. "Umm, that's great," he said. "Thanks. Yeah, I think I saw you at that place, whatever they call it. You were with some other people, right?"

"Yeah, we were just hanging around."

"Um hmm, me too," Jack said.

Gina and I were nursing our own cigarettes, listening intently to every word and watching Becky as she plied her body language. She would shift in her seat, pick at one of the several earrings in her left earlobe, twist a lock of her choppy black hair. We heard her ask, "You, um, take pictures of nudes?"

"Me?" Jack asked, surprised. "Nah—did you tell me your name?"

"Rebecca."

"Great name, Rebecca. I'm Jack."

"You told me."

"Sorry. Listen, Rebecca, my thing is trying to take pictures of people that make them look naked without having them take their clothes off. Do you understand that?"

"I don't know."

"To take pictures of people's souls. The way people really are without all the fake things they're always doing."

"I can relate to that," she said. "Are you famous?"

"A little, maybe. You can Google me when you get home. Whoops, I think I just saw the people I was waiting for coming in the front door. "Great talking to you, Rebecca. Sorry I don't have my camera with me." He picked up his cell phone from the bench and put it in his pocket. "I mean, my real camera. I'd love to have a picture of you. Maybe a series. There's just something . . . I don't know. Maybe I'll see you again."

"Okay."

"Thanks for the cigarette," he said.

"Okay."

As Jack walked back to the door leading into the room, Gina whispered to me, "You're raht about Jack."

I whispered back, "I've been having lewd thoughts about you all night."

"Sue-Ann!"

"Let's go finish our dinner," I said, smiling.

Back at the table, Jack handed me the cigarette butt. I looked at it carefully and put it away in my purse. I nodded at Gina. "One of the same brands," I said.

"Did I do okay?" Jack asked.

"Shit, Jack, that poor girl is creaming her panties."

"Yeah?" he smiled.

"Yeah."

"What was the cigarette for?"

"It's nothing you need to know about, but I found some cigarette butts at the scene of this thing I've been working on and I wanted to see if Goth Girl's is the same brand. It is."

"Is that bad?"

"Might be, unless I do something."

"Too bad. She seems like a really nice kid."

Our food was cold by now and our drinks room temperature, but we finished what we wanted and paid. The cashier was a young woman I had never seen before—Linda C must have Saturday nights off. Gina had stopped at the trash barrel below the SMASH THE DIXIE CHICKS sign. She rummaged around among the jewel cases and came out with two different titles and stuck them in her purse. Back outside, cars were still coming and going with difficulty. A horn blared and someone shouted, "Get the fuck out of the way, you moron!" I looked over to see a cowboy in a pickup shouting at a man in a red Jeep.

"Sue-Ann," Gina nudged me. "That's your friend in that Jeep."

She was right. Poor Benny was having trouble getting out of the parking lot and the bozo in the pickup—who had evidently just pulled in—wasn't making things easier. Benny was finally able to swerve around the man and I saw him hit his own horn on the way past. But instead of the honk I was expecting, a loud voice, metallic and digital, came from a loudspeaker bolted to the front bumper. "BITE ME!" it growled.

Before the cowboy could react, Benny was in the street and racing off. Heads turned and people on the deck were laughing.

"Heh heh," I chuckled.

Chapter 12

After we got home from Eat Now and Gina said her goodbyes, I shunted Jack into my mother's room, showed him the adjoining bathroom and towel closet, and helped clear Cindy's few remaining papers from the bed. As soon as he was settled, I went into my own room and closed the door. I knew I had to call Donny, had to sit down with him tomorrow and talk about Adam, but the idea of having him come to the house again, or even going to his, was a bad idea. And one of the main problems with Pine Oak is that there are no restaurants open on Sunday. Either you cook your own meals or drive to one of the adjoining towns. So when I managed to reach him on his cell phone—he was out on a call, not unusual for a Saturday night—I asked him to meet me for lunch at the Burger King between Pine Oak and Hanson's Quarry.

"What's it about, Sue-Ann?" he asked.

"I'll tell you when I see you," I told him.

He sputtered a little, but finally agreed.

After I hung up I sent Cal a lengthy email bringing him up to speed on what we had found out—Gina and I agreed that it was better coming from me than from her. I had gotten back a brief message: "Good work. Keep peeling that onion. C.D."

I spent the next morning trying to relax. First, I spent a quality half hour with Alikki in her pasture, brushing out her mane and gingerly picking out blackberry brambles from her tail. In the few days I had owned her, she had become an important and unique character in my life. I loved currying her, stroking her coat, or just watching her in the pasture swishing her tail lazily at gnats and walking as gracefully as she could from one lush patch of grass to another. Sometimes if I was too attentive to her, she would swish *me* with her tail, roll her eyes, or snort at me. I loved it all, but had learned to back off when she wanted me to.

That morning, after Alikki had dismissed me, I decided to practice my kyudo. I mentioned earlier that archery always relaxes me, and Japanese archery requires a zenlike, meditative state that is almost like being in a trance. I was anxious to escape from my surroundings for a while, but to shoot archery properly—especially kyudo—you can't have anything else on your mind. Despite the fact that I donned my white and blue practice uniform and thick, three-fingered glove, despite the fact that I did my best to empty my mind of all outside influences, the practice session was a mess. My shots missed the target with such consistency that I may as well have been blindfolded. The world was way too much with me.

First on my mind was the goat story—not only did I think over all the things I had found out so far, but I agonized over tasks I had yet to do. Like talking to Donny at lunch and maybe calling Ray Colley and Paul Hughes. And it was more important than ever that I make another trip into the woods.

Jack was second on the list of things I had to deal with. I was worried about him going to the Middle East and getting killed, while at the same time I realized that if he survived, the experience might give him enough confidence and self-sufficiency to be the person he was always meant to be. The idea for his book was tantalizing, his asking me to write the copy was tempting.

Bubbling under was concern about my thyroid. I had

almost decided on having the radioactive iodine treatment, but it would have to wait. Sex I could put off; in fact, being radioactive might give me an excuse for taking a rain check if I felt myself weakening in that direction around Jack or Donny or whoever. But endangering Alikki and her foal was out of the question.

And, of course, entwined through each of my thoughts was Gina. The last week had been more than hectic; I had felt as if there were far too few hours in the day to get anything done, yet through it all, what I wanted to do most was sit and talk to Gina. My growing friendship with her was a total surprise. She was able to calm down my frantic nature just by her presence; she didn't care if I couldn't be as strong as I would like to be all the time. The fact that she was seeing Cal sent my thoughts in directions more scattered than my arrows, and I knew that somewhere on the horizon, Cal was going to play a bigger part in how our friendship progressed.

Another good thing about Japanese archery is that the arrows are nearly twice as long as regular arrows. They're almost impossible to lose in the grass.

When I put everything away and went back inside, I found that Jack had gone out somewhere. My mother's bed was made but slightly rumpled, with one of my father's Zane Grey books on the pillow, a bookmark carefully sticking out the top.

The phone rang and I ran into my bedroom to answer it. "Hello?"

"Is this Sue-Ann?" The deep masculine drawl was familiar, but I couldn't put a name to it right away.

"That's right."

"This is Paul Hughes."

"Oh. Hey, Paul, how's it going?"

"Sorry to bother you on a Sunday morning, Sue-Ann,

but I need to talk to you."

"That's okay, Paul. What's on your mind?" I was pretty sure I already knew what was on his mind, and looked around automatically for a pack of cigarettes. Where was Gina or Goth Girl when I needed them? I steeled myself by sitting on the bed, my back against the headboard.

"I had a long talk with Cal Dent this morning," Paul began. "On the golf course. He told me you were still looking into that goat story."

"He gave me the go-ahead. But it's not just a goat story any more, Paul. Did Cal tell you about the dog and the chickens?"

"He told me a lot of things, and I'll have to tell you that it upset me some. No, it upset me a lot, because I quit after nine holes and came home. Sue-Ann, I'd like to ask you not to go any further with this. I'm asking you as a friend. Well, I guess if I'm going to be truthful, we really don't know each other well enough to be friends, but I can ask you as a colleague."

"I respect that, Paul. But I'm going to need to ask why you want me to stop."

"You know why, Sue-Ann. You've got it into your head that my son is somehow mixed up in some damned craziness."

"Tell me about your son, Paul," I said.

"About Pauley? What do you want me to say? He's a good kid, he just . . ."

"Just what?" I asked.

"Look, Sue-Ann. I'm not gonna sugar coat anything. I was in the Marines most of the time Pauley was growing up, and we moved around a lot. We lived in Kuwait for a while after Desert Storm, but when I retired we moved here to Pine Oak where my wife was born. I bought a nice place to live. Pauley got into a good school. But then after 9/11 they asked me to come back to Washington and help with some counterintelligence work. While I was gone, my wife found out she had cancer. It was the quickest thing I ever heard of—two weeks and she was gone. But I was out of the country and couldn't get back . . ."

"I'm sorry, Paul."

"Pauley was . . . he didn't handle it well. He blames me for not being there when Susan died. He doesn't understand the pressure I was under—you just can't leave a job like that with so much at stake for the country. It's all about responsibility and getting on with your life, and I don't know why the hell Pauley doesn't understand that. We don't talk any more, Sue-Ann. We just don't talk."

"It's okay, Paul. I've been meaning to call you about all this anyway. Did Cal mention any of Pauley's friends?"

"I don't think so. Who do you mean?"

"Adam Zimmer and Becky Colley."

"I know he sees them some, yeah."

"Well, the three of them have gotten into some strange rituals."

"Rituals? What the hell kind of rituals?"

"I think they see themselves as outcasts—in fact, I think they're proud of it. One of them found a book on the occult and it gave them an idea of being empowered— something they haven't found in their real lives. So they've been performing secret rites or sacrifices."

"I don't believe it," he said matter-of-factly.

"Ask your son," I said simply.

"Even if you're right, Sue-Ann, they haven't committed any crimes."

"Stealing livestock, killing animals for the sake of killing? Yeah, those are crimes. Breaking into my house and trashing it is a crime."

"Hold on now, you can't blame Pauley for—"

"I guess Cal forgot to tell you that part, too. But, yeah, those three kids were the ones that broke in."

"Damn it, Sue-Ann, you're making up things just to see your name on a byline."

"First of all, Paul," I said with asperity, "I don't need any more bylines. I had enough of those when I was in Baghdad and people from all over the *world* were trashing my reports in their fucking right-wing blogs. Second of all, I can *prove* that those kids broke into my house. Last but not least, none of this matters because I would never write up anything that would put you or your son—or Becky or Ray or Adam or Linda C—in a bad light if I could help it."

"You mean—?"

"I'm not a scandalmonger, Paul. I don't like people breaking into my house or killing animals just for drill, but if people want to go out in the woods and waste their time calling up voodoo demons, it's not any of my business."

"Sue-Ann, I—"

I interrupted him again. "There's a caveat."

"What's that?"

"A caveat is kind of an exception—"

"I know what a caveat is. Just tell me what you're going to tell me."

"Paul, what will happen when somebody *catches* them breaking into a house or stealing something? When that happens and they call the sheriff, there's no way in the world to keep it secret."

"Okay, I understand that. That's fair."

For some reason, I didn't tell him about my fear that the kids were in actual, physical danger. I guess I thought that a word to the wise was enough. I contented myself with saying, "So you'll talk to Pauley?"

I heard a deep breath on the other end of the line—

not the inhalation of a cigarette, but a deep sigh coming from Paul's very depths. "I can't do that, Sue-Ann. At least not right now."

"Why not, Paul?"

"When I got back home yesterday afternoon, Paul, Jr. had moved out. I don't know where he is."

~ ~ ~

Donny drove into the Burger King parking lot ten minutes late—he was driving his Harrison towing wrecker, so he was probably on call—but I didn't mind. It gave me time to get my story together and to eat a sandwich. I hoped that Donny could help me remove another layer of Cal's onion.

Donny was showered and clean shaven. His short, light hair was wind tossed and the work uniform he wore was clean and pressed. Although it was after noon, he looked tired and gave me barely a nod as he entered and made a beeline for the counter. After he had gotten his order of a large coffee and a fish sandwich, he made his way to my table. "Okay, what's so important, Sue-Ann, that you had to get me way out here on the one day of the week I might have stayed home?" he asked.

I came right out with it. "I think that Adam was the one who broke into my house."

Donny knitted his eyebrows. "You mean Linda C's Adam? No way, man. Why would Adam—"

"Remember you told me that you showed him some of my *Courier* stories?"

"Yeah?"

"Could one of the stories have been about that marijuana bust?"

"The one where the truck jackknifed off the road. Yeah, that was one. I helped get that truck back into Forester. I mean, after they got a crane out there to right it.

I told Adam I could have picked up a few of those bricks and brought them home with me, but that marijuana was for shit."

"Maybe Adam asked whether *I* might have picked one up and maybe taken it home as a souvenir."

"Naw, he . . ." His sentence trailed off and he was obviously remembering something.

"Donny, you're a nice guy, but you trust everyone too much. Most people aren't as honest or as innocent as you are—even kids. You must have told him and I'm not angry, I just wish you'd think. What if he had called the sheriff?"

"Well, I may have said something . . . I'm sorry, Sue-Ann. I guess I was just trying to be pals with the kid and didn't think about how it might get you in trouble. But Adam wouldn't say anything."

"Adam *did* say something, Donny. Last Friday night he overheard someone calling me on a cell phone asking me to go out and cover a story. He remembered my name and remembered about the pot, so he and maybe two of his friends hid outside my house and waited for me to go out. Then they broke in looking for that marijuana. They just about tore up the house, but it wasn't there. The only thing they took was that bottle of tequila you gave me."

"Sue-Ann. None of this makes any sense. Do you have any proof that it was Adam?"

I sighed and sat back in the plastic booth. "I do, yes, but having proof isn't the point. The point is that I'm afraid that something bad is going to happen to Adam or his friends if they don't stop what they're doing."

"You mean if they don't stop breaking into people's houses?"

"No. It goes way beyond that. What I'm going to tell you now may seem crazy but it's true. What you do about it—tell Linda C or Adam's father or even the sheriff—is up

219

to you."

"All right, Sue-Ann. Go ahead."

"Adam has gotten mixed up with a boy named Pauley Hughes and a girl named Becky Colley. There may be more of them, I don't know. They get together and dress all in black and have secret meetings. One of them—I think probably Pauley because he's a couple of years older—has gotten into the occult and thinks he can call up spirits or demons. . . ."

"Sue-Ann, do you know what you're saying?"

"It doesn't matter whether you believe me or not. It just matters that you hear me out. I've been investigating a story about a goat that someone killed and stuffed in a dumpster."

"You mentioned a goat last time I saw you. But what's a dead goat—"

"Donny, killing a goat and putting it in a dumpster doesn't make any sense. It's something that no one in the world would have done. It's something that just begged to be looked into. So I did some investigating and found the place in the woods where the goat was killed. There were voodoo symbols on the ground, blood all over, and an empty tequila bottle in the bushes. The same brand of tequila that was stolen from my house."

"Do you know how many bottles of that brand of tequila—"

"Donny, damn it, I don't care! Believe me, it was the same one. I brought it out of the woods and I can get Dilly to lift fingerprints off it if I have to. But if you listen to me and don't interrupt, I won't have to. What brand of cigarettes does Adam smoke?"

"How do you know he . . . Marlboro Light, same as me."

"I found Marlboro Light cigarette butts in the same

place I found the tequila bottle, as well as butts from two other brands—Newport and Doral." I brought my legal pad up from the seat and extracted a photo from between its pages. "Look at the kids in this photo."

"That's not—whoa, is that Adam?"

"And the girl is Becky Colley. Know what brand of cigarettes she smokes? Doral. Know whose goat it was that was killed? Her dad's."

"Her dad is Ray Colley?"

"Right. But it gets worse. A couple of days ago, someone broke in to a woman's chicken house out on Peg-leg Road and stole some chickens. While they were at it they killed the woman's dog by stringing it up and cutting its guts out. Just for thrills. Then they took the chickens out to that same place in the woods, cut their heads off, and burnt them in some kind of sacrifice."

"You saw this?"

"I saw the remains. And I'm not the only one. Are you starting to believe me?"

"I . . . I don't know. Why are you telling *me* this? Why not talk to Linda C?"

"I don't know her that well and she probably doesn't like me anyway. I'm giving you the heads up so that you can talk to her, so that you can take care of it."

"Why don't you talk to Ray Colley or that other boy's dad?"

"I spoke to Pauley's dad this morning," I said grimly.

"It just sounds so crazy," he said.

"Donny," I told him. "It *is* crazy. And I have a really bad feeling about it."

"Okay, Sue-Ann," Donny said. "I've heard you out and some of it might even make some sense, but there's one thing that just doesn't fit."

"What's that?" I asked.

"You said that nobody would have been crazy enough to kill a goat and put it in a dumpster."

"Yeah? What's your point?"

"I don't have six college degrees, Sue-Ann, but think about it. Someone *did* kill the goat and put it in the dumpster."

It was a point that someone with six college degrees might have missed, and I was pleased, somehow, that Donny had grabbed on to it. Luckily, I had an answer. "No, Donny. That didn't happen, and that's the scary part. The kids killed the goat. Someone else put it in the dumpster. Whoever it was scared them away the first time—next time they might not be so kind."

"Who?"

"Somebody who doesn't want them out there."

Donny crumpled up his sandwich wrapper and stuffed it in his empty coffee cup. "You said that dog was killed on Peg-leg Road, right?"

"Yeah, why?"

"Adam's dad lives near Peg-leg road—right out by our farm." He stood up and took a step, then backtracked. "I'm not promising anything, but if I get the chance, I'll ask Jerry if he knows anything about what Adam and Pauley have been doing."

"Thanks, Donny."

I stayed for a few minutes after Donny left. I even bought a piece of chocolate pie and felt good about my appetite coming back.

~ ~ ~

I arrived back home to find Jack standing in my mother's bedroom, ironing clothes. He was dressed in a white undershirt, checked boxer shorts, and white socks. He had turned on the radio and was singing along to "Mammas Don't Let Your Babies Grow Up to Be

Cowboys."

"When did you get into country music?" I asked.

"Didn't. I just turned on the radio and there it was."

"Why are you still here?" I asked. He had taken everything from his car and piled it on Cindy's bed. His suitcase was empty on the floor.

"Don't have anywhere else to go," he said. "I sublet my apartment for the rest of the summer."

"You—" I felt like stamping my foot, except that's another thing that people don't really do. Instead, I put my hands on my hips and glared at him. "You move out of your apartment and drive down here after not having seen me for a year and expect me to let you move in?" I shouted. "I can't believe this."

"It's only for a few days," he said reasonably. "My flight leaves from Tallahassee Wednesday."

"What, you're going to Iraq already?"

"I thought I told you."

"I thought you meant in a month or two."

"Wednesday."

"What are you going to do with your car?" I asked.

"Don't know. Leave it here I guess. Maybe your friend Gina could drive me to the airport."

"Fuck you, Jack."

"Think she would?"

"She's old enough to be your mother."

He looked at me sideways, puzzled.

"Private joke," I said. "*I'll* drive you."

His face lit up with a smile. "Hope you don't mind me using your laundry room," he said. "And your iron and stuff. And, oh, I set up a darkroom in that second bathroom."

"Just make yourself right at home."

"And, hey, I found a TV in that trashed-up bedroom,

but it doesn't work."

"I didn't pay the dish bill."

"Broke?"

"I just don't want to watch TV."

"What happened to that bedroom anyway?" he asked, folding the pair of pants he had finished ironing and placing them carefully in the suitcase.

"Look, Jack, there are a lot of things going on in my life right now that I don't want to talk about. That bedroom is one of them."

"What about that story you're working on?" He took up a shirt from a pile of clean laundry and placed it on the ironing board.

"Maybe later."

"What about relationships?" he asked. "Anyone new?"

"Maybe yes, maybe no."

"What's that mean?"

"It means that I don't want to talk about it."

A pop song had replaced the country one on the radio, and I recognized the lyrics, "Up, up and away, in my beautiful balloon." The popular '70s song had been covered by a hundred artists over the years, and I had heard it at least that many times. This time, though, there was something frightening about it, like the rustle of leaves behind you on a dark night in the woods. As Jack concentrated on his ironing—something he had done for the both of us when we lived together—the deejay Smokestack came on the air.

"Hey, I bet you're glad you got to hear that. You know, one of the great things about working here at K-B-O-Y, your shoot-em-up radio station, is the real pleasure of getting to know all these old songs and groups that were popular before I was even born. Give all the credit to our Program Director. And do you know who our program director is? That scary bastard we all call The Creeper."

"Sue—" I held up a hand to stop Jack from speaking.

"Shhh, I want to hear this," I told him.

Smokestack was continuing. "The Creeper is kind of like a vampire. Some of us here think that he has been around since the pharaohs and some even think that he's the reincarnation of a voodoo god, but one thing is for sure. He knows his way around music. Here's an LP he just handed me along with a note. The note says: 'This group was active in the south in the late sixties. Two of their members were on the Florida State University swim team.' Wow. And hey, this particular title is going for fifty smacks on eBay. It's called "Reach for the Sky," and it's by a group called Cowboy. Whoopee! Enjoy, y'all."

The song that came on was a pleasant enough mixture of rock and country. "Is it okay to talk now?" Jack asked.

"Sorry, Jack," I said. "It's just that that radio station creeps me out. What did you want to tell me?"

"Gina came over while you were gone," he said. "She left these for you." He pointed at a roll of maps lying on a chair. There was a note taped to them. I picked them up and read the note.

> *Sue-Ann:*
>
> *Sorry I missed you. Here's the maps and stuff I got from the Property Appraiser's office on Friday. I wrote a web address on the first map and directions on how to get whatever ownership information you want, right there online. Just type in the parcel number from the maps.*
> *Gina*

I had never seen Gina's handwriting before. It was neat and almost flowery with a left-handed slant. But when I was reading, I was hearing the words in her voice: Sorry ah missed ya.

"Thanks, Jack," I smiled. I left him to his ironing and hurried into my bedroom with the maps, which I only glanced at before turning on my iMac and pulling up my goat story file to add the bit of information I had gotten from Donny.

"What are you working on in there?" Jack yelled.

"I don't want to talk about it." I shouted back.

After I closed the file, I got my notes from the truck and wrote up kind of a fluff piece on the mounted shooting event I had seen the day before. I tried to make it seem exciting, competitive, and colorful. I described the outfits, the pistols, the course, and even the rain. The only thing I left out were the winners of the events, which I would plug in when I got them from Panhandle Slim.

By the time I switched off the iMac, it was getting on to 3:00, but I was full of energy. I thought I might get Jack to take the tractor and make a start at mowing the pasture—which was getting high with weeds and choking out the nice grass below—while I cleaned up the barn, but Jack had gone out somewhere. I put on some work clothes and went outside to see if the tractor still worked. I wanted Alikki in her stall while the tractor was out so I took a halter and lead rope out to the pasture. I couldn't see her, but she hadn't been in her stall either. It entered my mind that she might have gone into one of the other stalls, or that maybe she was lying down for a nap and I had missed her. Or maybe, I thought suddenly, she might have chosen this moment to have her foal. The idea made me feel like I was someone whose wife had gone into labor. I was about to run back and check the stalls again when I saw something that made me cry out in anguish.

A huge oak limb had crashed to the ground, taking with it both boards from a section of the back fence and leaving a gap large enough for an elephant to pass through. Alikki was gone. And in the far distance, I heard the pop pop pop of hunters' guns.

Chapter 13

I rushed through the gap in the fence still carrying the halter, but stopped about ten yards beyond the fence line. My mother had kept a path mowed out through the brush and into the forest for when she went trail riding, either alone or with Myra Van Hesse or some other riding buddy. I had gone with her, too, riding Facilitator while she rode Trifecta, Alikki's mother. Although the trail had not been mowed since Cindy's death, it was still easily discernable: the grass was high and there were a few weeds, but none of the brush or scrub oak or thick blackberry brambles that grew so thickly on either side had encroached.

The trail wound around a full-grown cedar and a few tall oaks until it came to a fifty-acre stand of pines planted in neat rows. The trail circled around the stand, but Cindy had also kept a path open through the center of the pines—that's the direction Facilitator and I had gone, and I remembered a cool, refreshing darkness with soft needles whispering beneath his hooves.

It's not hard to follow the trail of a 1400-pound animal; Alikki's hoofprints were embedded in the soft ground. I saw that she had turned, skirting the forest and continuing on the right-hand fork. I turned in that direction, too and called out: "Alikki! Come home, Alikki, come girl!" I heard no answering neigh, so I set out to follow her.

I had no idea how long she had been gone. If she had left just after the phone call from Paul Hughes, she had been gone about four hours. Then again, she might have left only minutes before I came looking for her. I could always hope.

The thought of Paul Hughes made me hurry my steps. Pauley was at large. If he was the one who had the penchant for killing animals in bloody ways—as I suspected he was—what would he do if he stumbled upon a very pregnant and relatively weak horse? I heard an occasional faraway shot, and the pops came from the direction I was headed. It's odd; even though I had almost gotten used to the constant shooting around Baghdad, it was now one of the most frightening sounds I could imagine. I walked quickly for another half hour—the pine stand on my left and thick, vegetative forest on my right— mentally thanking Cindy for keeping her trails so well mowed that they were easily traveled even after a year. But in time I came to the end of the pines and stopped for a breather. As I had known it did, the trail went left around the far side of the pines, as it circled back to the pasture, but I was surprised to find that it also turned right, through the thick forest. I looked for Alikki's hoofprints. There they were, to the right and into the forest. That made sense, since Alikki had probably been on these trails before with Cindy, perhaps many times, and knew what vegetation grew where. She may be looking for a particular nutrient— Cindy was convinced that Native American medicine men learned their wisdom by following horses into the woods. I wondered what Ossie Enemy Hunter would think of that. But I only took two steps before I stopped still, a chill finding its way up my backbone. This trail had been mowed recently; probably no more than a month ago. A very fresh manure pile told me that I was going in the right direction, but who had mowed the trail? As far as I knew, I had no neighbors for many miles in any direction. I hurried down the path for a while before I saw another of Alikki's hoofprints in a disturbance of sand that had probably been made by a rooting armadillo. I stopped. I looked again. They were hoofprints all right, but hooves with horseshoes, and Alikki had never worn shoes in her life.

I searched the ground frantically, wondering if I had been following the wrong trail all this time, but no; there was the track of a bare hoof just ahead, and I hurried after it. "Alikki!" I called. "Come, girl!" Sweat was dripping down my blouse and I had to wipe my forehead with the brim of my cap.

Although the trail made walking easy, the forest around me was getting thicker and darker. I called again and this time I heard a faint answering whinny. Alikki! I ran along the trail for a few more minutes until another gunshot halted me in my tracks. It was much closer than before; maybe only a few hundred yards. I walked slowly, breathing hard, until I saw that I was actually coming out of the forest. I heard more shots and carefully looked out from behind an enormous oak to confront what was probably the last thing I expected to see: a fenced-in compound of some kind, with fields, houses, shade trees, and bushes. I crouched down. I had come out at the very corner of the fence and the trail forked to follow both fence lines. The right-hand part of the trail was empty; on the left, grazing near the fence line, was Alikki. A few paces away was a gate made of heavy-gauge pipe and fastened with a chain and padlock.

The fence extended in both directions further than I could see. I peered closer into the compound. First, I saw acres and acres of pasture land. Past that I could make out tilled fields and buildings of some kind—a large house and half a dozen smaller buildings, but constructed in a style popular back in the days when most things were cobbled together from wood and tin by talented craftsmen. They were far enough away that I could make out no details other than they were shaded by an occasional oak and magnolia.

The gunfire had stopped. I walked slowly toward Alikki, not only because I didn't want to scare her, but because I was studying the compound. If I had been paying more attention to the ground, I wouldn't have stumbled over an old piece of lumber that someone had left there. I righted myself before I fell, but looked back at the offending board, which was just visible through the growth. Actually, there were a lot of boards, set into the ground in some kind of pattern, but the vegetation made it hard to discern. I bent down and tried to pick one up, but it was firmly embedded in the terrain. It looked and—when I touched it— felt, rough, old. Some of the boards were rotten, almost crumbly, but many were not. I saw a nail sticking from the end of one of the rotten boards and managed to pull it out easily. It might just have been the effect of the weather, but the shape of the nail was slightly different from nails I had seen and worked with before— sharper at the point and thinner at the head. I followed the pattern of the boards more closely and realized that, if they were up clear of the ground, they would resemble a deck, or maybe a wide bridge over a stream. The boards seemed to follow the line of fence that stretched out to my right. I looked behind me and saw that it continued out into the forest, although it was almost impossible to see more than a glimpse or two in the thick brush. Then I had it; it was a road. An ancient road made of boards.

A wooden road through a forest. Were the road and this compound connected? If so, the connection must have been in the distant past. As I peered inside I became aware of several figures, but they were so far in the distance that it was all I could do to make out that they were men and not women. At least one of them seemed to be carrying a rifle. The shots I heard came from the direction in which he was walking, but luckily, he was walking away from me, not toward me. I felt naked and vulnerable without my bow. It wasn't much against a rifle, but it was something, and I was careful to keep out of sight behind brush or trees as I made my way toward Alikki.

Alikki was grazing contentedly on grass near the fence line, but when I reached her side, her head came up and she began nuzzling my pockets. When she detected no sugar or carrot, she went back to grazing. I looked through to the other side of the fence—which was made up of heavy wood as well as a strand of hotwire—and I saw why she was so calm. A tall gray horse—the same one I had seen when I woke up in the woods and again at the cowboy-mounted shooting event—was standing close by, erect, in the posture of a guardian. Behind him, grazing unconcerned, were four other horses of different shades of brown and chestnut. As I approached, the gray horse's nostrils flared and his ears went back.

"Hey, Trigger," I said softly to the gray. "Is this your home?" I went close enough to the fence so he could sniff me and he visibly relaxed. His ears came back up and he nickered softly. He remembered me; knew that I was not someone he needed to fear. He watched without concern as I slipped the halter on Alikki.

I was scared of the men with guns. What were they doing here? What was this, this *place* doing here? How was Krista Torrington connected to all this? My solution was to get out of there quick and ask questions when my horse was back home. I led Alikki back the way I had come. After rounding the bend, though, I heard the hoofbeats of the other horses galloping away from the fence and toward the other side of the pasture. Alikki's head came up and she whirled around in the path. I held tight to the lead rope and said calming words until she relaxed. I was curious enough about what had spooked the other horses that I tied Alikki's lead rope to a branch and crept back to look through the fence from behind some shrubbery.

The horses had cantered toward two people who must have walked up by a path I hadn't noticed. They were close enough for me to see a short young woman with wild, strawberry-blonde hair carrying a feed bucket. Krista Torrington. The horses had not spooked after all; they were just running in for their dinner. As I watched, I saw Krista's companion—had she given Mark Patterson an invitation to visit?—turn in my direction. No, it wasn't Mark; in fact, the figure I saw couldn't have looked less like Mark and still been human. For, even at that distance and in shadows, I could make out sparse and scraggly black hair and a face so hideous that I thought at first I must be seeing the effects of light and shadow. The face had an unnatural shade of reddish brown—somewhat like Panhandle Slim's hair. It looked contorted, wrinkled, somehow, but not by age. I had seen enough burn victims in Baghdad to know that whoever the man was, he understood what fire could do to soft flesh.

I crept back from my hiding place and found Alikki restless, shaking the branch as she pulled against the lead rope. I quickly untied her, calmed her until her ears came back up, and began the dark walk home. I had found my horse again. She was safe.

The walk back was uneventful, but hot. Alikki walked

docilely and with a suppleness that told me that she was glad I was taking her home. She had seen other horses and she was happy; what she needed now was water. We did not see or hear anyone else on the trails. After I had put Aliki in her stall and fed and watered her, I went out to the gap in the fence and roped it off so she couldn't stray off again. I would have to shop for lumber before I could repair the fence properly.

As soon as I got inside the house, I switched on my iMac. I had new data but no idea what to do with it. What I wanted was to find information on the compound I had stumbled across and on the old wooden road that had almost been erased by the forest. The problem was, I didn't know what to search for. I didn't know the name of the compound nor the road, so I used general search questions. I typed in "wood road," and came up with zilch. I altered it a little, to "wooden roads," and had more success. In fact, in a very few minutes, I had the term I was looking for—one I should have guessed. What I had seen had been a plank road.

I turned from the computer and opened the history book I had gotten from Benny's. Because the book was a history of Jasper County as a whole, information about Pine Oak was limited, but it was interesting, and a lot of it concerned the Plank Festival. I searched the index under "plank road" and hit the jackpot. Under that listing there were sublistings such as "construction of," "cost of," and the like. Under "construction of," however, there was the sub-sublisting of "in Planktown." At the end of an hour of going between the computer and the book, I found out a lot of what I wanted to find, and most of it was a surprise.

As far as I could determine, a plank road was similar to a railroad track, but upside down. Wooden rails were set up on both sides of a level dirt road and parallel to it.

Across these were laid planks three or four inches thick, to form what might look today like a long deck. There were no ruts in a plank road and no mud. A six-day trip on a dirt road was cut to half a day on a well-maintained plank road. The first plank roads were built in 1844 in New York and Michigan and were so popular that they began a plank road craze that was to sweep across America for over two decades.

In 1830, Cecil Torrington, a settler from New Jersey, founded a small community in north Florida that he named after himself. Torrington existed mostly as a sleepy farming town until the plank road boom, when the population—suddenly wide-eyed—realized that they were living amid a vast wealth of oak and pine forests. Sawmills opened up, a railroad line was shunted in, and the small city was renamed Planktown. For twenty years, oak and pine logs were sent out on the rails, materials for hundreds of miles of plank roads, mostly in the north. It was during this heyday that the Plank Festival came into being—a citywide holiday that celebrated the area's wealth and importance in national transportation.

Unfortunately, after five or six years, the timber making up many of the plank roads began to warp or rot and had to be replaced. Maintenance on the roads soon became so expensive that the construction of new roads diminished and then died altogether. In 1875, with the dearth of new orders for roadbuilding timber, the town council voted to give the city its third name, and Pine Oak it has remained. Still, every year, on August 22nd, the city celebrates its rich past by holding the Plank Festival. Today, most of our harvested pines are trucked to another county, where they are pulped and used to make disposable diapers. Just thought I'd throw that in.

Yet the most interesting piece of information was

contained in a single paragraph in *The History of Jasper County*. It was the paragraph I read when I followed the last index reference under "plank road."

> *It is an irony that Planktown, which supplied great northern cities with materials for building hundreds of plank roads, had only one of its own, a five-mile stretch connecting the old Torrington homestead with the new railroad line. There is no record telling what the road's purpose was, although it can be assumed that it was used to haul timber over difficult terrain. The road, as well as the homestead, have been lost to the mysteries of time.*

What did that mean? That the location was lost? That the old homestead had burned down or was reclaimed by the forest? Well guess what, folks, I had found it, and I obviously wasn't the first.

Was Krista the descendent of Cecil Torrington? And could the compound be the original Torrington homesite? Who owned it now, I wondered; then I remembered the maps Gina had brought over. They, too, were the jackpot; Gina had done great.

When Jack returned about seven-thirty, I was hunched over the dining room table with the maps and a magic marker. He dropped off some groceries in the kitchen, then took his camera bag into his—into Cindy's—bedroom, where I heard him moving around for a few minutes. When he came back he started unpacking the grocery bags.

"Watcha got there?" he asked.

"I'm trying to get an idea of who owns the woods in back of the pasture here."

"Thinking of buying?" he asked.

"Who, me? No. Sorry, I'm a little distracted. You want me to talk you have to give me coffee."

Jack went to the coffeemaker and complied with my request, and in a few minutes he was sitting next to me at the table. Although I had vowed not to involve Jack in what I was doing, I began telling him the goat story. The truth is, I needed someone to talk to just then, and he was there. When I finished telling him about trips into the woods and what I had seen there, I began explaining what I was doing with the maps.

"The first map starts right here at the location of Meekins' Market. What I've been interested in is who owns the property in back of it—in other words who owns The Clearing; who owns the place where I shot the rattlesnake, and, more important, who owns what's further out? Those two people I saw walking out of the woods—where were they coming from?" I stopped and sipped from the cup of hot coffee and nodded toward the map. "As you can see, most of the parcels are pretty big: fifty acres at least. As I find out who owns each one, I'm outlining it with this marker and writing the owner's name on the map."

"Have you found anything interesting yet?" Jack asked.

"Lots. Look, Gina got *two* maps from the Property Appraiser's Office. One for in back of Meekins' Market and one for the neighborhood around my house."

"Yeah?"

"Well, the two intersect. See how one map fits right over the left side of the other?"

"What does that mean?" he asked.

"With the winding dirt roads and squirrelly trails, I didn't realize that I could walk out that path behind Meekins' Market and eventually get to my back door through the woods. It might take a lot of hours, and I'd have to take some twists and turns, but it could be done."

"So who owns all that land in back of you there?"

"I do."

"Not all of it?"

"Not all of it, no, but at least 400 acres, including 50 acres of pines. A lot more than I thought I owned. Well, actually, I didn't know I owned any—my mother bought most of it when she and my dad moved out here and she put the land in my name. But look here. Look back at this other part of the map. Clarence Meekins told me that he owned a few acres in back of the market. That was the first thing I found that was weird."

"Why was that weird?" Jack asked.

"He actually owns a thousand and six, so Clarence lied to me. And he lied to me again when he told me that the paper company owned some of the land out there. They don't. He also told me that a woman named Mae Barnes owned some property out that way. She doesn't; know why? Because Clarence Meekins bought it from her seven years ago."

"How do you know all this?" Jack asked.

"Gina got me a website for the Property Appraiser's Office. I call up a map of the county, pinpoint a certain area, then zoom in. Every single parcel of land in Jasper County is on that map, along with who owns it and who that person bought it from."

"Holy wow."

"Here's something else that's weird," I went on. See these next five or six parcels in back of the one Clarence owns? From the dates I found online, the parcels have been bought up slowly over the last hundred years by the same family.

"What family?"

"The same family that founded Pine Oak back in 1830. I mean, I never knew there were even any Torringtons left until I met Krista the other day."

"The girl with the gray horse?"

"Right. I think she's part of the original family."

"Why?"

"Because I saw her earlier today." I pointed to a place on the map that I had outlined with a large red rectangle. "Right here."

"You walked out in the woods today?" he asked.

"Alikki got out and I had to go find her." I summarized my trip, describing the compound, the plank road, the gunshots, Krista, and her scarred companion.

"So how does all this connect to the goat?" Jack asked.

"I have no idea in the world," I told him. "But, somehow, it does."

I had been working nonstop, with breaks only to feed and check on Alikki, whose teats were very distended and beginning to drip, so when Jack produced a glass of merlot while he cooked a spaghetti dinner, I was well content.

"Where have *you* been all day?" I asked him, moving my maps to the side and getting some dishes from the cupboard.

"Photo shoot," he replied. He was working with tomato sauce, sautéed chicken bites, green peppers, onions, and a few spices—all of which he must have bought when he was out.

"Photos of what?" I asked, amazed at his ability to take his work wherever he went, at his ability to *be* his work.

"I'll show you in a minute. Watch the sauce; it'll still take fifteen minutes or so. I have something cooking in the bathroom. I mean, the darkroom." He disappeared into his bedroom.

When he had been gone ten minutes, I went to the stove and finished the cooking. I had just put the food on plates when he came back in. He sat down and handed me a still-wet contact sheet with photographs of what looked to be a dozen teenage girls. Different hair styles, different outfits, different expressions, doing different things. "Who are . . ." I began, and then stopped. Different degrees of makeup. Different . . . One of the photos showed a girl dressed in a fashionable black gown, with black hair, dark black eyebrows, and bright red lipstick, in fact, the lipstick was the only color in the photo. It was Becky Colley as she had never seen herself before. "Jack, this is extraordinary!" I said. I looked closer. Different outfits, different hair styles, different locations, different everything but subject. *All* the pictures were of Becky Colley. And every one of them showed a different side of the confused girl.

"She called my cell," he explained.

"Where did you take these?" I asked.

"Either in her house or on the grounds outside. Some of the outfits she had in her closet, some were her mother's, some we went out and bought."

"You were alone with a sixteen year old in an empty house?"

"Nah, her mother was with us most of the time. Rebecca talked her into letting me do the shoot. Is she sixteen?"

"I don't know how old she is. I don't see any nudes here, though, so I guess it's all right."

"You know I don't do those kinds of pictures," he said. "I saw her naked, though, because she changed clothes in front of me when her mother was on the phone in the kitchen."

"You let her?" I exclaimed. "Jack, don't you know what kind of trouble—"

"Don't worry about it, Sue-Ann," he interrupted. "I think it meant a lot to her to have me see her naked. I told her she looked great naked, but between you and me I thought she was a little on the skinny side."

The rest of the dinner was peaceful; I mean, if things can be peaceful on the outside while my mind was humming like a gyroscope. We ate, drank wine, and puzzled together over the maps. We did the dishes, and when they were put away, Jack was content to go back to his Zane Grey book while I went back to work.

As soon as I sat back down at my desk, I found an email from Panhandle Slim. The petite cowboy sent me not only a brief bio on the eventual winners of the cowboy-mounted shooting event, but the entire list of the competitors, presumably so that I could see how many classes there were and how many competitors were in each. Or maybe he was expecting *The Courier* to print the whole list. Dream on. I pulled up the background piece I had written earlier, and spent a half hour plugging in details about the winners. I saved the file and emailed a copy to Cal at *The Courier*. I was printing out a copy of the finished story for my records, when Jack walked into the room in his boxer shorts and t-shirt holding another photo.

This was a finished color glossy that showed Krista riding bust-ass for leather at the mounted shooting event. She was racing toward the camera, pigtails flying, leaning toward the row of balloons with an expression of delicious freedom. It was a photo that captured not only her delight, but showed the exact moment her pistol went off, a shower of hot powder grains spewing from the barrel toward an exploding balloon a few feet away. "I printed this up for that girl we met," he said. "Maybe her boyfriend can give it to her."

It was a wonderful photo and I considered asking Jack to make a copy for me. Problem was, if I had copies of every one of Jack's photos that I wanted, I'd have to empty my archery stuff out of the barn to make room for them.

"I'll give it to her myself," I told him.

"You're planning on seeing her again?"

"Oh, yes."

Jack seemed satisfied with that answer and went off to bed. It had been a long day and I was tired, but before I could shut the computer down I heard another ding telling me I had email. I clicked on it and was surprised to see what looked like a moving valentine—a throbbing heart—in the middle of the screen. No words, just the heart. I looked at the sender window.

It said ginette@thecourier.com.

I smiled.

Chapter 14

One of my favorite books is *Traditional Archery,* written by a stickbow lover named Sam Fadala. I took a copy with me to the hospital on Monday morning in case I had to wait a few minutes before getting my stitches taken out. Although it is a beginning book for recurve or longbow shooters, I enjoy going back through it every year or so to confirm some of my ideas or habits. It contains a little history, a bit of practical lore, and many enjoyable suggestions. This is the book that introduced me to stump-shooting, for instance. What it avoids are the technologically advanced target bows that are used in the Olympics and most national championships. And for good reason. Olympic bows, with their long adjustable carbon stabilizers, counter balancers with weights for precision tuning, clickers, doinkers, plunger buttons, mechanical arrow rests, double-click target sights, and unbreakable carbon limbs, are to recurves what robots are to humans. Whenever I shot one, I felt like a cyborg—and looked like one.

But shot them I did, spurred on by my old mentor Crookneck Smith. When Crookneck had won the world championship back in the 1970s, they didn't have all this folderol, but he had kept up with the newest innovations and encouraged me to upgrade.

"If you weren't good enough," he told me, "I wouldn't say anything."

And that was kind of nice. Crookneck had long ago

had to hock his championship bows for food and booze, but the archery store—which just managed to pay its own way—let him keep his hand in. As I mentioned earlier, he once shamed me by mentioning that my equipment was not of the highest quality. I suppose that's one of the reasons I sold my Martin Mamba and bought a Hoyt Axis with its machined and forged metal riser.

But the higher the technology the closer we come to perfection, and when I shot my first perfect end at 30 meters and later broke 600 in a 72-arrow final at 70 meters, I felt like I had when I had shot Crookneck Smith's souped-up compound half a dozen years before in his ratty little archery shop outside Huckleberry Spring, North Carolina. I began to feel less human and more robotic and, after my sojourn in Sydney for the 2000 Olympics, I sold my target monstrosities and began relearning how to shoot naturally. With my wooden bows I could strive to get better throughout my life, knowing that whatever I achieved, I did it with steady hands, keen eyesight, and firm instinct.

"Doctor Morris will see you now."

I looked up from my book with a start, then got up and followed the nurse into a small examining room. Dr. Morris, brown hair disheveled as much in the morning as in the evening, stood waiting, holding his ever-present clipboard in both hands and his well-chewed pencil in his mouth.

"Mmm, mmmmph," I said, as I entered.

He took the pencil from his mouth, grinned at me, and asked me to have a seat.

It was a fun visit. He took out the stitches from my scalp, made some silly comment about my gorgeous, silky, long, dark tresses, and proceeded to ask me about how my medication was working out. I was feeling better, getting stronger, and had decided to go with the radioactive iodine treatment option. I told him I'd have to wait at least a month because of Alikki's foal, which was going to be born any day and who I wanted to imprint without fear of giving it radiation poisoning. This was all cool with Dr. Morris; in fact, it would give him more time to study the effects of the initial drugs. Then, when he had replaced the small patch on my scalp, he looked at his watch.

"I've been here since five a.m.," he told me, "and I haven't had anything to eat. Come on down to the cafeteria and I'll buy you a coffee."

"Coffee?" I answered. "How could I say no to that?"

The cafeteria had only a few tables and was kind of dingy, but I got a coffee, a yogurt, and a banana. Dr. Morris had a breakfast that looked like it came out of a frozen package, but he seemed satisfied. He looked at the book I had put on the table on top of my purse.

"What's traditional archery?" he asked.

"Shooting with wooden bows," I answered.

"Aren't all bows wooden?"

"They should be."

"You shoot?"

"Some," I said. I really didn't want to be long winded so I deflected the question by asking, "Did you know that archery is the national sport of Bhutan?"

"Where's Bhutan?" he asked.

"Near Nepal," I told him.

"Ah," he nodded. "Well, everyone should have a sport, but why did I get the impression that you were a soccer player?"

"Through an over-vivid imagination," I smiled. "Although I did eat at the same table with Mia Hamm once."

"Really?" he asked. "Where was that?"

"Long story that I don't really want to get into right now. But, I mean, we weren't friends or anything."

Dr. Morris concentrated on the last of his food, then looked up. "Ever play golf?" he asked.

"Nope. That's a sport I missed out on. Isn't it kind of boring, though?"

"I guess it is for people who don't play," he admitted. "But hey, look who's talking."

I laughed. "Point for you," I told him. "But if you think archery is boring, you should watch my other sport."

"Other sport?"

"Dressage." It wasn't an outright lie; after all, I *had* taken dressage lessons, although only a handful. What was slightly disconcerting was the thought that I had subconsciously made the decision to start riding again—to actually start getting serious about dressage.

"You've got me there," he said. "Is it the national sport of Nepal?"

"It's kind of like horse ballet," I told him. "My mother used to say that watching dressage was about as exciting as watching hair grow. I won't be riding for a while, though. Why are you smiling? Do I have banana on my face?"

"No. You're a careful eater. I was thinking of something that happened at the golf course on Sunday. Something not so boring."

"Tell me about it."

"Okay, you know what a driving range is?"

I nodded. "It's a practice area, right? It's got yardage markers."

"Exactly. At the Jasper County Country Club, the practice range is right near the second tee. On Sunday morning I was carrying a bucket of balls out to the range. There was a foursome on the tee and eight or nine players hitting balls at the driving range. The guy next to me was an incredible golfer—beautiful swing, great follow-through, and he was hitting a one iron, something that most people don't even own. He was hitting long, low line drives. One of the guys on the second tee was just addressing his ball when this guy next to me smacks one right into the center of the 150-yard marker, and all of a sudden, *bong*! It sounded like the Chinese army was being called into battle. The guy on the second tee must have jumped three feet in the air and missed his tee shot completely."

"Bong?" I said. Something about Dr. Morris' story sounded familiar.

He started laughing. "The country club had just replaced the old wooden markers with Chinese gongs. What a sound."

"Gongs," I repeated.

"Boy, was that guy on the tee pissed off. But the number of people using the driving range has quadrupled in the last week. They even have a new slogan: 'Are you good enough to ring the gong.'"

I was amazed. Benny had told me about those gongs; they were his invention. Benny had actually sold one of his inventions, or more likely, he had told someone about it and *they* had sold it. I had a lot more respect for the little guy. I was going to mention this to Dr. Morris when his beeper went off. He glanced at it, then told me, "Gotta go. Ambulance just came in with an emergency."

"Thanks for breakfast," I shouted at his retreating figure. "Or lunch."

"My pleasure," he shouted back.

I gathered up my purse and book and made for the exit, where I almost got knocked down by a red-headed man about twice my size. As I looked after him, thinking of telling him about himself, a man that could have been his twin sent me spinning in the opposite direction.

"I'm not a dreidel!" I shouted after him.

"Surprisingly, the second man stopped, turned, and asked in a puzzled voice, "What's a dreidel? Oh, hey there Sue-Ann."

I suddenly recognized the man as one of Donny's half brothers. "Chad? What's going on? Is someone hurt? Has something happened to Donny?"

"Naw, Donny's okay. It's Pop. Tractor tire blew while he was trying to drive it out of a ditch and it fell over sideways, pinned him down. It was all Tad and I could do to lift it up and get him out. Broke his arm, maybe some ribs, too." He looked around and saw that his brother was talking to someone at the main desk. "I want to help, but I guess there's nothin I can do."

"Just let the doctor do his work," I told him. "Come over here and sit down."

Reluctantly, the big man trundled over to a bank of maroon chairs and couches set in a rough rectangle, and parked his bulk on one of the couches. I sat nearby in a matching chair. "I'm sure your father's going to be all right," I told him. "He's too tough an old bird to be hurt bad."

Chad smiled wanly, then said, "You didn't have to pull him out from under that tractor. And darn it, I told him those tires were shot and not fit to drive on."

At that point, Tad Brassfield joined his brother on the couch, and even though they sat at the ends, they filled it. Both stand over six feet but look bigger because they each weigh over 300 pounds. Because of their weight, both wear overalls most of the time. Their tee shirts bulged in front and showed the dirt and sweat of having to dig their father out from under his machine. Tad is older and slightly taller; Chad weighs more and has a beard to go with his unruly red hair.

Tad nodded at me. "What are you doin here, Sue-Ann?" he asked.

"Fell and hit my head a while back," I told him. "Got the stitches out today. Did you get your dad checked in okay?"

"I guess."

"I'm sure he'll be fine."

"I guess." Tad sat for a while, then looked up at me. "You probably know that none of us have any reason to like the old man much." I kept silent and let him continue. "But seein him lyin there, tryin to breathe, lookin up at me to help . . ." He shook his head. "And at the end of it, if he gets well and comes home, it'll be the same all over again. He'll probably even blame us for not gettin him out soon enough." He stopped, gathering his words together in his head. "Sue-Ann, Chad and I, we don't think much, don't have the time, but I've been wonderin the whole time we were drivin over here, what if he dies? What are we goin to do if he dies?"

"You're grown men, Tad," I told him. "You know the farm like the back of your hand. You'll both be fine. Anyway, Ed's not going to die."

From his corner, Chad spoke up for the first time since Tad had sat down. "We can't let it be the same," he said simply.

"What are you sayin?" his brother asked.

"I don't know. We need to get Donny."

"Need to get him for what?" asked Tad.

"We need to get him," Chad insisted.

"I'll call him," I said.

"That's not what I mean," said Chad. "But yeah, I guess we should call him."

Donny was working a wreck on the other side of the county, but he said he'd get to the hospital when he got free. I sat with the brothers for another hour. We didn't talk much, but I got the idea that this was a changing point—that they dimly realized that from that day forward, their lives were to be different in some way. It scared them and excited them at the same time. They reminded me of draft horses—used to pulling plows and wagons—who were suddenly faced with being saddled. When Donny came in, looking both pissed and worried, I got up and went to him. I nodded my head toward Chad and Tad, "They need you," I told him. "I'll call you later." Then I got in my truck and drove toward Pine Oak. I had my maps on the front seat and I was on my way to *The Courier* offices to show Gina what I had found.

I felt no sympathy for Ed Brassfield, but couldn't help feeling sorry for Tad and Chad, who were both suffering. Well, if their father died they would be free. That's pretty blunt, pretty harsh, but true, and, although I tried to keep it deep in the back of my mind where it belonged, I wondered if my father had felt the same way when Cindy died.

To get my mind off the situation, I turned on the truck's radio, set as always to the pirate station. I heard a few songs without paying much attention. Then my back went up as I heard the scratchy, whiny voice of The Creeper waffle up out of the speakers, sounding like fingernails on a saw. I turned up the volume.

"Lot of people think they find supernatural beings in a church; or maybe they think they conjure up demons with black cats and bones. One or two think they have angels on their shoulders, yas, but all these people are wiggy like mice. You ask me where there are demons and I say they are in the swamps and the forests. You ask me where there are spirits and I tell you that there are spirits in the trees.

"Don't you fools go near the old dead oaks in the woods. They

are the darkest; they hold the fiercest and oldest spirits of highwaymen and thieves; their bare branches are weapons. Some of them got hung in those branches. No, the dark trees you don't want to mess with. The trees don't got eyes, but they see you just the same.

"Sometimes spirits can call up snakes to come out and eat you; sometimes demons ride white horses through the trees.

"Magnolia trees hold the spirits of all little girls that died on their way to church, yas. The flowers the same color as their little dresses.

"Cypress, now, they got lots of different spirits, but some of the spirits be sailors and slaves who died a hundred and fifty years ago. Know how they died? Demons got em.

"You don't know this, but I do: some weeds and shrubs got demons, too. Little demons, like bugs or chickens. Feel that thistle? That's chickens pecking at you; that's no-see-ums getting their chow down.

"And those long rows of pines on your neighbor's land? You see em? Yas, those pines have grabbed the spirits of dead soldiers so you can be safe when you walk through them. You can rest. You can lean on them. Those soldiers, they can rest now, too.

Some say that when we die we come back as something else—a cow, a pig, a roach. But maybe we come back as mango trees.

"And if my spirit is in a mango tree, maybe people, maybe birds, come to feed off me and I will be satisfied, I will provide."

Well, that was even stranger than usual, vaguely depressing but uplifting at the same time. And complicated and maddening. What did he know about snake spirits, stands of pines? Not for the first time, I felt that The Creeper could somehow reach out over the airwaves and read minds, see things that he shouldn't be able to see. Yet he had enough of the Delphic Oracle in him that I could never find anything concrete that would help to identify him or pin anything on him as precise as a prediction.

Gina's PT Cruiser was not in the parking lot, but I went in anyway. Betty was sitting in Gina's desk, talking on the phone, but she hung up when I entered.

"Hey, Betty," I said. "Is Ginette out selling ads?"

"She's out all right, but out sick," she said.

"Did she say what was wrong?"

"No, just that she wasn't feeling well. Said she'd be in tomorrow."

"I'll check back tomorrow, then," I told her. Instead, I went across to the Piggly Wiggly and bought two cans of chicken noodle soup and drove across town to Gina's house.

I knocked at the door, but didn't get a response, although I heard the sound of Gina's guitar coming from a back room. I tried the door and it was open. I walked in, feeling pretty sure that I wasn't interrupting an intimate meeting. The music was coming from the left and I could see Gina sitting crosslegged on a mattress, bent over a guitar. It was a different guitar than I had seen the last time I had been here—long and sleek and colored in a golden-brown sunburst. And, although she was playing it left handed, the pick guard was positioned properly at the bottom. The song she was playing was not country this time; it was more of a chant. I heard:

> *You always were,*
> *you always are,*
> *and you always will be.*
> *You are everywhere,*
> *you are in everything.*

While she sang, I had the opportunity to look around the room. It was the simplest room I had ever seen: a king-size mattress was centered against the back wall, a nightstand held a clock and a lamp. There was a bare, but well-made dresser across from the bed, and on the wall a picture of an odd-looking old man with long hair and a hook nose. Doors led to a closet and bathroom, but both were closed. Gina herself was dressed in flannel pajamas and had her hair tied back in a ponytail.

Gina looked up and saw me, but her eyes were expressionless, as they had been the first time I had visited her. I saw that she was in a funk, so I tried to cheer her up. "Does nothing ever surprise you?" I asked. "I mean, what if I was a thief?"

"You are a thief," she said.

I was taken aback. "What have I taken?" I asked.

"You know what you've taken, Sue-Ann. You've taken over mah lahf. Ah caint go out of the house without thinkin that maybe ah'll catch a glimpse of you somewhere. Ah've put your number on my speed dial and have to slap mah own hand a hundred tahms a day to keep from callin you."

"I want you to call me," I told her.

"Whah? So you can screw around with mah mind?"

I swear to you that I had no intention of replying as I did; it just came out, like water from a faucet. "I love you," I said softly, and almost gasped at my own audacity. But Gina's reaction was even more unexpected. She jumped up from the bed and stomped barefooted into the living room where she found a pack of cigarettes and lit one. I was left standing in the middle of her bedroom and she glared at me through the open door.

"God damn it Sue-Ann," she cried. "Can't you see that you're scarin the shit outta me?"

"You don't want me to love you?"

"No! Yes. Ah don't fuckin know!" she shouted, tears rolling down her cheeks.

"I've never seen you cry before," I said.

"Fuck you, Sue-Ann. Just fuck you."

"That kiss in the woods that day didn't mean anything?"

"It meant *everythin*!" she wailed.

"Then why . . . what did you say?"

"Ah said it meant everythin. Everythin ah've ever wanted in mah whole lahf was in that kiss. But ah'm not you. Ah just can't jump into boilin water without wonderin how bad ah'm goin to get scalded."

"I won't burn you."

"Everyone that's ever meant more than shit to me has left me hangin."

"I won't leave you."

"How do ah know that?" She was calming down some. She wiped her eyes on the sleeve of her pajamas.

"You've got to trust me."

"Ah want to, ah do," she said, blowing smoke.

"Here. I brought us some chicken soup."

"Ah'm not really sick," Gina said. "Ah jist . . ."

"I can see that," I smiled. "But let's eat it anyway." I showed her the two cans of chicken noodle soup. "Just like mother used to make," I said.

"An granma, too," she smiled back at me.

Over the soup, which you should heat—contrary to the directions on the can—without adding any water, Gina started to brighten up. By the time I had recounted my adventure in rounding up Alikki, she was back to normal and wide eyed.

"Sue-Ann!" she cried. "What was that girl Krista doin way out there?"

"I expect she lives there," I said.

"And who was that awful-lookin man that was with her?"

"I don't know, but I'ma find out."

"How?"

"I need to show you on the maps," I said. I looked around for a place to spread them out. The dining room table was small and covered with soup bowls and stuff. I took the maps back into her bedroom and spread them out on the mattress.

"These are the same maps I got from the Property Appraiser's Office," Gina said.

"Right. But I've pasted them together to make one big map instead of two smaller ones so you can see how they intersect."

For the next hour I pointed out how the trail from Meekins' Market, if you followed it far enough, would almost have to dead end at the west side of Krista's Compound. The trail I had followed looking for Alikki came out at the south side. That meant that if I had followed the trail that had been mowed around The Compound fence, I would have struck the eastern trail. In other words, there was an actual, if serpentine, trail from Meekins' Market to my own back yard.

"Well, what are we goin to do next?" she asked.

"First I've got to make sure I'm right."

"How?" she asked.

"By following the trail to the end."

"To The Compound?"

"To The Compound."

Gina had gone to the head of the mattress and folded herself into her lotus posture. I was sprawled out at the foot and my eye caught the picture of the man on the wall.

"Who's that, I asked.

"Baba."

I thought I had misheard her. "Your papa?"

"No, silly. Baba. He was a spiritual leader. An avatar."

"What, Hindu?" I guessed

254

"Kahnd of a funny mix of Hindu and Sufi and Muslim."

"You're, like, into mystics?" I asked carefully.

"Naw, but Baba is kahnd of special to me."

"Why?"

"Ah don't know if ah kin explain it. . . did you know that Cal went to college in London for a year?"

"No, I didn't, but what—"

"It's somethin that was kinda lahk a crossroads for him. He made friends there, he did things he'd never done, he felt real free . . ."

"My father did that!" I remembered, "Except that he studied in Florence."

"And does he always say things lahk," she deepened her voice to a man's timber and said, 'Ah remember that back in Florence we were so pore that we had to eat the bark off the trees.'"

"Or, 'We rode a train for six days without getting off,'" I laughed.

"Raht," she smiled. "They compare everything they do now with what they did in London or Florence. Ah suspect that you'll always be thinkin about bein in Iraq."

"It will be hard to forget it," I admitted.

"Well, ah've never been out of the U S of A, but ah have memories jist lahk Cal has about London, except ah got mahn in Myrtle Beach, South Carolina."

"South Carolina?" I asked.

"Ah spent almost six months in Myrtle Beach," she said. "Didn't ya know?"

"Of course not. What were you doing in Myrtle Beach?" I asked.

"You're gonna laugh," she said.

"I won't."

"Ah was at the Meher Spiritual Center," she said.

"Mayor . . . ?"

"Baba," she said. "You really never heard of Meher Baba?"

"Vaguely, maybe. But back up, what were you doing in Myrtle Beach?"

"Okay, lookit," she began. "Back when ah got divorced from Jimmy, ah wanted to leave Pine Oak for awahle. Ah tried college for a couple of years, but it wasn't a success. So ah got in mah car and jist drove around the country. Ah visited mah parents in Texas for a few days, but when ah was supposed to come home, ah didn't. Ah wanted to see new things and didn't know if ah'd ever git another chance. Ah went up into Colorado and got a job workin horses for a whahl. When that ended, ah drove up through Chicago and went to Boston and New York for a few days. Ah walked around Washington, D. C., and ah stood on the banks of the Potomac River. It was all new and excitin and ah was lonely as ah could be. Ah lived in Nashville for a couple of months waitin tables and listenin to music til three in the a.m. Ah wanted to play, too, but ah wasn't near good enough and ah knew it. Ah still didn't want to come back home, but ah didn't have anything else ah wanted neither. Ah was livin out of mah car some of the tahm, tryin to save money, and ah was feelin real bad about mahself. Ah didn't feel ah had any future. There wasn't nothin ah was good at and everythin ah trahed went sourer than milk left out in the sun."

"What do you mean?" I asked. Listening to her story was fascinating, not because it was exciting or unique, but because it was so unexpected, so totally out of character from the Ginette Cartwright I had known most of my life.

"Come on, Sue-Ann," she answered. "Ah had jist got divorced, ah lost mah baby, mah professor boyfriend dumped me, ah flunked out of college, and ah couldn't play guitar no better'n a ropin horse. Things just weren't goin mah way."

"That's what I felt when I came back from Baghdad," I told her.

"Ah know," she said. "Wah do you think ah came over that first day? Ah could see mahself in every move you made."

"You . . . I can't believe that you . . ." I could hardly speak. I changed the subject abruptly. "So what about this Baba?" I asked.

"One day ah was drivin from Ah-Donno to Who-Knows-Where, havin lunch in a diner in Myrtle Beach and ah saw a flyer on the door. It said somethin lahk 'Lost? Come and fahnd yourself.' Ah know it was silly, but it gave an address and a tahm for later that evenin and there was a picture of a really strange little man with a big nose and mustache and underneath that there was a slogan that said, 'Don't Worry, Be Happy.' An ah decided ah wanted to be happy." Gina stopped and lit a cigarette. My own craving was strong, but maybe not as strong as it had been a few days before, and I was able to hold off asking her for one.

"You know anything about eastern religions?" she asked.

"Well, I'm kind of an expert on Islam right now."

"Sorry, ah wasn't thinkin."

"And I know that most people in Bhutan are Tibetan Buddhists," I added lamely.

"Where's Bhutan?" she asked.

"Never mind. Tell me about Baba."

"Course ah never met the man," she said, blowing smoke at the ceiling. "He dahd before ah was born. But he wasn't part of any major religion; he just took what he wanted from Hinduism and Sufiism and some of the others and made a philosophy out of em. He made things seem simple and easy. He didn't want us to do any rituals or anything lahk that, but some of us lahk to keep a picture of him around to look at an to remember."

"I guess I can understand that," I said.

"He was just a lil ole man who thought he was special. He thought he was so special that he was god. And a lot of other people thought so too—still think so. Can you imagine being special enough to someone that they actually think that you're god? I keep that picture near me so that ah'll remember that anybody can be special if they trah hard enough." She took a hit of her cigarette and continued, "He lahked music, too, and some of us would go down to the beach at naht and play our instruments and sing some of his poems that we'd put music to. Ah was playin one when you walked in. An that's where ah got mah Gretsch. Bought it off a guy that was givin away all his worldly goods. He gave me a good deal because it was custom made for a lefty."

"Where did you learn to play?" I asked.

"Mah daddy played some and ah got it off him, but Myrtle Beach is where I really learned my chops."

I rolled up my maps and stood up. "I have to go feed Alikki," I said. "And there's still some things I need to get settled with Jack. He's leaving on Wednesday."

"He's not goin to take mah picture?" she asked.

"Next time," I said, and walked toward the door.

Sue-Ann?" her voice made me turn my head.

"Umm?"

"You really love me?"

If ever there was a time when I blushed, that was it. If there was a place I could have hidden my face, I would have hidden it. "God," I managed. "I can't believe I really said that to you."

"You *really* love me?" she persisted, but this time it was

as if the words had finally sunk in, and there was wonder in her voice.

I only nodded. "I'll see you," I said.

"Call me every day or ah'll kill you," she said.

Chapter 15

That night I lay awake again, but this time it was a pleasant wakefulness. Never in my life had I entertained feelings for another woman. But unless my thyroid was turning my mind inside out, the feelings I had for Gina were not only real, but more powerful and more calming than I had ever had for anyone else. It was all so new and strange that I felt like I was fifteen again. Had I known that I loved her before I actually said it? The thought gave me a chill.

I don't know if I dreamed of Gina when I finally fell asleep, but let's say I did, and when I woke up just after dawn, I was happy and refreshed.

I walked into the kitchen in a short nightgown and turned on the coffeemaker. Kitty Amin walked between my legs and out his cat door and I thought I heard a low whicker from outside. I opened the door and in the half darkness I saw Alikki standing in the barnyard, a long rope of placenta trailing from her birth cavity, watching a tiny horse taking wobbly steps toward her. Forgetting the coffee, I ran outside almost as naked as the foal. I slowed my approach almost to a tiptoe and reached them just as the baby was rooting around for a teat. I heard slurping and gulping. I petted and cooed over Alikki, then, with hesitation, put my hand on the foal, which looked to be totally black. She was a filly and she was still wet. As I touched her, she turned her head and looked at me curiously, then went back to nursing.

I ran into the house for towels and iodine and carrots, then looked into Cindy's room and screamed, "Jack. I have a baby horse! Get up! Get your camera! Quick!" Without waiting to do more than see Jack open his eyes and grunt, I grabbed what I had been wearing the day before and ran back outside. The foal was still nursing. Being as gentle as I could be, I swathed the baby's navel stump with iodine. As I was getting into my clothes, the foal pulled away from mama and faced me. I was captivated and moved closer. I looked into her eyes and breathed into her nostrils. After a while I moved around her so that I could contain her in my arms, one arm around her rump and the other across her neck. I spoke many words to her so that she would get used to my voice. I traced my hand down each perfect leg and cupped her fluffy little tail.

I fed Alikki half a carrot, and she crunched it with the satisfaction of a horse that has done a pretty fine morning's work. I could tell she was proud of her little girl and I was proud of her. I had only had her a few days, but already she had settled down into her new life with me and she was getting more comfortable and healthier each day. Her hide was growing new hair where the raw places had been. I could even see where her bones were gradually receding into her flesh, rewarded by access to real feed, pasture, and exercise. Kitty Amin was perched on the stall door, watching what was going on with interest. When Jack came out with his camera, my face was resting on the neck of the baby and Alikki's face was resting on my shoulder. No picture that Jack ever takes will be worth more.

She was a beautiful little filly and I decided then and there to call her Enemy Hunter; little Emmy. After all, an A-line Hanovarian mare crossed with an offspring of Billie Gay Bar was an unbeatable combination. I hoped that if I ever saw her namesake again that he would approve.

Emmy was getting curious and began walking around the barnyard, followed closely by her mama, still trailing her afterbirth. The vet had warned me about this and told me what to do, so I caught up to her and, with effort, tied the placenta in a knot so that it wouldn't drag in the dirt. After a while, Emmy had enough of baby steps and now began a long-legged canter around the barnyard, followed again by Alikki, who whickered softly once or twice. Jack was snapping away and I just sat back and watched this new part of my life as she scampered and gamboled. I could hardly believe it—she was less than two hours old and she was already cantering like a Grand Prix winner.

After fifteen minutes or so, the placenta disengaged from Alikki. I knew it should be examined for completeness—any afterbirth that stayed inside her could cause serious infection—but I had never examined a placenta for completeness before. Only then did I think of calling the vet, and I rushed inside and dialed his number. When he answered, I found I couldn't speak fast enough and I began throwing out armfuls of words at once. He stopped me by asking, "Who is this?"

"Sorry," I said. "I'm a little excited. This is Sue-Ann McKeown on Pine Basin Road. You came out last week to check on my mare."

"Oh, right. So I guess she had her foal."

"A couple of hours ago. Can you come out and take a look at them? I would have called you last night if I had known it was going to happen."

"Horses have been giving birth by themselves for

thousands of years."

"I know," I said. "But this is *my* horse."

"I'll be out in an hour or two, but from that jumble of information you gave me at first, it sounds like mother and daughter are doing fine."

"Should she be running around the barnyard like she is? Should I put her in a stall?"

"Let her run around."

"I saved the placenta," I told him.

"I'll see you in a while," he told me.

As soon as he hung up, I called Gina at the office.

"Pahn Oak Courier, Ginette Cartwraht speakin'."

"Gina," I told her excitedly, "Alikki had her foal this morning. We have a baby horse!"

"Already? Wowie zowie. Ah cain't wait to see—it's a filly?"

"How did you know?"

"Ah jist knew. Ah cain't wait to see her. Did you give her a name yet?"

"Enemy Hunter. It's a long story. I call her Emmy."

"It's a nahce name, honey," she told me. "Weird but nahce. Ah'll try to come out about lunch tahm."

The vet came and went before Gina arrived. Emmy had gotten a clean bill of health and Alikki was much better than she had been the first time he had seen her. He went ahead and gave her West Nile vaccine and took blood for a Coggins test. He also took a check for a couple hundred dollars that I hoped wouldn't bounce. Jack had gone out to buy a few things he needed for his trip.

Gina seemed preoccupied when she arrived, but she brightened up when she saw Emmy. "Little Enemy Hunter," she said. I showed Gina how to imprint herself on the filly, petting her, looking her in the eyes, breathing her breath, containing her, letting the filly sniff her. I brought soft drinks outside where we sat in lawn chairs and watched Alikki munch hay while Emmy zonked out at her feet.

"I can't believe that all these good things are happening to me," I told her.

Gina took my hand and held it. "In three or four years, mebbe we can take these two out on a trail together," she said.

"I can show you the plank road," I told her.

"The what?"

"Oh my god, I forgot to tell you about the plank road last night. You remember Cal asking me to write up something about the Plank Festival?"

"Um hmm. But that's a ways off yet, ain't it?"

"A ways, but I wanted to get a head start on it so I did some research."

I briefly described the mention of a plank road in *The History of Jasper County*, then I told her about my actually finding part of the road near The Compound. "Here's something else I forgot to mention," I continued,. "Pine Oak used to be called Torrington."

"Ah never heard that."

"The town was founded by a guy named Cecil Torrington in 1830."

"The same last name as Krista," Gina said.

"Right, and according to the information I got online, The Compound is owned by somebody named Ashley Torrington."

"Descendents of the original settlers?" she asked.

"It seems likely."

"Think Krista has anything to do with the goat?"

"No," I answered, then reflected. "I don't know. Damn it, Gina, I'm this close to figuring it all out, but it seems that everything new I learn complicates things

Iza Moreau

more." I brushed a few strands of hay off my shirt.

"Do you know that Pauley Hughes has disappeared?" I asked her.

"Cal told me. Sue-Ann, ah think that boy's twisted a couple a turns too taht."

"I think so too," I said.

Gina brightened up suddenly. "But guess what?" she began. "Goth Girl's not Goth Girl any more."

"What do you mean?"

"I saw her."

"Where?"

"Well, um, Cal came over after you left yesterday and we talked some. Then we went over to Ray Colley's for a few minutes—he wanted to show Cal his new driver. While we were there, Becky came out of her room dressed like a normal teenager."

"She's in love," I told her.

"With who?"

"With Jack."

"You don't mean *your* Jack? Ah mean the Jack that's stayin here?"

"Well, yeah, that Jack. But Jack has made her love herself, too. He went over to her house and took some pictures yesterday. *She* called *him*. They went through every outfit she had and then went out and bought more. The pictures are great. She has a dozen different ways to be Becky; she doesn't need to be Goth Girl and hang around losers."

"Anyway, Ray said it was just about the shock of his lahf. Becky wants him to take her shopping for cameras."

"Cameras?" I said. "Well, I guess Jack's not the worst person in the world to emulate." But it was hard for me to think about Becky Colley. All I could think about was that Cal had gone over to Gina's after I left. That they had

264

talked some.

"You think Pauley's out there in those woods?" Gina asked.

"I don't know. Maybe. I'll take a bow when I go out there."

"You'll take *me* when you go out there. And maybe ah'll take a bow, too. When are you going to go?"

"I don't know. Soon. I'll let you know."

We quieted down for a few seconds and could hear the rapid breathing of the filly, the munching of hay by her mother.

"I need to tell you about her name," I began. I took a breath and continued. "When I was in Baghdad I met this marine lieutenant from Montana. He's a Crow Indian named Oscar Enemy Hunter. I only knew him for twenty-four hours, but in a way he made me look past all the bureaucratic bullshit that was going on, all the fighting and killing and well drilling. He joined the cavalry so he could be near horses. And when he got to Baghdad he gravitated to the Iraqi horses—fabulous Arabians with thousands of years of breeding. He made me see that some things are universal, some kinds of love and respect, and I wanted to honor him by giving our horse his name. She's the Enemy Hunter, and the enemies are hate and distrust and greed and prejudice. And chaos. The day I spent with Ossie Enemy Hunter was my last day in Iraq. I never saw him again or heard from him. Maybe someday you and I can go up to Montana to the Crow Fair that he told me about, where the whole tribe gets together to celebrate like we celebrate the Plank Festival."

We were silent for a while, gazing out over the forest. The pines looked like giant arrows and the sky was target blue. In the paddock, Alikki still kept watch over her sleepy foal, Gina stroked my hand, and all seemed right with the world.

"Sue-Ann," Gina said at last.

"Hmm?"

"Cal asked me to marry him," she said. It was pretty much a mood breaker and I pulled my hand away.

"I slept with Jack last night," I lied stupidly. "What did you tell him?"

"Ah said ah'd think about it," she said. "Whah did you sleep with him?"

"I don't know. I was drunk. "What do you mean you'd think about it? Why didn't you just say yes?"

"You know whah," she began, but I cut her off.

"And damn it, Gina, if you want me to smoke you have to give me cigarettes."

"What?"

"Give me a goddam fucking cigarette!"

We were both smoking like trains before I finally spoke again. "Are you pregnant?"

"That's a nasty question, Sue-Ann," Gina said carefully. "Ah caint get mad because if ah were you, ahd've ast the same thing. But the answer's no, ah'm not."

"Do you love Cal?" Gina didn't answer. "Do you?" I repeated.

"Not as much as ah love you," she said softly.

I jumped up from my chair with half a thought of practicing my archery, or maybe taking a walk in the woods. Instead, I turned around to look at her. She was sitting kind of slumped in her lawn chair, holding her cigarette tightly. I blinked. "You love me?" I asked blankly.

Gina nodded. "Ah do."

"And you're going to marry Cal?"

"Ah didn't say that. Ah said that he'd ast me."

I sat back down beside her but purposefully looked away into the distance. I took up her pack of cigarettes and lit another for myself without offering one to her.

"Sue-Ann," she began. "We're both girls. How could we make it work? What if someone found out? You know how the news travels."

I nodded. "You're right. What's the point of taking that kind of chance? You should do it. He's the best man in Pine Oak and you're the best woman. You're natural together. You'll have nice kids. You'll be great on the PTA board." My voice was rising, but I couldn't control it. "You can buy a station wagon and be a soccer mom. You can—"

"Maybe ah should jist go." Gina stood up. I stood up and faced her.

"Maybe you should. Maybe you should never have come over in the first place. I should have just told you to get the hell out like I'm doing now or kicked your ass like I should have done in high school. Go on home to your fuckboy and have a good screw—and whah don't you take your "hosses" with you? Here's a heads up: better keep lookin over that pale whaht shoulder of yours because now that ah'm not sick, stealin Cal away from your skinny butt will be easier'n pickin a ripe peach from a low branch."

Gina stepped forward until our faces were only inches apart. She had dropped her cigarette and both hands were fists. Mine were, too. "Bring it on, bitch," she began. She stopped and I saw her face working, her eyes searching for something inside herself. Her mouth twitched and turned until it finally twisted itself into a smile. "Fuckboy?" she asked.

I couldn't help myself; I smiled at my own ridiculousness. Within seconds we both were laughing so hard tears came. Then we were just crying and holding onto each other, our faces buried in each other's necks.

In the paddock, Emmy had gotten up from her nap,

taken a few sucks of milk, and started cantering to and fro. She ran up to the two of us and stared, then ran away again, squealing. To her, and to the rest of the world, nothing had happened.

"Think about what you want to do and do it," I told her at last.

"It's not somethin ah'm goin to rush into," she said. "See you around?"

"If you don't call me every day, I'll kill you," I said.

Gina had told me that she loved me. It was something I had been hoping to hear more then anything else, but when she walked out of the paddock, I thought she was walking out of my life.

For the rest of the day, I went around the house numb. I cleaned up some, read a chapter of the horse mystery, and tried to work up my research into an article on the Plank Festival. I longed for some diversion, but Jack was still out, and the pirate radio station was off the air.

I called Donny at his apartment and Linda C answered the phone.

"Hello."

"Hey, um, Linda C, is Donny there?"

"Who's this?"

"Sue-Ann. Sue-Ann McKeown. Is he there? I want to ask him about his dad. I was at the hospital yesterday when they brought him in."

"Oh. Okay, I'll get him."

"I don't want to bother y'all."

"No. I'll get him."

Well, that was awkward, I thought as I listened to a clunk and then dead air. I had not spoken to Linda C since she and Donny had become attached. I hadn't expected her to be at Donny's; I knew that her own house was much larger and more comfortable, and the last thing I wanted was for her to think that I was—

"Hello? Sue-Ann?"

"Donny, hi. I wanted to find out about Ed."

"Yeah, well. He's busted up pretty bad. He'll recover, all right, but he won't be strong. One of his arms will be almost useless and his lungs were damaged by some broken ribs."

"I'm sorry," I said. "How are Chad and Tad?"

I heard Donny light a cigarette and blow smoke. "For a while, I thought they were worse off than Ed. It was like, if he died, they wouldn't know which overalls to put on in the morning."

"When I was at the hospital, Chad said something about wanting you for—"

"They want me to come back to the farm," he said.

"They've asked you to do that before," I said, reminded of our first meeting.

"They want me to come back to the farm and run it," he said.

"But what about Ed?" I asked.

"Chad and Tad are pretty dim most of the time," Donny said. "But they finally figured out that Ed has run the farm just about as far into the ground as it can go. They're going to talk to Ed and make him give me his power of attorney. In the next couple of days the three of us are going to sit down and go through Ed's bank accounts and farm papers. Chad and Tad aren't like me; they don't know nothing except the farm. If it had to be sold for taxes or something, they wouldn't be able to find jobs."

"Is it as bad as that?" I asked.

"You mean are we gonna lose the fram? I don't think so. Once we've figure out where we stand financially, we're going to go to the bank and see if we can get a loan for some new farm equipment."

"You mean you're going to do it?" I asked.

"I'll try it for a while, I guess," he said. "But I'll still have to keep my job at Harrison's part time."

"That's great, Donny. I'm really happy for you. I was driving by the farm the other day and thought what a really nice place it could be with a little work. Well, with a lot of work."

"That's one thing Chad and Tad don't mind," he said. "I guess my job will be to make sure that what they're doin is useful instead of crazy. If we're lucky, maybe the bank will lend us enough to buy a new John Deere with some mower and bailer attachments. We're going to stop growing corn and go into the hay business."

I let him talk for a few more minutes about his plans, listening to him as he made them, really. Then I said, "I have two horses now. I'll be your first customer."

"They must be paying you more than I thought at *The Courier*," he said.

"It's a long story, but look Donny, did you follow up on what I told you about Adam?"

There was hesitation on his end, and when he spoke he lowered his voice. "You're off base, there, Sue-Ann."

"You talked to him?" I asked.

"Yeah, but I can't . . ."

"You can't talk because Linda C is there?"

"Right."

"Listen, Donny. This is important. That other boy I told you about, Pauley Hughes, ran away from home and he's crazy as a bug. I'm afraid that he might—"

"Forget it, Sue-Ann. But thanks for asking about Ed."

"I'll call you at work tomorrow," I said, and hung up.

Chapter 16

It was Wednesday morning and I was up early again. I fed and spent some time with the horses, then came in and made breakfast. With two pieces of bread in the toaster, I went into Cindy's room to wake up Jack.

"Up, sleepyhead," I told him. "We're off to the wars."

I was trying to make light of the fact that Jack was leaving that afternoon, flying from Tallahassee to make his connection to Iraq. I might never see him again. Strange how awful, devastating even, that possible loss seemed now when two weeks ago I would have all but assumed that he was gone from my life forever and not cared. We can be the leavers, but not the left. Gina was going to marry her good man and my good man was going off to the world's biggest bombsite to get himself blown up. I looked at the eggs, sausage, grits, and coffee like it was a last meal.

Jack had taken the darkroom materials from Cindy's bathroom the night before after developing a few shots he had taken of me shooting both my yumi bow—dressed in full Japanese kyudo regalia, and my colorful Black Widow recurve, although I was still not strong enough to pull it more than a couple of times. He also printed out a copy of the picture he had taken of me, Alikki, and Emmy just hours after the filly was born. He had packed his bags and loaded his car except for his toilet articles and the clothes he would be wearing.

Jack came in bathed, dressed, and combed. He seemed to be in a cheerful mood but ate without saying much. He washed and put away the dishes while I dressed. I found that if I combed my hair a certain way and pinned it, my bald spot was hidden and it felt good to be able to go out of the house without wearing a ballcap.

"Okay, what's our first stop?" Jack asked, holding the front door open for me.

"*The Courier* office. Wednesday morning briefing. I've been missing a lot of meetings because of my thyroid, but I want to get back in the mix." I had also gotten an email from Cal asking that I attend, so I knew that something was up.

"Sounds good."

We took Jack's car because it was new and had gas, while mine was old and dry. I drove. Jack looked out at the surroundings like it was his last time seeing them. I guess that's how he sees things: either for the first time or the last. In between doesn't count with Jack.

We arrived at the office a few minutes early. Cal and Gina were already there and so was Paul Hughes, who was looking glum and put out. Cal was sitting at the head of the table, his back to the window. Paul sat on his right and Gina sat next to Paul.

Cal only then noticed that I had brought a guest. He reached over and put out his hand. "Cal Dent," he told Jack. "I'm the editor here."

"Jack Stafford," Jack replied. "I used to work with Sue-Ann at—"

"At *The Richmond Times-Dispatch*," Cal finished. "It's a real pleasure, Jack. I'm a fan of your work."

"You are?" Jack asked.

"You are?" I asked.

"Are you kidding? I was hoping you'd win the Pulitzer Prize last year for those photos of the Jessup factory explosion, but even before that I knew your work on the terrorist attack in Washington—and that Philip Morris tobacco worker strike, that was priceless."

"Jack's on his way to Baghdad," I told Cal.

"Following in Sue-Ann's giant footsteps, eh?" he said.

"That's what I do best," Jack replied.

"Sue-Ann's giant footsteps?" I said.

"Your work, Sue-Ann, not your feet," said Gina. And on cue, I felt Gina's bare foot stroke my leg. I looked at her wide-eyed.

Cal looked up at a movement in the doorway. "Mark. Come in. Mark Patterson, this is Jack Stafford."

"Mark and I have already had the pleasure," said Jack, showing most of his perfectly white teeth.

Mark sat down and looked at Jack expectantly. "Coming to work here Jack?" he asked.

"Just passing through," Jack answered.

Cal spoke up. "We're still waiting for—wait, here they come now." The outside door to *The Courier* offices opened and two figures stepped inside, looked around, and headed for the conference room.

I had never met Ray Colley even though he had served several terms on the County Commission, but I had seen his picture in *The Courier*. He was a smallish man, kind of stocky, with brown hair and gold-rimmed glasses. The only thing kind of odd about him was that he wore a string tie with his brown suit. Half a step behind, I saw that his daughter was with him, no longer Goth Girl, but not yet Princess Barbie either. She was wearing plain blue jeans, a white tee shirt and faded running shoes. Her hair was still dyed black, but she had shaped it subtly into a style that was both appealing and stylish. She slouched a bit and her body language told everyone who cared to look that she was scared and ill at ease, but that she still retained some of her punk swagger. It was an interesting combination. When she saw Jack it looked like she wanted to hide her face and expand her chest at the same time.

Jack had no idea what was going on, but that never stopped him from being Jack. He stood up and, ignoring her father, walked up to the girl and held out his hand. "Rebecca," he said, sounding genuinely happy, "It's so good to see you again." She put her hand out timidly and Jack took it in his own. She totally melted. Jack led her to a chair and pulled it out for her. Then he turned to her father and put out his hand. "Jack Stafford," he said. "I had the pleasure of meeting Rebecca this weekend."

"Ray Colley," said the surprised commissioner.

"Good morning, Ray, Becky," Cal said.

Paul barely nodded to Ray Colley and totally ignored his daughter.

"Okay, everyone," Cal said. "Let's start the meeting. I told Betty to come in later because we have some private things to discuss—some things that Sue-Ann has been working on. It might be a good idea, though, if Jack—"

"Jack knows everything," I cut in.

Cal looked at Paul. "Okay, Paul?" he said.

Paul shrugged.

"Let Jack stay," said Becky hurriedly. "Please?"

"Becky," said Ray Colley sternly, "that's enough." Then he turned to Cal and said, "I guess it's all right."

"Okay, then. But nothing we say here is to leave this room, got it?"

We all nodded, even Mark, to whom everything must have been as clear as paint.

"I'm going to break things down as simply as I can. Sue-Ann, if I get anything wrong, correct me."

I nodded.

"All right. Two Fridays ago, Clarence Meekins found a dead goat in his dumpster." Cal looked at Ray Colley. "It was one of your goats, Ray. Sue-Ann thinks that it was stolen from your pasture by three kids, then taken into the woods and killed. You want to tell us anything about that, Becky?"

Becky, who had been shamefaced a few seconds before, turned to me with angry eyes. She jutted out her chin and said, "Who's she?"

Cal said grimly. "As far as you're concerned, young lady, she's God. She's found out enough about the three of you to have you all arrested. Now please address the question."

She hung her head a little. It might have been an act, because her bottom lip was still pointed in my direction. "It was Pauley," she said.

"What was Pauley?" Cal asked.

"He read something about voodoo in a book. He got all crazy like. The three of us—me, him, and Adam Zimmer—were riding around kind of smashed when he decides to, you know, steal this goat. It sounded like a good idea so I caught one for him. We took it out in the woods and tied it to a tree while Adam made all these voodoo symbols on the ground. Pauley killed the goat and started to, you know, cut it open. Auntie Adam threw up, but I'm not squeamish. I wanted to see what the goat looked like inside and I wanted to see if any voodoo stuff would happen." The girl stopped and a look of fear passed across her face like a shadow. Jack had to prod her to continue.

"What happened then, Rebecca?" he asked.

"Then I . . . I saw something in the woods behind us. It was a face—really gross, like in a horror movie. Pauley saw it too, and it was way up on a white horse and the horse reared up and the face made this horrible noise and we all ran." Becky had been so caught up in her memory that her voice almost broke. She stopped and regrouped.

She said, "Pauley said that it was one of the four horsemen of the apocalypse."

"And you believed him?" Cal asked.

"I don't know, maybe. What else could it be? I mean, you didn't *see* this thing. Pauley didn't even stop to pick up his book."

"Tell us about the chickens," Cal said.

"A couple of days later, Pauley wanted to try out another spell that he remembered from the book. Adam didn't want to go back in those woods, but me and Pauley convinced him—Pauley could convince Adam to stand on his head in the middle of I-10 if he wanted to. Adam even knew an old lady who had some chickens so we went and stole some. I got one and Adam got the other. But a dog started barking at us and Pauley killed it. Then he started to cut it up until I told him to quit." Becky went silent for a moment, remembering. "I didn't think he should have done that. I mean, goats are the worst, but dogs are all right. But then we went back out in the woods and we killed the chickens and burned them in a fire. We were all plastered on this tequila we had. Adam made some symbols on the ground and Pauley started dancing around and calling on the loas—that's what, you know, they call the voodoo gods—but nothing happened. I think that Adam probably got the symbols wrong because of the book."

"What book?" asked Cal.

"You know, that book we left in the woods the first time."

"What about it?"

"It was gone. Adam had to try to make the symbols from memory and he's a dim bulb sometimes."

"Sue-Ann?" Cal looked at me, wanting to know if I had any questions. I did.

"What were the three of you doing at the Ag Center

last weekend?" I asked.

The rebel in her flared up again. "None of your damn business," she said. Her father raised a hand to slap her but Cal caught his wrist and shook his head almost imperceptibly.

It was Jack who got her to speak. "Sue-Ann's an old friend of mine, Rebecca. She's good people and you can trust her."

Becky shrugged, and spoke, but to Jack and not to me. "Pauley wanted to hang out. He's got a thing for this girl. He met her a couple of months ago and tried to get cozy with her but she blew him off. Later on he was at Meekins' Market and thought he saw her going into the woods behind the dumpster, so he went in after her. I think he was just high, but that's when he found the clearing. It was a great place for meetings."

"And the Ag Center?" Jack asked gently.

"I was getting to that, I was," Becky replied. "You know that night we killed the goat? Well, after that ghost thing chased us out of the woods, Pauley drove us all to Eat Now to hang out and plan what we were going to do next. And that girl was there; the one with the crazy hair. She was with this guy," she pointed across the table at Mark Patterson. "So we snuck up and sat in the next booth so we could hear what they were saying. He was trying to pick her up but I could tell she was about to blow him off, too, but his cell phone rang."

"Hey," interjected Mark. "She didn't blow me off. That was probably the call from Cal telling me about Clarence finding the goat in his dumpster and . . ."

I saved his bacon here. Again. "So what did Krista say when you told her you had a tip to check out?"

"She, um, told me she had to get back home but if I wanted to see her again, she'd be at the Ag Center on

Saturday."

"Right," said Becky. "So that's how we knew she'd be there. We were going to follow her home from the Ag Center but we got thrown out. That's the last time I saw Pauley. Last time I saw Adam, too. They were supposed to meet me at Eat Now but they never showed."

It was Paul's turn to talk. "Becky," he began in a tired preacher's voice, "Pauley's run away. Do you have any idea where he might have gone?"

Becky shook her head. "I donno. Maybe back out in those woods."

"Whah d'you think that?" Gina asked.

"He, um, thinks that the reason the last sacrifice didn't work was because the animals were too little. He's got some plans, but he didn't tell us what they were. He says he hears weird voices on the radio, but I listen to the same station and I never heard them." She rubbed her eyes and looked around the table, and I could see that her bravado was ebbing away. She even looked a little scared as she continued. "He bought this new knife on eBay," she said. "It's like one of the old sacrificial knives—kind of curved and really sharp. It was pretty expensive but he had his daddy's credit card number. I really wanted to see him use that knife . . ." Then she looked Jack in the face and blushed, if people actually do that, and changed course. "But I'm not into that any more," she told him.

Cal looked at Paul. "You think we need to bring the police in, Paul?" he asked.

Paul looked much older than he had when the meeting started. It was as if he had only just been convinced that Pauley had gone off in the head. "I don't know anything any more," he said. "Let's give Paul Jr. another twenty-four hours. He's run away before, but he's always come back."

"We'll leave it to you, then," said Cal. "Sue-Ann, I

guess this story you've spent so much time on will have to be our secret. Excellent work, though." He took a breath and looked around the table. "All right, let's get our assignments straight for this week; I'm sure we all have places to go and people to see."

Jack, Ray, and Becky left the room and I saw the three of them talking quietly outside as Cal gave out assignments—including one for me; I guess I didn't look as sick as I had the week before. Gina, who had kept her feet to herself through most of the meeting, stroked my leg again under the table.

The meeting adjourned and we broke up into other groups. I took Gina aside and whispered, "Are you trying to make me completely lose it during a meeting?"

"Ah wanted t'see if ah could," she smiled.

Cal, Ray, and Paul had gone into Cal's office and closed the door. Jack was talking to Becky. I noticed a seriousness in his demeanor and Becky was nodding her head, trying through her shyness around him to be equally serious. Jack took something shiny out of his pocket and handed it to her and she looked up at him with a puzzled expression. He nodded at it and kept talking. Gina was asking about Emmy the Enemy Hunter when Cal's office door opened and the three men came out. Ray quickly collected his daughter and they left the building. I saw them get in Ray's SUV and drive away. Cal went back in the meeting room to collect his notes and, to my surprise, Jack went in and joined him, closing the door.

"What's that about?" Gina asked.

"No idea," I answered.

I talked to Gina about my assignment—there was a rumor circulating that the owner of a local car dealership was thinking of running for the state house. I had to interview the guy and do a people-on-the-street survey of what the locals thought about his chances. Gina had an appointment later in the week with Marty Harrison—the owner of the place Donny worked—to wrangle him into an advertising contract, and to get him to rethink his slogan of "Don't blow it! Tow it! With Harrison's!"

I had my own opinion. "I don't know, Gina, that slogan is pretty hard to—"

Cal's door opened and Jack came out smiling. "Time to go, I guess," he said. He took Gina's hand and told her, "Maybe if I get back in town, we can do a shoot."

"Ah'd lahk that," she replied. "Ah think."

I told Gina I'd see her later and walked outside with Jack. He was headed for the car, but I stopped him. "What was that all about with Cal?" I asked.

"I wanted to make him a proposition."

"What proposition?" I asked.

"I wanted him to hire Rebecca," he said.

"At *The Courier*?"

"Of course."

"Right. So on the masthead it would say Editor: Cal Dent, Reporter: Mark Patterson, Goth Girl: Becky Colley. Are you out of your mind?"

"It's not like that. I asked if he would take her on as an unpaid intern. She likes photography and I want to help her. It'll mostly be gopher work, maybe some typing, but it'll keep her out of trouble. Maybe she'll even get a chance to take some pictures."

"She doesn't know the first thing about photography!" I told him. "She just wants to do it because you do it."

"And that's okay. Every photographer has to start somewhere, and when I get through with her she'll know a lot."

"What do you mean, when you get through with her?"

"I'm going to give her a correspondence course.

Whatever pictures she takes she sends to me in Iraq or Richmond or wherever I happen to be, and I'll critique them. I'll give her advice on cameras, and explain darkroom techniques, and suggest books to read." He stopped for a second and looked away. "Besides," he finished, "she needs me."

That was a switch, I thought, but I kept it to myself.

"What was that you gave her in there?" I asked.

"A camera phone. I told her to call me whenever she wanted."

"She already has a crush on you. You want her to fall in love with you big time?

"I don't mind," he said.

And, I realized, I didn't either. Being needed was something I had had way too much of; it was the thing that was ultimately responsible for our breakup. But I don't think Jack had ever really been needed before. I mean, it wasn't as if he wanted to marry the girl, and even if he did, I wasn't the one to accuse someone else of choosing an unlikely partner. I put my arm around his waist. "You go, boy," I told him. "If I wanted to be a photographer, you'd be the one I'd want to teach me."

Jack was looking around the parking lot. "Is that a bookstore?" he asked.

"Only one in town," I said.

"Can we go in there for a minute?" he asked. "I read one of your Zane Grey books and it was pretty good. Maybe I can find a couple, to take with me."

"Sure," I said.

For once, there were several customers in the store and Benny was bobbing and nodding and clearing his throat in his best style. Jack's eye was immediately drawn to the small shelf of westerns and he began to browse through them. The customers were all strangers to me, older women with bags of mysteries or romances to trade. I was casually sifting through the self-help section when Benny extracted himself from the other customers and waddled toward me.

"Hoping you'd come in," he began.

"Do I owe you money?" I asked.

"Naw. Nope. We're square. I got some news."

"What kind of news?" I asked.

"I, ha, I had a customer," he said.

"And you want me to write a column about it?" I asked playfully. "You've got four or five customers here now. Maybe we can get a photographer and run a full-page story."

"Naw," he smiled. "I mean somebody came in the other day and bought one of the new books on Santeria I just got in. And I talked him into a couple of Aleister Crowleys. I, um, I'm not sure I ever saw him before, but just wanted you to know. Got his name from his credit card."

"Hughes, right," I said. "When did you say he came in?"

"Hughes? Naw. Hmm. Zimmer."

"Adam Zimmer?" I asked. "Are you sure?"

"Yeah, uh, wrote it down. Not Adam, though. Card said Gerald. Early forties, heavy salt and pepper beard. Looked kind of like a rumrunner."

Adam's father? I thought to myself, while my mouth was asking, "Benny, what does a rumrunner look like?"

"I, um, hmm, kinda thin, wrinkled clothes, you know."

"Listen, Benny. That might be really important information. See that guy over there, the one that doesn't look like a rumrunner? Will you help him find some Zane Grey books and tell him I'll be right back? I have to run back to the office for a minute."

"Ho ho. *Wild Horse Mesa, Wildfire, Horse Heaven Hill, Valley of the Wild Horses*—"

I stopped in mid-step. "Did you say *Horse Heaven Hill?*" I asked. Is that a Zane Grey book?"

"You betcha," Benny said, then continued, "*Mysterious Rider, The Thundering Herd* . . ."

I was out the door, rushing back to the office, knowing at last that my father had a good reason to choose Mr. Moon's Horse Heaven Ranch when he sold Alikki. Moon and my father were both Zane Grey fans.

I almost bopped Paul Hughes with the door as I went in. "Wait, Paul," I told him and looked around the room. Betty Dickson had come in and was back in her corner working on ads, but she was the only one I saw. "Where's everyone else?"

"They all went out," he said.

"That's all right. You're the one I wanted to talk to."

"Me?"

"Right. I just found out where that voodoo book came from—the one Pauley is so interested in."

"I was wondering that myself."

"Adam Zimmer's father. Either his father gave it to him or Adam stole it from his collection. What do you know about Gerald Zimmer?" I asked.

"Jerry, I think he calls himself. Nothing. I've met him once when I took Adam home from my house. Seems like a loner. I think he works nights as a security guard at one of the interstate rest stops. So you think he's into, what, the occult?" he asked incredulously.

"I don't think anything, Paul. I'm just giving you a head's up. Gotta go. Hope Paul Jr. shows up."

Back in the car, me still driving, I felt sad that Jack was leaving, not just because of the danger, but because he wouldn't be around when I got to the bottom of my goat story, which, despite what Cal and the others might think, wasn't nearly finished yet.

"Do you still have a cell phone or did you give your only one to the Goth Girl that was?"

"I bought that one for her yesterday. I was going to ask you to give it to her, but then she showed up at that meeting." He pulled another phone from his coat pocket and handed it to me. I dialed Donny's cell number from memory. From the sound effects on his end, Donny was driving his truck and listening to the radio. "Donny, it's me. Turn down your radio."

"Who? Sue-Ann?"

"Right. Listen—"

"Hold it, Sue-Ann." He turned down his radio to the point where I could barely hear it. "After we talked on Sunday I went over to Jerry Zimmer's place and asked him some questions. He said I was nuts! Adam was there, too, and he told me to bug off. I don't need any more advice that—"

"Donny, stop! Do you know where Adam is?"

"I guess he's at home, why?"

"Linda C's or Jerry Zimmer's?"

"Jerry's. Linda only has him—"

"I told you last night that I think Pauley Hughes is out of control. I think it's a good idea if you'd find Adam and keep him with you until we know where Pauley is."

"What about that girl? Becky?"

"She's safe. I spoke to her earlier today. She told me about the three of them stealing the goat and chickens and everything else I told you the other morning. And she said that Pauley is getting weirder and weirder and Adam seems to idolize him, will do anything for him. Adam needs somebody with him right now that's not his father."

"I don't know, Sue-Ann. I'm on my way home from

an accident right now; I've got a totaled Ford in tow, and I'm already not welcome at Adam's father's house. Linda C is a wreck and—"

"Listen to me. I just found out that Pauley is carrying around an old sacrificial knife, and that he plans to use it. I also found out that he's been reading books on the occult that he got from Jerry Zimmer. I know these things for a fact. Just go over there to see if everything's okay. Apologize for what you were saying the other day. Go out for drinks, buy them dinner, ask Jerry who does his landscaping, whatever. What can it hurt? Then take Adam with you in your truck. Tell him he can see a lot of accidents and wrecked cars. He'll love it."

"All right, Sue-Ann. I'll think about it."

I hung up and handed the phone back to Jack.

"You okay?" Jack asked me.

"Just a little tired."

"Who were you talking to?"

"Adam Zimmer's mother's boyfriend. Adam's mother is divorced and the father has custody. Donny has been trying to straighten the kid up. I hope he'll go over and find Adam before Pauley does."

"Is it like this in Baghdad?" he asked, smiling.

"Maybe it's this bad everywhere," I replied, smiling in my turn. "But maybe it doesn't have to be."

"You thought about writing the text of that book yet?"

"What, you mean your book? I don't know. Probably. I mean, it sounds like something I'd like to do. How do you want to work it?"

"Well, after I've been there awhile, I'll select some photos. I'll email you a scan along with everything I find out, like whether something was destroyed by a U.S. missile or by a suicide bomber, or whatever."

"Be as specific as you can."

Driving down the interstate is something you do unconsciously; unless there's a wreck or a hurricane there's never anything interesting to see. But it's an easy drive for conversation and, for another hour, Jack and I talked. Or I should say, I talked. I gave him names of contacts both inside and outside The Green Zone in Baghdad, I told him some places where local cuisine was almost worth getting shot for. I told him about the Baghdad Zoo and the 19 Arabian horses in the Iraqi National herd.

"My first shot," Jack said, breaking his silence.

"What?"

"The horses. That national herd. The "after" shot. I'll try to round up pictures of the horses before the war."

"Good choice. Very good choice."

When we got into Tallahassee we still had hours to spare, so I pulled into the parking lot of one of the malls to have lunch in a Thai restaurant I had been to once or twice before. After that, we strolled along the mall, looking into shop windows and talking about how we would like to either have or not have whatever was displayed. In front of a jewelry shop I halted so suddenly that Jack almost knocked me over.

"What's wrong?" he asked.

"Nothing. I just, uh, I think it's getting late. It's a weird airport. You have to get there like a decade before your flight leaves because of all the added security. They've got some shops there we can look in if we have any extra time."

"Suits me, I guess."

We hurried out to the car and I never told Jack the real reason that I suddenly got all rattled and silent for the few hours more we spent together that afternoon. Glancing through the window of the jewelry store, I saw Gina and Cal standing at a counter being waited on by a man in a black suit. The couple was holding hands and Gina's head with her long beautiful blonde hair was leaning languidly against Cal's neck as he pointed into the case. Jack didn't have to memorialize the scene with his camera; it's burned into my brain like acid on a metal plate.

Iza Moreau

Chapter 17

It was the telephone with its horrible jangle that woke me up again. I tried to will myself awake and sound halfway intelligent when I answered, but all that came out was, "Wha?" And I guess that wasn't all that bad for having been as stoned as I had gotten the night before. Gina was getting married so fuck it. The thought struck me like a slap in the face and only the voice at the other end of the line kept me from slipping back under the covers.

"Sue-Ann! Sue-Ann, are you there?"

"Who the hell? Dilly? What?"

"Sue-Ann. Bill Dollar. Something's come up. Something big this time."

I was waking up quickly. "What is it?" I asked. "And why are you calling *me*?"

"I can't get Mr. Dent on his cell phone. I called the office and left a message, but nobody will get it until later this morning. I called his house, but no answer."

"What's happened?" I asked again.

"There's been an accident. A farmer found a body in his pasture about an hour ago, kicked to death by one of his horses."

I was instantly awake. "Who was it, Billy?" I asked, but I felt I already knew the answer.

"Nobody knows yet. But it's a kid, maybe twenty, maybe younger, kind of heavy set. Dressed all in black with weird markings on his face, I mean on what's left of his face."

288

"When do you get off duty?" I asked.

"I just got off a few minutes ago."

"Can you meet me somewhere?"

"Sure, I guess, but there's no place in Pine Oak that's open yet."

I thought as fast as I could. "Make it *The Courier* office then. Half an hour. Nobody will be there except us. I have a key and there's a coffeemaker there. Listen Billy, do you know Linda C's son Adam?"

"Sure. I heard he's gotten a little weird lately, but I guess he's okay, why?"

"You're sure the dead boy wasn't Adam?"

"No, no, you're on the wrong track there, Sue-Ann. This boy was older and bigger, and like I said, I know Adam by sight."

"In that case," I told him grimly, "you might want to give Paul Hughes a call. I hope it's not true, but I'm pretty sure the boy you described is his son."

It was probably close to seven a.m. when I pulled into the parking lot of *The Courier* offices. Dilly Dollar was already there, sitting in his squad car and smoking. I unlocked the door and ushered him in, asking him to go back near Betty's space, out of sight of the window, while I made coffee. I was shocked almost out of my mind by the news, but not surprised, and I would have thought that to be impossible. A young man was dead who I had seen only a few days before, the son of someone I saw regularly, who I worked with, who was part of my extended newspaper family. And behind the shock was guilt—the guilt of having known something was going to happen and failed to prevent it. The if-onlies pinged around the inside of my skull again. If only I had talked to Pauley myself; if only I had gone to his father with my suspicions earlier; if only I hadn't taken that brick of marijuana from a crime scene.

Causes and effects twisted and entwined themselves into tight knots. But I was through with crying. The last dozen or so hours had numbed me like a bathtub full of Novocain.

So this would have been a happier story if I had never gotten the opportunity to describe Officer William Dollar of the Jasper County Sheriff's Department, but things can't be all good all the time. At just after seven a.m. he and I were seated across from each other in the paste-up cubicle of a small-town newspaper office drinking coffee. Billy Dollar is a sandy-haired, wide-smiling man who looks much younger than his 34 years. His smile makes up for his average looks, and his erect posture and neatly pressed uniforms disguise his too-thin frame. I had known Dilly even longer than I had known Gina. We had gone to grade school together, then middle school and high school. I had graduated near the top of my class, Dilly near the bottom, but what he lacks in intelligence he makes up for with his keen sense of self-preservation. He may not deserve much, but neither does he need much and is among the happiest of my old classmates. This morning, though, he showed none of his teeth and cracked no jokes. Seeing death up close does that to you, and Dilly had been the first officer at the scene. He would get a bonus for giving me the tip, but I knew that was the last thing on his mind as, slumped forward in his seat, he told me of his night on patrol.

It was just before five a.m. when a farmer named Coonbottom Mason woke up to the sound of his four dogs barking outside in the horse pasture. He yelled at them to shut up, but they kept on, so he pulled on some overalls and went out to investigate. Coonbottom is in his seventies, so it took him a few minutes to get to where his dogs were running back and forth, growling and barking. He thought they had trapped one of the wild pigs in the area so he was a little careful. He noticed that his half dozen horses were on the far side of the pasture and that they too seemed jumpy. He almost didn't see the body until he was right up on it because the black clothes blended in with the night, but it was there, all right. The boy had been kicked in the face by a large animal and it didn't take a veterinarian to see the shape of a hoof mark imprinted on his skull. He was lying on his side, almost as if he had lain down and gone to sleep in that position. There were a couple of odd things about the body. One was the white greasepaint symbols that he wore on his face, like tribal war paint or maybe the tattoos of South Sea Islanders that Coonbottom had seen when he served in the navy. The other odd thing was that a few inches from the boy's hand, a curved, razor-sharp, eastern-looking knife lay in the cropped grass.

Just as Dilly got through with the story, his cell phone rang. He flipped it open, spoke a few words, and closed it back again. "Paul Hughes has identified his son's body," he said.

"Shit."

Dilly ran his hand through his thick brown hair. "You know, Sue-Ann," he said. "I've seen a lot of accidents in the last dozen years, and I've had to stop fights in bars. I've seen abused kids and wives, but there was something about seeing that boy lying in the field that just wrenched my gut around."

"I feel it too, Bill."

And there were a few seconds there, if things had been just the slightest bit different, like maybe if the moon had been shining in through the window or if I had been smoking a cigarette, I could have found myself holding on to Billy; when he might have been able to persuade me to do things he had never persuaded me to do before. But those seconds passed. I knew that Billy was aware of that tiny window of opportunity and was equally aware of its passing. He smiled wryly, stood up, and put on his hat. "I've gotta go home an get some sleep," he said. "You staying here?"

"Yeah, I've got to write this up. Tell me one more thing before you go, though. Where is Coonbottom's farm?"

"Way out east of town on the Waxahatchee road."

It was as far away from the Torrington property—and from my own, for that matter—as it could be and still be in Jasper County.

"Are you doing okay, Billy?" I asked.

"Hanging in there," he said. "Nights like this are a little hard."

"You and Milly okay? Your two girls?"

He looked over at me and understood. He straightened his body almost imperceptibly. "They're safe, Sue-Ann."

"Be good, Bill," I told him.

I spent the next hour writing up what I knew about the death of Paul Hughes, Jr. on Cal's computer. Betty Dickson walked in while I was taping a note to the computer screen and I told her the whole story.

"Listen, Betty," I told her. "Will you tell Cal that I've written up the story on his computer when he gets in? I printed out a copy and put it on his desk."

"Cal's taking the day off," she told me. "Ginette, too. I'll be the only one in the office today."

"Will you keep trying to get him or Ginette on the phone then? I'm sure Cal'll want to be with Paul and we need to find out what to do with the story."

"What about you?" she asked.

"I have something I have to do."

Although it was only just after eight in the morning, it was heating up outside. Clouds were rolling in from the west and it was going to be a hot, muggy day with maybe a storm or two. Not something I was looking forward to being out in. I drove slowly, thinking and planning. When I got home I changed into hiking gear—white tank top over sports bra, a pair of camo-colored slacks and thick hiking boots. I choked down some cold spaghetti, then went into the barn for my tackle. This time I chose my smallest bow—a Saluki Turk, incredibly light and fast, if only I was strong enough to pull it. I selected half a dozen arrows with fierce broadheads, made sure that my fannypack had everything I might need, then went back out to Jack's car.

I didn't want Clarence to see me, so I parked in front of a defunct Pure Oil station down the block from the market, gathered my stuff together, and set off into thick woods at an angle toward the path that led to The Clearing. The summer growth made things tough and bristly, but I finally made it, although not without a few scratches.

No one was on the path, but I could see evidence that it had been recently used—a shoeprint, a couple of broken branches making it easier to pass by, several green leaves strewn ahead as if someone had grabbed a handful from the nearest bush and flung them down. The light bow and the trampled path made the trip easier than my previous one, but it was hotter and sweat ran down my face and neck like tears. The back of my shirt became quickly soaked. Vines as thick as my wrist came up from the ground, crawled their way up the oak trees, and finished, high in the branches, as splotches of color even greener than the oak leaves themselves. Baby vines did the same to scrub oak, but these vines were green and sprouted hundreds of prickly needles. There were blackberry bushes, too—bare this late in the season—that would rip the laces from your shoes if you didn't step carefully. I did. My footsteps were quick but precise, and I hurried on across billions of dead leaves and over occasional fallen branches. When I arrived at the clearing, I was beat. It was then I realized that my heart was beating too quickly, my breath coming too fast. I had forgotten to take my thyroid pill before I left home and, come to think of it, I may have missed the day before.

I sat down on the log, breathing and sweating heavily, and looked around me. The cornstarch circle was almost completely faded and no new symbols had been added to its perimeter. I did, however, find a cigarette butt that looked and smelled recently smoked. A Newport. Then I found something else, something that left no doubt in my mind that I was on the right track, although it also warned me that I might be walking into very dangerous territory. It was the stub of a white grease pencil.

Pauley Hughes had been here, probably not long before he was killed.

Although I couldn't do anything to help him now, I got up, went back to the path, and continued my trip through the woods. I knew almost everything now, but the few things that were still mysteries would determine my next moves. I needed to confront someone with what I knew. Trouble was, I didn't know who I was going to confront or what I would say to them if I ever did. But I had to keep on.

I traveled mostly in the canopy of the great forest, walking across an occasional clearing of dead trees or high grass. I may have been walking for an hour when I came to the place where I had killed the rattlesnake, so I sat down and rested again on a log. I searched and found the tip of the arrow that remained in the tree when Clarence had unscrewed it. It was tinted a rusty red. Overhead, the sky was darkening and rain clouds were coming my way fast. I got up and kept following the path, and this part of the path was new to me. Instead of thinning out into a dog or rabbit path as I had once suspected it would, it actually began to widen and after I had gone another half hour through steaming leaves I came to a swath cut by a tractor. And recently cut, too; from the look of the grass and weeds that had been mowed, it had been done less than a week before—probably at the same time as the one I had found when I had gone out searching for Alikki.

Walking was easier now, I felt freer, although very tired. I took an arrow from my quiver and held it nocked on the string in my left hand. If I needed to, it would only take me an instant to draw and fire. The trail was irregular because whoever was riding the tractor had to pick their way carefully through thick forest and very heavy brush. Some low, overhanging branches had been cut down and thrown to the side. A brown shape in the path made me stop. A coiled snake? No, horse manure, but at least several days old judging from the fact that rain had turned it into a flat mushy pile.

Subtly, the nature of my surroundings was changing. A few pinecones on the trail attested to the presence of very tall trees, but they were sparse—the forest was thinning out. It had suddenly gotten dark; I looked up and saw that the storm clouds were now almost directly overhead.

As I turned around a bend to my left, I saw it. Just beyond a towering magnolia tree was a four-board fence at least five feet high. A heavy metal gate that must have been wrought a hundred years before was affixed to new-looking fence posts and fastened with a chain and padlock. I approached the fence warily and peered out from behind the magnolia. The scene might have been an aged photo torn from the pages of the *History of Jasper County*. Not just one, but a wide sweep of five buildings shaded by several oak and magnolia trees. The buildings were old, brown, and by modern reckoning, misshapen, with gables and extra rooms built on seemingly willy nilly. Three houses, it looked like, with a large, two-story barn to the side and one other structure—with a high, modern metal tower jutting up behind it—that could have been either barn or dwelling. A couple of the roofs were obviously newer than the others because their silvery tin outshone the rusty brown. All three of the houses had wooden porches. The largest— almost a mansion—had a veranda running completely around it. I saw some machine equipment parked near the barns, but no cars.

There was no doubt about it. I had found The Compound again, but from another angle. This then, was where the two backpackers had come from.

None of the people I had seen earlier were in sight, and for once, I heard no rifle shots. I tried the padlock, but it was fastened. The boards of the fence were too close together for me to squeeze through so I handed my bow through to the other side and started climbing. It was only when I had gotten to the top that I realized that my heart was beating so fast I was about to pass out. As I swung my leg over the top board and began to climb down, a wave of vertigo swept over me. My foot missed the next board and I slipped from the top of the fence onto the soft grass on the other side. I tried to cry out, but the wind had been knocked out of me and my voice wouldn't work.

I turned my head. Two or three men had come out of the barn and were walking toward the field; they looked to be carrying rifles. On the porch of the largest house, someone else was moving but male or female I couldn't tell. I lay back for what must have been a few minutes but, although my breath came back in thick bursts, my strength was gone. I put my hand out and touched my bow. The arrow I had been carrying with it was just out of reach, but I shifted my body enough to take it in my fingers. It was probably the hardest physical thing I ever had to do, but I somehow raised myself to my knees and drew the bow. The house was nearly a hundred yards away so I had to pull hard and allow for plenty of arc. With my strength now completely gone, I let the string slide over my fingers and felt the arrow fly.

I saw nothing else, felt nothing at all. I just lay there in the grass. A horse neighed in the distance. An instant later, thunder growled like wild dogs and the sky cracked open.

Chapter 18

I woke up in an antique store.

There was a chair with doilies, what looked like tintypes framed on the thick paneled walls, tiny toy animals and other bric-a-brac on shelves and tables. Shaded lamps with fringe. Even the bed I was lying in was a large, four-poster with quilted coverlet and white, white sheets. There was a fireplace against the far wall with a solid oak mantle. I heard rain splinking against the tin roof.

"Are you all right?" I heard a soft masculine voice from the corner and tried to turn my head in that direction. It was an effort. All my energy seemed drained away like blood from a corpse. In the corner, sitting in what appeared to be a mahogany rocker, was a pretty young man in his early twenties. His black hair was wavy and long, his face clear and dreamy. Short, from the way his feet didn't quite meet the ground as he sat in the rocker. He looked tired, concerned.

"Umm," I tried to speak.

"What's wrong with you?" he asked. "Are you hurt?"

"I . . . I think I just had . . . I think I just had a thyroid storm," I managed. That's what you get if you don't take your medicine, boys and girls.

"What's that?"

"I . . . have a thyroid condition. I have medicine but I didn't bring it." My voice was getting warmed up and I was finding it easier to speak. "If I don't take it my body releases too many hormones. Have I seen you before? You look familiar."

"I don't think so."

"What's your name?"

"Smokey."

"Listen, Smokey—cool name by the way—where am I?"

"Don't you know?"

"I'm in an old house somewhere. In a strange bed."

A new voice, familiar but stern, came from the direction of the doorway. "You're in Torrington."

"Clarence?"

Clarence Meekins came in the room and stood before me looking seriously worried. "It's me, Sue-Ann. God's family jewels, what made you come out here?"

"I'm too sick to talk about it right now, Clarence, but you know why."

"Didn't I try to tell you—"

"If you want me to talk, you have to give me pills."

"Pills?"

"I need my thyroid medication."

"Where is it?"

"I left the bottle in my purse. White Lexus, parked at that old Pure station near the market. The key is in my . . . where's my pants?"

"I'll get them," said the young man named Smokey. I watched him leave and suddenly had a powerful déjà vu. I may never have seen his face before, but I had very definitely seen the back of his head. Clean, longish hair, carefully cut and combed. He left the room for only a few seconds and came back in with a pair of wet and muddy camos in his hand.

"Right-hand pocket," I said.

"Want me to take care of it?" asked Smokey.

"I'll go," said Clarence. "But you and me, Sue-Ann, are

going to have a long talk when I get back."

"Bring it on," I said, and passed out.

When I woke up again the room was dimmer. I didn't know how much time had passed and there was no one in the room to ask. I felt somewhat better and managed to sit up a bit. "Hey!" I shouted. I heard footsteps in the hall and Smokey came back in the room.

"You awake?" he asked.

"My horses," I said. "I have to feed my horses." I thought of asking for a phone, but who would I call? Gina and Cal were who knows where, Jack was gone. I had to get up and do it myself, but I doubted I could even make it to the door.

A new voice from the doorway, feminine this time and vaguely familiar, said, "I can do it." Krista Torrington walked in carrying a glass of water and my purse. She was wearing new Nike running shoes which made no noise on the wooden floor. Her long, reddish-blonde hair was combed over her ears and curled down in a cascade over her shoulders. She was much more attractive than I had remembered.

"I told you we'd meet again," I told her.

"Here's your pills," she said, taking the bottle from the purse. She helped me to get one down my gullet by lifting my head and letting me have a sip of water. She laid my head back gently on the pillow. Smokey had left the room again and I was alone with the girl. "Why'd you come here?" she asked me.

"Where's Clarence?" I countered.

"He'll be back later," she said. "He had something to do outside. Where are your horses?"

Slowly—I couldn't believe how much effort it took me even to think, much less give directions—I told her how to get to my house, where the feed was, and how much Alikki

The News in Small Towns

got. "Check the water buckets and make sure they have hay in their stall."

"I have horses," Krista reminded me.

Smokey came back in the room carrying a tray. "I brought you some tea and toast," he told me. Krista made to leave.

"Wait," I told her. "I need to thank you," I managed. "Both of you."

"For what?" the girl asked.

"For saving my life," I told her. "This makes twice, doesn't it?"

"I don't know what you're talking about," she said. "And don't thank us yet." Then she left the room.

"What did she mean by that?" I asked Smokey.

He sat back down in the rocker and smiled thinly. "Don't know," he said.

Now that I was awake and at least halfway observant, I realized that his was the first smile I had seen since I had been there. An aura of gloom surrounded the house like thick fog and I felt like I had stepped out of time into the middle of a nineteenth-century funeral.

I managed to take a sip of tea and a bite of toast and I was suddenly very hungry. I took more bites until the toast was gone. I drank half the tea and put it back on the table near the bed. "Did I ask you how I got in this bed?" I asked.

"Jeremy was coming around the side of the house when your arrow almost knocked off his cap before it smacked the side of the house. Made a hell of a noise, even with all the thunder. It took five ex-marines fifteen minutes to get to where you were lying. So scared of a woman with a bow that they were ducking from tree to tree and crawling through the grass and the mud. They liked it, really."

301

"Who *really* found me?" I asked.

"I just told you. Jeremy and some of his buds."

"I saw men with guns," I remembered.

"Yeah, that would be them. They're all ex-combat troops."

"Did someone pick up my bow?" I asked. "If it's left out in the rain, the laminations might—"

"It's in the other room. Why did you try to kill Jeremy?"

"I—I didn't. I was about to pass out and I couldn't get my voice to work. I was just trying to get someone's attention."

"You got it. Listen, if you're so sick, why did you come way out here?"

"I wanted to tell you . . . I wanted to tell you—all of you—that you were safe. You don't have to worry."

Smokey seemed to think about that for a while, then got up and went out of the room. I heard some vague noises somewhere in the house, heard the wind blow droplets of rain from the overarching oaks onto the tin roof. I must have dozed off again, because the next thing I heard was a commotion from outside the room. It was totally dark now. I tried to sit up again and half succeeded, reached out and found the lamp chain and pulled it. A soft light allowed me to see movement from the doorway. The voices got louder. I heard the words "Don't—" and "You can't—." Then a louder voice broke in, a very familiar voice.

"Ain't neither of y'all any bigger than a minute, so git your little butts outta mah way," and the next thing I knew, Gina was in the room, standing at my bedside. Krista and Smokey crowded in behind her, arguing.

"Hi, darlin," Gina said.

"Gina."

"These kids takin care of you okay?" she asked.

"Yeah, sure," I said. "How did you find me?"

"Ah was in your house waitin for you when that little gal showed up. Ah convinced her to bring me here."

"How?" I was still so astonished to see her that I could hardly speak.

"Told her ah'd call Dilly and have her arrested for stealin Jack's car."

"Gina. I . . . I saw you with Cal in the jewelry store. Did y'all elope? Are you married?"

"No, baby."

"But—"

"We'll talk about all that later. Raht now ah want to fahnd out how you're feelin."

I had to think about it. "I'm okay, I think," I told her. "I've gotten some strength back and my heart seems to be about back to normal. Gamma gave me a pill a while back."

"Who?" Gina asked.

"That girl. Krista. She calls herself Gamma when she's on the radio."

I looked at the two young people and smiled. Smokey shrugged his shoulders at Krista and said, "*I* didn't tell her."

"Gina, this is Gamma and Smokestack, my two favorite deejays. Smokey, you and Krista related?"

"She's my sister," he said.

"So you're a Torrington, too."

"Yeah. You really listen to our shows?"

"They keep me going. They also scare the shit out of me."

"Cool."

A clump of thick footsteps on the wooden floor made us turn our faces toward the door in time to see Clarence.

He looked in a hurry, but stopped dead when he saw Gina at my bedside. He looked at both Krista and Smokey with disbelief. "How did Ginette get here?" he asked them.

"She just . . . came," shrugged Krista.

"God's titties, Krista!" Clarence exclaimed. "What's your grampa going to say?"

"The Zombie can kiss my tush," Krista replied sulkily. "I'm tired of all this secrecy shit."

"And all these fucking guns and arrows around here are weirding us out," added her brother.

"What's everybody talkin about?" Gina broke in.

"Butt out, Ginette," said Clarence. "The less you know the better off you'll be."

"All right, Clarence," I butted in, "We're going to have all this out right now, while I'm still alive and awake."

"God's—" We never got a chance to hear what part of that deity's private anatomy Clarence was going to call upon next, because I didn't let him finish.

"Clarence," I said firmly. "You can stand or get chairs. We're going to be here awhile."

"Come on, Clarence," said Smokey.

The three of them left and I was alone with Gina, which was pretty much all I wanted in the world at that moment. She sat on the side of the bed and stroked my hair.

"Betty called mah cell and told me about Pauley," she told me softly. "We came back as fast as we could. We read your story as soon as we got to the office. Cal went to fahnd Paul and ah went to your house. Ah thought you maht do something stupid and ah was raht."

"Stupid for not taking my pills," I said.

"Stupid for not takin *me*," she corrected.

Clarence, Krista, and Smokey came back in, carrying matching chairs that looked like they were borrowed from a nineteenth-century dining room. Smokey presented Gina with the chair he brought in and took his place in the rocker.

When everyone was seated, I struggled until I was sitting upright. I noticed that I was wearing a thick cotton shift, soft and warm. I took a breath, and began.

"Which one of you put the goat in the dumpster?" I asked.

"Both of us," Smokey answered. "Me and Krista. Clarence, too."

I looked at Clarence with daggers, but he just shrugged.

"I had to lie to you, Sue-Ann," he said. "Torrington's been a secret for over a hundred years. This is where the first settlers of Pine Oak built their homestead. And there are a lot of reasons why this place needs to stay a secret."

"I'll have to take your word for that," I said. "But let's get back to the goat. How did you find the goat in the first place?"

"Granpa and I were out riding in the woods," Krista began. "He was on Trigger and I was on a mare named Bob. We heard some voices and some kind of chanting, so we rode closer. The bushes were really thick near the trail so we were able to ride close without anybody seeing us. Then one of the kids threw up and the noise or the smell must've spooked Trigger, because he reared up and the other two kids saw him. The girl screamed and they all ran like demons were after them. I picked up the book they left and gave it to grandpa. We rode home, called Clarence, and the four of us made a plan."

"It was a good plan, too," I said grudgingly, looking in Clarence's direction. "If you leave the goat out in the woods, nobody knows about it except you and the kids that stole it."

"We thought if we called attention to it," Clarence said, "those kids might get in trouble with either their parents or the police."

"And they wouldn't come back into our woods," Krista added.

"And then your secret would have been safe," I finished.

"It would *still* be safe if you hadn't followed that blood trail out into the woods," Clarence said.

"I don't think so, Clarence. Pauley went from one obsession to another: Krista, the radio station, Santeria. He thought there was something in the woods that would help him or save him or give him some great insight or bring his mother back from the dead, whatever. He was going to keep coming back until he found this place or until somebody killed him."

"But we never touched hi—" Smokey began, and was interrupted by Gina.

"But Sue-Ann," she exclaimed. "You aren't sayin that somebody *killed* him are you? You told Betty he was kicked by a horse. And if Pauley's mind was so set on *this* place, what was he doin way out on the other sahd of town last naht?"

"He was dumped in that pasture, Gina. Probably by some of those guys outside. But he *was* kicked by a horse. Was it Trigger, Krista?"

Krista nodded and started to cry.

Smokey spoke for her. "The goth kid must've followed the mowed trail and climbed the fence near the pasture where we keep the horses. . . ."

"He had a big knife," Krista cried through her tears and her voice went up in timbre until it was almost a scream. "He was going to kill one of the horses for some stupid ritual!"

Gina looked at me with a question in her eyes. I nodded. "That's what I thought," I told her. "No way Pauley would decide to go on the other side of town when what he wanted was in these woods. He knew Krista lived back here somewhere and he knew she had a horse. I found the grease pencil he used to paint his face back in the clearing. It's in my fannypack. I've seen Trigger. He's big and he's kind of wild. I doubt there's anyone that can manage him except an expert rider like you."

"Only me and Granpa," she sniffed. "Anyone tries to get near him when we're not there and he spooks. Some horses like to kick out with their hind legs; Trigger just rears and strikes."

"My mother believed that horses can read a person's feelings," I told her.

Krista looked up at me with wet doe eyes and asked, "You're not going to have him destroyed, are you?"

"No one's going to destroy anything," I told her. "And no one is going to *say* anything."

"You mean—" Clarence began.

"I mean that this is our secret. Pauley's death was an accident. Whatever you all are hiding out here has nothing to do with it and is nobody's business but your own. My newspaper story—and *The Courier* has to run one—says that Paul Hughes, Jr. was killed in a tragic accident on Coonbottom Mason's farm. Even if there's an autopsy and the coroner suspects that he was killed somewhere else and moved, there's still no way to connect his death with this place because no one will know that this place exists. No one will know about Pauley's obsessions or about his painted face or about that knife he carried because none of that is in the story."

Clarence looked astonished but relieved. He glanced at Gina, and formed a question. "What about you, Ginette?

Are you—"

"Ah think that Sue-Ann is raht as a rock and just as hard headed," she smiled.

Clarence blinked and seemed to remember something. "Sue-Ann," he said. "I got your doctor's name off the bottle of medicine and called him. He told me that if you weren't dead already you'd probably be okay as long as you got one of those pills down you. He said you shouldn't be moved tonight, but that we should bring you in to the hospital as soon as we could."

"Thanks, Clarence."

That was it for the night. I wanted to rest. Krista and Smokey took Gina off to another guest room and Clarence went home, saying he'd be back the next day. I must have been really tired or sick or something, because when I woke up early the next morning, Gina was under the covers and snuggled up against me. She was sleeping like someone who had not slept well in ages, and she didn't wake up when I softly stroked her hair.

I was long due for a visit to the bathroom and got out of bed as silently as I could. I felt much stronger than the day before. I could stand without any problem. I took a few steps and didn't fall, so I tried a couple more—everything seemed to be all right in the walking department. In the hall I found my clothes, washed, dried, and folded, atop a mahogany table. I took them into a bathroom I found off the main hall. I used the toilet, then the ancient, clawfooted bathtub, and when I came out, I was fully dressed except for my shoes. I walked in my socks over the buffed wooden floor that may have been cut from the same trees as the old plank road outside. No one else seemed to be up, so I decided to explore the house, wondering vaguely if I was a prisoner here. What if the soldiers outside thought that Gina and I might reveal their secret if we were allowed to leave? If so, I at least wanted to find out what that secret was. I passed two doors made of thick wood inlaid with a delicate filigree design and came out into a large drawing room. A half dozen chairs with their backs shaped like shells were spaced regularly around the room, which also had a bookshelf on one wall, a long secretary with many drawers, a rolltop desk, and portrait upon portrait in hand-worked walnut frames. All gave the appearance of being part of an ancient haunted house except for a section of framed photographs near the door. One of these was of a young man in his twenties dressed in an American Marine uniform. Two others, obviously taken quite recently, were of Krista and Smokey.

A high, twisted, breathy voice came from behind me. "We get into all kinds of trouble when we are young, yas?"

I whirled around to face the grotesque vision of a thing that looked half man, half corpse. Dressed in a silky-looking pair of baggy Persian trousers and a light, white, short-sleeved shirt, the figure's face was mostly old burn scars. One eye looked fixedly on me, the other was burned away. Some of the skull was bare scar tissue, the rest tufted out in black scraggly hair that grew out and down beyond his shoulders. Only one of the shoulders, though, had an arm connected to it. The man sat languidly in an armchair studying me. I was startled, of course, but I managed to look him in the eye and reply. "Sometimes that's what being young is for," I told him. I'd seen this man once before and had expected to find him somewhere in the compound. But being across from him in a drawing room was not the same as glimpsing him through vegetation from a distance of a hundred yards.

"The sight of me does not shock you?" he said. I recognized the whining tone and unusual cadence and I realized that his larynx was probably damaged as well as his skin.

"I'm always shocked at what brutality does, but I was in Baghdad," I told him. "You're prettier than a lot of the bits and pieces I saw over there, but I can imagine how you must have scared those goth kids in the woods, especially if you were riding a huge white horse. You're The Creeper, aren't you?"

"Smokey calls me that, yas, although what Krista calls me is not so kind. My real name? Ashley Torrington at your service. And riding? It is one of the few things I still do well."

"Sue-Ann McKeown."

"Yas. I've been hearing stories." The effect of twisting his face into a smile—even a genuine one—was grotesque. "Please, why don't you sit down and we can have a chat."

It was at that moment that I knew that this scarred old gentleman was in total charge of The Compound. I also knew that I had nothing to fear from him.

I was glad to slip into one of the huge chairs, although I had to turn it a little so that it would face him. As I did so, I noticed a feature of the room I had not yet seen: a bank of shelves holding expensive-looking audio equipment—a turntable, a cassette player, a CD player, and much more.

"Yas," he said, following my gaze. "That's my other little obsession: I sometimes think only my music keeps me alive."

Mr. Torrington's face was hard to look at—mostly a mass of shiny reddish wrinkles and only a nub where his right ear once was—but I forced myself. "What happened to you?" I asked.

He shrugged. "I was in the middle of a napalm attack in Vietnam. Should not have been where I was, no, but there you are."

"I'm sorry," I said. "So when you got well, you came back here?"

"As you see, I never got well. But yas, I came to Torrington. It is the oldest settlement in this county. Cut off from the rest of the world for one hundred and fifty years."

"But these houses," I said. "They're old, but, I mean, wouldn't the forest have taken over in a hundred and fifty years?"

"But these houses have never been empty, no. There have always been Torringtons here, living in silence, tilling fields, making repairs, all of these. Until the kids came here it has mostly been a place for the sick or the insane."

"Krista and Smokey are your grandchildren?" I asked.

"Yas. They grew up with my son and his wife in Phoenix. My son owns a big-ass fiber optics company and lives in houses here and there—mostly there, as Phil Ochs once said."

"Where does the money come from to keep this place up?" I asked.

"We have pensions, we grow and make things and sell them. My son and his wife never come here, no, but he gives me guilt money—more money than we need. I built a radio station with his "contribution.""

"So that's where the radio station comes in," I said. "And you know a lot about music."

"Music is my mistress," he said. "Mostly the music of my contemporaries. In fact, 'Music is My Mistress' is the title of a song by Linda Hargrove. I once met her at the dog track in Jefferson County when I was whole. But I try to listen to many newer things as well. I have thousands of records, CDs, cassettes. And, ha ha, if I want anything else, right now, I can get it off Napster for ninety-nine cents."

"In case you have a special need for, say, *Goat's Head*

Soup, and don't have a copy handy."

"Ummm, yas. I imagine musical stories; I live out my memories, and even the experiences of those close to me through songs."

"So when Krista rode in that cowboy-mounted shooting event, you helped Smokey choreograph it in music for his show. He played songs about cowboys, balloons, shooting." The Creeper nodded. "And when the goth kids killed the chickens, you came up with an old group that had a drummer named Chicken."

The Creeper shook his head and sighed. "I really did not think anyone would catch that one, but, hmmm, you always hope."

I had a moment of clarity. "But if you've been putting pieces of yourself into that radio station all along, shuffling sections of your memory, making your own unique connections to things, leaving little coded messages, you . . . you wanted someone to find you."

"And you did, no? Ah, it's too bad I didn't meet you when I was younger," the old man said. "It might not seem so now, but I have brains. When you have only yourself for company for almost forty years, you begin to think more than others. But you and I could have . . ." He let his voice trail off into a creak.

"Are you hitting on me, Mr. Torrington?" I smiled.

He made a grotesque squeaking laugh, coughed, and said, "Maybe, yas, maybe I am. You were looking at my picture on the wall there by Krista and Smokey."

"You were a fine looking man," I told him. "Did you enlist?"

"Yas I did. I was in a military family. I took ROTC in college. I didn't want to go to Vietnam, but I went anyway. It's what was expected of me."

"Boys and girls are still going to other Vietnams

against their will," I told him.

"Yas," he said.

"The men who found me yesterday: who are they?"

"Ex-marines from all the wars that ever were. All shot up or fucked up in many ways. They live here until they are ready to go back to the world."

"And none of them that left have ever let on that this place is here?" I asked.

"Semper Fi," he said.

"What happens in Torrington stays in Torrington."

"Yas. And Clarence seems to think that you and your friend are going to keep our little community a secret."

"Only if you'll let us come out and visit you sometimes."

"Hmmph."

"I'll take that as a yes."

"I am finding that I like visitors, even though you are the only visitor I have ever had. This friend of yours; I hear she's very pretty, yas?"

"She's young enough to be your daughter," I told him. "Besides, she likes girls."

"Yas?" He cocked his one eyebrow at me curiously. "And you?" he asked.

"I like *her.*"

"A risky secret to carry around in a small town," he said.

"We're in Torrington, now," I whispered.

When he smiled, I no longer saw the twisting and the grimacing effort it took him; all I saw was the amusement. "I hear others moving around," he said. "Go through that door and eat. We have a very good cook who once ran the mess hall at Camp Lejeune."

"Just one more question. What does Clarence have to do with all this?"

"Clarence? Umm, a distant cousin. His father lived here for years when he retired from the market. It made him happy to think that he was alive and everyone thought he was dead. Clarence sees and hears things for us. Clarence was a good soldier."

"Clarence is still a good soldier," I said. "Ciao."

"Chow down," he answered. "Come back when you're well."

"You know about my—" but the man who was once Ashley Torrington, waved me away.

After breakfast, the four of us—Krista, Smokey, Gina, and I—took a tour of the 300-acre community. I swallowed another pill and was spared the labor of walking when Smokey rolled up to the front door with an electric golf cart. Gina sat in front with the driver while Krista and I sat in back, holding on to the side rails.

Torrington has an average of a dozen residents. Except for the younger Torringtons, all are ex-military men or women and their spouses, who live in the two large outbuildings I had seen on the way in. Miniature versions of the house I had been brought to, they had undergone various kinds of repairs and improvements over time—all mod cons, for instance, new roofs, fluted replacement pillars for the porches. We passed close to three or four fields, each planted with a different crop. I saw cabbage, watermelon, and one I couldn't identify. "So this is how Clarence gets his produce so fresh," I said to Krista as we whisked along.

"Some of it," she replied. "Some of the community even makes, I guess you'd call them crafts, that he sells for us."

"What kind of crafts?"

"Have you ever seen the eye-pillows he sells? Those come from here. Quilts, too, and quilt potholders. Even junk from the old attics. Sometimes Smokey and I will get our backpacks and take a load in to Clarence. I guess you saw us once, huh?"

"So that's what you were doing out there," I said. "And Clarence *did* see you and got you to help carry me out of the woods."

"I carried the snake," she said.

"The service medals," I remembered. "They come from here too, don't they?"

"The people who live here try to forget they were in the service," she said. "They'll let go of everything but their guns."

"I've heard them shooting ever since I moved back to Pine Oak," I said. "At first I thought they were hunters, but I can tell the sound of a glock from a pea-shooter."

"They're always out shootin stuff. Trees, deer, whatever," said Krista. "They're okay, I guess. A couple of them make pretty good deejays, but they're really strange. They never go into town and don't want anybody to even know they're alive."

"That's why Sam and Jason ran when you snuck up on them that morning," Smokey added.

I was genuinely puzzled. "Sam and Jason?" I asked.

"That first morning," Krista explained. "They had found a load of 1930s magazines in one of the old rooms and schlepped them through the woods to Clarence's. The dumpster was their drop-off point. They didn't know anything about the goat or they probably would have waited a day or two."

Gina, who had been listening to Krista's and my conversation, spoke up. "Ah'd been wonderin who it was you heard that morning.

I didn't reply. It was the last piece of the puzzle—one so small I had all but forgotten about it, but without that, there could have been no puzzle at all, no story, I would have had to use all these words for some other purpose.

The golf cart's tires crunched over the trails we were driving on. "Y'all don't sound like you grew up around here," Gina remarked to Smokey.

"Naw. We're from Arizona. Born and raised. We came down to help Grampa with his radio station. We've both worked in a college radio station in Phoenix, but nobody knows music like Grampa."

"How have you kept the FCC from shutting you down?" I asked. "It's not like you're broadcasting from a ship somewhere like some pirate stations and can move from place to place."

Krista giggled the laugh I had come to associate with Gamma. "It's a jape," she said.

"What's a jape?" asked Gina.

"A joke!" Krista cried. "We're not really a pirate station—we just *say* we are."

"We're a fully licensed, dues-paid radio station," Smokey added. "But we can get away with a lot because nobody thinks we are. I mean, what real station doesn't advertise and doesn't have pledge drives? We play exactly what we want; Krista can spout her poetry—"

"And I can make up recipes," she giggled, "and hope I don't poison anybody."

"It's your poetry that might poison people," I quipped. "Really, *Poultrygeist?*"

Krista giggled again.

We had passed by the stables and I saw Trigger and several other horses—chestnut, black, and bay—grazing in a nearby pasture. I was so intent on the horses that I almost didn't see the row of boards just to the outside of the encroaching forest. "Hold it!" I shouted. "Stop for a minute." I jumped out even before the cart stopped and walked—not ran, Dr. Morris—toward the structure. I bent down and felt the roughness of he old boards—part of the old plank road I had seen just outside the fence the day Alikki had run away.

The others had gotten out of the cart as well. "There's more of it further down," Smokey said. "Grampa said to leave it alone, but I don't know what the big deal is."

"This is the ruins of the oldest plank road in the world," I said. "That's why the original town's name was changed from Torrington to Planktown."

"Didn't ya know?" Gina asked.

"We learned that from a Jasper County history book," I told them. "But the author said that its location was unknown. I guess that's the line I'm going to have to take when I write my history of the Plank Festival."

"What's that?" Smokey asked.

"Just an old Pine Oak tradition," I said. 'Like a small town Fourth of July."

I walked back to the cart. "I've gotta get back home and feed my horses. Then I need to pay a visit to my doctor. Gina, do you know how to drive us out of here?"

"There's a dirt road that comes in from the opposite sahd of those fields. Krista told me that it's mostly used for trucking out produce."

"Or trailering out her horse to go to wild west shows," I added.

"She's on restriction for that," said Smokey.

"Let me know when you get off," I told her. "Maybe you can teach me to ride as good as you do."

"Tell Mark I'll call him sometime," she told me.

"Who's Mark," Smokey asked suspiciously.

I winked at her.

Chapter 19

I'm getting pretty near the end of this story, and I've just realized that I haven't finished telling you about Crookneck Smith. So I'll do it now.

From the day I bought my first bow until the day he gave me my last lesson, Crookneck Smith became my confessor as well as my coach. He knew about my classes, marveled as my accent began to change from the Pine Oak drawl to the anonymity of the news anchor I once thought I wanted to be. He learned about my boyfriends, parents, and news assignments and never offered a harsh criticism unless maybe I plucked the bowstring or took my eye off the target when I was shooting.

And over the years, I learned something about him, too, both in his own words and from his daughter Beth, who worked in the shop sometimes. Archery had been his life—too much his life—and his constant traveling had ruined his marriage. This and the waning of his ability as an archer caused him to drink more heavily, and his problems snowballed. I found out that "Crookneck's Archery and Hunting Supplies" was just a front for the taxidermy business next door, and although it paid him a living wage, he spent most of it on high-tech archery supplies and Kentucky bourbon. He told me once that he planned to enter the world championship for senior compound bow shooters, but he never did. Another thing he never did was drink in my presence.

Whenever I dropped in, he set up regulation FITA

targets on his old cotton bale and had me practice until my fingers were nearly raw and my arms shook like the tail of a rattlesnake. Crookneck became not only my unofficial coach—he refused to take any money for his advice—but also my unofficial father. While Mike had never really paid much attention to me—being too concerned with his own shortcomings—Crookneck Smith went out of his way to further my archery education. He provided me with books and videos, researched and signed me up for various shooting matches: indoor, outdoor, and 3-D, whatever he could find within driving distance.

And after he had convinced me to change to the more sophisticated target recurves with their shiny protruding paraphernalia, he accompanied me to regional, then national meets. This continued even after I accepted a job 150 miles away in Richmond, Virginia. He was a spectator when I won the National Championship in 1999. My mother was in the audience, too—she knew what it meant to compete in a minor sport—but Crookneck preferred to sit by himself, away from the crowd—small as it was—wearing a baseball cap that said "Crookneck's Archery."

When I had loosed my last arrow, which cemented my win in the finals, my mother was cheering mightily, even whistling with exuberant happiness. But she was not the first person I searched out in the stands, to whom I raised my bow in triumph. It was Crookneck, who sat alone in the far corner of one of the bleachers. But he was not so far away that I couldn't see the redness around his eyes or the tears streaming from his face.

That was the last match that Crookneck attended. He still drank heavily, still suffered from his wife's defection and his increasing feebleness, and months later, when the Olympic trials rolled around, I heard from his daughter that he had a liver ailment and was confined to his bed.

Maybe because of his absence, I didn't shoot as well as I was capable and finished fourth. Because it was a three-woman team, I was named first alternate.

At this time I was dating a lawyer a dozen years older than me and was enwhirled in a hectic life, and when I returned to Richmond from the trials, I became swept up in that life again and couldn't drive up to see Crookneck for several weeks. When I finally drove out, I was surprised to find him at his workbench, thinner and weaker, but still smiling.

"There she is!" he said as I walked in. I grabbed a push broom and began a sweeping operation that had not varied since I had purchased the broom several years before. I swept for a while in silence, before he continued, "Ye know, fourth is not that bad."

"Nobody wants to be fourth at anything," I told him. "I missed you in the stands."

"Yeah, waal, ye know, I was planning to go, but my guts started acting up and Beth had to take me to the hospital. Next time ye get a coach, don't get someone who's at death's door."

"I won't get another coach at all," I told him. "And you're not at death's door." But his face was more emaciated than I had seen it, his hands twitched as he tried to work his Bitzenburger fletching jig. For an hour or so I helped him fletch a couple dozen shafts and we traded shooting stories. I told him that when I was practicing for the Olympics I had to shoot around the outside line of the center circle because when I would aim at the exact center I would end up hitting my previous arrows and breaking them. He told me about the time he had lost a contest because his opponent had nicked his previous arrow—which was in the 7 point range—and deflected it into the center. I hugged him as I left. It was the first time I had

320

ever done that, and it was the last time I ever saw him.

The day before I left for Sydney, I got a call from Beth. Crookneck's heart had stopped in the night. One of the last things he said was that he hoped someone on my team would break her arm so that I'd get a chance to beat the best in the world.

But of course that didn't happen. I spent a lot of time walking around the fabulous city, shopping with my teammates, ogling the more famous athletes like the Williams sisters, Lance Armstrong, and Lisa Leslie. I wanted badly to get Robert Dover's autograph for my mother, but I was too shy. I loved the sunshine and the Olympic village and all the people, but, oddly, I didn't think about the possibility of Karen or Denise or Janet breaking an arm. And in my practice sessions, I shot splendidly, better than ever in my life, but I knew that my competitiveness was dying down; I knew without ever having thought about it that I wouldn't attempt to compete in 2004.

The truth is, I was getting deeper into my real profession with *The Richmond Times-Dispatch*. My new boyfriend Jack put on a good front, but he was just not that interested in my archery. But most of all, with Crookneck Smith not around to ruffle me with his calm drawl and his boisterous conversation, I no longer felt the draw of competitive archery. The scores in the finals of the 2000 Olympics were staggering, and would get higher still in subsequent Olympics. I remembered my Martin Mamba with pleasure and, a few months after I got back from Sydney, I sold my Olympic tackle and bought another recurve—the Black Widow takedown I still have.

And I never had another coach.

~ ~ ~

The cemetery in Pine Oak is called Shady Rest for a

reason. Nestled into a dozen acres alongside one of the many pine forests in the area, it is dotted not only with pines, which carpet the gravesites with their soft brown needles, but a few live oaks and two large magnolias as well.

Pauley Hughes' funeral took place the day after Gina drove me home from Torrington. I hadn't had to stay in the hospital, but Will Morris was furious with me, telling me how upset he would be if the first patient he ever had died because she refused to take her medicine in a timely manner. No walking in the woods, no archery, no soccer.

It was a drizzly day, but the rain kept it from being swelteringly hot. Most of us carried umbrellas and shared with those few that did not. I had missed the funerals of the two people who meant the most to me, and as I walked from my car through patches of wet grass, years of memories of Cindy McKeown and Crookneck Smith cantered through my mind.

Pauley was buried next to his mother, which would have pleased him had he known. Paul Sr. was dazed throughout the entire service, possibly a drug-induced daze. I'd have drugged myself silly, too, if, in the course of a couple of years I had lost both wife and only child. Cal was standing next to him at the gravesite, but Paul didn't respond to anything he said. Betty Dickson was there, dressed more somberly than usual, and surprisingly, she was weeping. I liked her better then, and still do. In the group around Paul were his two other golf buddies, Ray Colley and Joe Rooney. Ray had come with his wife and Becky, although they were standing somewhat apart. I noticed that Becky stared directly forward throughout the entire service with a kind of fierceness that was hard to interpret.

Some of Pauley's other schoolmates were there, but

looked ill at ease, as if they would have rather been in class. There were a few people who I had not expected to see. Donny, for one, with Linda C and her son Adam. Adam was dressed in a black suit and had his hair cut and combed. Adam, too, was crying, although trying not to show it. I wondered which direction he would go; the next few weeks would probably be a big test for him and for Becky Colley.

Gina, who I had expected to see standing next to Cal, was unaccountably absent and I worried that she might be sick.

About halfway through the service, I spotted Krista and Smokey Torrington, standing motionless without umbrellas under a tall magnolia tree some hundred yards away. They were standing so close to each other that their shoulders were touching, twins except for the color of their hair. They looked like figures painted in a gothic landscape.

I was walking back to my truck after the service when I heard footsteps behind me, then a female voice. "Sue-Ann," I stopped, looked around, and waited for her to catch me up. "Sue-Ann," she repeated.

"Linda C," I responded. Linda was dressed in a long, lightweight dress with a dark flower pattern. She wore her white waitress shoes and I could only assume that she had been preoccupied when she left the house. Her dishwater blonde hair was done up nicely, though, and pinned. Her face held a few lines, but maybe not as many as mine. I had no idea what she wanted; I simply hoped she wouldn't make the morning any more unpleasant than it already was.

"I know we don't know each other very well," she began, "but I wanted to thank you."

"Me? For what? Here, get under my umbrella."

"I think you saved my son's life."

"That's news to me," I told her. "I've never spoken a

word to the kid."

"You gave Donny that head's up on my ex. I knew he was into weird stuff—that's one of the reasons we divorced—but I never thought he was dangerous—all those occult books . . ."

"I don't think many books are dangerous, Linda C," I told her.

"You don't understand. When you called Donny and told him to keep an eye on Adam, Donny hauled the wrecked car he was towing all the way to Jerry's. When he opened the door and went in, Pauley was there. He wanted to take Adam somewhere and Adam was rarin to go. Donny said he didn't think that was a good idea. Jerry got riled—said Adam was his son and he could hang out with whoever he wanted." Linda C stopped and looked at me kind of shyly. "You probly know that Donny don't lahk to argue."

I did know. His inferiority complex usually caused him to lose arguments, even when he was right. I nodded.

"So Donny just punched him out."

"No he didn't!"

"I should smile he did!" she smiled. "And then Adam started screeching somethin nasty, so Donny slapped shit out of him."

"I can't believe it!" I told her. In my heart I was saying, you go, boy.

"And that's not all. Donny ast Pauley if he wanted some too, but Pauley just ran out swearin and cursin. Ah don't lahk to speak ill of the dead, but Pauley could be a real nasty little boy." Linda C stopped and rummaged in her black handbag for a pack of cigarettes. She lit one and offered the pack my way; I shook my head.

"What ah'm tryin to say, Sue-Ann, is that if you hadn't told Donny to watch out for Adam, it might have been

Adam that got kicked by that horse." Linda C took a long puff on her cigarette. "And you know what? Adam knows that when Donny smacked him, he mighta saved his life. It's a start, Sue-Ann."

"Thanks, Linda. That makes me feel better. Adam sounds like a smart kid, but I feel like I should have been able to save Pauley, too."

"If there's . . . if there's ever anything ah can do for you, ah hope you'll call."

"I will, Linda. Now go home and dry off before you catch pneumonia and I have to go to another funeral."

I wanted to thank Krista for feeding my horses when I had been so weak, but when I looked toward the magnolia tree where she and Smokey had been standing, they were gone. It was as if they had gradually blended into the mist.

Chapter 20

A week passed, slowly. I was concerned enough about my health that I stayed home and piddled. I read a few Zane Grey books—the ones Benny had mentioned sounded horsey, and they were. I pulled up my goat story file and put the finishing touches on it. I fed and groomed Alikki and Emmy. I spent hours putting fresh oil on my bows and waxing bowstrings. I fletched some shafts I had gotten online and kept an eye out for a used O. L. Adcock two-piece longbow on eBay.

Gina stopped over once or twice but only for quick lunches. She was busier than usual at work going over the plans for expanding *The Courier* to three issues a week. She wouldn't explain why she had missed Pauley Hughes' funeral and she was equally mum about the state of her relationship with Cal. Something was weighing on her mind, but when I asked her about it she told me she was just tired. I had an email from Jack, who had arrived in Baghdad and was getting acclimatized. That was pretty much my entire social life.

Another Friday arrived. It was approaching evening and I had just finished *Wildfire*. I wanted to kill Zane Grey for making his male characters such a bunch of sexist prudes, but I enjoyed the stories. He seemed to like horses. I had already washed the dishes, fed and groomed Alikki and Emmy, taken out the trash, bathed, whatever I could think of. In other words, I was getting cabin fever in a big way. I was going through the other Zane Grey titles on the shelf when the phone rang. I let it ring twice just to let whoever was calling know that I wasn't sitting by the phone.

"It's me, darlin," came Gina's voice through the wire.

"Gina," I said. "You sound happy. Did you get all your work done? What's up?"

"It's a girl's naht out," she told me.

"What?"

"You ever been to Sahpress Lake Lodge?" she asked.

Cypress Lake Lodge. I thought a moment, then remembered an old group of cabins, recently renovated, on the banks of Okachokeme River. Years before it had been a tourist trap for bass anglers. "You mean that place out by the state park?" I asked.

"That's it."

"What about it?"

"That's where ah am."

"What are you doing there" I asked, genuinely curious. Was she trying to get the owners to buy an ad? Or maybe she and Cal . . .

"Ah'm waitin for you, silly," she said.

"Are you serious?" I asked. My mouth was so wide open I could have stuffed a tennis ball in it. "I mean, really?"

"Ah'm in cabin 15."

"I'll be—I mean, I want to—should I bring anything?" I was glad she couldn't see me. My mouth had suddenly turned all smile.

"An appetaht. Now git in your truck."

I got, but it was forty-five minutes before I pulled into the parking lot. The Cypress Lake Lodge is a motel made up of twenty log cabins set in a semicircle on the lake shore. It took me a few minutes to find cabin 15, which was only a few steps from the dock. It had just turned dark and about half the cabins had lights showing through the windows. I knocked, and felt my knees wanting to knock as well. They were jelly knees. "Sue-Ann," I heard from somewhere in the cabin, "damn it, git in here."

I got again, and as soon as I closed the door behind me, I was surrounded by the smell of good food. The inside of the cabin was decorated in a rustic motel-room motif. The walls were logs, but professionally chinked and sealed. A small fireplace lay dormant on one wall. A curtained window looked out toward the lake. A small table had been set—complete with cloth napkins and gleaming silverware. In the center was a large silver bowl steaming with what looked and smelled like thick gumbo. There was a loaf of home-made bread and a bottle of red wine. The plates were patterned china and the wine glasses crystal. A matching crystal vase held two roses. There were two chairs at the table and in one of them sat Gina, attired in a long white dress patterned with what appeared to be magnolia blossoms. She wore a string of pearls around her neck and her hair was carefully combed and set in a jaunty wave along her shoulders. Just beyond, under the window, was a queen-sized bed. The covers were already peeled down revealing fluffy-looking pillows. I looked at Gina, then at the bed, and back again. I swallowed.

"You're . . . gorgeous," I told her. "I feel so baggy, why didn't you tell me to dress up? Where did you get this food?"

"Ah made it. An you look exactly the way you should look."

"Can I sit down," I asked stupidly.

"Ah was hopin you would. Now ah want you to eat. Ah spent all day makin this stuff—this cabin's got a nahce little kitchen." She served us both with bowls of the gumbo and cut thick slices of the bread. A butter knife and a stick of butter took care of the rest. Then she uncorked the bottle and poured us both a goblet of wine. I put the gumbo on my tongue and tasted fish, shrimp, oysters, rice, okra. I took a sip of wine, which went directly to my head. I dipped the bread in the gumbo. I realized I was hungry and also that I was way too nervous to talk. Gina watched me with kind of a sly smile, which made me even more nervous. I had a second bowl of gumbo and we finished the bottle of wine.

"That was probably the best dinner I've ever had," I told her. There were tears in my eyes that I blinked away.

"You don't wanna leave?" she asked.

"I don't think I ever want to leave," I told her. "But I don't understand. What about you and Cal. . . . ?"

"We'll leave Cal at home tonaht," she said. "We'll talk about him tomorrow, but not tonaht."

"Those are beautiful roses," I remarked. "Everything.... You've made everything so perfect."

"Never got a rose from a girl before, ah guess."

"No."

"Finished eatin?" she asked. "Want anythin else?"

"I want to kiss you," I said.

"Me? Whah?" she teased.

"Because I like you . . . I like you more than archery."

"How could a girl say no to that?" she said, and stood up. I stood up, too, but my stomach was in half a dozen knots having nothing to do with the food. We came together, she standing still, me reaching out and touching her cheek, running both hands through her hair, looking in her eyes as she looked into mine. I leaned forward just a bit and placed my lips against hers, and only then did Gina move. She put her arms around me and returned the kiss, her lips exploring mine as mine explored hers. Then our tongues met and our bodies came together. I reached around and began unzipping her beautiful gown. She moved back a step and let me. The dress fell to her bare feet and she stepped out of it, perfectly naked except for the string of white white pearls. She was so beautiful I almost fainted. Then I felt her lifting up my t-shirt and pulling it over my head. I suppose I must have given her some help, but I don't remember. Then my bra was gone and she had unzipped my jeans. When we were both unclothed, she dimmed the lights and led me to the bed. We lay down, side by side and held each other. We kissed again, gently. I ran my hands along her pale shoulders.

"Gina," I whispered. "I don't know how to start. I mean, which of us is on top? Tell me what to do."

She pointed to her mouth. Start here," she said. "And work your way down."

We kissed and kissed. I licked the smooth softness of her underarms and trailed my tongue across her neck and chest. Her breasts were slightly smaller than I had imagined in my fantasies, and maybe not as firm as they had been when she was a teenager, but firm enough. I had a lot of fun with them and I believe that she enjoyed it vicariously. And I kept going down, along her thighs, legs, to her feet, which I had wanted to marry the first time I had seen them, and then back up again, and when I made her shudder and squeal, and buck her hips like a wild mare, I knew I had finally accomplished something important in my life.

I moved back up to where I could kiss her lips, let her taste herself.

"It was okay?" I whispered.

"Ah, really do love you, you know," she said. "Ah do."

"Show me," I breathed.

And in the next half hour, she did, with her tongue and her lips and her fingers and her breath. My own bucking and writhing and moaning was different from hers, but had the same result.

Flushed and sweaty, we took a shower together, and anyone who has never cupped a beautiful woman's soapy breasts from behind has missed something special. There were more kisses under the full spray of the shower.

"Ah've always wanted breasts as big as yours," she told me.

"And now you have them," I smiled.

We dried off and got back into bed. I sat back against the headboard, my head propped up on both pillows. Gina sat crosslegged at my feet and pulled out a manicure kit. She took one of my feet in her lap and began filing my nails.

"Gina?"

"Umm?"

"Do you think that someday we'll be two old dykes in slippers and separate armchairs watching reruns on TV?"

"Shush, Sue-Ann."

Gina kept her eyes on what she was doing, while my mind raced with odd thoughts. "Isn't one of us supposed to be kind of butch?" I asked. "I don't feel butch. I feel really feminine. I mean, I've never felt so feminine before. But do you want me to cut my hair? I will if you want me to."

"Shush."

Gina was painting my toenails—something I had done maybe twice in my life— with a brownish red polish,. I lay back and closed my eyes and felt her hands as she gently manipulated my feet. I felt her breath as she blew the polish dry.

"Listen. If we got married . . . I mean if there was anywhere in the world that would let us, would one of us have to be the husband?"

"Shhhh, shhh."

"You know," I babbled. "you can have a baby through AI if you want to. I can be its mother, too, or maybe its father, it's pretty confusing. Or maybe I could carry the baby if you didn't want to ruin your figure. . . ."

"Sue-Ann. Quit."

The wine and the softness of her hands nearly made me fall asleep, but I didn't want to sleep through any of this.

"Gina?"

"What, baby?"

"Do, um, do you think we'll ever get to do this again? I mean, if we couldn't, I think I'd have to kill myself."

"Me, too."

She started giving me a foot massage, kneading the balls of my foot and twirling each toe gently. I realized I was moaning and opened my eyes. I looked in Gina's eyes; she was looking in mine. I looked at my feet and gasped.

"God, Gina, you've made my feet so gorgeous I want to have sex with *myself*."

"Can ah watch?" she smiled.

"You can help," I told her, and we ended up doing the same thing we had done earlier, but different. You want details, go rent a video.

I woke up early the next morning and realized that it was the happiest morning of my life. Gina was curled up beside me, breathing softly in sleep, her thigh touching mine under the covers. We had turned the air conditioning on high and had kept each other warm throughout the night. I stole out of bed, dressed, and looked in the cabin's small kitchen. Gina had stocked it almost for a siege, and by the time she woke up and joined me with a sleepy smile, I had strips of crisp bacon and a scrambled egg and cheese omelet already sitting at the table and I was working on getting the last pancake out of the skillet. And coffee, natch, but if I hadn't said it, would you have known?

We didn't say much as we ate, just smiled at each other shyly every once in a while. Finally, on our second coffee, I said, "I don't want to leave, but I have to get back and feed the horses."

"Krista's feedin for you this weekend," she said. "So you're stayin here with me."

"What, you called her?"

"You didn't think ah was goin to let mah horses starve, didja?"

"What time do we have to check out?" I asked.

"That would be Monday," she said. "Ah guess ah should have told you that this was our girls' *weekend* out."

After we ate, we cleared the table and did the dishes. We sat down in a sofa made of small logs and large cushions, our bare feet touching on the one footstool. Gina smoked, I watched. Then she went into the bedroom and came out with a couple of shopping bags with carrying straps. "For you," she said. "Sorry ah didn't have tahm to wrap em."

"But it's not my birthday yet," I said.

"But ah missed all your other birthdays," she smiled.

"You hated me on all my other birthdays," I reminded her.

"Ah don't now."

From the first bag I pulled out a complete hiking outfit from L. L Bean, complete with lace-up, high-topped boots that were remarkably light. From the other, smaller bag I extracted a two-piece swim suit and leather beach sandals.

"Ah hope they're your sahz," she said.

"I don't know what to say."

"Then get dressed. We're goin on a canoe rahd."

333

Gina had already rented a canoe from the office and it was waiting for us at the dock. Neither Gina nor I had much experience paddling, so our ride started out as a zigzag adventure. After a while, though, we made it across the small Cypress Lake and into the almost pristine Okachokeme River, bordered by cypress trees festooned with Spanish moss. Always cosmetically prepared, Gina produced a bottle of suntan lotion and applied it to both of us. It was a lazy ride, both of us too intent on our paddling or our steering to do much talking. We were just enjoying the moment and each other's company, pointing out a leaping bass and a small flock of storks. We made small talk, of course, but just trivial stuff about Benny Benedict or maybe going out to visit The Creeper sometime, as Gina still hadn't met him. Yet as we turned to go back to the lodge, I could tell that Gina's mood was turning darker. She answered my casual questions in monosyllables, keeping her eyes on the bottom of the canoe. It was such a switch from earlier in the morning that I had no idea what to say to her. We paddled back into Cypress Lake before she looked up, took a deep breath, and began to speak.

"Sue-Ann," she said. "Ah told Cal ah wasn't goin to marry him."

I was glad to hear this, but Gina's demeanor told me that there was more to it. "You did?" I asked cautiously.

"But ah ain't goin to leave him neither."

"What do you mean?" I asked.

"Ah don't know if Cal loves me, ah don't. He doesn't talk about love much. Maybe he's love shy after things not working out with his wahf. But he was the first person in mah lahf to think that maybe ah was special. He gave me some responsibility, an ah never had that. Ah've done some good for the paper; he says that without me he'd have never even thought of goin to three a week, much less daily. We're kinda a team."

"So you're, what, going to stay with Cal? You're going to keep being his girlfriend?"

"If you and ah moved in together, there'd be talk. Both of us'd probly lose our jobs and that wouldn't be the worst part. That's okay for you, Sue-Ann; you've already given up a career, but ah caint do that. But if ah stay with Cal, ah can help build a better paper and ah can feel good about mah abilities."

"So," I continued numbly, "you're going to move in with Cal?"

"Ah won't marry him and ah won't move in with him. Sometahms he'll spend the night at mah place and sometahms we'll stay at his. Most of the tahm we'll be apart. Sometahms we'll go out to a movie or somethin, but nothin formal. Ah told him that we could date and we could be lovers, but that ah didn't want people to see us as a couple. That's whah ah didn't go to Pauley's funeral. It hurt him some, it did, but ah couldn't tell him whah ah've changed. Ah *won't* tell him. And here's somethin else ah didn't tell him: that if he wants me to have his baby, ah will."

"But if you get pregnant, you'll *have* to move in with him. You'll have to—"

"No, Sue-Ann. ah won't." Gina stopped and took a deep breath. "If you don't want to see me or be with me again, ah'll understand."

"You mean you still want to be . . . you want us *both*?" I burst out.

Gina just looked into the water like she was looking for a floating body.

I didn't bother looking, I just jumped out of the boat and started swimming toward shore. With any luck I would have overturned the boat; with better luck I would have drowned, but neither happened. When I reached the shore I glanced back out and saw that the boat was still upright, Gina still sitting on her seat clutching an oar but making no attempt to use it.

I shouted at her: "Damn it, Gina. You sent me a throbbing heart!" I turned away and rushed into the cabin where I snatched off the bathing suit Gina had bought me and left it puddling on the wooden floor. I ignored the bag of hiking clothes, dressed myself in what I had arrived in, and flew out the door to my truck. And I drove and drove.

I'm not sure how long I was on the road and I don't remember where I went. I was angry and hurt beyond belief and took no note whatever of my surroundings until I looked at my gas gauge and realized that I was dangerously low on fuel. I found a gas station, filled up and bought a hot dog from their deli. It was atrocious, but far better than eating anything Gina cooked. I took a thyroid pill and drove on. But instead of finding myself in Tallahassee or Panama City or somewhere with a bar or a movie theater I could lose myself in; instead of calling Donny and telling him that we were back on; instead of showing up naked at Cal's apartment, I found myself, hours later, pulling back in to the parking lot of the Cypress Lakes Lodge.

I parked and got out of the truck like a linebacker moving toward a loose football. I opened the door of number 15 and slammed it behind me. Gina was sitting back against the headboard of the bed, arms around her knees, staring at the floor. I noticed that my bathing suit was no longer lying on the floor and the wet patch had been mopped up.

Gina looked up at me finally and said, with a sadness in her voice, "Forgit somethin?"

"Fucking A I forgot something. I forgot to tell you

about yourself."

"Go raht ahead, doesn't matter." Her voice was mechanical, like words were coming from her mouth without her making any conscious effort to speak.

I was fighting back tears, had been fighting them back for hours. "Remember what I said to you last night?"

"All of it."

"Well, everything I said was a lie. I don't love . . . I don't like you better than archery. You're still the slithery bitch you always were. I was testing you to see how far you'd go. I faked all those orgasms, too. I was really convincing, right?"

"Then why are you cryin?"

"I have Graves' disease."

"Problem is, you do love me." Her voice had been getting slowly less mechanical. I blinked and saw that she had folded herself into a lotus position. Her eyes were brighter, her voice steadier.

I wiped my eyes. "I do, and yes, it's a problem."

Gina didn't answer, just kept looking at me.

"I can't help it," I continued. "Even if I come in the office next week and you treat me like a stranger, I'm still going to want to be with you, I'm going to want to touch you, to travel to different countries with you, to sit and talk to you about philosophy and economics at the breakfast table."

"Ah want those things, too, Sue-Ann, except the philosophy part scares me a little."

I smiled; I couldn't help it. I couldn't help walking toward the bed.

We kissed, we made love, we shouted at each other, and we cried and cried.

And in the morning we got in separate cars and drove in different directions.

Iza Moreau

Epilogue

The next months passed quietly. The medication Dr. Morris had given me had allowed me to get back most of the weight I had lost and I was looking and feeling almost as good as new. It was still another Friday and I had scheduled my iodine radiation therapy for early in the coming week. There was no danger, but I was sad to be destroying a part of my body that had given me good service for many years, sad to know that I would need to take replacement hormones for the rest of my life.

In many ways it was a goodbye-to-the-old-era day. Earlier that morning, I had set up an old 55-gallon steel drum and started burning all of Cindy's old bank statements and unnecessary files. Then I decided to burn pretty much everything in my father's room—an easy way to finally clear up the clutter that the goths and vandals—and Mike himself—had left. In addition, I had a lot of jetsam from the pasture to burn—old hay twine and scrap lumber from the cross fence I had just put up for when I decided to wean Enemy Hunter.

When Gina got off work that afternoon she found me in the back practicing archery with my Black Widow. With a wave, she went into the barn to change her clothes and get out her own archery gear.

No, Gina hasn't moved in with me although I'm still hoping that someday she will. We visit each other in secret and love each other when we can. She is still the bright star in my sky, the one person who can hold me perfectly still and content. But every story doesn't end exactly the way you might think it should. Gina and I could move to a larger city and live together openly. I could get a job with almost any newspaper in the country, but if we moved to a city, I wouldn't be able to keep Alikki and Emmy, and I had grown as attached to them as I had to Gina.

And I no longer wanted a star-studded career. I was excited at the changes we were making at *The Courier* and delighted about getting back into riding again. I had begun work on writing the text of Jack's book of Iraq photographs and had a couple projects of my own in mind. I had queried a few publishers about possibly writing a book on my Baghdad experiences; a couple of similar books had come out already and they were popular. I was also thinking about organizing my mother's dressage aphorisms into a small, easy to read book, possibly using photographs or illustrations. I had become familiar enough with some of the equine publications to know that they were always looking for new material.

"At least it's not summer," Gina said, fumbling to fasten the wrist guard around her right arm.

I loosed an arrow, hit the red portion of the bull's-eye target, and smiled.

"What's with the burnin?" she asked, doing a type of tai chi warm-up exercise I had taught her.

"House cleaning day," I told her.

Our practice sessions were always casual, with more emphasis on form than on hitting anything. In fact, it was identical to the instruction that I had received from Crookneck Smith, who I often spoke to her about with affection. Soon I would teach her the ability to concentrate, but for now, it was common to catch up on the day's activities while a portable radio sent out its messages from the chair it was sitting on. Because they knew that we listened, Gamma and Smokestack sometimes played with us. As Gina continued to limber up, we heard Smokestack say,

"Hey, out there. This is WJAPE—the most fun you'll ever have with a pirate radio station. Listen, folks, we know we've been saying this for a while, but there's a little horse farm out on Highway 77 and Cedar Road—I can't say its name because it would embarrass the owner—but this little place needs some TLC cause the guy running it's not as young as he used to be. He needs some hay and feed and he needs some volunteers to muck out his stalls so the poor horses don't have to stand around in poop 24-7. But most of all, people, he needs advice. Go on out there and give it to him, huh? The horses will thank you for it."

We had heard this spiel before and could imagine Mr. Moon's fury when people stopped to throw hay into his bare fields or, manure rakes in hand, gave him their opinions of turnout, proper stall care, or the disposal of barnyard waste. This was Gina's doing—she had kept her word to Moon and this was her way to monitor his horse activities.

"And for all those in our listening area that are 'that way,' here's a gay little tune by Jonathan Richman called 'I Was Dancing in the Lesbian Bar.' Ooo ooo ooo, y'all."

"What!" I exclaimed.

I looked at Gina to see if she had noticed. She had. Her eyes were wide open and she was shaking her head. "Anyone in the listening area mah ass," she said. "Ah'm gonna git that boy."

"Take soft breaths," I suggested. "Pull, point, and release. Let the arrow roll off your fingers like a wheel rolling off a cliff."

The fire was going out and I suddenly realized I still had something that needed to be burned; that should have been burned long ago. "I'll be right back," I told Gina. "Keep practicing."

I ran around the side of the house to my truck, pushed up the seat, and took out the brick of marijuana. When I got back and Gina saw what I was holding, she exclaimed. "You're not gonna—" Then she stopped and shrugged. "Ah guess it's jist as well," she said. "We've been doin all raht without it."

I began breaking the thick rectangle of marijuana into small chunks, then into flakes, and dropping them in the barrel. "You know," I said, "this is what started all that trouble,"

"The goat story," Gina said.

"I never told you this," I said, "but I wrote up that story. It was a really good piece of investigative work. It's just that the more we found out the more impossible it became to actually print it."

Just then Smokestack played "Good enough for Granddad," a rollicking boogie by the Squirrel Nut Zippers wherein the vocalist crooned that if something was good enough for his old pap, it was good enough for him. Its refrain had become the "pirate" radio station's theme song.

"You couldn't give away Torrington's secrets," Gina agreed. She had put her new left-handed Martin Mamba aside and was helping me sprinkle the last shreds of grass into the burn barrel, trying not to breathe too much of the thick smoke. Torrington had become special to us for many reasons and we had spent several nights there together. I was thinking of giving archery lessons to the recuperating ex-soldiers. We had gone trail riding with Krista on Torrington horses and Gina had finally met The Creeper himself, Ashley Torrington, and they had become friends.

"I wouldn't want anyone to know about how far

Pauley Hughes had gone over the edge," I continued. "That reminds me. I got an email from Jack this morning. He told me he saw Paul Senior in The Green Zone the other day. I guess he got that job with Halliburton he wanted."

"Ah guess. And Mark has been covering Paul's old territory pretty well."

"I put us in the story, too," I said.

"You did?"

I nodded. "And unless we want everyone in Jasper County knowing about us, it's like Paul said in that first meeting: there's no story."

"Just because it can't be printed, Sue-Ann, doesn't mean there's not a story."

A voice from around the side of the house made us turn from the barrel. "Anybody back here?"

"Clarence!"

"I didn't know if I had the right—God's banana, Sue-Ann; what are the two of you burning?"

"Bout fahv thousand dollars' worth of grade-A weed," Gina told him. "Somethin Sue-Ann picked up when she shouldn't have." She took a deep sniff. "Ah think ah'm gittin hah," she said.

"But why are you burning it?" he cried.

"Smoking is bad for your health," I responded. "What brings you out here?"

He took a close look at the burn barrel, then looked in my direction. "I just wanted to see your place," he said. "Krista told me all about this archery range. And I want to see this horse the two of you saved."

"I've—we've got three horses now, Clarence. Come on out to the pasture and we'll introduce you."

A minute or two later we were all leaning over a board fence that looked out into both sides of the pasture. Alikki was grazing to our right, looking every bit of her 16.3 hands. "That's her, Clarence," I said. "Her name is Alikki and she's a registered Hanovarian."

"She sure don't look sick any more," Clarence said.

"I figure she's gained three or four hundred pounds since I got her," I told him. I pointed to the field on our left. "That's her baby," I said. "We just weaned her. And that gray horse is an Andalusian Clydesdale cross named Hurricane Irene. That's Gina's riding horse and right now she's kind of an aunt to the baby."

"What about you?" he asked. "Are you riding?"

"I've been practicing on Irene and on a couple of the Torrington horses," I said. "I'm just lunging Alikki now, trying to get her strong enough to support a rider again. Krista'll probably be the first one to sit on her. She's a better rider than we are and she's lighter. When I can ride her, I'm going to start taking dressage lessons from one of my mother's old friends."

"But Sue-Ann," Clarence said. "Krista told me that she was the horse your mom was riding when she . . ." His voice tailed off.

"Alikki's not responsible," I told him. "If Cindy were here right now, and I really wish she was, she would tell all three of us that what happened was her own fault for riding alone and riding too near something that Alikki wasn't familiar with, like a tractor or a wheelbarrow. It might have been one of those commandos from Torrington shooting too near the house. She might have stepped in a nest of ground wasps. Thunder," I added. I looked at Gina and remembered my first rated show. "A flapping banner."

We stood there for a few minutes just watching the horses grazing in the rays of the setting sun. As we were walking back toward the barn, out of nowhere, Clarence asked Gina. "Have you moved in with Sue-Ann yet?"

"God, Clarence," I exclaimed. "It's so weird that you know about us. What the hell was The Creeper thinking?"

"Oh, I'm a pretty good person with a secret," he said.

"Yeah, I guess you are," I admitted. "Including keeping back everything I wanted to know about—"

"No, ah haven't moved in," Gina broke in, preventing the argument that usually ensued when Clarence and I got together. "There's a man ah don't want to hurt. It's complicated."

The smoke from the barrel was wafting our way and I felt lightheaded. "Whooeee," I cried. "That smoke is making me feel real good." I hung my bow on the pole and took off my wrist guard.

"Anything new at the market, Clarence?" Gina asked.

"Peanuts," he said.

"Peanuts?"

"I got a call from a guy out in Micanopy who's developed this new strain of peanut and he wanted me to look at em. Hey, that reminds me, there was something weird about that trip—maybe you can do a story about it. I was driving over the Suwannee River on Highway 90 when all of a sudden I hear this song playing in my head. The Suwannee River song. Then I realized it wasn't in my head at all, that somehow it was coming from the tires of my truck. It was making my whole truck vibrate. You know." He sang the line "'Way down upon the Suwannee River.' Just one time, then it was gone."

"You heard this on the bridge itself?" I asked.

"Right. I mean, one of those extension bridges with the iron gratings. Those things always make a kind of hum, but this one hummed a tune. It was the damndest thing. God's great gourds, Sue-Ann; now I think *I'm* getting high."

345

Iza Moreau

About the Author

Iza Moreau is a two-time Rainbow Award Winner, a two-time Lesfic Bard Award Winner and a Golden Crown Finalist. She lives in the Deep South and counts Sarah Waters, Maggie Estep, and the Bronte sisters—Acton, Currer, and Ellis—among her literary influences. She is also the author of the popular Elodie Fontaine Mysteries.

She can be reached at:

authorizamoreau@gmail.com

www.ingramcontent.com/pod-product-compliance
Lightning Source LLC
Chambersburg PA
CBHW070624260626
47161CB00007B/2575